The Clitheroe Prime Minister

Steven Suttie

Thanks...

I must say a very special thank you to Dave Walton, who kindly leant me his laptop to write this. I'd taken a few weeks off work to get stuck into writing this story and then dropped my laptop on the floor when answering the phone. (It was a call about P.P.I.) Cheers Dave, I'll bring it back soon.

Thank you to David and Mary at Banana News in Clitheroe town centre for such brilliant support since I first mentioned using their shop in the story.

Thanks also to Jill Bowyer for her constant interest in this writing project, and ongoing support. Thanks Jill.

Thanks to my wife Liz for her support and feedback.

Thanks to my Mum and Julie for the constant interest in my progress with this.

Thanks to my family for their ridicupation with Soap Opera. Your ignorance has forced me to find something else to do for a few hours each night, and this is the result. I'll start on another one soon.

Thanks to everybody else who has been handed a scruffy pile of papers and asked to read it, and to everyone who has listened to me whine on and on about this for ages...

This novel is dedicated to Kay Moon, who gave me the confidence to write. It's now my favourite hobby, and you are an excellent teacher. I will always be indebted for such brilliant support and encouragement.

Thank you Kay. I hope you like this one...

"Same again?" mouthed Sandra from behind the bar, pointing at the empty beer glasses on the table. Jim Arkwright held his thumb up and gestured on behalf of his drinking pals Dave and Phil. Sandra sensed an unusually tense atmosphere in the Snug, the small room adjacent to the main bar area. Dave was in the middle of telling a hot-blooded story, so Sandra had taken the initiative. It was clear that something was wrong, she knew better than anybody that her regular tea time customers seldom nursed an empty glass after a hard day at work.

"And the thing was," continued Dave, wearing his customary orange railway overalls, "the whole line was closed down for three hours, through all of the morning rush hour – all because some little bastard kids had thrown a shopping trolley down onto the track from a bridge near Blackburn last night. Instead of just moving the damn thing – the transport police wanted to do a crime scene investigation and all that, having to wait for a crew to come down from Manchester."

"Bloody Norah!" said Phil.

"Exactly! So now we'll be paying out fines for the trains that didn't run, taxi fairs for passengers, replacement bus costs and all that. All told, this will have cost fifty grand at least!" Dave's friends raised their eyebrows at the cost. Jim whistled a surprised tone at the significant figure.

"Fifty bleeding grand! They could have just put the trolley to one side!" continued Dave, his voice getting slightly louder with each detail. "And even if they do get hold of the little shits responsible, nowt will happen to 'em any road!"

Jim and Phil were listening intently, sympathetically shaking their heads as Dave recounted another frustrating day working as a senior trackside engineer on the railway. Sandra appeared and delicately placed two pints down on the table before quietly heading back to the bar to fetch the third.

"Cheers love," said Phil.

"So, I said to my boss," continued Dave, "Why don't they just take the trolley off the flipping train track and do their finger printing and DNA stuff somewhere else, and we can get the line moving? My boss said they need to do it on the track because there could be other clues nearby!" Dave threw his hands in the air in exasperation. "It's my ability that is called into question when the targets aren't met. But when I tell them how to get things moving, no one takes a blind bit of notice of me!" The sheer frustration of it all made him really mad, despite Dave usually being one of the most laid back and relaxed people around. He took a huge swig from the fresh pint of ale. Almost a third of the drink had disappeared as he placed it down loudly and wiped the froth from his lips.

"What? So they are going to all this trouble, disrupting all these people that are trying to get to work," asked Phil, "and costing all this money to the railway, even though they know its probably kids high jinx and nothing will happen to them if they're caught anyway?" Jim tried to lighten the mood and laughed sarcastically.

"Exactly!" exclaimed Dave, "But the transport police have their procedures to follow you see, and its bollocks to everything else!"

Sandra reappeared and carefully placed the third beer glass down onto the table. She turned and asked the two younger visitors if they were alright. They were unfamiliar faces and had sat opposite Phil, Jim and Dave. Sandra was worried that it may be a bit too intense sat in this room at the present. The two young men insisted they were fine as Sandra wiped their table.

The three regulars mulled over the stupidity of the situation for a minute and got stuck into their beer.

"I'll go and settle up at the bar," said Jim, as he stood and followed Sandra out of the Snug – quietly relieved by the opportunity to break away for a minute.

The landlady of the New Inn was an attractive auburn haired divorcee in her forties. Like most of the people in Clitheroe, she grew up in the town and had gone to school with many of her regulars, including Jim.

"Is that £9.90, love?" he enquired. Jim's tanned bald head and five o' clock shadow made him look quite rugged and mature, but Sandra still thought of Jim as the good looking, funny young lad that she and many of her girlfriends had fancied at Ribblesdale School thirty or so years earlier.

"It's not gone up since 4 o clock chuck!" she said as she threw her cloth in the sink. "Hey, what's up with Dave? In all the years he's been coming in here I can't remember seeing him so wound up!" Sandra asked the question as she took Jims £10 note and rang the figures into the till.

"Oh, he's just letting off a bit of steam about work. His targets for making sure the trains are on time have been affected by some kids mucking about, and now his bonus is looking a bit doubtful," explained Jim.

"Its typical – he's a hard working, conscientious bloke, trying his best but gets shat on because of the behaviour of other folk. It's not right." Jim held out his hand for the change.

"No tip?"

"I wouldn't insult you!" Jim laughed as he took

the ten pence coin and put it in his pocket.

"Well you go and cheer Dave up, you're good at that."

"Aye, I'll try and change the subject love, we don't want him turning the air blue."

"Oh don't worry about that, I've heard it all Jim. Hey, I thought you were picking Albert up from the airport anyway? You said you wouldn't be coming in today." Sandra reminded Jim that he had issued her with a profits warning the previous day, as his father was due back from holiday.

"Flights were cancelled, strike by the Spanish air controllers. Dads over the moon, he's got an extra day out of it! Maybe even longer! So he got straight in a taxi back to the resort."

"Lucky sod!" said Sandra as she smiled at the thought of Jims old Dad raving and misbehaving in Tenerife.

Jim returned to the table and sat down to hear Phil summarise the whole railway situation with his typical rundown.

"Aye. It's a load of shite Dave, that's what this is."

"Hey, look, it's the Prime Minister - perhaps he's making a statement about the shopping trolley!" Jim was pointing at the TV screen above them as he made his way back to his friends. He wore a mischievous smile and there was a glint in his eye. Everybody that knew Jim would recognise that grin as the precursor of a wind-up. His sarcastic comment received a wry chuckle from his friends and from the two young men sat just opposite. They couldn't have helped but overhear Dave heatedly explaining his work troubles over the previous ten minutes.

On the screen above them in the corner of the

Snug, the TV news channel was showing live pictures from Parliament. The Prime Minister was standing behind the famous dispatch box in the House of Commons reading out a statement. The volume was down and Jim saw this as the perfect opportunity to change the subject from Dave's work troubles and lighten the mood a little. Jim only came to the pub for the chance to relax, have a good laugh and mellow out after a long day at work.

Jim began imitating the Prime Ministers famous voice, surprisingly well - to the amusement of his drinking friends.

"And I say to my right honourable friend, that the shopping trolley should have been taken in the back of a police van, so the line could be re-opened, and I recommend to the house that Dave should get his bonus!"

The surreal monologue managed to get a vague chuckle from Dave, as Phil laughed out loud and began to clap. Sandra was watching on from the bar as the two young men also enjoyed Jim's impromptu, unrehearsed impression of the PM.

"And when we find the vermin little bastards who threw the trolley onto the railway line, we're going to shove them down a man-hole and make them clean all the shit off the sewer walls for a week, with their finger nails!" This comment received a huge laugh, mainly because the PM triumphantly punched the air just in time with Jim's impression.

"Let's see how they like that!"

"Hear Hear!" said Dave, raising his pint glass high in the air.

"We need to get to grips with the problems that are killing our society. We have towns and cities over run with people who are doing pointless things that cause endless, expensive problems and its ordinary citizens who have to pay the bill. I tell the house that from today, we're sorting it out once and for all. Britain is the joke of the world and it's easy to see why. We have people committing crimes - just so they can get back into prison because life is better there. We've gangs of kids who walk around looking for people to hit, things to steal or break, and they know there are no bad consequences for it. For most young adults, drunken violence is just part of a night out. We've got single young women becoming pregnant just so they can move out of their parents house. We've got alcoholic MP's, junkie celebrities, benefit fraud Mayors. There's no end of crap role models. And telly isn't as good as it used to be!"

The small audience laughed. Jim kept going, pretty sure that the PM's image would disappear off the screen any moment.

"Look all around you, what do you see? Broken communities, unemployed youths, dysfunctional families, inadequate schools, and worst of all – the lying, cheating, free-loading, hypocritical MPs that are so busy looking after their own back pockets – they don't have the time to take any action in the communities that they are paid to serve!"

Jim's tiny audience was enjoying the performance, and to their delight the muted footage of the Prime Minister continued to show on the screen. Jim didn't know where his spontaneous rant was going, he just kept chattering away, trying his best to be as disdainful as possible. He was just pleased that Dave was finally calming down and getting over his anger. Jim took a hearty swig of his ale and launched back into the spur-of-the-moment speech, egged on by the unrelenting encouragement.

"From now on, this government doesn't give a shit about the feral kids, the imbecile chavs, the druggies, the drunks or any of the incompetent gobby yobbo's that waste all our police time, choke up our courts and hoover up our tax money with their stupid, self imposed problems! From this day onwards, we're putting a stop to being understanding and supportive towards society's tossers. From this day on, our main priority will be to support the members of society who do the right thing! No more faffing about, wasting our time and money on the scum, the lazy, the wide boys and gob-shites. We're going to make Britain great again, by sorting out all these pathetic useless scumbags that believe we owe them a favour!"

Jim's ridiculous rant, in a near perfect imitation of the Prime Ministers voice, got another hearty laugh and a round of applause from everyone in the Snug. Dave stood up to buy the next round of drinks, looking much happier and a lot more relaxed than he had done just a little while earlier. The television channel returned to its newsreader. Phil laughed as he stood too.

"You need your head testing Jim, I've always said it." Phil was shaking his head as he went on his way to the Gents.

"That was really funny, mate!" said one of the two younger men sat opposite.

"Can you imagine if the Prime Minister actually said all that! There'd be riots and God knows what!" added his friend.

"Ha ha, Ah thanks, only mucking about, that's all." replied Jim, as he finished his pint. "I've not seen you lads in here before. You do know you have to be over forty five to come in here don't you?"

"No you bloody don't!" yelled Sandra from behind the bar, shooting a mock look of anger at Jim.

"Ignore him!"

"Haha, we're just visiting for the day." Said the first of the two.

"Someone on the street recommended we come in here for a good pint and friendly banter." The other visitor spoke this time, as he fiddled about with his mobile phone.

"Ah well, you've come to the right place, they pride themselves on having the best selection of guest beers in town," replied Jim, glancing over at the bar for Sandra's approval, but she was busy serving Dave and missed the rare, but genuinely meant compliment.

"We're up from Manchester, we run a skateboarding magazine and we're doing a feature about Clitheroe Skate Park. But we're just waiting to go home now." said the first one as his friend continued to play with the phone.

"In fact, we'd better sup up, the train will be leaving in five minutes."

"Well, nice to have met you. Come back to Clitheroe again, it's a good little town, and more outsiders are needed to help dilute the gene pool." Jim smiled as Dave returned with the pints and Phil also made his way back from the gents, still laughing at Jim's crazy impersonation.

"Cheers, thanks." The lads clearly hadn't understood what Jim had meant about the gene pool. Jim chuckled.

"Seeya." The two young men left.

Jim thanked Dave for his fresh pint of locally brewed beer.

"Nice lads them, for Mancs!" quipped Jim. Little was he to know that after this brief encounter with the two young Mancunian chaps, his life was about to be changed beyond all recognition.

Chapter Two
Arkwright Household, Clitheroe Saturday 19th May

"Dad! Dad! Come in here, quick!" wailed Jim's teenage daughter Lucy from the dining room. Jim was startled, he'd been blissfully slipping into the beguiling semi-conscious lull of his Saturday afternoon doze on the settee. He opened his eyes and focused.

"Dad, I'm serious. You're drunk, on the internet!" continued Lucy.

"DAD - derr!" she bellowed at the top of her voice.

Jim was intrigued, in fact - he jumped up off the sofa with a start. What on earth was Lucy talking about he wondered, as he stumbled half awake through to the dining room where Lucy and her friend Jess were watching the computer.

"You freak Dad! Look at the state of you, why have you done this?" Lucy was clearly annoyed at what she was seeing on the screen, whilst her friend was in fits of giggles as Jims rather nasal, but incredibly accurate impression of the Prime Minister played out.

Jim was just puzzled. He stared hard at the computer screen and watched himself talking about naughty kids scraping shit off sewer walls.

"What's going on?" asked Jim, indisputably confused by the bizarre situation. Lucy pointed at the screen.

"Well Dad, that's you, drunk and embarrassing." She moved her finger up to the top of the screen, "And that's YouTube, the world's most popular video sharing site." Lucy then held up her thumb and forefinger to Jims face. "And this Dad, is my credibility right now. Thanks a lot Dad, great idea!"

"Wait, wait a minute Lucy. This hasn't got

anything to do with me. Well, obviously - that's me. But I don't understand why it's in there?" He pointed at the pc screen.

At that moment, Jim remembered the two Manchester lads in the pub at the time he was messing about. He sat down at the table.

"Oh, shit!" he said. Jess laughed nervously as Lucy stared harshly at her parent.

"I was just having a laugh in the pub. I wasn't drunk, I was just being daft, that's all. But I don't get why it's gone on the internet." Lucy's friend Jess was transfixed by the video as it continued to play.

"Because SK8M8 has put it on there Dad, look! He's called it "The Clitheroe Prime Minister." Why did you even let him film you anyway?" asked Lucy, furious with the situation, anticipating the amount of abuse this will attract from her peers.

"I didn't!" said Jim, "Of course I didn't! I was in the pub with the lads and the news was on and I started messing about. No one was filming me. There were a couple of tourists in, two young blokes in their 20's, said they were over from Manchester, they run a skateboard magazine or something. They must have taped me." Jim was pleading for Lucy to believe him, that this was as much of a shock to him as it was to her.

Jess was still watching the screen and sniggering at the video.

"It's really funny!" she said.

"No its not!" shrieked Lucy as she stormed out of the room and slammed the door behind her. The family portrait of Jim, his wife Karen and their three kids, Lucy, Jonathan and Victoria which hung on the wall shook violently as Lucy's footsteps thumped up the stairs and then another door slammed. Jim looked across at the video, still playing on the computer and held his hands up.

"I didn't know somebody was taping me. How can someone do that without me knowing Jess?" he asked, meekly embarrassed by his very limited knowledge of computers and gadgets.

"It looks like it was done on a phone. Did you not notice anyone holding a phone up while you were doing that weird voice?" Jess was still smiling. Jim shook his head, and covered his face with his hands. He was embarrassed and was becoming increasingly annoyed as his nasal speech continued through the speakers.

"It's not that bad," she said reassuringly. "It's funny!"

"I'd better go and speak to Lucy. She's really upset." Jim was sincerely confused by everything that had gone on in the last few minutes. He opened the door gently and went upstairs. He tapped on the girls' bedroom door.

"Go away Dad. You're a mong!" It was said between heavy sobs.

"Hey now! You keep a civil tongue Lucy Arkwright! I came to say I'm sorry." Jim had raised his voice just enough to remind Lucy who she was speaking to. A moment passed before the door clicked and Lucy appeared. She was visibly upset and shaking.

"Sorry Dad. But it's so weird, all my friends are going to crucify me at school. Everyone's laughing at it already, it's all over Facebook."

"What do you mean? Can't we just take it off, delete it or something?" asked Jim, his naivety of all this stuff was really in the spotlight, to the frustration of his 15 year old daughter.

"Dad, I know you don't get it but it's like this okay. Ben Jackson, one of the kids from the Skate Park is constantly searching *Clitheroe* into video search engines to see any new skate videos that are posted. Last night, he did this as usual and the only new video from Clitheroe is that freaky thing with you in! Now he's put it on Facebook so everyone at school can see. He even wrote "Lucy Arkwright's Dad acting the goat in the pub!" Everyone is going to hate me now." She started crying again, big, heavy emotional sobs.

Jim hugged her, and was beginning to get a vague idea of how upsetting this could be for the young lass – but was also confused by why those lads from Manchester had gone to all this trouble in the first place. As far as Jim was concerned he was only having a lark with his friends, trying to cheer Dave up a bit after a tough day, there was nothing more to it. It was just a standard few minutes in the pub.

"How can I get in touch with the bloke who put it on there?" he asked Lucy. "I'll ask him to get rid of it. I'll sort this out, don't you worry."

"Dad, everyone has seen it now, there's no point. Half of my friends have reposted it. Everyone in Clitheroe, God - everyone in Lancashire my age will have seen it by now." They were interrupted by Jess, shouting excitedly from downstairs.

"Lucy! Jim! Oh my God! Come here, quick!" It didn't sound like bad news as Jess repeated "Oh my God" in some kind of slowed down ecstatic shrill.

Lucy wiped her face and brushed past her father and headed down the stairs. Jim felt wrung out and bemused by the whole situation, and now with all the techno jargon that Lucy was using he just felt like laughing. This was totally surreal. He followed Lucy down the stairs to see what Jess was so getting excited about.

"Look –look how many views it's had! It's on

the Youtube featured page, it's had twenty one thousand views since yesterday! Watch this as well," Jess was talking really fast and all of it was going over Jims head, but Lucy looked very interested so he assumed that it was constructive information.

"Read the comments – they're unbelievable!" added Jess, clearly thrilled and struggling to catch her breath.

The three of them looked at the screen, at the column beneath the video. Jess began scrolling down the page. There were dozens upon dozens, possibly hundreds of similarly positive comments, most of them saying

"OMG, Legend!" or

"Hahaha Love this guy!" or

"Sick!"

"What does that mean – that it's sick?" asked Jim. Lucy laughed, wiping the tears from her eyes.

"It means its really good Dad!" Lucy laughed again. Jim was relieved to see the usual smile was returning to his daughters face.

"Look at this one," said Jess with a chuckle, "it says "talks more sense than the real Prime Minister!""

Lucy was laughing properly now and seemed to be enjoying what she was reading. Her tears of a moment or so earlier seemed long forgotten, as can sometimes be the case with teenagers. Jim could cope, he was used to tantrums and traumas, it was all in a days work for the parent of three kids.

"Sorry, girls – can I just ask one question that I don't understand?" he asked, hovering behind the teenagers. "Why would those lads video me having a laugh in the pub and just put it on the web? It makes no sense to me. Have they done it to annoy you, Lucy?"

"No Dad, course not. He must have just thought you were funny and started recording you. Everyone does it nowadays. Everyone wants something cool or funny to upload onto Youtube. You were just in the wrong place at the wrong time Dad."

"What! I was in the pub, at the normal time! It's those flipping strangers that are out of order!"

"Chill Dad, it's cool." Lucy wanted Jim to go away now so she could read the comments, see what people were saying about her Dad.

"Yes, seriously Jim, this is immensely cool!" added Jess.

"So, you're not upset anymore?" asked Jim, trying for the life of him to grasp the current mindset of his adolescent daughter.

"No, its cool Dad, look at how many comments you've got, and look at what the video description says – its amazing!"

On the screen was a small description box to promote the video. It read:

"The Clitheroe Prime Minister ---→OH MY GOD :-D Went to Clitheroe to check out the Skate Park facilities and met the coolest old man in the whole world. This guy is just way too funny!!MUST SEE PMSL :-D Share this film, legend, old man, lol, clitheroe, lancashire, UK, hahaha, cool"

Lucy kissed her father on the cheek, giggling.

Jim wandered off towards the kitchen to make himself a brew, surprised and irritated to be described as an old man at the age of 45. All he could hear was the hyperactive giddy chattering of the girls reading out comment after comment and laughing, giggling or screaming after each one. He made his drink and went to sit down in the front room, just as his only son, 13 year old Jonathan burst in through the front door, laughing.

"Dad! Guess what!" he shouted as he slammed the front door behind him and threw his bag on the stairs. "Someone's put you on the internet! It's well funny! I've just been at Harry's house and his Dad showed it to us! He said I had to say to you, well done!" Jonathan was beaming from ear to ear, struggling to catch his breath.

"I know, I know, Lucy has just shown it to me." Jim laughed and Jonathan walked over to him and gave his Dad a high five.

"You're a legend Dad! Can't believe it! Harry's Dad watched it about three times, he couldn't stop laughing! What has Mum said?"

"She doesn't know. She's out shopping with Vic." Replied Jim, wondering for the first time what his wife Karen will make of all this.

"Ha ha, Dad, this is the coolest thing ever! I'm phoning Granddad, he's going to love this!" Jonathan wandered off to the phone, laughing as he went. Jim sat down on the settee with his brew and stared out through the front room window at the Castle. He realised he was grinning, and wondered if the day could get anymore peculiar. Just then Karen walked in the front door with their youngest daughter Victoria.

"Mum! Mum!" shouted Lucy as soon as she heard her Mother arrive home. "Come here, this is awesome!" she shouted, jumping up and down and waving her hands dramatically and enthusiastically. Karen burst out laughing.

"I know, I know, I've heard all about it. I've been stopped by everyone. Your Dad eh? What's he like?"

"Your hair looks amazing!" said Jim, spellbound by Karen's new style.

"Good!" said Karen. "You noticed!" She gave

him a kiss on the cheek. "Make us a brew love, and don't try and change the subject! Right, lets have a look at this video that your Dads made."

"I haven't made...." Jim stopped himself. Karen had waltzed through to the other room and wasn't listening anyway. Jim shuffled back to the kitchen to follow his instructions.

"Anyone else want a brew?"

"Go on then!" shouted Jonathan.

"Coffee please Dad!" yelled Lucy.

"Please can I have a tea, two sugars Jim?" asked Jess, politely shouting over the sound of Karen's laughter at her husband's bizarre video.

Chapter Three
Taste of India Restaurant, Clitheroe, Saturday Night

The Arkwright family were in very high spirits, enjoying a fun night at the only Indian restaurant in town. They were indulging themselves with a lavish meal to celebrate Jim and Karen's 25th "first snog" anniversary. The meal had been planned for several weeks, because Saturday nights were always fully booked at the Taste of India.

In Jim's eyes, Karen had always made a concerted effort to look good and had always carried it off - but tonight she looked even more stunning than ever. She had been to have her jet black hair cut into a dramatic new "bob" style especially for the occasion and although she had been unsure at first, the reaction to her funky new style had certainly been positive. Jim couldn't stop looking at her, nor complimenting her on the sexy new look. It was a bold step for Karen who had always been comfortable keeping to the same practical style. There was no doubt that this new bob was making her feel more confident and attractive tonight though as the relentless positive comments and admiring glances continued.

Jim had been holding his wife's hand for most of the evening, the couple were evidently still happy with one another after reaching their quarter century together. The children, Lucy and Jonathan had dressed very smartly for the occasion, and 9 year old Victoria - the baby of the family, was making everybody laugh with her cheeky remarks and questions.

"Did Daddy have hair, or was he still bald when you first met him?" had been her best one-liner so far.

The family were also merry due to the amount of people that had wandered over to comment on Jim's internet appearance. It seemed that practically everybody that the Arkwrights knew in the restaurant had seen the clip, and had congratulated Jim on his impression - and had laughed at the simple joke of it all becoming so popular.

"You'd get my vote fellah!" had become a regular comment.

The few people that hadn't yet seen it had certainly heard about it, thanks to the instant sharing over Facebook, Twitter and e-mails. The Clitheroe Prime Minister video was the talk of the small market town, still an old fashioned place with a very close knit community spirit. Most people know one another other in Clitheroe. And if they don't know one another they generally know *something* about one another. The mood in the restaurant was exuberant and everybody was having a great time, most notably the Arkwrights.

Karen and Jim had their first date in 1987, after Jim took her to the pictures in Blackburn to watch Dirty Dancing. His first choice had been Predator, but Karen had swiftly convinced him in no uncertain terms that her choice would be the only film being watched by the pair that evening. Karen had skilfully set her stall out, right from the very beginning, on that very first date. Her modus operandi of "what I say goes" still stood firm twenty five years down the line.

"And your Dad had a moustache at the time, and he used to get little bits of food stuck in it!" The table erupted in laughter as Karen poked fun at Jim.

"Well, it was less of a moustache, more of a baby caterpillar." Jonathan's eyes were watering and his face was bright red, he was laughing so much. Karen did her kids favourite party trick, and rubbed Jim's bald head and made her "squeak squeak" sound that made the kids roar with laughter.

Jim was lapping it up, and didn't mind the abuse at all. He was having a really wonderful evening with his family. To him, Karen still looked as young and as beautiful as she had done on that very first night they briefly snogged on the bus back from Blackburn. That first passionate embrace was only interrupted when the bus took a corner too fast and Jims lap got covered in his lukewarm portion of chips and gravy. The family burst into laughter again, as Jim recounted the story of how he had tried but failed to conceal the mess on his brand new baggy white flannelling trousers by holding the newspaper wrapper in front of himself, so their Mum wouldn't see the mess as they got off the bus.

"I saw it straight away – I actually thought he'd diarrhoea'd himself!"

Lucy was almost crying with tears of laughter as story after story was retold of her parents as youngsters, kids themselves, just getting together. She felt enormous pride for her parents who have always seemed more like best friends than an ordinary husband and wife. She decided to say something, but without any idea of how profound an impact her words would have on Karen and Jim.

"Mum, and Dad, I think its amazing that you two have been together for so long, and that you still get on." This comment received another hearty laugh at the table. Lucy continued, not intending to amuse her family, but delighted that she had. "Most of my friends Mum and Dads have split, some friends even say to me that they are jealous, because I've got a Mum and Dad who still love each other, always laughing and having fun and still living together - the way that it's supposed to be."

This short, unplanned and impromptu speech brought a tear to both Karen and Jim's eyes, they were holding hands on the table and caught a glance at each other. Jims chin began to quiver as his eyes welled up.

"So I just wanted to say to you guys, that even though Dad had a really creepy moustache, thanks for getting together and thanks for literally being the best parents any kids could ever hope for." Jonathan and Victoria were nodding in agreement at their big sisters words and started a round of applause. The couple glanced at each other once again and laughed an awkward, emotional sob as they tried to hide their embarrassment at feeling so touched. Jim extended his fingers and wafted them quickly before his eyes, blinking rapidly - which got another laugh from around the table. Jims mocking impressions of emotional women and overtly camp men were excellent and well appreciated when TV talent shows were on, but this was the first time he'd had to do the actions to real emotion. Karen lifted her glass and led the toast.

"Cheers!"

"Thank you Lucy," said Jim, through a cracked voice. "But let's change the topic eh? You're breaking my bloody heart!" Jim wiped away his tears as Karen rubbed her eyes. They were red and teary but the smile on her face was beaming.

The rest of the evening went as well as it had begun. The 25th anniversary of that notorious snog on the back seat of the 225 home from Blackburn had been a memorable evening for the Arkwrights.

The family walked the short distance home through the Clitheroe Castle grounds. It was a cool, still night and Jim and Karen held hands all of the way home.

As Lucy, Jonathan and Victoria went off to their beds, Karen poured Jim a scotch and herself a large glass of red wine. They Snuggled up on the settee and had a cuddle. Jim let out the biggest belch of his life and groaned.

"You scruffy bastard."

"Sorry love."

"You're a bleeding dosser, I'll tell you that Jim!" Karen smacked him round the head. "That stinks you filthy rotten bastard!"

"Sorry. It's on the move that curry though." Jim lifted his leg as he apologised and started to force a trump.

"Ooh. Maybe not." He put his leg back down and laughed at Karen's disapproving look. "Will you put a bog roll in the fridge for me? It's gonna be a stinger in the morning, that." Jim laughed again. He was really making himself laugh tonight and Karen found it very amusing.

"Happy snogerversary Jim, you old tit."

"Same to you. I've had a great time tonight love, absolutely brilliant night, that."

"I have as well. Best night out we've ever had, the five of us. That was gorgeous what Lucy said wasn't it? She really hit a nerve she did, bless her." Karen looked like she was going to fill up with emotion again.

"It was really from the heart weren't it? I felt like a right dickhead crying though." Jim was beaming from ear to ear as he remembered how awkward he'd felt. He took a sip from his generous portion of whiskey.

"It's been a great night. I love you Jim."

"Cheers. I love you too. Hey, I was thinking about it tonight. If that was the anniversary of our first snog, it'll only be a couple of weeks until the anniversary of our first heavy petting in your garden shed."

Karen gave him another crack around the head.

Chapter Four
Sunday Morning, Burnley Canal

"Well, we've certainly got the weather."

"The only trouble is, the warmer it gets, the smellier these dog shits become."

"Aye, well you have to ignore that Dad. Let the beauty of your surroundings take over."

"It were a lot nicer than this in Tenerife, all the young women walking about with no tops on over there. You've never seen nowt like it!"

"Ah, so thats why you're out of breath, you dirty old beggar?"

"Not at all!"

"Well, there's a very good chance you might see some tits along here as well, but they'll not be the type you mean. They keep their hoodys on around here Dad, and their Adidas tracksuit pants, whatever the weather."

Jim and his father were out on their weekly Sunday morning walk. Albert had chosen this route as it was flat, steady ground along the canal bank, but he also loved the scenery all around the old crumbling mills and tall chimneys, some with baby trees and bushes growing out the top of them now. This part of the Leeds to Liverpool canal was very near to the back-to-back terraced streets where Albert had grown up and started working in the cotton mills as a cloth lapper after he'd left school almost sixty years earlier. Albert would normally thunder along this path, taking in the sights and reminiscing his younger days. However, his pace was sluggish today, the all inclusive holiday he had just got back from had seen him indulge a little too much in the heavy food and free drink. The excesses were clear to see and Albert felt far from sprightly.

"I can't see you finishing this walk Dad, you're knackered already." Jim was mocking in his tone, rather than concerned.

"Give over, I'm right. Just a bit rusty is all, I've been sat by that pool for two weeks lad, haven't gone the length of myself!"

"Sat by the bloody bar more like." Jim affectionately grabbed his father round the back of the neck and shook it gently. "What would Mum say if she knew you were getting a fat knacker?" He shoved his Dads neck tenderly in a toy fighting kind of way. Albert chuckled.

"Leave her out of it Jim. Besides, I'm not getting fat. It's relaxed muscle this!"

"Ha ha, relaxed muscle. You wish." Jim grinned at his Dad, it impressed him that he still had an answer for everything despite all that he'd been through over the past couple of years.

"She'd say, "you have as much of what you like and you enjoy your life Bertie!" Albert sniggered mischievously to himself as he walked, knowing it was a complete lie. Jim smiled as well, more at the unlikelihood of his Mum ever calling her husband "Bertie," even in jest.

"You're such a bloody bullshitter! She'd say no such thing *Bertie!* She'd have you on a diet faster than you could say "two more steak and kidney puddings," God rest her soul."

"Aye, she would. She would Jim, you're right enough about that."

Albert could see that the conversation was about to fray into the familiarly depressing territory of his life as a widower. Albert dreaded these awkward, inevitable chats with his son. He didn't mind talking his problems through with anyone else, but he didn't like to worry

Jim. Despite anticipating that the topic of "life after Mum" would inevitably come up at some point on the walk, Albert decided to postpone it for a while and changed the subject quickly and very skilfully before the conversation drifted into it.

"Hey, have I told you about these drinks I had, by God – I can't remember what they were called. Black Russians I think, Black Belgians, something like that. Anyway listen, you'll love this. They pour you a pint of cider, then they top it up with a Pernod and a dash of blackcurrant! All you have to pay for is the Pernod which is one Euro. It's gorgeous Jim, honest to God, it's like a cocktail, but for blokes. I've never had a cocktail before but flippin' heck they're nice! They're so refreshing in the hot weather and you get absolutely hammered off them!" Jim laughed loudly at his Dad, he couldn't help it – even though he knew that he shouldn't encourage that kind of behaviour in the slightest.

"You're a bloody one off you Dad, you really are!"

They walked on a bit further through the heavily industrial part of the canal known as the Weavers Triangle. They meandered along at a slow pace on the gritted tow path in relative silence really, becoming lost in their own thoughts. Albert was mainly preoccupied with memories from the distant past that were being stirred up by the surroundings and the brilliant views all across Burnley.

Jim on the other hand was more concerned about the present, and the big job at work that was starting the following day.

As the pair continued to walk, Jim became more and more shocked by the decaying state of the area.

"Look at all that litter in the canal. Its disgusting, that far bank over there is absolutely full of it. It'd take a skip at least just to clear up that bit."

"Its getting a heck of a lot worse Jim, I was just thinking the same thing myself."

"It's a scandal, we should have people clearing it all up. Not just the litter, I mean everything you see that's wrong. All along the canal, for over a hundred miles we have these derelict and rotten old mills, just standing here, doing nothing. All that property that could be made use of is just standing idle. And that's only on this canal – there's over a hundred canals in Britain. This is only one of them!"

"Half of this lot wants bulldozering to be honest Jim."

"Yes, but what I'm getting at Dad, Why don't we get the million unemployed youths in this country working on all this? Fixing the canal walls, cleaning up the graffiti, replacing the broken windows, mending all these fences? It'd give them skills, training and work experience, and a bloody good pride in their surroundings."

"Aye, well that's a fair comment Jim. They certainly need more than a lick of paint to be honest." Albert knew the buildings were in decline, and had been since the mills stopped working in the seventies and eighties. That was around the time that the cotton trade had finally stopped in Britain after 200 years of incredible toil and labour. Despite the industrial revolution starting all around here in Burnley and across the Pennine towns of the north of England, production eventually moved to cheaper countries with less regulations, lower wages and minimal workers rights. It left towns like Burnley lost, unable to provide alternative work for its tens of thousands of cotton workers. The remaining decay and rot that Jim and Albert were looking at had become the legacy of all that.

"They shouldn't be sat at home doing nothing on benefits, getting depressed and feeling worthless – there's plenty of work to go at here. The authorities should be on top of all this, teaching them building skills by renovating these old mills, turning them into flats and offices. They could let them out at minimal rents to get the housing crisis under control."

"Aye, well they're not doing a right lot now are they? You're right enough lad."

"Look, like that one there, needs pulling down as you say. There will be some that are past hope. But the ones that need to be demolished could be used to train the next generation of demolition workers. It's so obvious, it really makes me really bloody angry when I see how shite our country is."

"I know son, and I don't think many people would disagree with you. I've never understood why you never tried your hand at politics. You'd have been bloody good at it Jim, you really would."

"No time Dad. How can you seriously commit yourself to working in politics with a young family and a business to run? You can't if you're working class. Now if you had been a multi millionaire and sent me off to an exclusive private school, I could have probably looked into it!"

"Cheeky get." Albert shoved Jim towards the waters edge and laughed as his son almost lost his footing.

"I nearly went in then, you mad old loon!" Jim laughed at his Dad, even though it shocked him that this gentle old man was still as mental as ever.

"Well you show some respect to your elders or you *will* go in next time!" Albert was smiling, faking offence at Jims comment.

"Well, you know what I mean Dad. The people

who can afford to go into politics don't come from round here, they probably don't even know that all this still exists. That's all I'm saying."

"I know what you're saying son – but your business is going very well. You could still have a go, you're young enough still."

The thought hung in the air a while, both men were walking and looking around at all the opportunities that this area held for training young builders and apprentices and regenerating the area. Once he'd started weighing everything up, it didn't take long for Albert to see the amount of potential in Jim's suggestion.

"Let's have a sit down here eh Dad, have a butty and a brew." Jim put the back pack down and pulled out a small fold up chair for his father and then the other for himself. Albert unfolded his seat and sat down, making a loud appreciative noise as he took the weight off his feet and slumped in the chair.

"Watch you don't rip that chair Dad."

"Funny today aren't we?" asked Albert, again feigning offence. Jim set up his own seat and sat beside his father, facing towards the slow rippling, muddy water. A half sunk bottle of Ace cider was bobbing lazily in the water as the sunlight illuminated the neon blue plastic, forcing dazzling shimmers of bright, reflected light to ripple and twinkle on the top of the mucky water.

"I know I'm moaning, but I do love it here Dad, it was a good choice for our walk today. I used to love coming fishing down here with you and Granddad. We'd always have a good laugh. Never caught nowt though!" Jim looked pleased just to recall those long hazy days with the two men that he had loved and admired the most.

"There was always boats passing through an' all.

Not seen a single one yet today."

"I know, it's all changed forever now lad. Unrecognisable really to when I was a nipper. Hey, do you remember that time when your Granddad brought that massive cod along and tied it to the line? It was enormous! You'd been for a wee in the trees and you came back and caught him just as he was about to chuck it in?" Albert laughed at the memory, his Dad had been embarrassed to be caught red handed trying to play the prank on his Grandson. "He'd been up to the market that morning for that fish, just to play that joke on you."

"God, yeah. I'd forgotten all about that Dad. He was a top man my Granddad." Jim and Albert were lost for a moment, staring out into the bobbling reflections of the old red brick mills dancing and swaying silently in the canal. A few moments of comfortable quiet passed.

"He used to tell me that he built all these mills. He told me all about this canal, said he dug it all out with his mate, all the way from Leeds to Liverpool. He had a story about everything! He was very proud of all this wasn't he?" Jim poured his Dad a brew from the flask.

"Aye. He was a good man your Granddad. I bloody miss him, I do. I wouldn't believe everything that he told you though. He told me he built Blackpool tower with his mate when I was little."

"Did he? He was some story teller!"

"Bullshitter more like. Most of these mills had been up best part of a hundred years before he was born! He should have gone into politics, the amount of bullshit he used to come out with!"

Jim laughed at his Dads comments, amused at him calling his own father names but in such a proudly affectionate way.

"What's on't buttys today lad?" Albert looked up and over at his son who was unwrapping the tin foil that held the neat little parcel of sandwiches together.

"Cheese and pickle."

"Real do. Thanks." Jim shared out the pack up that Karen had lovingly prepared earlier that morning. The two men stared gormlessly into the canal, once again getting lost in their own thoughts as the water gently lapped up against the stone kerbing. A distant droning noise that had been faintly buzzing in the distance slowly began to get louder, eventually building up enough volume and reverberation to shatter the peace and tranquillity and put the two men on edge. As the noise got louder it became clear that it was a motorbike that was headed along the canal towards Jim and Albert.

Just a couple of minutes passed before two teenage lads appeared through a cloud of dust round the bend on the towpath. Both of them were wearing shorts and T shirts, and without a crash helmet between them. They noisily and carelessly rode the moped scooter, laughing and shouting as they tore up the gravel path riding the scooter to its top speed.

"Yeah! You fucking dickheads!" shouted the kid on the back as they zoomed past Jim and Albert, a matter of inches away from the back of the pensioners chair.

The incident was a total mood changer and both men were left feeling angry and alert, a sudden burst of adrenaline was racing through their veins as dust, the smell of petrol, the noise of the scooters engine and the boy's laughter hung menacingly and rebelliously in the air.

"Little baskets." Said Albert under his breath. Jim had jumped up out of his chair and had somehow managed to stop himself from chasing after them. If his Dad hadn't been there, he was sure that he would have run after the scooter and dragged them off it by their throats.

"If they come back Dad, they're going in that canal with the bike. I'll boot them in there myself." The look on Jims face was unmistakable anger. He was incensed at the hostile, hateful attitude of the two lads that he had never laid eyes on before.

"What was the need for that Dad? Seriously?"

Albert just stared down into the shadowy water as Jim watched the scooter disappear from view in a thick cloud of dry dust.

"If they come back, and you kick them into the cut, you'll be going to jail - simple as that. No one will want to hear your side of the story – you'll just be seen as a mad bloke who is a danger to young kids. Just leave it Jim. Forget about them son."

"They could have hit you Dad! Could have hit both of us. They could have killed us."

"Aye. Well, they didn't and that's the main thing. You need to keep a cool head Jim. You really worry me when you get a temper."

"Don't worry about me, I stopped myself from chasing them Dad. I'm more bothered about you, what they could have done to you. You're an old man, why are they driving a bike at you and laughing and shouting abuse like that? What was the point?" Jim sat back down and saw that he'd dropped his sandwich on the floor as he'd jumped out of his seat.

"Little bastards."

Despite more than five seconds having elapsed since he'd dropped the butty, Jim considered whether the five second rule should still count on a spot popular with dog walkers. He decided that it wasn't worth the risk, a mouthful of dog dirt would really ruin the morning. He kicked the sandwich into the canal which attracted a couple of ducks to flap enthusiastically and float across from the other embankment to tuck in, forcing the cider bottle to drift a tiny bit further along on its slow journey toward the canal bank.

"If I did boot them into the canal, at least it would make the little bastards stop and think in the future!"

Albert didn't reply. He waited a few moments to let Jim simmer down before he spoke again. "See, the thing is Jim," he paused, taking a sip of tea from the flask cup, "what you've got to ask yourself is this." Another long pause passed before Albert continued. "There's nowt you can do about them lads. But ask yourself this question, could you imagine our Jonathan doing that?"

"No. No chance Dad, never in a month of Sundays."

"Well, there you are. As long as you know that your kids know right from wrong, that's all you have to worry about. Them two lads there won't have a Dad like you at home, teaching them what's what. They probably just have a stressed out mother who can't control them. It's nowt for you to get involved with. If we'd decided to walk up Pendle Hill today, instead of coming here, them lads would still have driven down here on that bike. It's not personal you see, it's just the way kids are now."

"Fair enough Dad. Fair point."

"Now if they do come back, you just keep your cool and let them go on their way. No hassle." Albert ripped his sandwich in half and gave a piece to Jim.

"Aw, thanks Dad. Sorry, but I just get really annoyed by the pointlessness of things like that. They could have slowed down, gone past sensibly. There's just no need for it, but more and more of the kids seem to be going about trying to piss someone off, with that couldn't-give-a-shit attitude. It makes me wonder where it will all end up." Jim bit into the sandwich he'd been given.

Albert thought about what Jim said for a few moments before offering the flask and cup over, and decided to change the topic.

"Hey, what was this that Jonathan was talking about on the phone yesterday? He said you're a star on the internet!" Albert slapped his son on the knee and laughed. "It's not a flippin' porno is it?"

The pair laughed at the joke, and in a small way it helped to lift the gloom that the scooter riders had brought.

Once Jim had explained the discovery of the internet video and everything that had happened the previous day, Albert looked as though he'd only really understood some of it.

"I'll be glad when everyone's forgotten about it Dad. It's so creepy that someone can just sit there and film you like that without you even knowing anything about it. And then to top it off, they put it on the computer and everyone in the world can see it!" Jim shook his head. Albert looked solemnly across the water, and up once again at the enormous, unused mills and the giant chimney stacks that towered all around this once heavily industrialised place.

"I don't really understand anything to do with all that Jim. Nothing makes sense to me. The whole thing with computers and internet, and these mobile phones everywhere, it's slowly becoming like the computers are taking over. Don't get me wrong, I like some of the things they can do. Jonathan and Lucy had me looking into the back yard from a satellite in space the other day. Now I enjoyed that - that was something else! You could see my flippin' wheely bins! But the things are taking over – you have to put your shopping through these computerised tills now at the supermarket. I refuse to do it! I say to them – that's a job there, someone could be earning a wage there. But no-one listens to an old biff like me. Now if everybody stood together and refused, we'd stand half a chance!"

"No I know. I can't really understand all the computer stuff myself Dad, I think I get it off you."

"It's dangerous though you know. It's never been possible for people to communicate in the ways they twitter and send videos through their phones. But it's going to cause a lot of harm you know Jim, people have too much freedom to organise themselves now – look at the riots – all organised by phones and twitter. It's a dangerous thing the government are doing allowing all this freedom to organise protests and disputes. Its like they are willingly losing control."

"On the other hand though, people go online now to protest, and it's much nicer than trashing towns or burning down buildings! They sign petitions and write angry comments on the internet, and then they feel like they've done their bit. I bet the government are laughing, all the anger is deep but it's all very civilised, all the protesting takes place on laptops and smart phones Dad. Wi fi Warriors!"

"Aye, well it's all weird Jim. I remember seeing something on Tomorrows World about all that in the eighties, and I didn't like the sound of it then."

"The thing is with this video Dad, Karen is convinced it'll get bigger and bigger. She reckons the reason it's got this popular is because people all agree with the things I said. I wouldn't mind, I was only joking about with it! If they heard my true thoughts about everything, I doubt it'd be so popular!"

"Oh, I don't know. You've got a great brain in that head, always have had. You see logical solutions to problems really quickly. You've always been like it. Me and your Mum was always saying it when you were a kid."

"Well, listen Dad, I think it'll be hard work for Lucy at school after the holidays, but then after that it'll all be forgotten about soon enough."

Jims phone vibrated in his pocket. He took it out and saw that he had a text. It was from Karen. It read; "The video just hit 100,000 views!!!!!!!" Jim put it back in his pocket without saying anything about the message to Albert.

"Its 8.20 on BBC Radio 2, and this morning we're trying to track down the latest British internet superstar! If you haven't seen the Clitheroe Prime Minister impression video that has gone crazy over the weekend – check out the BBC Radio 2 homepage, we've uploaded a link there for you. It's absolutely hilarious – and this morning we're asking Great Britain the question "who is the guy?" We know he comes from Clitheroe in Lancashire, and that he does an awesome impression of the Prime Minister, in fact some people are saying he talks more sense – but that's all we know about him. So, please help us, we want to get him on the show this morning! So, get in touch if you know who he is! Back to 1976 now, Here's Elton John and Kiki Dee, with their classic number one smash hit - Don't go breaking my heart."

"Jesus Jim! Did you hear that? Are you going to ring in?" asked Eggy, one of Jims younger staff members at the welding workshop that he runs. The big job of the week was a school railings replacement that needed finishing to a tight deadline. The school was on a week's holiday and the project had to be completed on time. Jim didn't have any time to waste, this job for the local council had the potential to become the start of a very lucrative and ongoing contract. Jim was determined to do a first class job, on time. Jim had waited for years for an opportunity to become one the council's trusted contractors. He'd worked for months on the finer details, and he was determined that his company would put in an exceptional job on this trial contract.

"Bollocks, we've no time for dicking about lads, get that first load of 30 panels on the wagon, we need to be out of here in 5 minutes flat. Make sure they're fastened down properly Jason."

With that Jim walked off towards his tiny office in the corner of the dusty unit to answer the phone that had been ringing for the past minute or so.

"He's being a bit of a miserable bastard today isn't he?" said Eggy, quietly in the general direction of his co-workers. They didn't answer, they just continued to load up the heavy railing sections onto the back of the truck. But his colleagues understood the point that Eggy was making. They had all burst into work excitedly, expecting Jim to be in a great mood considering his video's success over the weekend. Everyone in Clitheroe had seen it now.

"Hello, Metal Makers, Jim speaking…"

"Jim, it's me." It was Karen.

"Oh, how do. What's up?" He was surprised. Karen didn't usually bother him at work unless it was really important.

"Jim, my phone hasn't stopped ringing all morning! Radio 2 are doing a competition to find out who you are. It's crazy, all my friends are ringing asking if they can phone in! I know you've got this big job on love, but think of the publicity you could get for the company from all this. The video is on half a million views now, and that number is growing by about ten thousand an hour!" Karen had spent the whole of Sunday lunch trying to convince Jim to "cash in" on this opportunity. Jim still thought it was a load of old nonsense and remained resolute that it will all soon blow over.

"I know, I just heard them saying it a minute a go. Eggy reckoned I should phone in as well. Its not my cup of tea isn't all this Karen, and if I don't do a good job on St Michaels school railings I could lose out on a shit load of future work. Now I'd rather us have that council contract more than I want 5 minutes talking shit on the radio. Any how, if I did it, then I'll be mithered to do summat else, then summat else after that. Now I'm getting off, need to get this fence up. I'll seeya tonight."

Knowing that as far as Karen was concerned - that was not the end of the conversation, Jim shouted "I'm just coming lads, shut up!" at the top of his voice just as he placed the receiver down, so although he had hung up, it was a polite way of hanging up. The conversation would have to wait until later on.

"I'm getting sick to death of this already," he muttered to himself as he grabbed the school drawings and plans, and flew out of the office, knocking off the light as he went.

"Right, Eggy and Daz, there's not enough room in the cab for you two so I want you both to jog over to the far side of St Michaels school field, near the traffic lights. If you get there before me, I'll buy you both a sausage butty from Joyces."

"Eh?" asked Eggy.

"No worries boss!" said Daz, shoving Eggy gently in the back. "We'll piss it Jim, we'll be there in no time - you'll have to go all round the one way system. Come on Eggy!" With that, Daz started jogging out of the unit, as his colleague Eggy followed and gave reluctant chase.

Jim laughed as he fired up the engine on the flat bed truck and eased it out of the unit, laden with the first sections of fencing for the school perimeter. "See you laters" he shouted out of the cab to the rest of the staff who would be making the rest of the panels while

Jim's small team would be installing them.

"Muppets!" said Jason, laughing at the two younger lads as they jogged out of view around the corner. Jason, and indeed all of the Metal Makers lads had been through these daft rituals before. Jim knew full well that he'd make it to the site before them. But Jim had always done things like that to judge the character of his lads. He found that it was a great way of getting an insight into their attitude.

Over the years, Jim had had plenty of occasions where employees have refused to do things, or argued the toss. The way that Jim viewed it was very simple. He pays well, works hard and runs a happy shop. He personally gives the lads trade skills that are of real value to them for the rest of their life. Jim knows that if he's got a 17 year old apprentice who is going to sulk and whinge about things, they are not going to fit in and make it as a member of his team. Daz knew this, and that was why he shoved Eggy in the back before he could start mouthing off and questioning Jims request that they run across town to the site.

It's a very simple technique that works for Jim, it helps him to sort the wheat from the chaff. He'd learnt it the hard way himself, when he was an apprentice thirty years earlier. Jim had to laugh it off and smile through his own embarrassment several times as his older colleagues laughed and jeered when he came back from the factory stores with a box of uncompressed oxygen, quick burning sawdust, and a fallopian tube.

All the staff at Metal Makers have funny stories of how Jim has done "character building" exercises on his staff. Most can take it, and generally become higher in rank and responsibility within the close knit team. Others can't take it and decide that Metal Makers isn't the right place for them.

On one occasion, a young lad called Russ who had a real chip on his shoulder started at Metal Makers. He was a big, strong rugby playing lad, and very intimidating. Russ believed that he was faster, harder working, wittier and more intelligent than anyone else there. He genuinely felt that everybody in the company was a moron, including Jim, and he made no secret of his megalomania by mouthing off at the staff all day long.

One morning, after hearing just about enough of this lad tormenting, boasting and generally upsetting the workshop mood, Jim went over to the fridge and brought Russ a slice of bacon. He asked him if he would take it over to Dawsons and get them to scan it into their colour matching machine and mix 1 litre of bacon coloured gloss. "Make sure he scans it in the middle bit, not on the streaky fat bits. It wants to be proper bacon colour!" said Jim, and handed the lad a ten pound note with the slice of meat.

Russ came back fifteen minutes later, without any paint.

"Eh? Where is my paint?" Jim had asked, while the rest of the Metal Makers staff tried to keep a straight face as they went about their work.

"They can't scan bacon into the machine!" said the lad sneerily, still arrogant.

"Why not?" asked Jim. "I've got to paint the railings at the butchers this afternoon! Go and try the decorating shop down near Booths lad!" Jim turned his back on Russ and carried on welding. As the conceited young lad left the yard and went round the corner with his slice of bacon dangling beside him, the whole team erupted in laughter. He returned a little while later, once again without any paint.

"Are you taking the micky Russ? Where's my

bacon paint?" demanded Jim, trying to stifle a grin.

"They can't scan meat. The scanner doesn't work on meat they said."

"Oh aye! Sorry Russ, I knew that! I'd totally forgot! Bacon your pardon mate." Jim smiled at Russ as the rest of the lads burst out laughing.

"What did you say?" said Russ, going red in the face, mainly through rage but also embarrassment. The rest of Jim's lads were enjoying this, Russ was finally getting his just desserts from their boss, the master of wind ups and mickey takes.

"I said bacon your pardon. Because I forgot that they can't scan meat into those scanners." Jim laughed in his face.

"Are you taking the piss out of me Jim?" shouted Russ. Jim laughed again.

"Yes, I was. You've been winding up my lads for weeks now. So I thought I'd have a look and see how you like it, give you a taste of your own medicine if you like. Now go and put my bacon back in the fridge, start treating my lads with some respect, or you can get your jacket and get out of my yard. It's entirely up to you, I couldn't give a tinkers cuss either way."

Jim had remained smiling throughout the conversation. Russ immediately got his coat and left. The rest of Metal Makers staff were delighted to see the back of the boy, who confidently swaggered out of the yard as though the company was doomed and about to go bankrupt without his input.

"Right lads, I'll share the remainder of his wage out amongst you all on Friday for having to put up with the wanker for so long!"

Instantly, the mood at Metal Makers returned to the happy, content and hard working atmosphere that it had previously enjoyed until Russ started wearing everybody down.

Jim had recounted the event later that day in the pub with his after work drinking pals Dave and Phil. Dave had told Jim that he was envious of the fact that Jim could treat his staff like that, and could actively encourage them to walk out. Dave explained that on the railways, you couldn't get away with anything like that for fear of being accused of harassment, or even being called a bully.

The comment had angered Jim, because the implication was that Jim was guilty of bullying. Dave had unwittingly found himself on the other end of a severe lecture for his trouble.

"You see that's precisely the kind of bullshit that has brought this country to its knees Dave!" Jim hadn't meant to raise his voice but noticed, partly thanks to the raised eyebrow expression on Phil's face as Dave attempted to back track.

"No, I'm not saying…"

"You're saying that if you treated a lad on the railway like I treated this Russ, you'd be accused of bullying. Well, I'm not a bully, I'm the boss. I'm the one who runs that company, I'm responsible for all my lads wages. I've got to get the jobs done on time and I've got my own family to support. Its my business – mine." Jim stuck his finger at his chest. "And if I give a lad a chance and he blows it because he can't behave – it's my right to take the piss out of him and send him packing if I want to."

Jim took a big swig out of his pint glass. He was clearly annoyed by the suggestion of bullying, regardless of how loosely it connected with the reality of what had happened at Metal Makers with Russ' bad attitude and the bacon paint.

Jim continued as Dave and Phil listened

intently. "Its actually good that toss-pots come along from time to time because I get to show my lads what's expected with stuff like this. When I show somebody up, it helps the rest of them feel valued and part of a team, as well as reminding them where the line is drawn. The trouble with this country is its gone so soft, the powers that be would prefer we all walk around trying not to offend people. But this lad has been threatening, annoying and taking the piss out of my staff for weeks. He's had plenty of bollockings but he doesn't hear any of them. If he is too thick, or arrogant to rein his attitude in and knuckle down to the requirements of the job, well it's his misfortune. I'm not a bully Dave. In all walks of life, if somebody works against their team they are outcast. It's basic human nature, and it's no different in my little workshop - and no amount of government legislation can change that fact."

"I totally agree Jim!" said Dave, "But all I'm saying is, the human resources rules about these things wouldn't allow me to send a lad off for bacon coloured paint on the railway because it would be against his human rights to be subjected to undue infringement of his dignified something or other." Phil laughed, Jim smiled.

"He's right," said Phil, offering Dave a bit of back up. "It's a different game now with all these giant companies getting sued left right and centre for work related stuff. You've to be careful about how nicely you bollock someone nowadays Jim, you have to be able to prove that you were constructive and supportive to the employee."

"Yes," added Dave. "We have to give "feedback" to rail staff. It's better known as a shit sandwich. If someone's late, we have to package the message up around positive comments, so the shit bit is in the middle. No word of a lie! So, we'll say "Hey, you did a really great job of being on time on Monday and Tuesday. But we're really disappointed that you came late today because it meant that a train was cancelled and it has a really bad impact on the railway, the staff and most importantly our customers, so please don't be late again or you'll be sacked as this is your final warning. But listen lets not dwell on that - on the positive side, you were absolutely brilliant at arriving at work on time on Monday and Tuesday!"

Dave's example received a huge laugh from Phil and Jim. Dave had summed up the stupidity of modern working life perfectly as far as his friends were concerned.

"Absolute joke!" said Phil, shaking his head as he spoke.

Jim totally understood the point Dave was making, but was still angered at the thought of his behaviour towards this daft young lad could be construed as bullying. It was Russ who was the bully, he spent every minute of every day bullying the other lads – saying whatever he wanted, knowing full well that none of the others would come over and give him anything back due to his size and reputation as a tough nut.

"It's not right though, this kind of pandering to toss-pots, and then calling the managers bullies. It isn't progress in my view. Its this kind of sentiment that's just encouraging the lazy, can't be arsed generation that are making the country unsustainable. All these youngsters do now is look around for somebody to sue against, and you can't call them names because it might hurt their feelings. We're deliberately forcing the younger generations to be lazy, thick, soft bastards. If I was ever accused of bullying I'd want to see black eyes and fag burns on my victims at the very least, I can tell you that for nowt."

Arriving at the school railings job, Jim and Jason pulled up in the truck outside the school entrance to find Eggy and Daz waiting. Jim wound his window down and looked down at the lads. They were fresh faced and slightly breathless.

"Ha ha! Told you we'd beat you Jim, piece of piss!" Daz was clearly very pleased with himself, and Eggy was smiling too. Both lads seemed delighted with themselves for beating the boss.

"Well done lads! I didn't think you'd manage it!" said Jim, sarcastically looking over at Jason. "I suppose I owe you both a sausage butty now!"

"Bleedin' right you do!" said Daz.

"Better had do!" said Eggy.

"Here you go then." Jim threw them each a white paper bag containing a sausage butty wrapped in tin foil.

"Now if I hadn't had to stop at Joyce's and wait for them to be cooked, you'd have had no chance lads!" Jim jumped out of the cab laughing, clutching his own sausage butty.

"Let's get these munched and then its all hands on."

Jim wandered around the lads pointing at the old fencing and explaining who needed to do what between bites of his sandwich.

A short while later, the lads had set to work digging out the old concrete posts that held up the perished criss-cross wire fencing. The faded and rusting fence had withstood everything that the great northern weather had been able to throw at it for over thirty years. The 1980's school boundary was now beyond repair and had to come down, to be replaced by Metal

Makers traditional railings.

Just as the first mix of concrete was poured into the new holes, Jim took a call on his mobile phone. It was a familiar voice at the local radio station Lancashire FM, with very exciting news.

Chapter Six
Monday Tea Time - New Inn

"Look, can we just give over talking about this bloody video on the internet. It's starting to peck my head." Jim had heard about little else over the past 48 hours and it was beginning to take its toll. He had hoped to get a reprieve here in the sanctuary of the New Inn. But with the video still going viral all across Britain and further a field, it was definitely right at the top of everybody's agenda at the pub where it originated from.

"Yes, but come on Jim, whichever way you look at it, it's a bit creepy – sitting there with a concealed camera and recording people. I'm sure there's some law against that."

For the life of him, Dave couldn't understand the reason why those young chaps had sat there and recorded the trio the previous Wednesday afternoon. Himself, Phil and Jim were now recognisable faces on the internet thanks to that video, and Sandra had accidentally let it slip that she had noticed one of them holding a phone up as Jim was horsing about. She felt bad for not mentioning anything at the time, but had no idea they were recording her customers. All of this had come as a big shock to them all, partly because it was nothing special. The video that was causing such a fuss on the internet was a typical afternoon's messing about for these three proud, hard working Lancashire men.

"Well, its one of those things, isn't it? It wouldn't have happened if we knew that this kind of thing went on. It's a learning curve, we can all take a lesson from it," suggested Phil. "And Sandra, you can start by putting a sign up. No videoing folk allowed."

"Right, okay Phil. Do you want me to put it next to the No Dickheads Allowed one?" asked Sandra, slyly ribbing Phil who had made many requests for signs, most of which were devoid of any political correctness. But Sandra had conceded that the "No Dickheads" sign allowed her a great deal of discretion. She was also still thinking about Phil's "No Dogshit On Your Shoes Allowed - Under Any Circumstances" idea.

Jim had an entirely different point of view on the topic.

"What bothers me right, about these youngsters nowadays, they are all so bloody obsessed with popularity. They want the most amount of Facebook friends, most followers on Twitter. This video thing just goes to show how they'll do anything for attention, to get popularity or status amongst their friends. Our Lucy and her pal were explaining it all to me. Apparently, the lad who put the video on the internet is classed as a legend now. And it was me who did all the donkey work!" Jim did a mock look of exasperation as his friends chuckled.

"That's half of what's going wrong with our country fellahs," offered Dave. "But don't be stupid, don't fall into the trap and blame the youngsters. The younger generations are being forced into this life of petty stupidity and silliness. They work hard on trying to get popular videos and a good reputation now, because there's nothing else for them to apply themselves to. They concentrate on all this pointless shite, like Twitter and Youtube because the big stuff, the important stuff in life that we aimed for at that age has been robbed off them."

"Hear, hear" shouted Sandra from her stool beside the bar, sympathetic to Dave's argument as the mother of teenagers herself.

"Think about it, they can't work towards decent jobs because there's none," continued Dave. "They can't buy their first houses and do them up, because they are far too expensive. They can't learn to drive because if they do they would never afford the insurance. They can't go to University anymore, because it's too bloody expensive. They are just being forced to get pissed, shag around and act daft, think about it there's nowt else for them. But that's not the way the telly news says it – they make out as though all these youngsters are deranged or something, they go on about bloody Broken Britain, politicians trying to shift the blame onto the kids rather than doing the noble thing and admit that since the seventies and eighties, they've screwed the country up and now the youth have no reasonable opportunities available to them in this country."

"Bloody well said!" shouted Phil.

"It's no bleeding wonder they act like idiots if you ask me. Our generation – their parents have failed them, good and proper!" Dave was pleased with the nodding and supportive gestures from his two drinking pals and the landlady who was sat on her stool by the bar, eavesdropping as she often did with the conversations of her favourite customers.

"Too bloody true! And they idolise footballers and pop stars who wouldn't get out of their Bentleys to piss on them if they were on fire!" Everybody laughed at Phil's quip, mainly because it was so true.

Jim was pleased that the subject had got round to this. His own kids baffled him with their insular and shallow views around the topic of heroes and idols.

"I was watching a programme about the worlds biggest structures with my lad, and we saw some truly incredible stuff on there – and the Shard came on, that three hundred metre high glass pyramid tower in London. I said to our Jonathan, he's some man Renzo Piano, he's built some of the most amazing buildings in the world. But he just stared at me. He'd never heard of him before. He knew what the Shard was, but not the name of the guy who designed the bloody thing! For me, designing a building like that is a hell of a lot more impressive than singing someone else's song!"

"Too true Jim, spot on." Dave couldn't agree more.

"How can kids know the names of people that didn't quite get through to the final on a crumby TV talent show three weeks ago – but they don't know any of the people who are doing really amazing things in the real world, building, designing and creating mind blowing structures like that? What are they taught these days in school?"

"I don't get it, I really don't. It's like they are force fed pointless information and celebrity news as a distraction. I'd rather it was important stuff that would inspire them, or motivate them into useful interests that could set them up for leaving school and college. But there's none of that." Sandra rarely butted in to these conversations but she identified with the point that Jim was making, her own kids were also oblivious to anything outside mobile phones, Saturday night TV and fashion.

"Tell you what is funny, I asked my Lucy why she wasn't going out the other day, you know what she said? She said "C.B.A." It turns out it means "can't be arsed" – so they can't even be arsed anymore, to say that they can't be arsed!"
The regulars had a chuckle at the twisted irony.

"Seriously though Sandra, you know in the Victorian era, when they discovered steam power and swapped farming for industry, Britain became the richest, most powerful and influential country on earth. Not bad for a tiny island! And it certainly wasn't a footballer, or a singer, or an actor that the people idolised, it was a bloke called Isambard Kingdom Brunel. He was an engineer, and he really was the most exciting celebrity in Britain. Word would spread up and down the land about him and his latest projects and achievements. Victorians would stand and talk about him on street corners and chat about his latest accomplishments, hoping that one day they might actually get to see one of his creations – whether that was the first ever metal ship that was built, or the aquaducts, viaducts, railway bridges, docks and engines that he designed."

"Didn't he design the Clifton suspension bridge in Bristol?" asked Dave.

"Yes, that's the fellah! He designed it, the first suspension bridge to cover such a height and distance, but he never saw it. Listen up – good pub quiz fact this. He died of a stroke before it was built. He was only in his fifties when he died, but I'll tell you what, his contribution to this country in his short life was off the scale. His comparison in our culture today would have to score 40 goals in a season, then win a celebrity insect eating competition and have a pair of false tits attached to his ears to get that famous! Britain has become a really pathetic race of people and we seriously need to change it. As the achievements of our biggest idols have shrunk, our ambitions and dreams have shrivelled up too."

"Couldn't agree more!" Phil loved it when Jim went on one like this.

"One of the country's biggest industries is football! This was a game our ancestors played to take their minds off the hard graft of industry! We're sat here, drinking beer in Lancashire - the birthplace of the world's industrial revolution – not Manchester's, or

Britain's, or Europe's – this was the whole world's classroom 200 years ago this place. And now look at us. Football is our main industry. Says it all doesn't it?"

"Bravo! A round of applause for Mr Arkwright please lady and gentlemen!" Jim laughed as Phil held up his beer glass in salute of Jims well considered rant.

"Let me get you a pint!" he offered as Dave too held up his tankard. Jim held up his hand in a rare protest. "No, no. I wish I could. But I'm just having the one tonight – got a radio interview at six on Lancashire FM!" Jim was clearly pleased with himself.

"They've got some big wigs on from the Council and they wanted a small business owner to go on and say things about the difficulties we're facing at the moment."

"Hey that's great stuff Jim. Nice one mate." Said Dave, patting his pal on the back.

"Well make sure you mention how crippling the tax system is. It's no wonder all the work has gone overseas. The Government have strangled the life out of industry in this country with their greed and meddling. But the jokes on them now, because all that tax is spent paying people benefits because there's no jobs or industry left. They've snookered themselves tell 'em! Serves them right, the short sighted, greedy bastards!" Phil was getting himself worked up at the very thought of Jim's opportunity to set the record straight with the powers that be.

"Don't you worry yourself folks. I'll give a good account of myself!" With that Jim swallowed the remainder of his beer and stood to leave.

"We'll be listening Jim. Give them a good telling love!" Sandra seemed genuinely excited by the thought of Jim laying some of his views on the line on the radio. She'd long thought many of his beliefs and opinions should be heard beyond the four walls of the Snug, and the same went for Dave and Phil. All three of them were very wise, deep thinkers in Sandra's eyes, but it was Jim that had what northerners called "the gift of the gab."

"Well, it's only a local radio talk show. Don't expect the revolution to start just yet. I'll see you lot tomorrow, where you can all take the piss out my posh speaking voice! Cheers."

"Aye, have a good 'en fellah." Shouted Dave as Jim retreated through the door and out past the doorway smokers into the summer sunshine, heading home to smarten himself up.

Chapter Seven
Lancashire FM Studios – Monday Evening

"Ah, Jim, a genuine pleasure to meet you."

Jim had arrived at the radio station in Preston feeling nervous, but excited. He had been completely taken aback when he was instantly recognised by the presenter Alan Proctor as he'd entered the reception area. Alan had invited him onto his radio show to talk about the financial struggle for local businesses in Lancashire.

This was a weird moment for Jim, he'd never been "recognised" before, it gave him a surprising jolt and made him feel a little embarrassed. Alan realised, and explained that he had seen the video.

"Sorry, how stupid of me – I recognised you from the Clitheroe Prime Minister video on the net. Ha ha, I see you've had over a million views now! It's absolutely hilarious, we had a right laugh watching it in the office. The guys in the newsroom think you'd make a far more sensible Prime Minister!" Both men laughed, although it occurred to Jim for the first time that maybe his invitation onto the show wasn't exclusively because of his standing as a local businessman, as had been suggested earlier that morning when the DJ phoned. None the less, Jim knew that this was a great opportunity to promote his company for free on the popular local radio station. "Come on through," said Alan, "I'll introduce you to my other guests." The short, quite chubby radio presenter looked absolutely nothing as Jim had imagined. Jim had heard the Alan Proctor show many times over the years, and had developed a very different mental image of the man. It made Jim smile to himself as he followed Alan along a glass walled corridor which had radio studios on either side.

"And, just in here we are." Alan opened a door and waved Jim through. "Now, we're all here. Let me introduce all of you guys to one another." Jim wandered into the small glass walled room which contained two rather reticent, serious looking people. They were sat awkwardly upright on a leather couch and the atmosphere was a little frosty. Behind them was a coffee machine. Jim smiled at both, but from the austere glances he received back he felt as though he might have gotten out of his depth, like he'd staggered into a high class dining room clutching a donner kebab, spilling garlic mayo everywhere.

"This is County Councillor Fred Norton, who is coming onto the programme tonight to represent the County's Chamber of Trade in his capacity of Chairman." Alan wagged his arm towards a miserable looking large, fat man with a huge red nose. "And this is Mandy Cunningham from Pennine Business Action." To Jim she looked exactly like a bossy middle management consultant, heavily made up and arguably 15 years too old for the revealing clothes she wore, and he could sense she had a huge opinion of herself. Jim would have bet his salary that she drove a bright red convertible.

"Fred, Mandy, I know that you guys already know one another, but please let me introduce you to Jim Arkwright."

"Hello!" said Jim cheerily, raising his hand with a friendly, nervous wave.

"Jim is a local businessman who runs a small metal fabrication firm over in Clitheroe." Alan was good at introductions but his guests it seemed were poor at social grace.

"How do you do?" asked Mandy Cunningham, whilst County Councillor Fred Norton simply nodded vaguely in Jim's direction and turned to Alan. "Is that it? Someone from a little firm? I was told senior management from British Aerospace and Vauxhall were coming on?" He looked thoroughly disgusted as he glanced again in Jim's direction. Jim laughed nervously, mostly out of shock and embarrassment at the rudeness of the man.

"No Fred, tonight's show is about the impact of the crisis on small businesses — your secretary was told we were talking to a smaller local business to see what can be done to help them." Alan desperately wanted to apologise on behalf of the councillor. He gave Jim a panicky glance that tried to sum up his embarrassment, and Jim got the message loud and clear.

"Listen mate, you'll probably learn more about the problems with this economy from talking to little firms than you will the bigger ones. Our firms are at the grass roots." Jim was offering an olive branch but Councillor Norton still looked as though he was being asked to share a phone box with a man who had just farted.

Alan became concerned about the mood amongst the guests. His experience and intuition told him that a harsh atmosphere could help make for an interesting programme, but he felt very awkward regardless, particularly for Jim - who really hadn't done anything wrong.

To help pass the ten minutes before his talk show was due on air, Alan began rabbiting on about the programme, the radio station and anything else that popped into his head.

Jim listened with interest to Alan's ramblings and observed the others. He wondered if Mandy and Fred were alright, they seemed totally out of their comfort zones. But then it occurred to him that the stakes were very high for them if either of them stepped out of line, or if they said something wrong. In his own case, Jim could say pretty much whatever he liked about the challenges of running a small business in the difficult economic times and wouldn't face any grief from anyone.

Under the circumstances, Mandy and Fred probably had a lot to fear from Jim, and from the radio stations listeners - as they all had the potential to question, embarrass or belittle the professionals who were here to promote themselves and their work. In Jim's mind, the thought made sense, and explained the Councillors unnecessary and hostile behaviour. A representative from British Aerospace would be finely tuned to talking about things in a political manner, whereas a small independent chap like Jim may not share the same heirs and graces. To these professionals, Jim was nothing more than an unpredictable wildcard.

This realisation empowered Jim, as his nerves began to jangle as the clock got closer to the hour mark. He began to feel restless, his palms suddenly felt sweaty and he got butterflies in his stomach. Alan stood up and clasped his hands together enthusiastically.

"Okay, lets go through to the studio guys."

After the introductions and pleasantries on the air, the Alan Proctor show got going and was enjoying a lot of audience interaction with plenty of phone calls, tweets and e-mails, mainly from listeners with a vested interest in the topics that the radio programme was talking about.

The conversation had so far stalled at the basic fact that banks were simply not lending any money to businesses, and this was the primary reason that firms were losing contracts and going bust. Alan read out an e-mail from a local business in Chorley. The owner had recently tendered for and won a major contract to build

50 huge recycling skips for the local authority. The deal was signed off, and the business had asked its bank for a loan of £67,000 to help towards the cost of raw materials. The total deal was worth £800,000 but the bank would not lend, so the business had to decline the job. The work was then awarded overseas to a contractor in Poland.

The point that Alan was making by reading the message was about how it was impossible for growth to happen and for a recovery to take place with such financial constraints on companies.

"I'll tell you what makes me laugh about this Alan," said Jim. "These TV shows they put on, showing some bloke who has got a problem with chucking stuff out. You know the kind I mean – an old guy who has completely filled his house with old newspapers and magazines – stacks upon stacks of them all through the house, can't stop doing it since his Mum died. I saw one a few months ago on Channel 4 – and the "hoarder" as he was called couldn't even get into his own house for all the stuff."

"Yes, we've all seen the programmes, it's a serious psychological condition, it's not really something to "laugh about" Jim!" The Lancashire FM radio show host was skillfully making sure that his station was immune from any potential complaints about "hoarders" or other sufferers of mental illness.

"No, no, I don't mean that they make me laugh because what they do is funny Alan. What makes me laugh is that we label them, as you say – having psychological problems – or we even think they are a bit mad, off their rockers like!" Jim laughed into the microphone. The two gloomy studio guests looked at him inquisitively, wondering if it was Jim who was having trouble mentally.

"We all ridicule him, wondering what it must be like to want to hoard all those papers – yet when some powerful businessman does the very same thing with bank notes in a bank vault, we are all supposed to think he's a fantastic success!"

"What is the point that you're making Jim, I must hurry you," asked Alan, aware that Councillor Norton was eager to make a point too.

"Well, think of a mega rich bloke who has billions stashed away, doing nothing in a bank, or all these massive corporate companies that are just sitting there on their cash, waiting for the crisis to end. What sense is there in that? These billionaires are hoarding the money while most people in society are finding that there is less and less of the stuff to go around. One of the main reasons we're in such a mess is down to this hoarding by the rich and the banks, their unwillingness to let go of the money and put it into circulation. It's exactly the same thing as keeping the ten years of newspapers on your stairs. It's absolutely crackers, and it's wrong – but nobody is doing anything about it." Jim noticed that his voice had got a little louder at the end of his rant.

"You're listening to Lancashire FM – It's me Alan Proctor on the air talking about the difficulties facing local business across the Red Rose county. My guests are experts on the subject so if you have any questions get in touch."

Alan turned to Councillor Norton. "Did you want to pick up on the point Jim made there Fred?" he asked. Councillor Norton shifted uncomfortably in his chair as he opened his mouth to speak.

"Yes, yes, I think it's absurd to compare the banks and the crisis they are all facing with the story of a hoarder. It's a silly, pointless remark which won't help matters at all. The problem that faces our economy started in America and…"

The comment incensed Jim, he hit back straight away, rudely and ruthlessly interrupting the Councils Chamber of Trade Chairman and cutting him short.

"Don't be an idiot Councillor. You must be a bit backwards if you want to come on here and start defending the banks!" Jim was not taking any grief from this stuffy old bloke who he sensed knew very little about the real troubles that companies like Metal Makers, and the tens of thousands like it were currently struggling with - despite him being the local authority's talking head on the matter.

"Jim, I think we should let Councillor Norton finish the point he is making." Alan interjected with a tone of authority, but Jim wasn't for listening.

"No, sorry Alan. I've not come all the way here to listen to politicians talk yet more crap and tell even more lies – I've heard it all before, we all have, you could have just put a tape of that crap on and saved me a journey. I'm here to talk about what's going wrong, and to talk about ways we can sort the mess out. This Councillor wants to tow the party line and confuse everyone with his silly talk about banks and defects and quantative easing and blah blah blah. We need to change the record! That stupid jibberish talk makes no sense! None of it does Councillor Norton and we are all just about sick to death of you and your politician mates trying to blag us all and treat us all like muppets."

The Councillor was furiously riled at the audacity of Jim Arkwright and his outburst. But as a time-served politician he knew exactly how to swerve a question and throw somebody a hot potato.

"So what's your answer then Mister?" The Councillor paused a moment as he looked at his paper work and spotted Jim's surname. "Mr Arkwright, yes, there it is. You appear to have all the answers – so please will you tell us how we can get out of this mess?" Fred gave Jim a sleazy, cocky wink. Alan watched on thinking that this was making great radio, despite the mood becoming even frostier in the studio.

"Ha ha, wink at me all you want Fred, that's exactly why I've come on here. I'm not like you, I haven't come down here to indulge my ego, and make myself seem all clever and in control. I'm here because of the problems that affect my business. And I'll tell you somat for nowt as well, I could kick-start this economy overnight Fred, get some money changing hands again. And if I could do it, why can't the flipping government do it?"

"Well Jim, its great to hear that you can save us all," interrupted the host, quite sarcastically, "– but we must go to a break. Please promise to reveal all after the adverts."

"I bloody will!" replied Jim energetically.

Alan pressed a button and the red light on the microphone went off. Alan looked across the desk at his guests.

"Everyone okay?" he asked as the speakers played an advert for a new film that was just out. Alan's guests nodded, Jim smiled and held his thumb up.

"Really enjoying it, thanks Alan, I've never been on the radio before." Councillor Fred made a harrumph sound. Jim laughed at him, and wondered if all politicians acted in this way, obnoxiously and with such arrogance.

"Are they all like this?" asked Jim looking at Mandy, pointing his finger at Councillor Fred. "Politicians, I mean." Jim didn't think Fred was a particularly inspiring person at all and he wondered how this guy had managed to get any votes to become elected. Jim put it down to the fact that nobody else probably wanted to do it. He had even less of an opinion on Mandy, the lady from Business Action, who so far had said nothing, and had just rolled her eyes at Jim when he tried to lighten the mood in the studio a little.

"Okay guys, back on air in ten seconds" advised Alan. "Jim, we'll come straight to you." Jim nodded, and again lifted his thumb up. It made him wonder if he seemed a little cheesy, but in any case he wasn't bothered, he was really enjoying himself. For the past three years or so, Jim had spent a couple of hours a day putting the world to rights in the New Inn. His revision was done and this live broadcast seemed like an excellent forum to express himself and his well versed frustrations.

"Welcome back to Lancashire FM. It's Alan Proctor 'til 8, and we're talking business tonight. Jim Arkwright joins us, the MD of Metal Makers of Clitheroe - and he has just been challenged by County Councillor Fred Norton to explain how he can fix the countries failed economy. Jim, the stage is set, you've got the entire Red Rose county listening - please tell us, and the government if they are listening - how you could sort this mess out?"

"Well, its really very simple Alan, me and my mates Dave and Phil were talking about this in the pub just the other week."

Once again, Councillor Fred harrumphed. Jim retaliated instantly, "Fred, let me say what I'm saying first, you're making a right dickhead of yourself man!"

"Come on Jim, we can't say things like that on Lancashire FM. Please, keep your personal views to one side." Alan was visibly shocked, yet trying hard not to laugh.

"Sorry Alan, but, I can see why they describe politics as showbiz for the ugly." Jim laughed again as he watched the Councillors reaction. He certainly knew how to wind the dignitary up.

"This is ridiculous, I'm not standing for this!" said Fred.

"Just pipe down! I've met some pricks in my time Councillor, but I have to say that you're the cactus."

"Jim! One more comment like that and you're off the air." Alan Proctor was very firm. Councillor Fred looked crest fallen, lost for a response.

"Okay, well listen. So far, right - the government has pumped three hundred and twenty five billion pounds into the banks to get them through the crisis. But as the company in Chorley mentioned earlier on Alan, the banks aren't parting with any of that money! It goes into a big black hole. So the economy has stalled again, and the Government are giving all of our money to the banks who are just sitting on it – not lending it out. It's completely mad."

"Yes, we know all of this Jim, so how would you solve the problem?" asked Alan.

"Well, I've got an idea - there are about twenty six million income tax payers in this country right? Imagine if the government gave them all a surprise bonus out of the blue, a cheque for five grand each to spend! There would be one rule though - that everybody who received it would have to spend it within 12 months on a British product, or a British service, or holiday." Jim was grinning at Councillor Norton who was avoiding eye contact with anybody.

"Wow! I think quite a few of our listeners would agree to that! But that's a lot of people, a hell of a lot of money Jim. How much money altogether?" Alan was clearly excited by the prospect of Jim's theoretical proposal.

"Well, it's roughly one third of the total amount that we've given to the banks so far - it would cost roughly a hundred and thirty billion pounds."

"A third of what has been given to the banks! This is just crazy." Alan was clearly impressed by Jim's argument.

"It would give the economy the kick up the backside it needs Alan, it's so simple. People could go and decorate, buy new carpets, build a conservatory, a new kitchen, buy a used car or put it towards a new one. In houses where two adults are working you'd be looking at a ten grand injection of cash overnight, money that they would have to spend almost immediately. It's so easy, but the powers that be are too thick to work this one out."

"Mr Arkwright, that's all very good in theory," interrupted Mandy Cunningham, the lady from Business Action, "however in reality, such an explosion of money into the economy would simply cause an instant bottle neck – products and services would get too much demand on them and it would cause a crash." Mandy's first and only contribution to the programme was to instantly dismiss Jim's idea, and in a really condescending and patronising manner.

"Ah, nice of you to get involved with your so called business action Mandy, it's a relief to see that you're not a cardboard cut out, the question had crossed my mind!"

"Well! That's an insult!" she seethed back.

"Not really Mandy, that's not an insult at all – it's an observation, and a fairly accurate one as well considering that you've only just piped up now, half way through the discussion – to slag my idea off. Now lets be straight here - you wouldn't have to send all the money out in one go Mandy, you could drip it out over 12 months, 18 months, 2 years or whatever. Send it out to folk on their date of birth as a birthday present, a little thank you for putting up with all the useless, slimy politicians that have wrecked our amazing country."

"So it's a birthday present?" scoffed Councillor Norton.

"My God, you people are so blinkered, you just look for quick ways to instantly explain how things won't work, or to make a sarcastic joke. If someone asks you a question you can't give a straight reply. No wonder you people are so detested. You make me die. The problem with people like you, the people who have influence over important things like business - is that you're all so insecure and scared of making a mistake – you do nothing! Rather than coming out and saying "sod it, yeah! Come on, let's have a bloody good look at it, let's have a crack at it, lets roll our sleeves up and get bloody stuck in!" you do nowt, you just hope the problem will go away by itself. That's where the country's problems really lie. Too many lazy, half hearted self serving dickheads like you two have a say in important matters. You're only here to promote yourselves – not to listen and help folk that are struggling to keep a business going, like me." Jim noticed that he was raising his voice, and tried to tone it down by reminding himself that this wasn't the New Inn but the areas biggest radio station.

"I've just told you how we can sort the economy out and give it a kick start and your immediate response is negative. If you people just listened, thought it all through, did your sums, this country wouldn't be in such a bad state."

Alan's face was filled with enthusiasm, he was listening to Jim and writing down notes. Mandy and Fred just stared blankly at the table top. Jim continued explaining his theory.

"Let the listeners weigh it up and we'll see if they think it's a good idea, stop me when I don't make sense Alan." Jim was really enjoying this, he could see he was annoying the hell out of the Councillor and the decision making "expert" Mandy, but could also see that the radio host was lapping it up. This was nothing more than a great night out for Jim, and he knew his mates Sandra, Dave and Phil would be listening intently, as would all the regulars down at the pub and they would certainly take the mick if Jim let himself down. He was determined to give a good account of himself for their sake – otherwise he'd never hear the end of it.
Jim launched into his explanation of how his idea would work.

"Let's think about it just from the point of view of the people who get a cheque for five grand and decide to buy a new settee with some of the money. All those sofa companies will see more demand, the sofa manufacturers will need to hire extra staff, the suppliers would need to order extra supplies and increase their staff to cope with the extra demand, the sales team would need more staff, the website programmers and accountants would see an increase in business, the trucks would need more drivers, and diesel, and servicing, the flipping cleaners will have more cleaning to do because more people would once again be making a mess in the canteen and skidding up the toilet. It's a simple domino effect, and one that is urgently, desperately needed in this country. Now, Mandy, Fred, our esteemed experts and leaders - I just told you how to get the economy moving again, and it'll be two thirds of the price cheaper than any of the bonkers schemes your colleagues in Whitehall have tried – schemes that have failed at enormous expense to me and my tax paying countrymen. You're all thick, and you're all crap at your jobs – and that's what's really wrong, the country is controlled, managed and influenced by thick, highly paid, self obsessed morons just like you two. Now, let me explain something - where I come from Mandy – that is what you call an insult. Hahaha."

All of the phone lines had lit up the switchboard at Lancashire FM. The e-mails, tweets and Facebook messages were pouring in. Over the next 24 hours the radio stations website wouldn't be able to cope with demand on its listen again function. Thanks to the Youtube video, interest in Jim Arkwright had been huge anyway before this radio appearance. But following this forthright, plain speaking broadcast, interest in Jim Arkwright suddenly stepped up a gear.

As Jim left the studios shortly after 8pm, he was stunned to find himself flashed by several photographers who had gathered outside the radio station. Regardless of his initial surprise he smiled and held up a two fingered victory salute as he walked to his car.

He could never have guessed that his smiling, triumphant picture would grace the front covers of two national newspapers the following morning.

Chapter Eight
Tuesday Morning – 22nd May 2012

"Well, it's very rare that we do this on BBC Radio 2, in fact it's so rare - I can't think of any other time that we've ever done it! But this morning we are going to play you a clip from another British radio station. Last night, the guy that has become an instant Youtube hit, the "Clitheroe Prime Minister" also known as Jim Arkwright appeared on a live radio debate on his local radio station Lancashire FM, and he totally wiped the floor with the politicians on the panel, just take a listen to this." The DJ started playing the previous evening's interview from the part where Jim explained his idea for how to get the economy working.

The presenter of the national BBC breakfast show was clearly excited by Jim's appearances in the media, this had been the second day that he had talked about it on the nations most listened to radio show.

Jim Arkwright's opinion on the economy really couldn't have landed on a bigger platform, and the public were instantly wowed by his laid back style and his straight to the point approach. He was proving popular purely and simply because he was just a normal person who had become sick to death of all the nonsense that he saw around him, and was articulate enough to talk about it. As far as the breakfast presenter on Radio 2 was concerned, this man was the only show in town and the production team desperately wanted to talk to him. The eight million listeners also wanted to hear more, and every single one of them wanted his £5,000 idea to be implemented with immediate effect.

*****

Whilst newspapers, radio stations and morning TV shows were reporting on Jim, the £5,000 bonus theory and the no nonsense approach, Jim himself was oblivious to it all as he was dismantling posts and digging holes on the school field with his staff, making preparations for the next section of upright supports for the railings. His mobile phone had starting going the previous night, and had carried on relentlessly after he turned it back on in the morning so he had left it, turned off on his desk in the office.

"Listen lads, we might have to put an extra hour in tonight. If we get this job nailed for Friday dinner time we'll all go home early, and I'll give you extra money for a chippy tea - and you'll all get Monday off an' all!" For some reason he made the whole announcement in a Welsh accent.

Jims trio of workers on the school field site were delighted with the prospect, and he knew that his more experienced workers back at the unit who were also working equally hard drilling, cutting, welding and constructing the railing sections would be just as pleased at the prospect of an early dart on Friday and a long weekend off. Jim had so far been very impressed with the commitment of his lads on this job, they had realised that it had great potential and that if Metal Makers could become a regular council contractor for big projects such as this one, the company would be on a more secure footing.

For the past few years, work had been extremely hit and miss - too busy one month and hiring new staff, then having no work on for the following month and having to lay the new staff off again. Jim absolutely hated that aspect of his business, but he had a really good feeling about this council job, it was a massive opportunity and he was absolutely determined to make the very most of it.

*****

At the Council headquarters, Councillor Fred Norton was in the civic chamber support office, furiously addressing the two council officers who had, albeit at his request, arranged his appearance on the Lancashire FM radio show the previous night.

"I don't know who this little jumpstart thinks he is!" he scolded, "but I will warn you two now that I will have your jobs if you ever, ever set me up for a stunt like that again." Both of the staff knew exactly how to respond; in complete silence.

"Find out everything you can about this Jim Arkwright, about his company and furthermore – if he has any business links with the County Council. No right minded person speaks to an elected County Councillor like that in a public forum. I've given 28 years loyal service on this council, and I will not be made a laughing stock of by this gob-shite. I will finish the bastard. I will be back in this office in two hours time and I want your reports on him, his business and if he has any - his links with this council. If there are any, they are going to be cut off today, immediately, am I understood?"

"Yes, Councillor Norton, without delay," said Sheila, the cabinet officer that had taken the brunt of his furious address. Councillor Norton walked briskly out and closed the door very calmly behind him as he left.

"Shit the bed! I have honestly never seen him that cross before!" Sheila was talking to her junior colleague Christine, a huge grin appeared all across her face, she was plainly delighted to have witnessed one of the most unpleasant and obtuse Councillors in the region in such a foul mood.

"Can he do that though?" asked Christine. "Just cut peoples business links off from us?"

"Of course he can. He can and he will, I've seen him do much worse hundreds of times, for a lot less than what this guy did to Councillor Norton last night. The bloke on the radio made a right show of him. He even said that he's met some pricks – but Councillor Norton was the cactus!" Christine laughed out loud at the audacity of the comment.

Sheila continued, "He will definitely stop any business dealings – but you just watch, it will be some council officer further down the line that does the dirty work and makes up a reason for it, insurance requirements have changed or they've identified a risk assessment failure, it will be something pathetic like that."

Christine looked really shocked. Sheila on the other hand had seen this kind of thing so many times before. It was just the modus operandi.

"He does it all the time. That's how it works with things around here, it's all about scratching each others backs. You'll pick it up Christine, it took me a while at first too."

"Jesus." Christine breathed in sharply and exhaled an exaggerated breath as she started her database search on Jim Arkwright and Metal Makers.

*****

Further afield, in London, Tim Dixon - the executive producer of TV's number one satirical political comedy panel show "Mock Off" had caught the Radio 2 playback of Jim's appearance and was trying his best to track him down, to invite him to be a panellist on this weeks show. He had plenty of budget available and was well known as one of the television industry's leading lights, mainly because he had a knack for getting exactly what he wanted.

In this case, he wanted Jim Arkwright on the show, this week whilst he was still at the top of the silly season agenda. But the only number available for him on Google was the Metal Makers factory, which was permanently engaged. Despite calling Lancashire FM and managing to charm them for Jim's mobile phone number, annoyingly, after finally getting the number - it just kept going straight to answer phone. It seemed that everybody in the media business wanted to talk to Jim. Tim sensed that the phone wasn't going to be answered, and the thought filled him with frustration.

"Bollocks to this. I'll drive up there."

*****

In the County Council offices, Councillor Norton had arrived promptly for his report into Jim Arkwright, and he was delighted to learn that Metal Makers were currently in the process of working on dismantling and replacing St Michael's school railings. He was even more pleased to hear that this was a probationary trial job that was on the contractor quality assessment and fulfilment evaluation scheme. He waltzed out of the office chuckling.

"Thanks girls!" he cheerfully, tunefully shouted as he left. Sheila held two fingers up at the door as it closed behind him.

"Arsehole." She muttered.

*****

Ian McEwan, the Business Editor for the Financial Times had listened with interest to the broadcast on Radio 2 and had set about testing Jim Arkwright's theory. He had spent several hours calculating and assessing the ins and outs, the pro's and cons of the idea.

So far, he was struggling to find any evidence to suggest that Jim Arkwright's £5,000 bonus scheme would not work, and the prospect of the initiative excited him. The only flaw that he could pick out was regarding the massive administration requirements of checking that each £5,000 was spent on British goods, but even this aspect promised new job opportunities. He was beginning to think that this small business operator from Lancashire had potentially put together a scheme that could seriously help to put the British economy back on the right track, manufacturing, producing and selling again.

It was without any doubt an audacious and outrageous economic strategy, but Ian's sums told him time and again that it would work. The economy would get the jump start that was necessary, and businesses would get the orders they needed. Off the record, he also agreed wholeheartedly with Jim's view that the quantitive easing schemes had made no impact whatsoever, they had merely propped the banks up from a certain collapse, effectively halting any prospect of growth. As he began writing his front page story for the following mornings paper – under the working title headline "£5K Bonus Initiative Would Work" Ian McEwan wasn't to know that the Jim Arkwright story was, by a funny quirk of fate, about to become the main news story in Britain.

*****

On the popular social network sites of Twitter and Facebook the terms "Clitheroe Prime Minister" "Radio 2 Prime Minister" "Clitheroe" and "Jim Arkwright" were trending. Tweets saying things like "Jim Arkwright for PM" and "Jim Arkwright's £5,000 bonus rocks" were typical examples of the tens of thousands of comments and statements from the general public.

There were also a great many "who is Jim Arkwright?" tweets that was keeping the trending alive. On Facebook several pages and groups had been set up. The most popular page had been called "Jim Arkwright – NBP Party - No Bullshit Politics."

On the page thousands of newly converted fans of Jim's wrote heartfelt messages of support and admiration, such as "You fucking legend mate."

*****

Around Clitheroe, Jim Arkwright was a familiar, and very popular character. His truck and vans were regularly seen around and about the town, the company managed to get plenty of work mending gates, replacing old metal drainpipes, fixing ancient metal window frames and even doing weird and wonderful projects like installing gigantic fire exit staircases onto the outside of buildings.

Metal Makers were the local firm that turned their hand to any metal fabrication job, however big or small. From time to time, they would feature in the local newspapers for their quirkier jobs.

One particularly memorable story had hit the Clitheroe Advertiser and Times front page a couple of years earlier when Jim and his team had been asked to construct a two metre diameter frying pan for the

Guinness world record attempt of making the biggest ever pancake. At Jim's insistence, the photo caption ran with the very cheeky "The Giant Frying Pan with Metal Makers boss Jim Arkwright and his tossers."

Jim himself was quite a well known man in the tiny town of just fifteen thousand people, having moved there from Burnley with his parents as a boy. Albert had secured a Foreman position at Castle Cement in the early 1970's and it made sense to buy a house in the town rather than face the daily commute to and from Burnley. Jim quickly fitted in around the area, and had never stopped making new friends.

All of the media attention that Jim was suddenly attracting was not such a big a surprise to those that knew him well, but great fun all the same. It made all of his friends, family, colleagues and neighbours laugh to learn that millions of people were talking about Jim Arkwright and one of his crazy ideas. There was little else being talked about in the town, the story of Jim being played on BBC Radio 2 running rings around the Councillor was becoming the natural successor and second part of the previous few days "have you seen the Clitheroe Prime Minister video on Youtube?" conversation.

Banana News was the main paper shop in the town centre and the topic of Jim Arkwright had been dominating the talk in the queue for magazines, ice creams and cigarettes since the weekend. The owners had begun to get quite sick of hearing the same old comments on loop from their local, fiercely proud customers who were all speaking affectionately of Jim. The whole thing had really caught the imagination of the Ribble Valley population.

But for all those that knew Jim and admired his audacity - there was still a great many people in

Clitheroe that had never heard of him until now, and they too were thrilled to hear about the local mans hearty triumph over the councillor, and that it was becoming a big news story throughout the country. But what happened next would make the whole silly story take on a completely different perspective.

Chapter Nine
Metal Makers Workshop – 2pm Tuesday Afternoon

There was a deafening amount of noise being made in the workshop as the staff were enthusiastically grinding, welding, drilling, painting and stacking the railing panels, all making a din that was competing against the radio - which was playing music at full blast. It was a very unusual place for Tim Dixon to find himself loitering.

Jim's supervisor Mark noticed the silhouette figure standing in the smoky, brightly lit entryway and stopped his work to walk over to the entrance of the dark, noisy unit to see what the visitor wanted.

"Alright mate, how can I help?" Mark was taking off his ear defenders as he spoke.

"Yeah, Hi, I'm looking for Jim."

"He's not here mate, he's out on a job. Is there out I can help you with? I'm his deputy like." Mark had a big cheerful face, one of those faces that make you feel instantly at ease, with big, kind hearted eyes.

"Well, I've got some work to offer him, if you could tell me where I could find him, that would be great. I've just driven up from London to see him."

"Bloody hell! You drove up here from London? Must be important mate. He never said he was expecting anyone though. He's just over at Saint Michael's school, they're putting some railings up while its school holidays like. What you want to do is take a left out of here, carry on until the lights," Mark started waving and pointing his hand into the air as he explained the way Tim should go. To an onlooker it could have looked as though he was trying to do a break dance move, but just with the one arm.

"Well thanks very much, you've been extremely

helpful. What did you say your name was again?"

"I don't think I did mate, but I'm Mark anyway."

"Well thanks again Mark, I'm sure I'll find him, much obliged."

Tim set off back towards his car as Mark returned to his work, wondering what job the bloke wanted doing so much as to drive up from London without an appointment.

Marks directions were straight forward enough. Tim soon found himself driving past the school field, the Metal Makers flat bed lorry and the small team of labourers in hi visibility vests. He spotted Jim, easily identifying him from the Youtube video that had kick started all of this interest in him just 5 days earlier. Tim parked his car outside Clitheroe Decorating Centre and walked across the pedestrian crossing towards the workers who were digging out just by the speed camera. He stood and watched them work for a minute, until Jim looked over at him.

"Hello, I'm Tim Dixon. I've just come from your factory – Mark told me where I could find you." Jim put his spade down.

"Carry on lads, excuse me a minute please," said Jim as he stepped over to where his visitor stood.

"Alright mate?" he extended a muddy hand "how can I help you?" he asked as he muddied Tim's clean hand with a firm shake.

"Well, I tried phoning this morning…"

"I know mate, forget all about that, my phone number is being rung up all hours of the day and night – newspapers and radio stations all wanting to talk to me. Is that where you're from?"

"Kind of, I'm in television, I'm the boss of the Mock Off show on Channel 4. Do you ever watch it?"

Jims face lit up as Tim asked the question. The name Tim Dixon now rang a bell with Jim, it was the last name on the credits at the end of the show. Tim is one of the best known directors in television, his CV is littered with some of TV's most popular programmes since the 1980s.

"Course I know Mock Off! It's my favourite programme. Jesus tonight! How do you do?" Jim extended his hand to shake Tim's for a second time.

"Well, I decided to drive up here and speak to you face to face."

Jims delight abated a little and he began to look slightly shocked. "Aye? Sounds a bit serious."

"I saw the video yesterday, which was a good laugh – but now with the radio appearance last night, you've really become the hot topic of conversation. I want you to be our star guest on the show this week."

Jim burst out laughing. He couldn't believe what he was hearing. He couldn't wait to tell Phil and Dave about this in the pub after work. They'll be pissing themselves laughing, he thought. He looked round at his lads who were working away, completely oblivious to the bizarre conversation that their boss was having with a top televison executive from London.

"This is a bleeding wind up!" said Jim, his mouth open slightly. Mock Off was pretty much the only programme that he regularly watched on TV. He simply couldn't believe that here was the Mock Off gaffer asking him to come on the show. Tim looked amused, appreciating what a strange situation this was for Jim.

"I knew you'd say that, as I drove up here I thought of what a ridiculous thing it was that I was doing. Our guests are always from within the media, I've never been out and approached a real person before," They both laughed. "But the thing is, that broadcast on Radio 2 this morning just put you in the Premier League Jim. People in this country are screaming for a change to our politics and what you've said so far has really grabbed everybody's attention. By next week, with all due respect - people won't know who Jim Arkwright is. But right now everyone is talking about you. I want you on the show this week. We record all day Thursday for Saturday nights transmission."

"What was on Radio 2? I knew they said sum 'ert about me yesterday, I heard them asking folk to ring in and tell them who I am." Jim chuckled again and Tim picked up for the first time that Jim was genuinely unaware of how popular he had instantly become.

"The local radio broadcast that you did last night was transmitted again on Radio 2 this morning! And everyone loved it, so that's why I drove all the way up here hoping to get hold of you before anybody else does. I'll pay you fifteen grand, lay on first class train travel, a limousine to pick you up, and a night in Hyde Park Hotel if you'll come on the show. Deal?"

Jim was stunned and flattered and was grinning like an excited kid, but depressingly for him, his overall concern was this school railing job. He started to explain the difficulty of just going off to London in the middle of the week with such a crucial job on the cards.

"I couldn't just leave the lads, I couldn't expect that of them while I'm off dicking about mate." Jim was seriously disappointed, it genuinely was beyond his wildest dreams what Tim was offering to him right now, the best day out imaginable, being a panellist on his favourite TV show - meeting the regulars on there, and seeing how it was all made - then staying at a top hotel as well, and getting a ridiculous sum of money on top. Karen would love it too. It really was the stuff of dreams. And Jim knew that he would have to turn it down.

"Bollocks Jim. I'm not taking no for an answer. Tell me what needs to happen here and I'll get you the best site managers in the world to come and deputise for you and I'll personally make sure this project is finished on time, and it'll be brilliant."

Jim laughed, and he felt incredibly flattered. It was a lot to think about and his mind was racing. But just as Jim was starting to think about how he could take Tim up on his extraordinary proposal, the Councils health and safety officer wandered over and interrupted the conversation.

"Afternoon Jim." He said, without much enthusiasm.

"Oh, Alright Matthew, didn't expect to see you here today. Is everything okay?"

"I'm afraid not Jim. I've got to take you off site, there's been some problem or other with the contracts for this job. I've been asked to come and get you to down tools and see you off the site straight away."

If Jim had been bemused moments earlier, he was completely bewildered now. But then a thought crossed his mind. He began to laugh.

"Ha ha, good one! You rotten bastard, I really believed you then Tim! I honestly thought you were telling the truth. Got to admit mate, you got me hook line and sinker there!" Both Tim and Matthew looked on with puzzled faces.

"It's a wind up isn't it? A hidden camera thing. Candid Camera! Beadles About! First of all I'm going to London on Mock Off and then I'm kicked off site when I've not even done a quarter of the job! It's a good one this!" Jim burst out laughing again, looking around for the presenter and a camera crew to come out from behind a bush.

Tim spoke first "Jim, I'm not taking the piss. I'm serious."

Matthew spoke next. "Seriously Jim, I don't know what's gone wrong, but I've been told to get down here toot sweet and get you and your lads off site straight away."

Jims face began to change from bemusement to raw anger. Tim however could see straight through the situation. He stood with his hands in his trouser pockets and shared his views with Jim, and Matthew.

"It'll be that Councillor you were winding up on the radio. That's what this is all about Jim, I'll bet you – he's squeezing your tit." Jim turned to Matthew, instantly realising that Tim's comment made perfect sense. It was the only explanation after more than six months of submitting tenders, negotiating contracts and all of the health and safety concurrence had been discussed, agreed and double checked for this job.

"That's it isn't it? Well you can tell that big fat fucking Fred to come and remove me off this site himself, the vindictive old bastard! I'm not going Matthew, no chance mate." Jim was practically spitting the words into the council representatives face.

Jim had raised his voice so much that his staff team of Jason, Eggy and Daz had downed tools and were watching him. They were reading between the lines as to what was going on. The staff had seen Jim annoyed and wound up before, many times - but they'd never seen him angry, not like this. It was unimaginable to see Jim this irate.

Matthew was standing there nervously, unsure of what to do next. He'd never had to ask a contractor to get off site before. With Jim refusing the request, he would have to go back to his superiors and ask them what the next step was. Tim could see that Matthew had just been sent on an errand, his failure to offer a justifiable reason for the suspension of work confirmed it.

"Matthew, have you ever seen Mock Off on TV?" asked Tim.

"Eh? Yes, of course I have. But what…"

"Matthew, that's my TV show. I run it. Your boss, whoever it was that sent you down here has just won this weeks shit-head of the week award, without a single doubt. Now I suggest you phone them up and ask them what to do next. You've been stitched up here Matthew, and I advise you to cover your arse." Tim took his hand out of his pocket and pointed a finger at Jim. "This bloke is on the front of the Daily Star today, so whoever has put you up to this must be either as thick as pig shit, or it's a career suicide. Now, watch your back – don't be the fall guy."

The young council officer was clearly as enraged by this as Jim was. Tim on the other hand was completely nonchalant and was acting as though he was having a mundane conversation about the weather.

"Phone them now Matthew and tell them that you're taking no further part in this political matter under any circumstances. One day, probably as soon as tomorrow you'll see that my advice has kept you in a job."

Tim was surprised, moreover shocked at how dim-witted Councillor Norton had been. He put his hand on Jims shoulder and began walking away from the health and safety officer as Matthew began speaking sternly into his mobile phone. Tim steered Jim onto the field and began to speak quietly and calmly to him.

"Jim, I came up here to invite you on my show and you effectively turned me down because this job is so important to you. Had you not said that, after I offered you fifteen grand, then I wouldn't get myself involved. But, you're obviously a genuine guy and I see how these arseholes operate every day. It makes my skin crawl the way these small town politicians behave, they are almost as sly and obnoxious as MPs, just a lot thicker. It looks like you're going to lose this important contract because you made a prick of that Councillor last night."

"I'm not mate, I'll not let him. Six months of meetings and paperwork and red tape bullshit have gone into getting this job, and it's only a fucking trial! I'm not having that useless bastard fuck it all up for me and my lads, there's more chance of Gary Glitter getting the Christmas number 1."

"That's the spirit." Said Tim, smiling. "Now listen, I know this bullshit world inside out. If you do exactly as I say, I'll make sure you get plenty more work from the local council Jim. If we make a big noise about this, they'll be offering you all the biggest jobs first. And then, the deal is that for thirty grand, you promise to come on my show this week?"

Jim nodded, "If you get this sorted out mate, I'll come on your show and I'll work all weekend if I have to." Tim extended his hand once again and the two men shook on the deal. Tim took out his phone and rang his friend Colin Glazier, the Duty Editor at Sky News.

"Colin, Hi it's Tim. I'm up north, yeah back home bothering sheep. Shut up. Listen. You know that favour I owe you? Well, I've wandered into a lovely little scoop here, it's a memorable one to do with the Clitheroe Prime Minister guy. Have you got a crew on standby in Lancashire? Yes, I'm in Clitheroe."

Chapter Ten
Tuesday tea time

It was fairly quiet in the Swan and Royal hotel, the historic town centre pub dating from the 1830's that had offered accommodation to such legendary historical figures as Sir Winston Churchill and Ghandi, and was also the birthplace of the Jet engine, when Sir Frank Whittle agreed the deal to mass produce his invention that would change the world forever.

The lunchtime rush hadn't really happened, but the bar staff were still confident that trade would pick up as the towns workers finished their day of work in the offices, factories and shops around the town and would pop in for a couple of scoops before heading home. They hoped so anyway, it was really boring standing behind the bar when there was nothing to do.

The TV was showing a daily tea time quiz show, but nobody was paying any attention to it. The few customers that were in the Swan were either talking to one another, or reading a newspaper. One of the pubs older regulars, Joe Turner got a call on his mobile. He started talking into the phone.

"I'm in the Swan." He said loudly, "What's the matter?" A few seconds later, he ended the call and slowly shuffled himself across to the bar. "That were the wife, she says that there's something going off in Clitheroe, it's on the Sky news channel now, she said. One of her friends from church just phoned her and told her."

The young man behind the bar took the remote control for the TV and scrolled through the channels to Sky News. The handful of customers were delighted to see their Castle on the TV screen and their initial, excitable reaction quickly abated as they listened to see what it was that was going on in their quiet little town that had attracted the interest of the international news channel.

*****

The Sky News satellite truck which had pulled up onto the field and parked beside the Metal Makers truck had attracted quite a crowd, which was growing all the time as youngsters text their friends and parents, and older residents came out into the streets to ask what was going on. All over the small town the message was very quickly going around that Clitheroe was on Sky News and residents were changing channels to watch it.

Up at the Castle Park, the town's main meeting point for young people, and the home to Lancashire's best equipped public skate park, the word was getting around about the TV crew, and wild speculation and rumours began circulating immediately.

Murder, child abduction, a plane crash and terrorism were all reasons cited for the Sky News truck to be broadcasting a BREAKING NEWS story, gossip that was recited breathlessly throughout the town; in the launderette, at bus stops and in supermarket queues. An exodus of teenagers walked the short journey down to Saint Michael's school field in an excitable bid to find out what was going on, and in the hope of possibly even getting their own faces on the telly as well.

*****

The "Clitheroe Prime Minister" story had gathered enough momentum in the media over the previous two days to make Sky News' exclusive coverage of Jim Arkwright in Clitheroe a must have story for all other news agencies too. As has become typical of any popular or tragic news story, the TV and press teams turn up en masse within minutes of each other, especially when a story showed this much promise.

Little over an hour after Sky began reporting, the local news teams from press and radio began to gather round, then other national channel's satellite trucks began arriving, hastily assembling and erecting their broadcast equipment and beginning live transmissions across their networks. The tiny, almost unheard of town of Clitheroe close to the Lancashire and Yorkshire border suddenly found that the country's powerful media spotlight was beaming firmly upon it.

*****

Apart from the story creating a buzz in the town where it was unfolding, the coverage was also proving to be a great story for the news channels in general, with feedback coming in thick and fast from the social networking sites - the tweets and Facebook comments from viewers were going crazy. Colin Glazier, the Duty Editor at Sky News was pleased with the story and the massive reaction. He sent a text to his friend Tim for giving him the heads up for the exclusive.

"This is sterling stuff" he wrote, "top result thanks mate. That favour is definitely repaid now!"

For several years, since the pair were working for another broadcaster, Colin had been confident that the "favour" was of such a magnitude, there was no way that Tim could ever repay it. But Colin was certainly impressed with this, and saw this story easily grabbing an award at the next Television News Awards ceremony.

The difficult task ahead was for Sky News and BBC News to try and keep an impartial balance, and report the story from a neutral standpoint. With the public reaction via Twitter already leaning heavily towards Jim Arkwright, by practically one hundred per cent approval – the job of keeping on the middle ground was destined to be awkward, particularly on the 24 hour, constant rolling news channels. This was where the all important time filling interviews with the general public are a major part of each hours output. The managing editors at both news channels knew that it was going to be quite impossible to keep a healthy balance on this particular story.

*****

None of the officers at Clitheroe police station had ever known a job like this one before, it had taken the small force completely by surprise. A typical Tuesday night would normally see a watch of six officers on patrol duty to police the small rural town of 15,000 people. There had been many instances of large crowds gathering in the town, and in many of the villages dotted around the area in the past, including the annual Beatherder festival that attracted thousands every year. But large gatherings had always been planned with plenty of forward notice and detailed information that was available in advance to ensure that the Lancashire Constabulary could match the manpower to meet the volume of people.

But this was extraordinary – by 7pm, St Michael's school field had a crowd well in excess of 1,000 people, all jostling and jeering, every one of the spectators was in very high spirits.

There was no trouble, but for Sergeant Andy Dawson, he was completely uncomfortable with the situation and needed it to end just as quickly as it had begun. He left the town's Victorian period police station on foot and walked the 5 minute journey to the school field where his four available officers were trying to make sense of the completely abnormal situation.

People, young and old, couples and entire families from all across the town were still making their way down towards the field, cheerfully enjoying the hazy summer sunlight as they walked, laughing and joking at the sheer audacity of one of their towns local characters becoming the main news item in Britain, and eager to see all the TV crews and satellite trucks in their quiet, unassuming little market town.

*****

After spending a good deal of time discussing the right strategy and providing Jim with some useful advice and tips on how to handle and manipulate the media interest that was destined to ensue, Tim Dixon was confident that the situation regarding the school railings would quickly be over-turned with Sky News covering the story. He took Jim's faithful word that he would be in London on Wednesday evening and available for the recording of Mock Off on Thursday before he bid the modest Lancashire man farewell and went back to his car.

Tim was heading back down South to try and catch up on some of the work that his unplanned trip north had disrupted. His parting words of advice had been, "If you play this straight, you'll be around a little while longer than the one week I credited you with earlier. Good luck Jim, it's been a real pleasure to meet you."

Tim was glad that he had followed his instincts and made the journey. He was confident that Jim's story was going to be a sensation on Sky News, but also pleased that once again, Mock Off had secured the latest person that was grabbing the political headlines.

Chapter Eleven
Tuesday 7.15pm, Sky News Live Transmission

"Good evening if you are just joining us. Our main story tonight – the so called *Clitheroe Prime Minister*, Jim Arkwright - who has become an internet sensation during this past week, has today launched a political protest in his home town of Clitheroe – and it's a protest that has already attracted around one thousand spectators from the local community. We can cross now, live to our northern England correspondent Guy James, who can tell us more about what's happening, as this story develops."

The screen changed from the studio newscaster to images of the reporter, stood with a huge microphone on the large school field that was now practically full of spectators, many of whom were jostling for a position near a TV camera. It looked more like the scene from a music festival than from a serious political protest, especially with the eminent 800 year old Norman Castle Keep on the horizon of every shot.

"Thank you Jeremy, yes I'm here this evening to report on a most extraordinary story." The backdrop of Guy James' report to camera was full of young people smiling, waving and shouting "hello Mum!"

"The atmosphere here can only be likened to that of a carnival, as the local people of this small market town of Clitheroe have come out onto the streets in force to support their local businessman, Jim Arkwright."

Guys voice was getting louder as he went on, trying to compete with the growing noise and frivolity taking place behind him on the school field. Back in London, the newscaster asked Guy what this was all about.

"Well Jeremy, details are extremely sketchy, but what I can tell you is that Jim Arkwright, a local metal structural builder, the man you can see chained to the fence here just behind me, has today inexplicably been told that he needs to get off this site, where he is currently contracted to work for the local council, on a major project replacing the boundary railings around this Primary school – but, he insists that he won't leave this site until the person who made that decision to remove his company from the tender comes down here and explains the reason to him, face to face."

"But there's a little more to it than that, isn't there Guy?" Asked the news anchor.

"Yes, absolutely Jeremy. The man who is chained up, well, who is actually welded by chains to the fence is a local businessman by the name of Jim Arkwright. Now, as many viewers will be aware, Mr Arkwright has been taking the internet by storm over the past few days as a video of him doing a mock announcement by the Prime Minister became a viral hit. The video has now been seen by an incredible 18 million people on the popular video sharing website Youtube."

"But just what is the argument here Guy? Surely having a successful video on the internet can't be a justifiable reason for a local company to be stripped of a council contract, can it?"

"No Jeremy, certainly not, and this is where the story really grows its own arms and legs. Last night, Jim Arkwright appeared on a local radio phone-in show with County Councillor Fred Norton, who is the Chair of the regional Chamber of Trade. Jim Arkwright basically annihilated and embarrassed the Councillor on the air, scoring several political points and winning many arguments. Jim Arkwright believes that as a reaction, in an act of petty retaliation - Councillor Norton has interfered with the contract to fulfil this work. As a result he has stated to us and other news agencies that he will not move from his position on this site until the relevant person comes down here and explains in plain English, why the contract has been torn up."

"Yes, well I can see it's a very complicated situation Guy. I see you are stood next to Mr Arkwright – can we get his response to the situation?"

Deep down, Jim was actually really enjoying himself, and he had to try very hard not to laugh and joke around with everybody who stepped over to wish him well or have their photos taken with him chained up to the railing. Hundreds of pictures were being uploaded to Twitter and Facebook under various tags such as "Legend!" and "Vote for Jim."

"Yes, well I can ask him if he would like to speak to us," said Guy as he walked the tiny distance backwards to where Jim was shackled to the steel railing panel.

"Jim, Guy James from Sky News. We're live on the network now."

"How do you do Guy? I'm very sorry to have caused all this fuss, I didn't think it would get this busy." Jim really wanted to break into a happy, cheerful mood with him being on the TV, but the point that he was here to make was not cheery at all. He would compromise his argument if he started clowning around and making it look like a personal publicity stunt rather than an important matter of corruption and abuse of power by the local Councillor. Despite the circus, his was a serious matter that if left unchecked would result in Jim's company facing serious financial struggle.

"Well, you certainly have got your point across Jim, can you tell our viewers why, or rather how, you came to be fixed by chains to these railings today?" Guy pushed his big grey outdoor fluffy microphone under Jims chin.

"Certainly Guy, I don't mind telling you at all. The reason why I'm doing this protest is because I want the person responsible for taking the decision to kick me and my employees off this site to come and tell me why to my face! My company has invested a hell of a lot of time and money into winning this contract and today I've been told that I've to leave the site without any more flaming information than that. The person responsible hasn't even had the good manners to think up a lie to explain it! So like I've said all afternoon, I'm not going nowhere until the person who made the decision to get me kicked off the site is here, telling me to my face, and to the media the exact reason why."

"Has anybody from the council been in touch with you about this yet Jim?" asked Guy.

"Nope, we had this young bloke who'd been sent down here to do the dirty work. But since I sent him on his way and told him I'm not going off site I've not heard nowt."

"Well Jim, we've been trying to get some reaction from the County Council ourselves and we haven't managed to get any official word. If the Council choose to ignore your protest what will you do?"

Jim had to try hard not to break into a smile. He already knew that the matter was definitely out in the open and was attracting significant news coverage. In the grand scheme of things, under normal circumstances - this wasn't a news story at all and Jim was fully aware of that. The interest was merely because of the Youtube video, and because the public have a huge appetite for anti-politician stories at the present time. British citizens were at the very end of their tether with politicians in general, and the potential of seeing yet another one come a cropper makes terrific news for broadcast and print.

But Jims over riding priority was to ensure that his company was treated fairly, and he wanted reinstating to the work that had been agreed.

"I'll stop here all night me, Guy. I'll stay all week if I have to, because I've got employees working for me who are relying on this job. I've got a mortgage that is relying on this job. If my work was no good, fair enough – but them railings are first class, look at them!"

Jim gestured at the metal rails that had been installed so far.

"The whole job is coming on lovely - so I want the council down here and explaining themselves. I'll stop here all month if that's what's required because it's sleazy, slimy, its underhand and its bloody out of order what's happened today. I just want to know why, because if it is simply because I gave that Councillor a good leathering on the radio last night, and he's chucking his toys out of his pram – I'll see him in court Guy, I really will. Its bang out of order, is this!"

Guy turned back to the camera, "Well Jeremy, that seems to be the story so far, but no word from the County Council yet. Keep in touch and we'll cover any developments here. But I guess we've only heard one side of this story and we will simply have to wait to hear the County Councils response in due course, but one thing is for sure here in Clitheroe Jeremy, Jim Arkwright isn't going quietly."

Back at the Sky New centre, the presenter thanked Guy for his report, and thanked Jim for the interview. "Well lets cross live now to our reporter Dianne Daniels who is standing outside Councillor Fred Norton's home in Preston. Dianne – any news from

Councillor Norton on this matter?" The view changed again, this time to a young news reporter stood outside an expensive looking red bricked semi-detached house.

"Good evening Jeremy. I'm afraid we've not had any reaction from Councillor Norton, but he is in there, and he doesn't look very happy with us being here. Despite knocking on his door and phoning him up, he seems very reluctant to speak to us."

"Okay, well keep trying Dianne. We will keep a close eye on this story as it develops, in other news now, a British Soldier on duty in Afghanistan has been killed in an explosion in the Helmand Province this morning…."

On the field the mood was getting happier and more frivolous as the time went on and the convoy of media crews beamed their stories and reports back to newsrooms up and down the land. Each report was packed with scores of young Clitheroenians, clearly having a good time and enjoying the bizarre situation on a lovely summer evening.

The well known yellow and white ice cream van "Purdy's Ices" a familiar site in the town turned up and negotiated through the crowds onto the field with the tuneful jingles playing was met with a triumphant cheer from the spectators.

Sergeant Andy Dawson had spoken to his small number of officers, and whilst he was satisfied that the crowd were behaving and keeping order, he was still becoming increasingly concerned that the amount of people milling around already, along with the growing number of people travelling from all over town - was going to become unsafe. He went across to speak to Jim after patiently waiting until the live news interview had been done.

"Hello Jim, becoming a bit of a star I see, front

of the papers this morning, now this." The two men vaguely knew one another already from around town. Sergeant Andy Dawson often enjoyed a few pints of real ale in the New Inn, and their paths had crossed at several events and functions through the years.

"Alright Sergeant Dawson? Look I'm sorry about all this, but I've been stitched up. My company is going to go bust if I lose this contract – I can't have it."

"I understand, my officers have been filling me in. I'm not mithered about you being chained to the railings mate, but this flipping circus is a real headache – its turning into Glastonbury here and we're not sure what we're meant to do. I've only got four staff on patrol duty – and if anything happens here, say for example a wasp stings someone, and there's screaming and a rush amongst the crowd and a kid falls over, gets trampled on, crushed to death, we'll all be on the front of the papers for the wrong reasons." Sergeant Dawson was being fair, but if Jim would just go home now, that would make his job a lot easier.

All around them the excitement was obvious, this was a completely unique event in Clitheroe, energised by the fine weather and general nosey culture of the town. Swarms of people were still heading towards the field from all directions.

Jim totally understood Sergeant Dawson's problem with all of the people, and agreed that it was getting silly. "I know what you mean, but that is surely a worst case scenario?"

The Sergeant smiled. "Of course it is, but I have to work in the worst case scenario field every day Jim. It's what policing is all about."

"I didn't expect all this, I thought that the Clitheroe Advertiser might come and take a picture. Lancashire Telegraph at a push. But now I need this flipping Councillor to hold his hands up and let me get on with finishing this school railings contract."

"So that's what it's about? You get your work reinstated here and it'll all stop? Okay, thanks Jim, I'll get on to them now and see what they're going to do about it."

"Er, well no, that's not it at all. If I say that's okay I'll get to finish the job. That will shut me up and then I'll never hear from the Council again. Nah, bollocks. I want the guy down here, and I want an explanation for the scandal. Sorry Sergeant Dawson, but that's what its really about, I've got a lot riding on this job being a success and that tosser from the Council can forget it if he thinks he's shafting my firm and getting away with it. Sorry, really I am, but I have to stand my ground. I've no choice."

"Okay, I get your drift. It's my problem now, I'll try and get the guy here for you in the interests of public safety, but I want a promise that you'll piss off straight after?"

"If it goes my way, yes I'll get my lads to cut these chains off. But if not, who knows?" Jim looked at the Sergeant with a serious expression.

"Well I'll be honest Jim, in my rank I won't be able to achieve much. I'll have to phone the Superintendent and ask him to phone the Chief Constable. It's all about power with these Councillors, he wouldn't talk to a Sergeant, but if anything went wrong here tonight, if somebody was hurt it would be me in the firing line. Leave me to see what can be sorted, I'll report back to you in a bit. In the meantime I'll have to get some more officers down here from other divisions."

Within thirty minutes of the conversation between the Sergeant and Jim, several police vans and minibuses containing officers from the neighbouring Lancashire Constabulary Divisions of Blackburn, Preston, Accrington and Burnley had arrived and the officers were deployed around the field and town centre – mainly as a visual presence, there had been absolutely no trouble.

Accountability was high on the police's agenda, and should anything go wrong, if the mood changed - at least there would be a token presence of officers on standby to try and manage any situation.

Tim Dixon was back in London, and smiling at his TV as the Sky News **BREAKING NEWS** banner flashed across the screen. The presenter announced that he was crossing to their reporter Dianne Daniels who was outside Councillor Fred Norton's house in Preston.

The Councillor had just pushed through the small press pack and got into a waiting car that had pulled up a few minutes earlier. The TV crew recorded him say "get out of my way you fucking parasites!" as he stomped aggressively through the reporters. The car sped off down the street.

"Well, could that be the first sign that Councillor Norton is on his way to Clitheroe to speak to Jim Arkwright?" Asked Dianne into the TV camera. "He certainly looked as though he was in a hurry. Back to you at the Sky News Centre."

Tim laughed out loud, trying to remember when such a petty, unimportant story had dominated the news.

"He's going to be a big star this guy." Tim held up his glass of red wine at the TV. "Cheers Jim!" he said as Sky re-ran the footage of the stressed out, overweight and thoroughly disenchanted looking Councillor pushing through the press pack, but on playback his vulgar comments were beeped out.

Chapter Twelve
Prime Ministers Office, 10 Downing Street

The British Prime Minister was receiving news of the bizarre story from the TV. The screen in the PM's lavishly decorated office was showing the BBC's coverage of the peaceful protest in Lancashire, now into its sixth hour. The reports were interspersed with clips of Jim Arkwright's famous rant in the pub that had become a sensation on the internet. It was the first time that the Prime Minister had seen it, and it was received with mild amusement.

To the relief of the police, much of the crowd had eroded away and the remaining straggling groups were also beginning to disperse. The predominantly young members of the audience had to be home. It may well have been an extraordinary gathering at a unique political protest, the likes of which had never been seen in Clitheroe before– but none the less, the young people knew what time they had to be in.

"We've potentially got a real problem on our hands here Prime Minister. If interest in this man continues, he's going to be more famous than most of the elected MPs."

The Prime Ministers senior advisor, Miles Wentworth Farlington was anxious that Jim Arkwright's national and international exposure was already becoming a distraction away from mainstream political stories.

The Prime Minister was watching the television and Miles was unsure if he was being heard as the BBC news reporter spoke into the camera, constantly repeating the same news that Councillor Norton still hadn't turned up at the site and that nobody knew where he was. Despite the rudeness of his boss seemingly ignoring him, Miles Wentworth Farlington continued talking.

"He is just a regular man, a commoner, so naturally he is making a significant connection with many members of the population, along with the fact that he seems to have a very endearing personality – dare I say it, the man is a naturally gifted politician. But scenes such as this one simply cannot be encouraged. If the general public see fit to chain themselves to railings at the drop of a hat, we'll have utter chaos on our hands." Miles Wentworth Farlington looked extremely stressed out as he awaited the Prime Ministers reaction. It seemed to take an age before his boss spoke.

"Well Miles, frankly I'm not surprised that he is angry. It's totally shameful what has happened to him, especially if it is true that some bloody County Councillor had him sacked for winning an argument." The PM appeared more bemused by the situation than concerned.

"He's denying it. He represents our opponents as you probably realise. I have spoken to him on the telephone earlier Prime Minister. He refuses to accept any involvement in it whatsoever. He claims that Jim Arkwright is crazy."

"So who is responsible? It sounds a little more than a general coincidence Miles."

"Well, I have managed to speak to the Civic Chamber support officer at the County Council up there, an officer of some thirty years standing and she has confirmed to me that the Councillor was in there this morning demanding information regarding this mans company. She added that he had verbally promised to cut any ties that Jim Arkwright had with the Council before the day was through, and all of this was said in front of another officer."

"So, he's hung drawn and quartered then? Stupid fucker!" The Prime Minister was becoming slightly irritable.

"We will need to tidy this up as soon as physically possible Miles. We need this Arkwright fellow to scuttle back into the anonymous little hole that he accidentally scampered out of. Get this Councillor shamed right away – put a press release out condemning his actions, make his position untenable, talk about democracy being integral to British politics, trust is a vital aspect etcetera – and make it clear in the statement that the PM will personally see to it that any work that Arkwright is currently doing will be reinstated with immediate effect."

"Yes Prime Minister, I'll get to work on that right away. Do you think that we ought to condemn Arkwright's actions though? We may be seen to pander to him – could be seen as weakness, an angle for the papers to press on with their agenda of discrediting the authority of your leadership." Miles was taking down notes and jotting down thoughts as he spoke. The PM's gaze was still squarely fixed on the TV, despite the story making no developments at all over the past two hours or so.

"No, I take your point Miles, but let's be clear – we'll be sullied if we condemn him, and in opposite effect we will be tainted if we back him. We need a solid middle ground. Apologise for the gross interference in the mans business interests, get this ridiculous Councillor out of the picture – and lets just hang fire and see if Arkwright disappears. If he doesn't we can discredit him in due course, once all of these flames have died down a tad."

"So you believe that he is simply going to

disappear after all of this?" Miles looked up from his notes at his uninspiring boss.

"Of course. I have no reason to think otherwise." The PM was spellbound by the TV screen as supportive vox pops from the public were broadcast, all offering encouragement and congratulations to Jim Arkwright.

"Well, I have it on excellent authority that he has today been booked as this week's star guest on Mock Off. And tomorrow morning the FT are running a front page editorial piece supporting his five thousand pound bonus scheme idea. I'm afraid that I don't share your optimism that he is going away." Miles looked quite stressed and worn out. His brow was creased and he was sweating slightly through his fiery complexion.

"Listen to me Miles, its great that this fellow has put his politics on the news agenda. It's a break for us, a diversion from the media simply discrediting us and our policies. I don't share your panic about him. If anything, I'm quite relieved to be getting a day off. Now take a series of deep breaths, produce the press release, get it wired and then take yourself off for a tall glass of something strong and try to relax."

"Of course. As long as you're sure he isn't going to become a threat?"

The Prime Minister laughed and waved Miles out of the office.

"A threat! Ha ha ha ha oh Miles you do make me smile, he's just a bloody northern pleb enjoying fifteen minutes of fame on the television. You do worry too much Miles, I've said this to you before."

"Good night Prime Minister." Miles left the UK's most powerful office and walked swiftly along the thickly carpeted Downing Street corridor and turned off into his own office, trying hard not to curse the PM under his breath. His gut feelings about things had always been laughed off by his boss, and once too many times his gut instincts had been proved correct.

Miles genuinely felt that Jim Arkwright had already become far too much of a working class phenomenon amongst the British public, and he knew that this was unchartered territory, especially for the struggling Government that he was employed to try to help.

Miles wanted to see a little more caution and considered planning, but he was reluctantly, slowly becoming as aware as most other MPs and media commentators that this Prime Minister was the most arrogant, pig headed, self assured and ultimately embarrassing politician that the country had ever encountered.

It made perfect sense to Miles why Jim Arkwright had become such an overnight sensation – in simple terms the public were sick to death of the disastrous Government in power – but felt powerless because the other parties were no better as a replacement. There seemed to be no alternative to upper class male politicians and much of the country felt that they were at stale mate. As a direct consequence interest in politics was at an all time low. People simply didn't want to know anymore. TV talent shows, celebrity gossip and football news were much more interesting to Joe and Joanne Public than politics.

Despite the texts on his phone that suggested otherwise, Miles was very well aware that he had a home to go to, and a wife that he had to try and keep interested in him. With the amount of stupid hours he'd been putting in recently his home life was suffering enormously. He began to write the Prime Ministers statement so that he could e-mail it straight to Number

10's Press Office for immediate release.

"As your Prime Minister, I cannot attempt to justify and cannot possibly try to defend the actions of County Councillor Frederick Norton of Chorley East. To interfere with a local council contract and remove business from a contractor with such a lack of conscience as a direct response to coming second best in a media argument is quite frankly a shocking and despicable demonstration of abuse and corruption of power.

I call for the immediate resignation of the Councillor who has called British political integrity into question, and I will make it my personal business to ensure that Mr Arkwright and his company are reinstated on the works contract. I will personally oversee an inquiry into how such wrong doing can take place in a modern and democratic society. Trust is the very foundation stone on which our democracy is built. I am as shocked and dissatisfied by this scandal as Mr Arkwright."

The press release was autographed digitally by the PM, a function only accessible by Miles, and sent off for immediate publication via the Number 10 press office to the associated press agency, where within moments it would be shared by every news broadcaster and journalist in the world. It was to be met with genuine delight by the news editors on the rolling news channels – the story desperately needed freshening up as it had become rather stale over the past couple of hours.

Chapter Thirteen
Tuesday 10.15pm, St James' School Field

The *BREAKING NEWS* banner had whooshed onto the Sky News' screen within seconds of the Prime Ministers statement being seen by the editors and journalists. Jim Arkwright was getting quite annoyed that the Councillor had obviously refused to come along and explain himself. It left Jim feeling angry and upset that despite all of this attention, he'd ultimately lost. It was all beginning to feel like a massive anti-climax.

Guy James, the Sky correspondent on the field would soon lift Jim's mood, as he walked across to Jim and read out the statement. There were loud cheers and laughter from the remaining supporters on the field.

Jim was clearly pleased, he had been determined to make sure that his work on the school was reinstated, as Tim Dixon from Mock Off had promised it would, but he was also pleased because he felt shattered after so many hours of standing up in his chains. For the first time he allowed himself a beaming smile and a celebratory punch of the air.

"Well that's good that Guy, and I hope Councillor Norton does the right thing and resigns. I'll get my lads to come and cut these chains off because I'd better get ready to come back here in the morning to get on with this job now it's all sorted out – it should never have happened all this."

"It's a pretty scathing attack from the Prime Minister against Councillor Norton, but the good news is that the PM is personally ensuring that you can get on with this job right away."

"Yes, like I've said Guy, I'm happy with that – but I'm not about to start congratulating the Prime Minister about it. It's the only right and proper opinion to have on the disgraceful stuff that's gone on today. But make no mistake Guy, if Councillor Norton and the Prime Minister were both from the same political party – you'd not be reading that statement out tonight. It's only because they're from opposite parties that the PM is making such a song and dance, its damaging for Norton's party, and scores points for the PM's party. I don't trust any of them anymore Guy. The corruption that this Councillor Norton is involved with runs right the way through the political system."

"But Jim, the PM has personally guaranteed an enquiry into this – and has said that your work here can carry on." Guy seemed quite mystified by Jim response to such excellent news.

"Look Guy, the Prime Minister making a promise about anything holds no water anymore. The TV cameras are here so of course it's all got to look neat and tidy but I'll see what happens after I've finished this job, and see if the phone rings with more work from the council. My bet is that it won't. But thanks any road for all your help Guy, at least I can get on with this one now. Can somebody tell one of my lads to come down with here with an angle grinder and cut me free so I can go for a pint at the New Inn? I'm absolutely gasping for a pint of Pendle Witch!"

A quarter of a mile away, a loud cheer went up around Jims local. The whole pub had been watching the performance, many of them had gone straight through from tea time. Now they were all delighted to hear that the night would be rounded off by Jim popping in himself.

The mood in the pub had been like a New Years Eve party, and Sandra had been rushed off her feet since the story came on TV at five o clock. It seemed that all of the New Inn's regulars had been onto the field at one time or another, and had then felt drawn to the pub to watch the news story unfold. As a result the place was crammed.

As the light faded, Sky News showed Jim being cut free from the railings and a final, almighty cheer went up around the remaining crowd of 60 or 70 hardcore locals that had stayed right until the bitter end.

Jim was finally laughing and having a joke with everybody, he'd had to keep his mood quite austere all day.

There was now a feeling of triumph and celebration in the air, and for those neutral viewers watching at home with no connection to Jim, or to Clitheroe, it was a quite extraordinary and almost inspirational evening of news reporting that would certainly live on in the memory of those who had watched it.

Jim had come across as a mild mannered, hard working and honest gentleman who had been treated outrageously. The whole thing had turned into a bureaucratic battle of David and Goliath proportions. It's not very often that a small town businessman can attract such attention to a relatively small fry case of wrong doing at the local council and cause such a fuss, even dragging the Prime Minister into it. But by a bizarre set of circumstances, all triggered by two strangers filming Jim having a laugh with his mates in the pub, that's exactly what had occurred within just a few days.

Not long after Jim had reached the pub and had been greeted like a rock star by his friends and associates, he was presented with his much craved for pint of ale. Jim quickly realised that he'd made a mistake telling the news crews where he was headed.

Outside the New Inn, the satellite trucks had set up and had begun broadcasting. The place erupted once again when the front of the establishment came onto the TV screen. The mood was ecstatic in the pub, and Jim had finished his pint within seconds. Guy James, the sky correspondent who had interviewed Jim a few times throughout the night came into the pub with a cameraman. This excited the already jovial crowd inside the New Inn.

Jim was sat down, getting into his second pint and was pleased to see his fellow patrons of the pub having such a good night. Guy was broadcasting on Sky News right there from within the pub. It was incredible, the broadcaster was asking the regulars what they thought of Jim, and all the fuss that was being made.

"He's a brilliant bloke – can't top him!"

"I'll tell you one thing for certain, he would make a far better Prime Minister than the shower we have now."

"Everyone loves Jim – you can't find a more genuine bloke."

"He'd do anything for anyone would Jim."

"One of the best!"

It was pretty conclusive stuff, and if there was anybody else in the country that still needed convincing about what a decent, honest, hardworking, intelligent and amusing man Jim Arkwright was, they would only have until the morning to wait and read all about Jim in every national and regional newspaper.

The days events had guaranteed the story would be on the front page of them all, with Jim Arkwright featuring on the front page of the FT too, as his "bonus scheme" idea was about to get full endorsement from the most serious of papers – the pink paper.

At the New Inn, Guy had eventually worked his way round the pub and was now stood near Jim, his familiar large grey fluffy microphone once more in front of Jims face.

"Jim, everybody in this pub is raving about you, joining millions on Twitter and Facebook who are claiming that you should be our Prime Minister! What's your reaction to that?"

Jim laughed, a big hearty laugh from the very pit of his stomach, fuelled by relief to be off the railings, feeling glad to have won the argument and a little merry from downing his first beer so quickly. He managed to compose himself enough to answer the question.

"Well, that wouldn't surprise me at all Guy, nothing in this country would surprise me where politics is concerned." The pub began to quieten down as people tried to hear what Jim was saying.

"You see Guy, this country has totally lost its way with politics now. The MPs expenses scandal, along with the scandal of cash for honours before it, and all those other examples of sleazy, scummy behaviour by MPs and the Lords has made people realise how pointless our democratic system is. It has left a very bad stain on people's opinions of politicians now, so much so, folk have started voting for the flipping brainless nazi parties."

The comment received applause and chants of "hear hear."

"Look at what this Councillor has done today – total abuse of power, just because I won an argument with him on't wireless last night. At one time we looked to our politicians as the pillars of our community, but nowadays most people view them with suspicion and assume that they entered politics for their own personal benefit, not to help the constituents that they get paid a hell of a lot of brass to serve. The big problem this country faces is a complete apathy for politics."

Once again the onlookers in the pub chanted and cheered their friend. Jim took a hefty swig of his drink before he continued. "Look, I'm just an ordinary bloke from an ordinary background and just have a look at how interested people have become in me in the past few days, I'm on the telly now! Hi Dad!" He waved and winked into the camera which got a huge laugh.

"This is your evidence that the British public are absolutely desperate for a change to the political system. Folk want something they can relate to – they can't relate to all these privately educated rich toffs who run things. We are seeing fewer and fewer voters going out to vote – because they just can't see the point, they don't see any difference between one party and the other. All they see of Parliament is a load of incompetent hooray Henry's shouting and jeering at each other, waving pieces of paper and acting like infants. Eighty per cent of the MPs in this country are millionaires. Whereas, by comparison to the country, less than one per cent of the population are millionaires – that fact alone shows you just how badly the system has failed."

"Spot on Jim!" shouted one patron of the pub.

"Go on Jim, get 'em told!" yelled another.

"Parliament is full of people who don't understand what real life is like for ninety nine per cent of the population! That's a fact. They just don't get it!" The rant attracted a rapturous applause and more supportive and encouraging shouts of;

"Give it 'em Jim!"

"Tell 'em Jim!"

"Fucking have it!"

"Normal British people who work hard, try their

best, help folk out and get along with their neighbours are not represented in Parliament. The ministers who are in charge of running the country have never even had a proper job anywhere! How can they run our country if they've never even run an errand?"

Another vigourous laugh rang out, and cheers of encouragement and applause waved through the crowd of the New Inn's familiar faces. It pleased Jim as it meant that he got a little break for another hearty swig of his well earned beer.

"I'm sure that deep down they are all probably really kind hearted, decent people who do care about Britain. But collectively, they are bloody useless. The Parliament that we have today only serves the MPs inside it, not the police, the nurses, the bin men, the teachers and the communities up and down Britain that keep us all going."

The pubs regulars, many of whom worked in the professions that Jim mentioned applauded the remark.

"I'll give you an example of what I mean. MP's voted for a ban on smoking in pubs, remember? – except, they kept a couple of bars exempt didn't they? In bloody Parliament! Haha, they told all us little silly people that we can't smoke in pubs because it's bad for us, but decided to keep their own ashtrays. Absolute tossers!"

The news reporter was about to ask another question but Jim carried on with his rant.

"Hey – they all send their kids to private schools as well – so it doesn't really affect them if they completely screw our schools up tinkering around with half baked ideas and changes – because their kids will be alright! And they have private medical care as well, so if they trash the health service – it won't affect them! Jesus! Enough is enough!"

Jim was beginning to go red in the face as the injustice of the British political system began to anger him. The regulars were egging him on, their chants and groans, boo's and applause for Jim's points was pushing him on.

"I reckon that to stand as an MP, you should have had to have at least fifteen or twenty years of work experience, in real jobs – not twelve months as a "researcher" in Parliament, or eighteen months at your cousins PR company – I'm talking about proper work in Britain, with proper British people – running a business, managing a railway, building up an enterprise, driving a bus – getting a good look at all the problems we face, getting a good idea of why we're in the state we are. One thing is for sure, this country is on the bones of its arse right now. Our politicians are supposed to lead the country to success. At this minute in time, it just feels like the Government are sitting around drinking expensive champagne and laughing at all us lot! So to answer your question Guy, I guess it's not a new Prime Minister that this country needs, it's a complete re-think about our political system!"

The vocal support and applause rippled through the pub once again, along with shouts of support "brilliant Jim! Get 'em told lad!"

Guy knew instinctively that he was getting great TV footage here, his gamble to follow Jim to his local had certainly paid dividends.

"Get us another beer in please Sandra!" shouted Jim over towards the crowded bar area. The mood was so pumped up in the bar, this remark also received an overjoyed welcome.

"So, Jim, what do you think is wrong with our politics then?" It was a rubbish question and Guy knew it, even as the words were coming out of his mouth. But luckily for him, Jim was in the mood he liked to be in the most – the mood that Karen described as "putting the world to rights." He approached Guys question with gusto, now almost oblivious to the TV camera and the fact that he was participating in his own live broadcast. He'd grown used to the media circus throughout the long, hot and peculiar day.

"I know precisely what's wrong with our politics Guy, and so does everybody else who isn't *in* politics. It's time that we all grow up and face facts Guy, but our Politicians won't, they argue and lie and twist things. We need a full stop, and we need to start everything again. This country is at tipping point, and the good people, the anonymous ninety nine per cent who put up and shut up are finally reaching the end of their tethers."

A huge cheer resonated around the building, causing distortion on the tv sound equipment.

"We don't have any law and order. We don't have mutual respect for one another. We buy all our stuff from overseas and then complain that there are no jobs or prospects here."

"Too bloody true!" shouted a voice from behind the TV camera.

"We drink too much, we moan too much, we pay too much for everything, we get ripped off by our own government daily, our economy is broken down, our youth have no prospects, our houses costs too much, we have cures for certain cancers but can't afford to pay for them and, despite all this - we only get angry about temporary traffic lights or late trains."

Another round of applause rattled around the pub.

"This nation has broken down, simple as that. It needs towing off the hard shoulder, taking back to the garage and having a complete overhaul. The last sixty years have been a total disaster – practically everything we did was a mistake, society has folded in on itself, it's completely broken down. We need Prime Ministers to stop talking about tough decisions and actually do them! Take some action to get Britain back on the right road. Frankly, the past few generations have screwed us over with short term ideals. I don't like it that my kids are growing up in this disgusting mess that we have all helped to create. We need to start again, we need to change course now."

"Would you care to elaborate on that point Jim. How exactly do you feel that we ought to change course?" asked Guy, kindly allowing Jim another wet of his pint.

"Because everyone in Parliament is too scared to admit it when they get it wrong. So they deny it, or ignore it altogether. But why can't we just face facts and admit it? Draw a fu... draw a bloody line and move on. We do most things wrong in this country, and then we all look at each other to say "told you so" afterwards. If you are trying to get to Scotland from Leeds, but your car is hurtling south down the M1 towards London, at what point do you hold your hands up, admit you've made a mistake and turn the car around? The way the current set of clowns running this country are going, we'd carry on past London, down to Dover and drive off the end of the flipping cliff!"

The applause around the New Inn was deafening once more, and many viewers sat at home were also applauding Jim, and his laid back style of delivering hurtfully true political views and observations.

The social media sites were ablaze with comments such as "OMG Sky News NOW!" and "This guy on Sky News now is truly awesome."

The Sun cartoon artist had been handed this one on a plate. The final versions of the following morning's newspapers were still being written as the drawing was submitted of a bus full of the Governments familiar looking Cabinet Ministers along with the Prime Ministers caricature sticking out of the drivers window, as the bus hurtled past an arrow pointing towards Dover.

"How long until we reach Glasgow?" was written in the speech bubble coming out of the Prime Ministers mouth.

"Nearly there now" was the caption above the mouth of the Chancellor of the Exchequer.

Chapter Fourteen
Wednesday Morning - Arkwright Household

"This alone will not iron the economy out!" pleaded the economist, to the presenters of the BBC Radio 4 Today programme, the UK's most listened to news and current affairs breakfast programme. "It will act merely as a sticking plaster, a short term scheme. I dread to think of what carnage such an initiative would have on the economy once everybody has spent their five thousand!"

Jim was listening to the broadcast on his alarm clock radio in his bedroom as he put his oily, paint splatted overalls on and brushed his teeth. Despite his initial pleasure of realising that his scheme was being discussed on the radio, Jim was becoming increasingly annoyed that his idea was being slated, particularly when he had no right to reply.

Jim felt that his words were being twisted and taken out of the context in which he had originally said them two days earlier on Lancashire FM. In Jim's view, he had floated the idea as a way of kick starting the dried out economy, a simple and effective way of getting money to change hands once again – he never made any statement that this action would be the answer to all of the nations financial problems forever, which was what it sounded like the economist guy was pontificating.

Jim was a long time listener to the Today programme, and he followed politics keenly. But this broadcast was annoying him so he switched the radio off and popped his head into the bathroom where Karen was showering. "Love, I'm going. Its ten past seven – I'm getting an early start."

"Alright cocker, see you later. Love ya," she shouted as the door closed.

At this point in time Jim was completely unaware that all of the papers were supporting him, championing his views and endorsing the £5,000 scheme. The Today programme would also end on a more positive point of view, with the Chancellor himself saying that Jim's idea "was being scrutinised with a keen eye."

But away from all the carry on with the media, and in spite of the stupidity that had played out the previous day, Jim was very keen to get on with this railings job, despite the fact that he had lost much of the enthusiasm that he'd had about Metal Makers prospects of securing future contracts.   Regardless, he still wanted to put in a sterling piece of work. There was no way that Jim would never allow anybody to suggest that his failure to attract further tenders was in anyway down to the workmanship of the railings that Metal Makers had put in.

It was a fine summer's morning and the birds were competing to be heard, all singing their own merry tune. The sun was already providing a good heat, but the ground was soaked in the morning dew – it was sure to be another hot one today, thought Jim as he leisurely wandered down to the school field, whistling as he went. He wanted a scout round to remind himself where they were up to and what still needed doing before he'd take a walk up to the factory and co-ordinate the days work for his staff. But it was hopeless. As soon as he got to the edge of the school, he could see a crew of waiting reporters.

"Aw for fucks sake," he said to himself. "They're still here."

Naively, Jim had considered the matters of the past 36 hours to be finished with, old news. He was absolutely astonished to see that the press pack had grown in size overnight. "What a set of freaky looking bastards." He muttered to himself as he crossed the school field to where they were assembled.

"Good morning Jim!"

"Hi Jim, Good morning!"

"Hello Jim."

It was quite bizarre this, thought Jim as he casually stepped towards the gathering.

"Have you lot not had enough of Clitheroe yet? We normally have to lock outsiders in the Castle to get them to stay here for this long!" Jim's lazy quip got a mild laugh.

"Seriously though," he said as he got right up to them, "Its all over now, I just need to get on with putting up these railings. There's nowt left of the story. I wanted the job reinstating, I've got what I wanted. You lot don't need to still be here."

This got a much bigger laugh than Jim's joke had. The media crews were surprised to learn that Jim was practically oblivious to his new found stardom. He was caught completely unawares as they showed him the newspapers that he was on the front cover of and told him about the millions of tweets and Facebook comments. The original Youtube video had reached 34 million views now, and clips of his other activities including the radio rant and the previous nights lambaste were getting some serious viewing figures too.

Jim's natural surprise and honest reaction to the front pages was being recorded on camera by Sky, ITN and BBC News and would soon be the latest footage to be played over and over.

"Nay! Bloody Norah! Look at the state of all this!" he said, the look of amazement completely spontaneous and unmistakably genuine.

For the first time, Jim was beginning to see how

massive his story had become. It was all completely ridiculous to him, and at that particular moment in time, extremely inconvenient as he just wanted to get on with his work. But the media were happy, they were getting even more brilliant coverage of this genuinely ordinary, down to earth man. Once Jim had given a couple of minutes of banter and general conversation – he made his excuses.

"Right, well thanks everyone for your interest and all that, but I'm afraid that's enough from me now, I've still got all these bloody railings to get ready and put up, so you can all get on your way now and I'll see you again sometime! Cheers!"

Jim walked back across the field, trying to remember how many panels were ready, and figure out how many more panels needed welding up today. His footprints left a fresh trail of bright green through the fine grey dew on the field.

"Is he taking the fucking piss?" asked one cameraman.

"Does he really think we're all just going to piss off now he's got everyone's attention?"

"You know what?" said a colleague, "I reckon he thinks exactly that – and that's only going to add weight to the theory that he isn't trying to get any limelight. That simple, chilled out bloke we're watching stroll across that field is going to be fucking running this country. You mark my words."

An hour later Jim had returned to the site with his wagon, laden with the day's panels that needed to be erected, fixed and painted. This next section would get the boundary fencing almost half way done, but despite the loss of almost four hours work the previous day, Jim was still confident his team could get back on schedule if they didn't hit any major setbacks.

But within minutes of starting, Jim realised that he couldn't get on with his work today with all these journalists and TV and radio crews milling about and standing in the way of their job. The media wanted his opinion on everything from tax to immigration, single parents to drug abuse. He was even asked his view about conflict in the Middle East.

"Here, listen. Gather round all of you. I'm not answering any questions today right, because me and my lads here have got this big job to sort out right. Now every time I stop working, to come over here and talk to you lot, my lads think I'm taking them for a ride. No more questions!"

Jim walked back to his small team. "I'm fucked if I know what to do with these lot lads, honestly, I am."

It was Eggy who had the best idea as they carried on with their work and discussed the media scrum standing over them.

"Just say you'll meet them in the pub after work and you'll answer anything they want to ask you then, but only if they piss off now!" Eggy looked really pleased as Jim slapped him on the back and cheered.

"You bleeding diamond! That's genius Eggy!"

Jim couldn't believe the simplicity of Eggy's solution.

"Right, excuse me one last time then lads, sorry." Jim walked over to the assembled media teams. "Okay, listen, I know you've got your jobs to do, and so have I – so if you lot just drive off somewhere, leave me and the lads to get stuck in with this lot, I'll come and meet you all in the New Inn at 5pm sharp and I'll answer anything you want answering then."

Jim Arkwright got his wish, the legion of reporters, photographers, journalists, radio presenters and TV news crews locked up their vans and went wandering around the idyllic rural market town at the foot of the famous Pendle Hill in the heart of the Ribble Valley.

Sky News and BBC News' viewers were being asked if there was "anything you'd like to ask the Clitheroe Prime Minister his views about?" Both channels were asking for questions and promising to put the best ones to Jim live on TV later that day.

Jim was beaming as he walked back to his team, satisfied at last that he would get some peace and quiet now to do this work.

"Bloody genius that was Eggy, I were gonna be in the New Inn at five any road mate!" His colleagues laughed. Jason summed the situation up perfectly.

"This is crackers this job Jim!"

The town was absolutely buzzing, all of this national media exposure had helped to draw an enormous amount of visitors to the place. The combination of the blazing summer weather and the schools half term holidays helped to convince families from all across the north of England to venture along to this lovely looking Castle town for a nosey around.

The media crews had besieged the town centre and the Castle grounds, grabbing "vox pops" from the public, excitedly asking questions about Jim, asking people if they knew him. The New Inn was also under a great deal of scrutiny as the exterior of the 18th century pub became the focal point for a lot of the news reporting.

"At five o' clock tonight, Jim Arkwright will be holding a special news conference right here to answer any questions that the public wish to put to him. We'll have the conference live here for you, with build up throughout the day." The Sky News anchor was normally seen in the studios in London, but had been sent up north to cover the story "on the ground" following the previous day's extraordinary scenes and the resulting political reaction to it.

Publicly, Councillor Fred Norton had still not been seen, nor heard of. The Leader of the County Council, Councillor Jack Francis had appeared on BBC Breakfast news earlier stating that he had received no news from Councillor Norton, but described his colleague's position at the present time as "untenable."

Chapter Fifteen
Wednesday Lunchtime – Colborne House Cafe

The ridiculousness of the situation was beginning to worry Jim's wife Karen. She had arranged to meet for lunch with her best friend Sarah in Swailes Café on Wellgate. The large, old fashioned family run "pie and peas" café was a firm favourite with the areas residents, particularly the older ones. It was almost like stepping into a time warp back to the 1970's inside the famous local café, red leather seats facing each other over cream formica topped tables. It even had the original 1970's poster promoting "Ice cold, nice cold Milk."

Karen was on her lunch break from work, and wanted to meet Sarah for a catch up and a chat about everything that was going on.

"You know what Jims like, he's not bothered by it all, he's just taking it all in his stride. But I'm worried that he's going to get too far involved with it all. What if he actually does end up getting properly involved with politics?" Karen wasn't her usual bubbly self, Sarah had noticed it straight away.

"I mean, he's bloody obsessed by politics, its all he talks about with his mates in the pub. So all this that he's saying on tv, its second nature for him to come out with all this stuff. I don't know half of what he's talking about most of the time – that's why I like it that he does it in the pub away from me!" Karen smiled, but the weight of worry was clear to see on her face. Sarah was unsure of what Karen was concerned about.

"I don't get you Kaz, he's obviously bloody good at whatever it is he's been doing, I got stopped by two cameramen on my way down here! Towns covered in news crews."

"I know – he is good, he knows exactly what people want the politicians to do - that's the trouble. What if he goes off to London and becomes a politician? That's what all the papers are saying he should do. But I'm scared of that. I like our life as it is. I don't want it to change Sarah. We've got enough money to get by, we're happy, the kids are settled. It's just all come out of the blue, and the phone-in on the radio at work this morning was all about how the Prime Minister should stand down and let Jim do the job! And all the callers were agreeing with it!"

Karen shrugged and gave her friend a look of exasperation. Sarah found the look hilarious and snorted into her coffee. It made Karen laugh for the first time that day. The pair of them were giggling at the total insanity of the situation, the thought of Jim as the Prime Minister. It was such a ridiculous concept to everybody who knows Jim, especially his wife.

"Honestly Sarah, I've got papers and radio stations phoning up at work trying to ask me questions. I swear to God I feel like it's a dream and I'm going to wake up in a minute!"

Sarah thought about what her oldest friend was saying. The pair had met at Edisford Primary school in 1981 and had been best friends for over thirty years. There wasn't anything that they didn't know about each other – and they always turned to each other for advice when it was needed.

"Listen, Jim is a bloody solid bloke, feet firmly on the ground. Me and Mike were pissing ourselves laughing at him on the telly last night. He's just dead down to earth and normal. I can't see why he would want to do politics, it's full of sleazy, arrogant, posh twats – he wouldn't want to hang around with them types of people."

Karen laughed again. It was a good idea to meet Sarah, she always helped to clear her worries up and made her laugh.

"But tell him how you feel Karen, and tell him that you're worried it's all getting a bit out of hand."

"It already is Sarah. Last night, after he got back from the pub, he told me that some guy from London had been up yesterday, driven up - and offered him fifteen grand to appear on *Mock Off*, you know that funny politics show?" Sarah held her hand up to her mouth and stifled a gasp.

"Fifteen grand?" she whispered, really loudly.

"Exactly. But Jim refused, said he can't go because he has too much work to do, so he only doubled it! Offered him thirty grand, there and then! And he's arranged for a senior foreman from Balfour Beatty to take over the factory while Jims away."

"Fucking hell! Serious?" Sarah was stunned. The question came out a little louder than Sarah had meant, causing a rattle of teacups from the old ladies sat at the table behind.

"Seriously! Honestly! Jim is taking me down there tonight, first class train, limousine travel, 5 star hotel in Hyde Park. They're recording the show tomorrow then we've got another night in London, coming back on Friday – we could have had longer because Jim's Dad is having the kids, but Jim wants to get back and make sure this jobs done right."

Karen had cheered up a bit now, Sarah's reaction had put her fears into perspective.

"I'm fucking jealous!" Sarah said it through clenched teeth, with a crazed look in her eyes.

"Why can't Mike ever do something really cool like this?"

Karen laughed again at her friend.

"I'm really excited, but I'm dreading it too. It's like a dream come true for Jim, he's said for years he'd love to go and watch them filming it. But what if he becomes a big star, really gets the taste for it?"

"Your trouble is that you're a neurotic bitch! Why do you always worry? Just go and have a lovely time with your husband and bloody enjoy yourself! Do your worrying later!"

"You're right. Thanks Sarah. I'm being a selfish cow I know, but I just like life as it is. I'm scared of what changes all this is going to bring."

"It'll be awesome! You've got an adventure and a half on your plate here. Just go with the flow and enjoy yourself you stupid bitch!"

"Alright, calm it with the insults you fucking trollop!" They both burst into laughter as a young chap on the table opposite looked up from his Daily Telegraph and gave a disapproving glance at the two friends. It took them a few seconds to compose themselves. Karen's eyes were watering.

"Look at your mascara! You look like Alice Cooper." Sarah set them both off laughing again. It had certainly been wise to come and talk to Sarah about everything.

"Seriously though Kaz, if it was any other bloke, the only thing that would be worrying me would be some gold digging pretty young slapper was going to try and get latched onto him. He's still a bit gorgeous you know, and getting a bit rough around the edges. A bit like a dossers Bruce Willis."

Their laughter filled the café once again as the shock of what Sarah said was stamped on Karen's face.

"Any other bloke would probably fall for some female attention like that, I know my Mike would. He'd fall right into that trap. But not your Jim, he's only got eyes for you that man. You're a very lucky woman Kaz, and I really mean that."

"Aw thanks babe. And you are too. Mikes a bloody good man too, I keep telling you this!" Karen was really glad to have had a laugh. Sarah was always good for turning serious stuff into a joke and making light of the things that Karen worried about.

"Mike's alright. I wish he had a bigger knob though."

Chapter Sixteen
New Inn, 5pm

It was pretty obvious to everybody that the New Inn wasn't a good venue to hold this "press conference" as the media types kept calling it. Jim had had to fight his way into the place, squeezing past all the journalists, TV crews and members of the public that had come along to hear what he would say. The bar area was four or five deep with people jostling and trying to get served. The mood in the place was extremely merry and enthusiastic. The noise of everybody chattering and laughing was deafening and it was awfully hot in the pub too, condensation was giving the walls an odorous sheen.

Jim finally fought his way to the bar hatch and let himself through. People were shouting "Here he is!" and "Alright Jim?" He went behind the bar where several people were frantically pulling pints, trying to keep up with demand. Jim tapped Sandra on the shoulder as she was pulling a pint of beer.

"Sorry about all this, love." He whispered to her.

"Don't be, its bloody good business." Sandra had been offered help from her friends from the other pubs in town, they'd fetched beer barrels in the boots of cars, brought along tables and chairs and some were even lending Sandra their staff to work behind the bar. There was an enormous sense of community spirit throughout the town, the locals were passionate about the place, and proud to see it looking so charming and idyllic on the TV. They were especially proud of their newly-famous representative Jim Arkwright too.

"I don't think we'll manage to do it in here though chuck. It's going to be a bloody health hazard.

When I said about this, it was to about 15 of them this morning. I didn't know it would get out of hand like this Sandra!" Jim looked genuinely sorry, worried that he had let his old friend down.

"That's £3.30 love," said Sandra as she handed the pint to the waiting customer.

"Jim, its fine – I'm the proud landlady of the most famous pub in Britain! They've been promoting it all day on telly. You're the main story on the bloody news man! There's been folk in all day, asking questions about you, talking about your idea for the five grand. It's totally off the scale all this is, off the richter scale!" Sandra closed the till and spun around to greet another waiting customer.

"Yes please love?"

"Two pints of Pendle Witch please love." Said the customer courteously, as he tried to ignore the fact he was being politely crushed by the ever increasing mass of people waiting behind him. Jim wasn't impressed by what he was seeing – he'd had no idea it would get this silly.

"Listen, we can't do this in here. I'll tell them we'll go round the back onto the Market Square– are they alright to take the glasses outside?"

"Of course Jim, no problem." Even under extreme duress, and glistening with sweat - Sandra still managed a carry off a very flirtatious manner with Jim.

"Have you seen Phil and Dave? I wanted to catch up with them but I can't see them anywhere?" The pub was absolutely full to the rafters, most of the people in there were looking directly at Jim, and blatantly talking about him.

"They're out in the beer garden. Good luck love!" Sandra kissed him on the cheek as he snatched the pint that she had just finished pulling for somebody else and went back through the hatch.

"You cheeky bloody bleeder!" Sandra was faking outrage.

"I'll pay you later!"

Jim walked into the middle of the pub.

"Right everyone – listen!" he shouted over everybody's head in the general direction of the door. A shuffled shush came from the crowd.

"I will be round the back of the pub. On the Market square – don't rush – buy your drinks and I'll answer the questions there, starting at half five."

Within seconds Sky and BBC news had over dramatised the simple message with *BREAKING NEWS* effects. The TV crews rushed out of the pub, causing an awkward and embarrassing bottle neck in the doorway. The press people rallied round to the back of the building and ran onto the market square, determined to grab the best spot and relieved to learn that the questions and answers session was no longer taking place inside the pub.

The market square itself was actually round, so there was some initial confusion about whether this place was the actual location that Jim was talking about. It was resolved by a local walking his dog.

"Aye, this is the Square, well, the round bit is."

The media people very quickly realised that Jim would be able to stand on the circular bench in the middle of the market square. They began setting up their microphones, tripods, cameras and sound equipment all around the bench.

"This is far better, this is ideal," said one to the agreement of his colleagues. There had been concerns that the acoustics and general scrum that would have ensued inside the pub would have resulted in a very poor standard of footage for broadcast. This was the perfect location, the sun still beating down heavily and barely a cloud could be seen in the deep blue sky.

Slowly, but surely the market square began filling up with spectators, the media pack were assembled all around the circular bench that enveloped around an old fashioned Victorian lamp post. Directly behind where Jim would address his questions stood the Norman Keep, known fondly as Clitheroe Castle.

The stage was now set for Jim to come along and keep his part of the bargain, and answer the media's many questions. Jim was with his long time drinking partners Dave and Phil as he walked quite casually into the crowded marketplace and made his way through the gathering crowds in the direction of the temporary media stage that had been spontaneously set up for him.

Dave and Phil stayed further back, looking forward to watching Jim in action. The things that he would inevitably say would not come as news to these two, they'd helped in the development of a great many theories and solutions over many hours, over many years, over many a real ale.

Jim was really surprised that he felt no nervousness or apprehension at all, as he put his freshly replenished pint pot down and ambled up onto the bench. Jim started talking, initially to the press people at the front.

"Thanks guys, for leaving me in peace to do my work today – it's a bloody big contract that's at stake and I had to make sure my company Metal Makers – the North's favourite metal fabrication company, no job too big or small, gave it our best shot." Jim winked into the cameras. His cheeky and audacious product placement got a laugh from the media crews. It seemed he could do no wrong, and he realised that he was thoroughly enjoying himself.

If this thing went the way he hoped, he'd basically be sharing all of his views and opinions to the whole nation, and – the best part of it, they all seemed to be listening to him. Normally he could only get his drinking pals to listen, even the lads at work dismissed him when the topic turned to politics.

"Oh fucking hell, he's going on one again," would be the typical snub from his colleagues who generally prefer women, football and car conversations.

But never in Jim's wildest dreams could he have imagined that one or two of his views could, potentially be heard by people who were actually in charge of government policy. To Jim, that was such an exciting possibility, it didn't bare thinking about.

"So, thanks a lot for giving us some peace and quiet today. Who wants to ask the first question then?" A noisy rabble erupted, but Jim pointed to a well known face stood right before him.

"Jim, Amanda Potter, Sky News – We've heard your idea about the five thousand pound windfall, do you have any more ideas on how we could fix our ailing economy?"

Jim looked at her and walked around the bench slightly to make full eye contact. He looked at her confidently as he spoke softly and affably.

"Thank you Amanda, did you have a good day here in Clitheroe?"

"Yes, it's been absolutely lovely, thank you." The well known, attractive news anchor who was a familiar sight on television every afternoon looked as though she might be blushing a tiny bit as Jim replied.

"Yes, it's a lovely town, and I hope that once all the media have lost interest in me, the name of the town will live on in everyone's memory, it really is a lovely place. A genuinely unspoilt, traditional English market town in an area of outstanding natural beauty."

Jims rambling attracted a wave of bemusement amongst some in the crowd who had come along expecting to hear hard hitting solutions to the UK's economic and social crisis, not cheerful tourism advice.

"Right, anyway where were we? Have I got any other ideas about how to help the economy? I've got loads Amanda. We could start with public bodies like councils, job centres, police, hospitals and benefits offices all adopting a policy of only buying British stuff. It makes no sense that public money is being spent on cheaper stuff from overseas in order to save cash. It's dumb, it's robbing Pete to pay Paul. The cash that's saved by buying from China then gets spent paying out Jobseekers allowance because there's no jobs here! So why don't they spend their budgets on British made office furniture, British vehicles, British stethoscopes and give work to the people? Think of the money that's diverted overseas through this kind of stupidity! Its money that should stay in our country, in our economy."

"Good point Jim! Well made!" shouted a member of the audience. It sounded like Dave but Jim couldn't be sure.

"Also – we should take a look at the supermarkets. We should force them to stock goods that were produced here in the UK. Ban them from selling stuff imported from overseas. Think of what an impact that would have if all the bacon we bought was British, not Danish. If the lamb for Sunday dinner was English, not imported from the other side of the world in New Zealand."

The Sky News anchor looked impressed with Jims answer and the two maintained eye contact as he expanded on his point.

"We should make the supermarkets behave more responsibly – make them operate in the interests of Britain, not just for their profit margins and share holders. This is the country where they make their money, they should have a bloody legal and ethical responsibility to make it flourish."

Jim was still talking directly to Amanda Potter, almost as though it was just the two of them standing there. He asked her "How many farms do you think there are right here in the Ribble Valley?"

Amanda gave an awkward, bewildered look and shrugged. It was her very first time in the area and she had absolutely no local knowledge.

"Well I'll tell you Amanda, there are hundreds! And how many of them supply the national supermarket chains here in Clitheroe? The answer is none of them. All that beef, that milk, all those spuds and carrots, cabbages and lambs and pigs that Ribble Valley farmers produce, and not one of them bought and sold on by any of the national supermarkets!"

The crowd were aware of the problem, but the expression on Amanda's face suggested that she had no idea or indeed any real interest in what Jim was talking about.

"Its total and utter madness, our farmers have to go to their markets to sell to independent butchers and grocers who can't afford to pay them very much because the supermarkets are driving down the price with their cheap imported stuff!"

Amanda was beginning to feel a little uncomfortable with Jim's mega personable response. She was starting to wish he'd finish the point, move on and answer somebody else's question. The audience however were lapping it up and applause at Jim's point was breaking out enthusiastically amongst the rural audience, many of whom were farmers themselves, or had strong ties to the areas farming heritage.

"So how does any of that make sense to anybody? We are closing down our own perfectly good businesses to buy the stuff from overseas, to save money! Meanwhile, our workers are made unemployed and as a result the country's economy has died because there is no money to spend on anything. These are the kind of economics that we need to get a handle on, right now. How can we allow the supermarkets to continue to buy from abroad and push the butchers and greengrocers out of business here? It makes no sense economically, or morally."

Jim stopped for a sip of his beer. But he was quick to continue and finish his point.

"So there are a couple of simple idea's that would make an enormous difference to the jobs market, the economy and more importantly, the survival of this country."

There was a positive chant of support from the crowd of onlookers. Many were regulars from the pub, but most were unfamiliar faces who had come for a nosey at the press conference after hearing about it all day on the news.

"We should force the supermarkets to have a strict list of products that must be sourced locally, I mean within like fifty miles of the store. And if they can't find local cabbages, they aren't allowed to sell cabbages in their store. Hey Presto, as if by magic – a cabbage farmer suddenly has a bloody opportunity to build up a nice business enterprise and take on some staff!"

Jim received yet another enthusiastic response from the ever increasing crowd that stood in the hot summer sunshine.

"We should make them work harder for the communities that support these massive supermarkets, right now they couldn't care less about the towns and cities that they serve." Jims point was now receiving a euphoric round of applause. But he still wasn't finished.

"And we should set limits on overseas goods that they are allowed to sell. We can do a hell of a lot with this economy – but we just have to think sensibly. It may be cheaper to buy our spuds from France – but its not providing any jobs to local people is it? So we all have to pay more in tax to support unemployed folk. Did I mention that this is madness? We could pay a few pennies more for our local spuds – safe in the knowledge that it is rebuilding our economy on a local level, that we are providing jobs and income for British farms and their staff."

Amanda looked relieved that he had finally finished his point. And then dismayed when she realised that he hadn't quite finished. Not just yet. Of all the politicians that she had ever met and interviewed, she could never recall getting such a detailed, passionate and well structured reply.

"But I've literally got hundreds of ideas of ways we could improve the British economy Amanda, there really are so many ways. Lets look at ourselves, lets start and think more about our problems. We buy our trainers from an American company who get them made in Indonesia, we import our sofas from Scandinavia, our clothes come from India, our furniture is from Russia, we buy our TVs from Asia, our cars come from Germany, we buy lager that's brewed in Belgium, our coal comes from bloody Peru! There's even a bloke who lives on my street who bought his wife from Thailand!"

There was an instant wave of laughter at the joke, which reassuringly pleased Jim - because even as he was saying it he wondered if he had perhaps crossed the PC line that was strangling the British sense of humour.

Jim let the laughter subside before continuing. Amanda had been on screen when he cracked that joke and her amusement was plain to see.

"Basically, what I'm saying is, we've become too lazy and started to buy all our stuff from abroad – instead of producing and buying our own stuff. Imagine if Britain made it the law that you can only sell British stuff in supermarkets – and any stuff that we can't grow or make here, like bananas for example should be imported from countries that trade with us in return. One box of pineapples imported, one box of leeks exported. Its easy in theory so why on earth don't we just do it?"

And with that, Jim was off, for the next hour or so his ideas and opinions would be broadcast all across the UK and Europe on the rolling news channels, and most of what he said in the first 30 minutes would be summarised on the mainstream TV news bulletins at 6pm.

In this quite surreal broadcast, this previously unknown local businessman would preach, dictate and empathise about many areas of ordinary, day to day life, in a way that would connect with the forgotten, normal people of Great Britain.

Jim Arkwright made himself crystal clear to everybody in the market place, and to the millions of viewers who were watching on television or listening on the radio. He set out his stall, calmly and lucidly saying,

"Now listen, some of you guys will be thinking "this bloody blokes trying to tell us what to do!" but I'm not trying to tell anybody what to do, or anything like that – I'm here to offer my opinions to the questions that you ask me. If you don't agree that we should try harder to buy British stuff, then that's fine, I really don't care, and feel free to stop listening to me! But right now, Britain is on its knees, socially, morally, financially, industrially – we're in a big massive hole and we keep on digging and digging in the hope we can dig our way out. Well it's never going to happen. All the real people like you and me in society recognise that, we just need the chance to convince the people who run the flipping country!" Listen, if we all agree to swallow our pride and admit we're doing things wrong, we can still climb out of the hole – but its going to mean a fresh start, a fresh new look at all the stuff that has put us in this big bloody hole in the first place. What I will say to you this afternoon is brutal, it's truthful, and it will be painful but most importantly, I'm being honest. I will probably upset a hell of a lot of people."

Once again Jim reached down and grabbed his pint. He took a long and thoughtful drink from it before placing the glass back down on the bench.

"No matter how upset people get by my opinions – please don't forget how upsetting life is right now for millions of people who can't get a job, or are living on lawless estates, burgled and robbed, beaten up by thugs for no reason, bullied, abused and left to rot by a system that's broken down.

Our pensioners are treated worse than the prisoners in our jails for Gods sake. That's not a cheeky little sound bite – it's a fact."

The audience on the market were applauding and whistling, cheering Jim on.

"Life is pretty damn bad in Britain for a lot of people. So I guess that what I'm trying to say is I'm not here to offer any ideas that can tweak the existing ways we do things – I'm saying stop digging! Get us a bloody ladder and let's start getting the hell out of the hole we're in!"

The speech won a rapturous round of applause. Jim went on to share his views on everything from Drugs, Unemployment, Disability, Crime and Punishment, Prisons, Youth, Education and Tax.

It became very clear from the moment Jim had stopped speaking on that bright hot sunny afternoon in Lancashire, that almost everything that he said had resonated with his audience and brought the public together. Practically everybody that had heard what Jim said was in agreement that the topics were the screaming priorities that were being ignored and neglected, allowed to fester and spread and get worse.

Some felt extremely strongly against one or two of the views and theories – but despite their strong views, the weight of what Jims objectors did agree with made even his most controversial policies easier to swallow and consider in a rational frame of mind.

This was totally surreal, it seemed that Britain had apparently found itself a new Leader, and it had all happened by mistake, an error. This simply had to be the work of fate. Jim Arkwright was supposed to have been picking his Dad up from the airport on the day that his PM impression video had been made just a week earlier. A series of peculiar coincidences had led to a most extraordinary case of being in the right place at the right time.

Politically, it had been considered impossible to achieve what Jim Arkwright had single handedly done. He had united all of the country on a wide range of serious issues. He was bringing the British people together again, and speaking in the way that they had craved for years – honestly and openly. But most importantly he spoke like they did. Jim Arkwright hadn't mentioned any particular party, or named any politicians that had got it wrong – and this was his most endearing quality, this was the thing that made him so different.

The public were sick and tired of the blame game culture of politics. The public didn't care how a pot hole got there, the public just want it filling in so they don't wreck their tyres every time they drive over it. If a bridge falls down, they just want it putting back up so they can get to work - not an inquiry lasting six months, that will find that the bridge was unstable. But politicians still couldn't grasp that basic fact and it was part of the reason that the public had given up listening or even caring what they said.

Jim Arkwright seemed like the kind of guy who would just get a damn pot hole mended, and put the bridge back up, and he'd roll his sleeves up himself to do it. This man was a breath of fresh air.

Politically, Jim Arkwright had caught the entire nation's attention, and this hadn't been done since World War Two, when Winston Churchill was elected to steer Britain through the crisis and defiantly declared to the nation that he had "nothing to offer but blood, toil, tears and sweat."

The enthusiastic media coverage of the public's reaction to Jim Arkwright, his straight to the point arguments and his "rough around the edges" style was something that all three of the major political parties had not failed to notice over the past 24 hours.

As the media hysterically reported on this "rough and ready" political giant, an urgent meeting between the UK's three leading political groups – the Conservative, Labour and Liberal Democratic Party Leaders and their party Chairmen was hastily being arranged at Number 10 Downing Street.

Unbeknown to the Prime Minister's senior advisor, Miles Wentworth Farlington at the time, this was to be a historical meeting that would go on throughout the night, and well into Thursday morning.

Chapter Seventeen
Wednesday Night - Virgin Trains Pendolino

"Hey this is the life isn't it?" Jim was grinning at his wife as he sat opposite her in the first class carriage of the train that was zipping along the rails in the direction of the capital.

The tinted view through the carriage window was mesmerising - the setting sun was creating a rippling pink and orange blaze of pastels, defiantly fighting against the darkening sky. Jim was staring out into the fading vapours, lost in his own little world.

"You've caught the sun you. Your nose is going to peel. Do you want me to put some moisturiser on it? I've got some in my bag." Karen was leaning over and prodding her husbands face.

"Don't be daft. I'm not sitting here with all moisturiser on my face. Don't be so preposterous!"

Karen laughed out loud, forcing a little bit of snot to burst out of her nose. "Preposterous!" she squeeled. "What kind of word is that?" She giggled, it was completely unheard of to hear Jim speak like that and it really tickled Karen. Jim laughed too.

"It's good innit? I'm practising with all the big words for tomorrow! I don't want to sound thick on Mock Off, do I?" They both laughed again and realised they were grinning from ear to ear as they watched the fading sunset grow darker. Jim did another little chuckle to himself and Karen laughed again. The train began to lose speed as it was announced that they would shortly be stopping at Birmingham New Street.

"Bloody hell, Birmingham already? They're nippy these trains aren't they?" Jim was posing the question to himself more than anybody else. It had been a long time since either of the Arkwrights had been down to London and the anticipation of what lay ahead on the short excursion was bubbling up inside both of them.

The first class seat just across the gangway from Jim and Karen's table had been empty until the carriage reached Birmingham. Now the train was losing some passengers and gaining new ones. It looked as though the Arkwrights were being joined for the second half of the journey. The man was dressed very smartly and looked to be in his early forties, a similar age to Karen and Jim. He seemed slightly embarrassed as he placed his laptop bag down on the table and removed his suit jacket.

"Hiya mate," said Jim with a nod, trying to break the ice. He could see the passenger looked a bit nervous and maybe felt like he was intruding. Karen followed her husbands lead and smiled warmly at the man.

"Oh, hello. Erm. Is it…. Are you Jim Arkwright?" asked the man. The question made Karen do a double take. Jim laughed, more at Karen's response than to the question itself. He'd become quite accustomed to being recognised over the past couple of days with all of the madness on the school field and then the media gangs all wanting an exclusive. But this was Karen's first experience of it and it was as strange for her as it had been for Jim just a few evenings earlier at the Lancashire FM studios.

"I am indeed." Said Jim cheerfully. "How do you do?" he asked of the passenger.

"I'm good. Thanks. I can't believe its you! That broadcast at tea time was something extra special. You've got the whole nation talking about you and here you are! Sat on the train beside me." He seemed to be at ease all of a sudden, it was as though Jim possessed a natural ability to make people feel good around him.

"Did you watch him? What did you think?" Asked Karen, desperate to find out how it had been received after missing most of it. Karen had been too busy arranging everything with Tim Dixon, and then packing and sorting the kids out for their stay with their Granddad.

"It was absolutely brilliant!" The man's face lit up as he spoke. "I'm not kidding, but I had goose pimples, and so did the others in the office as we watched. You've said exactly what everybody has been saying and thinking for years – except the difference is this is not just talk in a staff room or down at the pub – it was live on the fucking telly! Pardon my French!" He was staring straight at Jim, trying to get across how strongly he genuinely felt in his support for what had been said on TV just a few hours earlier.

"Don't apologise, we both speak French don't we love?"

Karen smiled at her husband and then at the man.

"Bonjour Monsieur!" She said in her broadest Lancashire accent and all three laughed.

"What's your name mate?" asked Jim as he opened himself a can of McEwan's Export that he'd bought from the trolley dolly earlier and began pouring it slowly into the plastic pint pot that he was carefully tipping with his other hand.

"Yes, sorry. I'm Stephen Parkin."

"Pleased to meet you Stephen, I'm Jim as you know and this is my missus Karen. What do you do mate?"

"I'm a Youth Development Manager for Camden council. I've been up here all day on a seminar. But to be honest, most of the day has been spent talking about you! I'm serious. I honestly can't believe I'm sat on the same train with you!"

"Jims going to be a star guest on Mock Off, we're going down there now for the recording tomorrow." Karen looked as though she could burst with pride at her husband's achievements in the last few days.

"Bloody hell, that's fantastic!" Stephen laughed at the idea. "That will be a brilliant episode! I didn't know it was recorded though, I always thought it was live."

"Yes, we did, didn't we Jim?" said Karen, kicking her husbands shin under the table, pleased to learn that it wasn't just them that had been duped.

"Ow. Jesus Karen, that was right on the bone you pillock. Aye, sorry Stephen - we didn't know it was recorded either – and we've been watching it for ten years!" Jim stopped rubbing his leg and inspected the head on his beer and took a sip.

"I'm a bit nervous about it though, you have to be dead funny on Mock Off. I'm scared I'll make a comment and no one will laugh!" Jim laughed, to himself mainly.

"So what does Youth Development work mean Stephen?" Karen asked. Stephen seemed delighted to respond, instantly demonstrating a real enthusiasm and passion for his work.

"I work on the estates. It means everything from making sure that there are enough activities going on in community centres and things like that, to going out and targeting under age drinking, substance abuse, drugs, under age sex. Then there's fundraising, trying to attract extra funding for new schemes and projects. It's good. It's an interesting job – but it's a losing battle, it gets harder each year."

"I bet its bad in London with all the gang culture as well isn't it?" Karen asked. Jim was listening intently to what their travelling companion had to say as the train was back in full motion and thundering along the rails.

"It is, gangs add to our problems, but there are lots of complex issues that are hard to tackle in today's society – lack of employment and training opportunities, absent parents, the breakdown of the extended family unit, parents suffering with depression problems, its all been building towards a new emerging culture of selfishness, self importance. The kids we see with the most serious issues are the next generation down from the first wave of societies drop outs, living in a sub culture of gangs and drugs and crime. And alarmingly, believe it or not, a growing number of teenagers are emerging from the second generation – meaning that their Grandparents started the entire process of existing on hand outs and welfare for their family. They refuse to accept rules, never had any boundaries put in place. It's like they live to a modern tribal type of rule and authority that is hidden away deep inside the estates."

"Jesus! It sounds scary" said Karen. Jim nodded in agreement.

"It is frightening, but my team work tirelessly with them, trying to get them on the right track, trying to show them a better way. It's hard, and we win some, we lose most. But our society is in a really peculiar place right now – and as I say, selfishness, self preservation and a really short term survival strategy is at the very heart of it."

"The parents are to blame aren't they? They should be punished." said Karen, shaking her head at the completely depressing picture of modern Britain that Stephen was portraying.

"Well, it's not as clear cut as that. I wish it was, and I also wish we were only talking about a minority of families but sadly that's not the case either. Almost half of the families in Greater London are living in poverty – in squalor and deprivation. It's like the third world on some of these estates. The London you see on the TV, with the tourist attractions and theatres and posh shops is a thin coating of gloss paint over the ugly, rotting reality beneath. And it's the same story in Birmingham, Manchester, up in Edinburgh and Glasgow. Honestly. And there are no straight forward answers to how we can fix all this, it's a big spiders web of complicated issues. And that's why everybody is getting so excited about you, Jim!"

"Well, we'll see. It's a bloody funny thing politics – a strange world that is mainly inhabited by financially fortunate, socially awkward, arrogant people who wouldn't be taken seriously or listened to if they were involved in any other walk of life. It's not often that a normal working man gets his voice heard amongst the posh folk who run things."

"No, that's very true Jim. And look at the fuss the media are making about you. I've never known anything like it!"

"It's really interesting what you are saying about the youths though Stephen. Me and Karen live in a lovely part of the country – it seems a million miles away from the inner city London that you describe mate. I'm glad my kids live up north, out in the sticks."

"Yes, we are lucky where we are Jim – but I still blame parents – I don't care how rich or poor you are, if you have a bloody kid, you should bloody well bring it up as best you can!" Karen was clearly agitated about this point.

"But, many of the parents were brought up in the same way, or even worse. So they don't know what bringing kids up properly means. I'll bet that you bring your kids up in a way that compliments the best of what your parents did with you both. If you were left to starve, were regularly beaten, neglected and abused by alcohol or drug dependent parents. You'd struggle to bring your kids up in a productive manner, if that kind of chaotic life was all you'd experienced. Some of our clients were put on the game by their own parents at the age of ten, eleven."

"Shit."

"Fucking hell."

"It's only going to get worse Karen – those of us who work in the social services sector know it's a ticking time bomb."

Stephen was knowledgeable about his subject, and he still sounded passionate and interested in finding answers and solutions to the problems that his department faced.

"Sorry Stephen, but Karen has hit the nail on the head, regardless of the circumstances – it is the parents! We can't just carry on living our lives working out answers and explanations as to why we're in a mess and being too scared to admit the problem. We need to draw a line under it, write it off and start working on proper ways to get ourselves out of the mess. The past is for the history books – the future is what our country needs to concentrate on. I just wish we could stop this inquiry culture we have. Instead of just having the courage to say stop, we carry on, tweaking things a bit after each inquiry. It *is* the parents fault Stephen, because it's nature's way to nurture your young, it happens in every species. But because British people have got so much cotton wool and bubble wrap and safety harnesses all around them all their lives, they are losing that basic human instinct. We've become inadequate people – we're losing the most basic instincts of survival, and it's down to welfare, that beautiful thought of providing care from the cradle to the grave. Nobody starves in this country and that's the biggest error that our society has ever made. Everything is handed on a plate. People know what they are entitled to. That's the word – the word that has crippled Britain – entitlement. So some, particularly the ones you're talking about Stephen – they give up and accept a life of free housing, free income and the only thing they need to achieve it is a kid. Or 5 kids if they want a big house and a bigger income. And if they want to supplement their income they can do a bit of crime on the side, burglary, prostitution, drugs, mugging or even a bit of shop lifting – or as you say, even selling their kids as prostitutes."

"Aw don't Jim, that turns my stomach," said Karen, still looking appalled at the point Stephen had made.

"Yes but, what I'm saying is, through trying to help people out, we have engineered our own sub species of human beings that have children as part of a process to getting a house and systematically indulge in crime as part of their culture. A kid is the equivalent to a passport photo to some of them, and even less of them have any concern about who fathers the poor little bastard! So with respect Stephen, let's put the political correctness bullshit to one side and run with the theory that it is the parents that are to blame for the shit you are faced with every day. It's the parents, egged on and encouraged by a totally incompetent policy on welfare."

"This is getting really complicated Jim. Why is the welfare state to blame?" asked Karen, seemingly overwhelmed with complex details. But Jim was happy to explain it to her, this was such a rare opportunity to have a decent discussion with his wife about the things that interested him the most.

"Because the welfare state not only allows them to doss about all day, it encourages them to go and do it! Without the welfare state, the estates wouldn't exist. But because of the welfare state working so brilliantly for the idle, we have to keep building more estates, each one replicating all the others with all the same social, health, economic, crime, education, and behaviour problems. When the hell are we supposed to say no! Stop! This shit doesn't work, it multiplies and grows like a mould, and it won't stop until it has covered everything!"

Stephen smiled. "So what is the answer Jim? I know this subject inside out. So you tell me how you would deal with the mould as you put it, and I'll tell you honestly if your solution would work."

It was obvious that Stephen was genuinely intrigued to hear Jim's ideas, and Karen still seemed quite interested as well. Jim took a hefty swig of his drink and looked out of the train window as he considered Stephens question for a few seconds as the lights of houses, kitchens, bedrooms and bathroom windows whizzed past at dazzling speed.

"This is a hard question Stephen but I'll give it my best shot. Most of this crap that we're talking about started on the day that the welfare state was introduced, which was at a similar time when women were given the contraceptive pill and the hippies passed their drugs around and said "free love" was the cool and trendy thing to do. It was the sixties. That was when the fibres of our society really started coming apart. As if that wasn't bad enough as a culture shock – the feminists started to spread the message that women should stop relying on men, and should stop fussing around their families and neighbours and they should go out and get careers. It all sounds bloody brilliant doesn't it? Go and get high, float about shagging whoever you like without the risk of pregnancy. And best of all, if you can't be arsed working, just stay at home and the government will pay you. And if you were a bored housewife, you could forget your domestic responsibilities and get a career!"

"Well yes," said Karen. "It sounds pretty fantastic to be honest!"

"Precisely!" said Jim, slapping the table. "Of course it does. It was like the basic rule book for everything the British people lived by for centuries had been ripped up. But fast forward fifty years and look around you - see what the desolate, soul gutting result of all that is. Blokes bringing up other blokes kids but not bothering to see their own, single parent families run by depressed mothers working like maniacs in minimum wage jobs that don't pay as well as unemployment, an army of tattoo covered alcoholic Grandfathers in ghetto like estates that are overflowing with feral youths that have little more to offer society except bullying, addiction, bad attitude, ill health, petty crime and anti social behaviour. And the feminists carved up the communities by driving mothers out to work, dropping their children off to be brought up in day care centres. All the time the proud, spotlessly clean communities that the housewives and mothers used to keep strong and close-knit have disappeared and disintegrated into anonymous multi cultured suburbs where everybody keeps themselves to themselves and nobody challenges anybody or anything. Houses and streets and estates and towns full of suspicious, depressed, docile soap opera viewers who don't think their neighbours like them."

Karen and Stephen offered a quiet round of applause. Jim laughed and took a sip of his ale.

"Well that was nicely put Jim!" Stephen was clearly impressed with Jims all reaching prognosis on what was wrong in the nations communities.

"Nice rant Jim! Is that what you and your mates sound like in the pub?" Karen was laughing.

"That's exactly what we sound like love! We put the whole world to rights in that little Snug."

"You didn't answer the question though Jim, you just explained why you think we're in the state that we're in. So I'd say that you're a naturally gifted politician!"

Stephen felt at ease enough to rib his new found associate. Jim smiled.

"You're right enough there mate. So yes, how I would sort it out would be very simple in theory, and it would create lots of jobs too! First off, I'd make it the law that if a male got a female pregnant, even if he was deaf and dumb - he would know beyond any doubt whatsoever before he put his dick anywhere near a fanny that he will pay for any child to be brought up, or he'd be going away to jail for sixteen years to break up big rocks into tiny little stones for 10 hours a day with no right to any appeals or time off for good behaviour or any bullshit like that. If we did that, I would guarantee you that we'd see a huge improvement on irresponsible Dads! And if we did that, we'd also save millions of extra pounds on treating these sexually transmitted diseases that are back in fashion. All we need to do is put proper, startling consequences in place. Make people think twice about their behaviour."

"Aw come on!" said Karen. "That's a bit strong isn't it?" she looked seriously disturbed by the solution Jim had put forward.

"Well, it's strong yes. But look where being weak and relaxed gets you – millions of kids being brought up by the state. It's a solution that would work, and it's a solution we need to get these walking hard-on's to take a little bit of responsibility for the fatherless kids they are irresponsibly spunking out all over the land."

"Jim! That's absolutely outrageous!"

"No, sorry love. You're judging it with that soft-touch liberal attitude that allows blokes to shag about, make babies and then when they get bored with the responsibility and normality, the realness of life, they head off into the sunset and repeat the cycle somewhere else. Kids need a proper family supporting them through childhood, not a stressed out, worn out mother and a series of step Dads."

"Jesus Jim!" said Stephen.

"Bollocks to being nice, look at the state we find ourselves in by being nice! This country has been lovely and nice with a cherry on top to everyone for fifty years, and it's got us nowhere – we're a joke to the rest of the world. We're a laughing stock! We need horrible, draconian laws to get people to wake up and stop taking the piss!"

"So that's the solution to fatherless kids sorted!" Stephen knew there was a much bigger picture that affected the circumstances in each case – not just a one size fits all answer. But Jim shook his head dismissively.

"It's bigger than that, there's more to it Stephen. It would be the start of something, a fresh approach to making people think responsibly, behave responsibly. It's not as much about Father-less kids as it is about people thinking twice about what the bloody hell they are doing with their lives."

"Well I can't see how you can start banging people up for not bothering with their children Jim."

"No. That's not what I said Stephen. Starting from now – from now." Jim bashed his finger against the table to help explain the point.

"You can't go back and start meddling with what's happened. But from tomorrow, you can make a difference. From tomorrow you can introduce new ways of clearing the mess up, start by getting some respect and standards back into society. Make it clear to people that they need to start to use their dicks responsibly, or they'll be facing a stiff penalty."

Karen burst out laughing. "Ha ha ha, did you mean that? Stiff penalty?" she asked, looking at her husband with a wide mouthed, shocked expression.

"Yes, of course I did." He smiled back at her. "It should be called the stiffy penalty."

All three of the adults laughed at the childish joke.

"Well, in principle I think it's a fair point Jim, but no MP would agree to that – how many absent fathers make up the electorate these days?" Stephen thought he'd thrown a curve ball to Jim.

"No MP would vote for anything that is controversial Stephen, otherwise we'd have reinstated the death penalty years ago, we'd have left the EU when we realised our membership actually worked against us. MP's wouldn't touch anything with real substance. They avoid stuff that divides opinion because they run the risk of being voted out at the next election, and they'd hate to lose their nice cushy job with all that fame, the extravagant expenses and all those shady business opportunities. So they do absolutely nothing. They just bullshit and bullshit hoping they'll continue to get away with it. That's all there is to it really! I genuinely can't see the point in them. But let's go back to answering your question. Now let's get back our lost community spirit! Since all the mums and housewives were morally bullied into going to work in supermarkets and travel agents, our neighbourhoods have totally lost any sense of community spirit, and a rising number of women are depressed and feel guilty about having drink problems through the alienation in their lives. We have to get back to talking to neighbours, becoming friends with the folks across the road again, getting to know the whole street. I'd make it policy that where a person can demonstrate they take an active role in helping to create a strong community spirit, they'd pay half council tax. If they are running an organisation like Scouts, or a football or cricket team – they get a 50% reduction on their council tax bill. Simple as that. If they can show that they go and get shopping for an elderly neighbour or cut their lawn for them, or say, organise a sports day or a street talent show, a neighbourhood watch scheme or a litter picking day for the kids. Anything like that, anything that helps to get folk communicating to each other and getting to know one another, they should pay half a bill."

"That's a great idea Jim. But many people in the communities that need this kind of help don't work anyway, so their council tax is paid for anyway. So it wouldn't motivate them." Said Stephen.

"The community problem of neighbours ignoring one another is everywhere mate. Not just in the council estates where you work, it's on practically every single street in Britain. We have allowed ourselves to get so wrapped up in the communities on telly, we don't know our own closest neighbours. We can name all of the residents of Albert bloody Square, but we don't know the name of the bloke next door but one! That needs sorting out, so we can start to build stronger communities that in time, can stand together and object against the vandalism, anti-social behaviour, drug culture, racism and gangs. It takes time, but the answer lies in building our communities back to how they were before the women abandoned them. I'll tell you now, women are the bloody back bone of anything that needs sorting out, and neighbourhoods need women back at the heart of them, organising them – keeping everybody in line. But how can they if they're on bloody shifts at the all night supermarket? Mothers and Grandmothers should be told that with immediate effect, they are under no obligation to go out to work. Their place is in the home, in the street and in the local community if that's where they want to be."

"And what's your answer to the other problem you mentioned? The one regarding people not working?" asked Stephen.

"That's the easiest one to fix of them all Stephen. We make everybody who can work, work. No more sitting around smoking and stinking, watching tv. We shouldn't pay out any benefits for worklessness at all, all it does is rot the mind of those who are stuck looking for things to occupy them all day and it just creates more problems which cost even more money and resources to fix. It generates crime, anti social behaviour and addiction through boredom, poor health through lack of activity, depression and mental health problems. We should have a big factory in every town and if people can't find work off their own back, they'd be taken into the factory, owned by the government, paying out the minimum wage. How long do you think those factories would be in existence before the kids in school cottoned on, and cleaned up their acts, pulled their socks up and gave one hundred per cent?"

"They'd refuse to go." Karen smiled smugly, and Stephen nodded at the comment.

"They'd refuse to go *now*, under the current "do what the bloody hell you like, anything goes" regime that is crippling us. But under a decent, strong society they'd be carted off and thrown in a cold damp jail if they refused to work. Think like that, hard, nasty, no bullshit and it would only take a few years to alter the attitude of mind that encourages people to think they can just take the piss out of the system. It's tragic when you think about it, because those who would suffer most at the start are those that have been ignored, neglected by governments for forty years and have known no better way of life than dossing on handouts, but that was never the idea of the system."

Karen was still offering her full attention, and Stephen was nodding as Jim continued to speak.

"During the industrial revolution – if you didn't work the day, you didn't take no pay – and you'd be hungry. Sick and lame people even had to get involved with what they could manage. The whole welfare state was just a dream for the Victorian and Edwardian people. It was supposed to give the sick people treatment, disabled people a better life, poor people a pair of shoes so they could walk without getting infected feet, cripples were supposed to get wheelchairs instead of needing to be carried around on peoples shoulders – it was meant to help people, give them dignity, hope and self respect."

"Come on Jim, our NHS is the envy of the world. It does work, it does help people." Stephen was really enjoying this discussion and most of all, Jim's quick-fire responses to the nit picking at his theories.

"In most cases, it does – and yes, we should be proud of our NHS and our schools and colleges and the social services that run alongside it all, I'm not saying anything bad against that. But somewhere down the line, we have deliberately ignored the countries poor people, built them big estates on the edge of town and encouraged them all to get their dole money and left them to it. But now, the newspapers want to demonise the poor, and we're all supposed to be angry and surprised that they've been breeding like rabbits because the moneys better that way. The system has actively encouraged them to find out what they are entitled to, what they can get for free, how they can get by in the shitty little system that's been provided for them. They found out how far they can push it, how much they can take, and who'd blame them? I don't! I'd have done exactly the same myself if my life had been different, if I'd been born into a world of closed doors and zero opportunities. Its obvious that you're going to get a bigger problem if you try and hide it. Well, if you want it sorting out, and I mean, sorting out for real, not a sticking plaster – then we have got to totally change the system for good."

"How do you do that Jim? Lets say I agree in principal with your theory – but I'm not sure how you can start a war against a whole section of society! And lets be honest here, you're talking exclusively about poor people."

"It's not a war Stephen, you sound like a newspaper columnist shit stirring it all up. These folks are desperate for a proper helping hand, and by taking away the system that helps them to rot away and feel worthless and empty inside, you'd be helping them, giving their life a sense of purpose and perspective. People need work, they need the camaraderie, the laughs and banter – they need to feel part of a team. People need to feel like they've done something with their day – it's a basic human need, like eating and shitting. We could easily find work for folk – look at the state of the nation – the roads are falling apart. Give them all jobs mending the roads for Gods sake. There just isn't any excuse for them not working other than the total and utter ineptitude of the government – half of these crime, drugs and asbo problems wouldn't exist if they'd just create the jobs!"

"But nobody wants to be forced into a job they'll hate, Jim. It's all well and good you saying all that – but people have rights." Stephen was playing devils advocate – but he was genuinely enticed by the clear thinking, straight talking approach that Jim seemed to tackle things with.

"If they don't like the work they're given - there's a college up the street where they can go to at night and study and work hard to better their prospects, like every bugger else has had to do."

"Fair comment!" said Karen.

"Everything I'm saying is fair – it's just been allowed to get so messed up and out of hand by useless governments that its going to seem unfair when it finally gets put right. But I know for a fact, once all these people are working, earning their pay, they'll be glad of it. They will feel a lot better off, they'll feel like they belong, like they've got a purpose in life."

"So how would you implement it, once all the factories and road laying facilities are in place – how do you actually do it Jim?" asked Stephen.

"Easy. You just say "if you don't come here tomorrow to work, we take your house and your benefits away." It'll be a shocker, don't get me wrong – a real kick in the ribs, make no mistake there. But hey, you can't make an omelette without cracking a few eggs – and after all Stephen – we can't carry on as we are. You said it yourself before – you win some, you lose most. Well bollocks to that. A bloke that tries as hard as you, who cares as much as you do should win them all. The simple reason that you don't is because the self interested pricks in government ignore what's going on - because in the short term – I mean, the four or five year term that the ministers are employed for on top pay - they don't want anything too big, or unpopular, or difficult to work on. Well I can see straight through it all. If I was in politics Stephen, I'd be there to work hard, make things happen and solve problems, create solutions, to improve the quality of life for people in Britain. That's the difference."

"Well, you've sold it to me!" said Stephen, smiling.

"And me." Said Karen.

"And I'd make a law that government ministers don't get paid if they fail hitting their targets. They get seventy quid a day food allowance anyway so they won't bloody starve!"

Karen and Stephen laughed.

"I'm not kidding. Stephen, if you get told to do something at work, and you don't do it – you'd get sacked wouldn't you?"

"Yes."

"Well these politicians get voted in to do things they promise to do, then don't do them, and still get paid. It's completely mental this system. The system should be – politician says they'd do something – thing gets done – they get paid. Thing doesn't get done – they don't get paid. See if you introduced that rule and see how much bullshit they offer before elections! See how many of the sly little worms resign straight away!"

"Bloody hell, can you imagine?" said Stephen.

"It's how it should be though. The majority of these privately educated goons in government are there for their own prestige and social standing among their rich families and friends. They don't enter politics to improve life for the people that you work to help Stephen, but they'll earn five or six times your salary, and that's before they fiddle their expenses and take a few bungs. I'll tell you now, the last person who entered the Houses of Parliament with honest intentions was Guy Fawkes."

Karen laughed as her phone started ringing. She looked at the screen and handed it across the table to her husband.

"It's Tim Dixon!" said Karen as Jim answered it.

"Hiya Tim."

"Hi Jim, where are you?" Tim sounded happy and excited, which made Jim begin to feel excited too, reminding him of the brilliant excursion he was on.

"Not far from London I don't think."

"I'll tell you something Jim, I think I might have a part time job working as your manager! My phone hasn't stopped since tea time!"

"Yeah? Why, what's happening?" asked Jim.

"Oh, words got around about you coming on Mock Off and now all the rags are trying to get your contact details off me. Anyway, listen — one of the calls was interesting. You know the daytime show "The Morning," its filmed from the same studios that we record the show — and they want you on for twenty minutes if you fancy doing it? They'll pay you twenty grand."

"Christ on a bike! That's a grand a minute!"

"I know! Welcome to the bullshit world of the media! So what do you think? It wouldn't affect the Mock Off schedule so I thought I'd let you know about it."

"That's crackers. What do they want me for?"

"Oh you know, they just want a quick chat about you being the most famous bloke in Britain right now."

"Right, well. That's fantastic news Tim. I'll tell Karen – put our name down. By the way, I'm talking to a great guy on the train – he works in Camden. Could you organise a couple of tickets for him for the recording tomorrow?"

"Sure. What's his name?"

"Stephen."

"Is that it?"

"What's your second name Stephen?"

"Parkin."

"Stephen Parkin."

"Yes, no probs – tell him to get to Elstree Studios for recording at 2.45pm. Right, I'll tell The Morning to schedule you on the show."

"Great stuff, see you tomorrow Tim, thanks a lot!"

"Cheers."

Jim handed the phone back to his wife and looked across at Stephen. "That's two tickets sorted for tomorrow if you can make it, it's at Elstree Studios, at quarter to one."

"Wow. That's brilliant Jim, thanks very much!" It was clear that Stephen was over the moon with the gesture.

"No worries, hey and Karen love – I'm going on The Morning in the morning!"

"Piss off! Oh my God! Seriously?" Karen's face lit up like a lottery winner checking her ticket. "That's unbelievable!" She started excitedly scrunching her fists together and stamping her feet on the floor, then began scrolling through her phone contacts.

"I've got to tell Sarah!"

"They're paying me twenty grand!" Jim was grinning from ear to ear.

"Oh my God!" Karen couldn't believe what she was hearing, and Stephen was smiling as well, happy to see the couple having such a good time.

"I'm so glad I've met you guys today. Really, it's great to see how genuine you are as well. I feel like history is about to be made with everything that's happening Jim!"

"Ah, don't be so bloody soft mate."

"Well listen Jim, do me a favour. If you ever do get the opportunity to sway any serious thinkers about the state of the nation and where we're headed – please promise me you'll put this abandoned generation of under 25's high on the agenda. It shouldn't take a genius to realise that these kids are going to be running things in 25 to thirty years time. It's at crisis point right now, they need saving, rescuing from a certain life of disinterest. Or there'll be a civil war, the poor versus the rich. The haves versus the have not's. And the way things are going Jim, the have not's will take everything in their path, the have not's are the vast majority remember! So please, I beg you, think of the single most dangerous prospect we face in society right now – a whole generation of young British people that hate their own country. Make a future for these youngsters before it's too late. There's no alternative."

It was a passionate speech, and Jim respected his travelling companion greatly for making it.

"Alright mate. I promise. I'll make sure I do, next chance I get."

"I hope so Jim. Because nobody else can get this on the agenda, God knows we've tried."

Chapter Eighteen
Thursday Morning

"Good Morning Big Jim!" said Karen teasingly as she drew open the curtains of the plush hotel suite and let the morning light flood the huge room. Sunlight illuminated the fine, sumptuous bedroom through the vast bay window that overlooks Hyde Park on the left and the busy London roads and buildings on the right.

"What you on about, Big Jim? What time is it?" Jim rubbed his eyes with the back of his hand, he needed a couple of seconds to get his bearings. Karen walked over towards him wearing the hotel issue luminous white fluffy bathrobe and stood beside the luxurious queen sized bed.

"Sweet Jesus, your breath stinks! You smell like a gammy foot!"

Karen wafted her hand at her husband in disgust. "Its eight o clock you lazy beggar, time to get up. You've got a big day lined up! There's a limo coming for us at nine. Look, you're on the front of all the papers again! They've started calling you Big Jim!" Her excitement and delight was plain to see.

"Ha ah, blinking Norah! Big Jim, that's a ridiculous name." Karen handed her husband the cup of coffee that she'd made for him as he chuckled at the daft nickname.

"Jesus, I needed that sleep love, slept like a little kid. This bed is amazing, comfiest bed I've ever known!" Jim took a greedy slurp of his coffee, dribbling a bit of it onto the posh white bedding.

"Jim you dosser – look at the state!"

"Its alright, it'll come out. Stop panicking," said Jim as he manoeuvred his cup away and shimmied out of the comfy bed. He stood in his underpants and Karen laughed at him. You've still got your socks on you scruffy bastard!"

"Hey, do you mind! I'm not saying nowt about you am I?" Jim took another slurp of his brew.

"So, are you not excited about reading the papers? I've ordered every single one for you!" Karen was clearly overjoyed by the exposure that her husband was getting.

"What are they saying? Am I getting slagged off?" Jim had already anticipated that some papers, particularly the more political ones would have started to rip his theories apart, unzip his arguments and disqualify his views like they generally did with mainstream politicians on a daily basis.

"No. Are they 'eck slagging you off! They are all in agreement with you. Every single one of them!"

Karen grabbed the Sun paper off the bed, opened it at the centre pages and held it up. Jim burst out laughing as he saw a double page poster, a giant picture of himself smiling. They had superimposed the V fingered salute picture from outside Lancashire FM and airbrushed him standing outside Number 10 Downing Street. The headline caption read "Big Jim for PM!"

"That's totally mental! I can't believe it!" The look on Jims face was one that Karen didn't recognise at all. She had never seen her husband look dumbfounded and elated, both at the same time. It was a peculiar look, and one that amused, and charmed her greatly as she wriggled out of her bathrobe and let it fall onto the ground.

"You gormless bugger, shut your mouth before a bloody moth flies in it. Are you coming for a shower? Its one of those double jobs! We could both get in!"

Jim didn't hear her, he was still gazing guilelessly at the newspaper.

"Jim. BIG JI- IM!" she raised her voice the second time. He looked up and saw that Karen was stood at the end of the bed, her robe on the floor at her feet. She was wearing nothing but a very cheeky look on her face.

"I'm going in for a shower. Coming?" She turned slowly and strutted off with a sexy swagger, reminding her husband that her body still remained in very good shape. Jim laughed, and he felt his heart beat race as the excitement of the moment caught him up with a judder.

At this time in their lives the couple got very little "quality time" with having two teenagers in the house. This was the perfect opportunity for a bit of careless fun for the couple. Jim followed his wife excitedly, awkwardly hobbling and running as he tried to pull his socks off as he went. Within seconds, the sound of laughter coming out of the steamy shower room echoed all around the posh hotel suite.

*****

Across all broadcast and written news reports Jim Arkwright and his market place broadcast was the only story of interest. The massive array of complicated topics that he had managed to cover and make sense of in his televised Q&A session was simply unparalleled. Some leading commentators said that Jim had made more political sense in 90 minutes than most senior politicians made in an entire career.

Aside from the general public - it was also evident to everybody in political life, and in the media too, that Jim Arkwright was quite simply an exceptional man. His views were straight from the hip, and in many cases controversial.

But behind every single point that he made was the unfaltering, undeniable argument that the alternative to what Jim was suggesting doesn't work. The alternative to what Jim was suggesting was what the country was already doing, and it quite simply was not working. He must have used the phrase "we tried that, it doesn't work, but we're still trying it" thirty or forty times during the marketplace session. It was the foundation and the cornerstone of almost everything that he said, and it was also the qualifying argument for why some of his most controversial views were not dismissed immediately.

Had Jim's views about reinstating capital punishment been presented by any other politician, it would normally be argued down and forgotten about within a matter of minutes. Hysterical campaigners and human rights experts would be all over the media to talk about miscarriages of justice and inhumane activities, quoting the bible and crying at the barbaric nature of it all. But on this occasion, Jim had presented his argument in such a crisp, informed and zippy way that no campaigners felt assured, or articulate enough to challenge his point of view. Jim had explained that miscarriages of justice such as executing innocent people were simply impossible with today's DNA evidence.

In the same way that he had spoken in tremendous detail about the economy with Sky News' Amanda Potter – he tackled every topic that he was asked about with as much zealous enthusiasm, research and knowledge. There could be no doubt that Jim Arkwright wasn't just another bigot with an opinion on everything and a solution to nothing. He was quite the opposite and his fresh new style had gripped the whole nation's imagination.

Jim had sewn up his capital punishment point by claiming that it was a miscarriage of justice every time a murderer gets locked away at tax payers expense, only to walk the streets again ten years later.

"That kind of wishy washy liberalism is a miscarriage of justice against society, against victims and their families and against our general belief in consequences. We will never start to get a handle on crime and disorder if we don't reinstate the death penalty for the crime of murder. Let's go back to a time when we had a deterrent."

To some, his broadcast had been so skilfully and professionally presented, that there were rumours and questions about how genuine he was. "Was it a conspiracy?" was the question on the lips of some.

But the majority of people in the country couldn't find any fault with a single word that he'd said. Most people saw in Jim Arkwright a long craved for politician that they could finally relate to; one who looked like them, spoke like them, shopped in the same shops as them and who'd had enough of the self serving politics of Great Britain, just like them. But what caught the public affection more than anything was Jim's ability to call a spade a spade and in the typical northern fashion – to say it as it was.

*****

After being greeted enthusiastically by Tim Dixon at the famous TV studios, Jim and Karen were given V.I.P. treatment by all of the staff and crew. Karen had been almost as excited as Jim to be spending the day at the making of such a massive TV show. She couldn't wait to start watching her husband appearing as the star guest on his favourite programme.

It was all very surreal to the couple as they wandered around the giant building following behind Tim, looking around and smiling at each other in a joyous, excitable daze.

"I couldn't stop laughing at you on telly the other night Jim," said Tim as he walked. "You are a real natural at all this – that advice I gave you the other day, you listened to it and it worked for you. You came across brilliantly, I really didn't expect it go so well, Jim!" Tim was clearly impressed as he kept nodding and enthusiastically trying to involve Karen in the conversation. "Has anybody heard anything from the councillor at all?" he asked.

"Not a thing." Said Jim. "I hope the rotten bastard has resigned, but I'll bet he's just keeping his big fat ugly head down, hoping it will all blow over!" Tim and Karen laughed loudly at the harsh ferocity of Jim's statement.

They continued to walk through the cavernous complex. TV stars, film stars and even the biggest chart pop band of the moment had all walked past the trio, as though they were casually wandering around a supermarket, trying to find margarine. Eventually they arrived at studio 1B, where the programme was filmed.

The Mock Off studio was exactly as Jim recognised it off the TV, but it was literally only the set that he recognised – the rest of the programme making process was a complete revelation to Jim and in many respects, spoiled his perception of the show, and the stars that appeared on it. Tim introduced the couple to the programmes host and explained how the rest of the day would pan out.

Jim was extremely surprised to learn that he would be in a one hour planning meeting with the panellists, joke and script writers, followed by a half hour break, during which he would be walked over to 7A, the "The Morning" studio for his appearance - then back to Mock Off for a rehearsal meeting before having a "dry run" rehearsal for about 45 minutes, then another break, followed by a three hour recording session to get all the material needed to edit it into a thirty minute programme.

In one sense Jim was beginning to wish the illusion hadn't been shattered – he'd always imagined that the stars of the show just turned up, made some brilliantly funny observations about the week's news for half an hour and then went home again.

Like many things on this peculiar and extraordinary week in Jim Arkwright's life, he was learning that things are not always what they first appear to be. But despite the surprises that were unfolding about the making of his favourite tv show, and seeing how normal and laid back the celebrities were in real life, Jim was still extremely excited and glad of the opportunity to have such an exclusive look behind the set and see how it all works.

Karen was even more ecstatic than Jim to learn that they would be chaperoned for the day by the star of the show, chirpy north east comedian Jed "Aye" Knight. Jim was even asked for some typical "northern man" cliché's to help Jed write his introduction for the special guest.

"Well, it might be the place where they have outside toilets and still insist on using chip pans, that's right ladies and gentlemen, I'm talking about the north! A place where they still only take one bath a week – and that's the whole fucking family – but here's a northern fellah who doesn't just say "bollocks" all the time – he actually spends his spare time making idiots of our politicians! We sent him a pigeon, inviting him on the show and he's been travelling down on his barge all week - Please welcome the cheekiest fucking northerner since me. Jim Arkwright! The Clitheroe Prime Minister guy!

*****

A lady called Donna Brierley from Norfolk had taken advantage of the governments E-petition function, and started a petition on the Number Ten dot Gov website. The petition subject was : "To make the Clitheroe Prime Minister the real Prime Minister." It was posted late on Tuesday night, at the time the television and news channels were broadcasting Jim's opinions and views from the New Inn – just after the railings protest had come to an end.

Between that time and Thursday morning the petition had gone viral. It had been copied and pasted onto Facebook, it was shared all over Twitter and had been sent around the nation's workers on e-mails too. By 11am, the petition had attracted its one millionth signature, and demand was still so high that the site kept crashing and jamming up. I.T. engineers had to keep re-booting the website server behind the most famous front door in Great Britain.

The Number 10 website policy on E-petitions stated that the government would aim to debate any topic that reached 100,000 signatures. This one had already amassed ten times that number in its first 36 hours, and had broken the British record for E-petition signatures. The previous record stood at 200,000 signatures and had taken six months of solid campaigning to amass such an impressive total.

There was absolutely no doubt left in Whitehall, this whole bizarre episode was doing a great job of getting the British public interested in politics again.

Chapter Nineteen
Studio 7A - The Morning – Live Transmission

"Well, as we have been mentioning all morning, we are very excited to announce that we have the most famous man in Britain sat with us on The Morning sofa."

The attractive female presenter Hilary Cassidy seemed genuinely delighted to be introducing Jim, who was sat smiling and awkwardly holding hands with his wife, who was there beside him on the best known TV set in Great Britain.

The idea of Karen joining Jim on the set was suggested as soon as the producers saw that their star guest had brought his wife along with him.

At first mention, Karen had been terrified by the idea of joining Jim on the couch in front of the national TV audience of several million people, and flatly refused – but the TV company immediately negotiated a £10,000 fee with her which quickly helped her to put her nerves into perspective. Besides, Jim had boosted her confidence by telling her that he'd feel a lot better about it if she was on there with him.

"And just in case you've been in a coma for the past week, and you haven't heard of Big Jim Arkwright" said Hilary's co-host Gary Bright, "here's a little report into how this ordinary man from Lancashire has become the most talked about person in the UK."

The red lights on the TV cameras went off as a video of Jim and his various antics over the past few days went out on the air. Gary Bright took the opportunity to brief his nervous looking guests and try and put them at some ease.

"Okay, Jim, we'll be going live again in about 45 seconds. First we'll come to you and ask you what you think about all the attention you're getting, and then Karen – we'll ask you what you make of all this. Is that okay?" Both nodded fretfully but enthusiastically.

"And then we'll open the lines and let the viewers ask you some questions Jim. Okay, lets standby, and we're going on the air in 10, 9...."

"Well, what a story. Its just like something out of a book isn't it?" Hilary was a great presenter, she was so relaxed and chatty in her style, she managed to put her guests at ease really quickly. Jim answered the question as honestly as he could.

"Well, to me, it is something out of a book. Even though it's weird with everything that happened with those two lads secretly filming me, and then it getting famous on the internet, it's all the other stuff that's happened since that really puzzles me."

"Well, as we saw on the film there, the story really started to get going when you took part in the radio phone in on Monday. It's now Thursday, just three days later and lots and lots of people are declaring that you should become our Prime Minister!"

"Yeah, like I say, it's unbelievable really. I wasn't even supposed to have been in the pub that day, I was meant to be picking my Dad up from the airport – so the whole thing is totally freaky anyway Gary."

"But how does it feel Jim, to find out that the British people are signing petitions in their tens of thousands, demanding to make you our Prime Minister?" asked Hilary.

"It's actually got a million on there now, I'm hearing!" said Gary.

"Bloody hell, has it? Well it hasn't really sunk in yet Hilary. It's a load of nonsense really, it'll all blow over soon enough. I just want to enjoy myself while it lasts, I mean it's fantastic to be coming here on a programme like this – it's beyond my wildest dreams really, so I just plan to enjoy the experience with my missus and you know, just sort of, I don't know really, it's mad. But it says a lot about how sick and tired people are with the normal politicians. It tells me that somebody in government needs sit up and to listen to all these people who feel so strongly about the current state of politics."

"You really think all this is going to blow over Jim? You've got five million people supporting your Facebook page! You're on the front of every single newspaper today." It was Gary asking the question, he appeared shocked that Jim seemed so blasé about the whole thing.

"Come on Gary – what people are getting excited about, if you think about it, is a bloke that's been on the news for saying "give everyone five grand!" and that's all its about really. If they ever got their five grand they'd soon forget about me mate, in a heartbeat."

Gary Bright laughed uncomfortably and looked over at Karen with an inquisitive expression of disbelief. He soon realised that Jim believed in what he was saying. Karen nodded as she gave Gary and Hilary an exasperated look which confirmed that her husband really was being quite genuine. Hilary looked back at the man who had got most of the nation talking passionately about politics again, and laughed.

"Well, I think you're selling yourself short Jim. In fact, I think that's the only thing that I've heard you say that I can honestly disagree with!" Hilary couldn't hide the fact that she was a fan. Karen saw the opportunity to jump in too.

"See! I've been telling him that as well!" She said, glad of another chance to press home her point that the people genuinely loved Jim, it was much bigger and a lot more real than he was giving it credit for.

"See Jim, listen to your wife if you know what's good for you!" laughed Hilary. "And it's a great pleasure to welcome you on The Morning sofa Karen, Jim's wife of twenty five years. I've got to say Karen, you don't look old enough to have possibly been married for so long!"

"Well, thanks very much. But people say that all the time. I even got asked for some ID to buy a bottle of wine in Asda's last year which really made my mates jealous!"

Everybody one the couches laughed and chuckled, and it seemed that the broadcast was going very well. The couple's nerves had settled down now.

"Well, you do look amazing Karen, and thank you for joining us. You'll have to come on again and give us your beauty tips." Karen blushed awkwardly but Hilary was being totally genuine.

"So what's it like living with the man that everybody wants as our next Prime Minister?" It was Gary that asked the question, trying to quickly manoeuvre the discussion away from girl talk that his colleague would happily spend the rest of the segment chatting about.

"Oh, I love this man more than words can say. He is a beautiful, kind, funny, hard working, caring man who goes out of his way to help everybody. He's a brilliant man, and a really amazing Dad to our kids - and I just couldn't be without him."

Tears began to well up in Jim's eyes and his chin began quivering. Karen noticed and laughed, rubbing and tapping on his shiny bald head to mock him further. "He's a right softy isn't he?" she asked, still laughing.

The programmes sharp eyed director had the

camera zoom straight in on this very personal, emotional and amusing moment.

"Well, what a lovely thing to say." Hilary looked spellbound by the moment as Gary tried again to steer the discussion on.

"Well, thanks Karen, its great to have you here with us. Now all morning we've been asking our viewers to get in touch if they have any questions to put to Jim. And we've had an incredible reaction and some fantastic questions as well. Let's go to line 1 and Nancy in Fife. Nancy, you're on the air with Big Jim!"

The screen changed to a map of Britain and a red telephone box graphic appeared on the map in the Fife region of Scotland, to help viewers to see exactly where in the UK the caller was ringing from. A close up of Jim's face took the bottom quarter of the screen up, covering Cornwall.

Jim was dabbing his eyes and looking a bit red faced and embarrassed.

"Oh well, that's lovely! Good morning Big Jim!" the caller sounded elderly and ever so softly spoken.

"Hello Nancy, nice to talk to you." Said Jim.

"So what's your question Nancy?" asked Hilary.

"Aye, well, I live beside a lot of druggies and they are forever causing a hell of a trouble all around the town and I just wanted to know what Big Jim thought of all that, and if he knew what to do?"

"Oh well, that's a great question Nancy, thank you very much. Well Jim, it's a complicated topic but please give us a brief answer, as we do have a lot of calls to get through."

"Okay, no problem. Hello Nancy, I'm sorry to hear that you're suffering because of this, just like a lot of people all over the country."

"Aye, I know, its getting bad everywhere now."

"Well, it could all be sorted out very easily to be honest. I reckon that we should legalise all drugs and if addicts want to get hard drugs and live their lives that way, they should be able to go down and get them at the chemists. If it's for party drugs like cocaine and ecstasy, you should be able to buy that at the corner shop, on the shelf next to the cigarettes and spirits. That might sound stupid Nancy, but sugar kills more people in this country than drugs do each year. But drugs are the cause of most of the countries crimes and misery. So we should make it legal and really easy to buy. Druggies wouldn't need to commit any crimes then, they could buy all the drugs they need, and most would probably get them for free if they are on benefits.

So yes, I'd say do that – there would be lots of great advantages from this, for example it'll cut crime down by about 90 per cent Nancy, and the best part is that the government would control the drugs and make all the profits. If we did it this way, the drugs would be better quality too, so Accident and Emergency staff wouldn't have to spend their days and nights working on addicts that have been tricked into injecting radox bath salts into their veins, and the doctors wouldn't have to spend all their time treating young blokes who've burnt their nostrils snorting Persil."

"Ach, well that sounds fine by me Big Jim! Lovely speaking to ya hen."

"Okay, thanks Nancy, up there in Fife. Our next caller is Daz, and he's in Middlesex. You're on the air Daz."

"Yes, thanks very much. Hi Jim!"

"Hello Daz, alright mate?"

"Yeah, listen Jim, I just want to say that what you're doing is perfect mate. It's about time this country had somebody real speaking up for us, someone we can identify with. Everything you've said, everything about you is so genuine and I just want to say thanks mate. I really do."

"Well, Daz, that's really nice of you, and like I was saying before to Hilary and Gary – if anything good comes out of all this, I hope the government and the MPs can see how easy it is to get people interested in politics if the general public can connect with you. Our MPs and Lords are walking around in the wrong century mate. They still think of you and me as the great unwashed, and that we should bow when they walk past. It's so wrong, so messed up, it would actually be funny, if these dickheads weren't messing up our country. Can I say dickheads?"

"Well, I just hope you do become Prime Minister Jim, I really do."

"Well, a great supporter there, thanks Daz in Middlesex," said Hilary, "and please excuse Jim's colourful language there!" Now here's Gordon in Macclesfield."

"Ah, thanks Hilary. Hello Jim, it's great to speak to you – and I agree with everything the last caller just said."

"Thanks Mate," said Jim.

"Now I just wanted to know what you think about my lad Connor. He's twenty years old and he's depressed because he's no job, no money. He just sleeps all day and then stops up all night on his x box or gets drunk with his mates and then owes all his jobseekers out when he gets it. It's driving me crackers Jim, I just want someone to give him a chance, its not right this."

"I know exactly what you mean Gordon, it's a disgrace. How old did you say he is?"

"Twenty."

"And how did he do at school?"

"Really good, and he's been to college and got his A Levels but there's nowhere now for him to go, he just needs to get a job, or training, or an apprenticeship."

"This really winds me up Gordon. I run my own business and I take young ones on every year, in the past few years I'm getting thirty or forty applications – it used to be four or five if I was lucky!"

"I know, but its murder Jim, when he applies nobody even bothers getting back to him, just to say he's been unsuccessful. He's given up, and he's not turned twenty one yet! I just wondered if you had some good ideas about how to sort the mess out?"

"I certainly do Gordon. You probably know that as well as your lad, we have over a million kids aged between sixteen and twenty five that don't have any skills or apprenticeships, who are just dossing about all day, being paid jobseekers allowance to do nothing. It's the equivalent to fifteen Wembley stadiums completely full of young people in the same shoes."

"Bloody hell! Really?"

"Yes, Gods honest truth Gordon. They've no job, no training, no prospects – and no promise of anything on the horizon either! Meanwhile we've got thousands and thousands of derelict homes waiting for demolition, at the same time as a housing crisis where we haven't got enough social housing to meet demand. There are young couples that can't afford to buy a house because they got so expensive during the boom. So why can't the powers that be think logically? We have over one million unemployed youths who are eager to get trained up and learn skills, and we have a housing crisis. Could they not be given the derelict homes to do up? Could we not employ some of our brilliant time served, unemployed builders to train them up? Train the kids up as scaffolders, roofers, joiners, brickies, plasterers, plumbers and sparkies. There'll be other training opportunites from that too, as architects, administrators, stock controllers, drivers, surveyors, buyers, foremen, canteen staff. I tell you Gordon, your Connor could easily be out there helping to do up all the derelict streets of houses, making them as good as new with an enormous army of keen, strong enthusiastic young people that are just desperate for a chance."

"Well that's a top suggestion Jim. And now you've said it, it's so obvious!"

"Yeah, but the prats in government will say we couldn't afford to do it. But after it's done, they could sell all the houses at affordable prices to cover the costs of rebuilding them and training the youngsters. I ask you, how is there a crisis Gordon? How? Why is your lad lay in his bed at lunchtime? I'll tell you why mate - because the people who run this country have got sausage rolls for brains!"

"Thank you Gordon, let's hope Jims answer was useful to you and young Connor and we wish you the best of luck with that."

"Thanks Jim, thanks Gary."

"You're welcome Gordon," said Hilary. "Our next caller is Don in Plymouth."

"Hello Don" said Jim, staring directly into camera, quite comfortable and relaxed in front of millions of housewives, pensioners, disabled and workless people.

"Jim, hello mate, what's the bloody chances of getting through? That's brilliant, thanks, its brilliant to get this chance to talk to you!"

"What did you want to speak to Jim about?" asked Hilary in a bid to get the conversation flowing.

"Well, I just think like what the other callers are saying that Jim is doing brilliant, really brilliant. I just think its time that we had an ordinary bloke saying, you know, standing up for ordinary folk. That's it really Jim. Just, thanks for what you're doing and we need you!" It was quite obvious that Don was struggling with nerves and excitement, and had clean forgotten his question.

"Well, there you go, a fine example of an ordinary British bloke, just went to all that trouble to say hello to me. Thanks very much indeed Don. You know, you are the kind of person that makes up more than ninety nine per cent of this country!

All we ever hear about is crime, unemployment, drugs, alcohol problems, murderers and paedophiles on the news and in our papers and magazines. But the fact of the matter is that when all you ever hear about is all that crap, you start believing that everyone in Britain is a wrong un! When you're battered with depressing news all the time its easy to forget that practically everybody in this country is a hard working, law abiding, nice, kind, friendly and funny person. Almost everyone in this country is courteous, polite and considerate person who has never committed a crime other than smoked a bit of pot or drove about without road tax for a fortnight until pay day. The massive majority of folk in Britain are lovely, warm hearted people that would stop to help a stranger if they fell over, just like Don there on the phone."

"Aw, thanks Jim!" said Don, his pleasure was unmistakeable.

"It's right though Don. We hardly ever hear about the times when good people do nice things. All we ever hear are reports about terrorism, hate crimes, racism, anti-gay bashing, animal cruelty and the bullying and victimising of vulnerable people in society. The reality is that life in this country goes about in a trouble free, hassle free way most of the time. The one per cent of misery we hear about fills our documentaries and news programmes and forms our opinions of life in Britain – creating a fear of life here and tricking us to believe we shouldn't go out at night. This needs to stop if we are ever going to have a trusting, harmonious society where our communities can grow and prosper together like they used to - instead of carrying on with the head down, don't get to know your neighbours culture that has taken over. Trust me everyone, most folk out there are like Don! So go and have a brew with your neighbour and see how you get on! And I'll tell you something else as well, I'd make the news channels and newspapers do balanced stories. If they report fifteen minutes of bad news, they would have to match it with fifteen minutes of positive, happy news. If its ten pages of bad news, the papers must have ten pages of good news. If they can only print eight pages of bad news! That should be the rule I think Don, to try and balance it out and stop people believing that everyone they walk past is a baddie. Show the bloody good stuff as well, the kindness, the friendly stories, all the achievements and charity success stories as well as the small amounts of grim stuff."

"Good idea Jim. That's a great idea that mate." Said Don.

"Okay, we're running against the time here Jim so we must move on." Gary intervened. "Next up is Margaret in Wolverhampton. What's your question Margaret?"

"Oh, hiya Jim."

"Hello Margaret, what did you phone up about

love?"

"Well I wanted to say, you and your lovely wife have been together now for twenty five years which is so rare in this day and age and I just think that's where we're going wrong with society. Couples don't seem to stay together for long these days and I wondered if you had some ideas on why? Or what you think makes a relationship last as long as yours because obviously, you two have managed it."

"Good God Margaret, that's a tough question! I doubt I'll be able to answer that now, that sounds like me and you need a couple of hours down the pub to get to grips with that one!"

"Oh, that would be hilarious!" giggled Margaret.

"But in brief, I think the main problem is that life is too bloody hard for couples nowadays. We're all taxed too hard. And we're not given incentives to build strong families anymore. Our values have changed so much in the past fifty years – its no longer about the achievements you make as a family that you are judged, its what labels you wear in your clothes, what car you drive that matters, how much you paid for your kitchen. It puts too much pressure on couples – they can't breathe because of all the material expectations they have to fulfil for their friends, families and neighbours and as a result the pressure is too much and they just snap, they give up. Today's view on success is very shallow, and it's the major stress in many people's lives. It's no longer about how well mannered your children are, it's about where you go on holiday that you're judged."

"That's true that Jim, I hadn't thought of that! But you're right."

"Listen right Margaret, see what you think of this - I know a bloke who doesn't eat properly because the repayments on his car are so expensive. But what good is that? He's tried to make it look like he's doing well by lending loads of money to pay off an expensive car, but then he can't afford the petrol to drive it anywhere! We need to get away from all that nonsense now, we need to just make fun of it all and accept that we've got our priorities all wrong. The government has to encourage people to stop creating a false image for themselves because it doesn't work. Depression rates have never been higher, alcohol sales have never been higher and as you say divorce rates, separation rates are through the roof – so it's not bringing any benefit to anyone. I say, let's go back to making families stronger and tighter. Stop Sunday trading for a start. All those parents forced to work in supermarkets or clothes shops instead of spending family time together with their partners and kids. It's no coincidence that since Sunday trading was allowed divorces and family break ups are up a thousand per cent. Family time is really important, and we always make plenty of time for it in our house Margaret."

"You see, that's so true Jim. You don't even think about it now do you, but shops used to be closed all day on Sundays!"

"I know love. I'd suggest that we should get Sundays back to being a day of rest, and also, I'd suggest that any family that stays together and brings their kids up well gets a nice little tax free cheque for twenty five grand as a thank you from the government! The parents that split up cost a lot more than that to tax payers in legal aid bills, administration work and benefits, and it costs a hell of a lot more if their kids go to jail! So why not reward couples who do the slog, knuckle down and face the tough parts of life and battle on through it all and do a good bloody job? I think if you knew that your effort would eventually be rewarded, you'd try and make the relationship work a bit better than simply walk away half way through. People give up too soon and I think they should try harder."

"Thanks Jim" said Hilary. "We're running out of time, but we could just squeeze another couple in if we're quick! Linda in Barnstaple is on line six. Hi Linda!"

"Hi Hilary, Hi Jim."

"Hi!"

"Well, what I wanted to say is, if you become Prime Minister Jim, I hope you can sort the bloody schools out. I was a teacher until two years ago and I took early retirement because the kids are just awful to control now."

"I know Linda! In fact I was talking to a lovely bloke about this kind of stuff on the train down yesterday. Hi Stephen – if you're watching!" Jim waved at the camera and pulled a cheesey face.

"Thing is Linda, the teachers have no powers anymore. Kids know it's just a game of cat and mouse now, with no real consequences available to the teaching staff. I wholeheartedly believe they should be allowed to do more discipline, to regain control. Put the ones who want to mess about in a cell for the day, see if they like that. If that doesn't work, just kick them out altogether, put them in a special school or better still - put them to work licking envelopes or something. Most of the school staffs energy goes into wasting time on the disruptive, unruly kids and there's nothing left to focus on the good ones. I reckon a good idea with the ones who mess about would be to kick them all out of school at 14 and make them do two years of mundane, minimum wage, relentless, boring, depressing factory work. Then, once they have sampled that monotony, start them back at school at 16 and tell them that if they don't want a lifetime full of that misery, they need to get their heads down and get stuck into the work. It's no good us lecturing our kids about the way they need to do things, we need to show them the penalty before they make the mistakes. A lot less kids will screw up their exams if they've already had a taste of life in the factory. With all the morons out of the way, assembling drain pipes or whatever, teachers can support our gifted kids to do a lot better, and not lose valuable, experienced staff like you Linda."

"But they'd just say no, and not go!" said Linda, who was well qualified to pass the comment.

"Well that would need changing as well, wouldn't it? Take a bit of control over them. That's all they need Linda. Give them punishments that will make them think twice, you don't have to be Albert Einstein to work that one out do you?"

"Oh God, Jim, I hope you do become Prime Minister. You'd be absolutely excellent!"

"Thanks love."

"Right then Jim, we are quickly running out of time!" said Hilary.

"It's been a great phone in this morning though hasn't it?" asked Gary – looking extremely pleased with how the programme was going.

"It's been absolutely fantastic Gary, and you must come and join us again some time Jim. And you will be most welcome as well Karen. Okay, our final call today is from Elizabeth in Carlisle. You're live on The Morning Elizabeth."

"Oh, thank you very much. I didn't think I'd get on!" The lady sounded very nervous, but excited too as the telephone box graphic appeared on the map over the far north of England.

"What did you want to talk about Elizabeth?" asked Jim, looking extremely calm and professional considering the fact this was a completely new experience for him.

"Well Jim, I've heard what you said about the ten point plan yesterday on telly. I'm a senior nurse at the hospital, and I just wanted to know what you think can be done to help the service. It's getting so difficult to do a good job with all the targets and percentages we have to reach. It's almost like the patients come second to the paperwork!"

"I know Elizabeth, my sister-in-law works in Blackburn hospital. She says the same thing. The problem we've got in the health service is the same that we've got in Parliament. People who don't know what they are talking about are telling people, who do know what they are doing - to do it differently. All of the health service managers who tell you that you're not treating enough folk, you're not turning over enough beds, waiting times are too high and all that nonsense are just University graduates who have never worked a day on the wards. How mental is that?
We have people with no idea what they are doing, running everything in this country. And then we are all supposed to be surprised when its announced that everything's all gone to cock! My recommendation would be that any manager in the Health Service needs to have at least ten years experience on the wards, at the very minimum."

"That would be brilliant Jim! We always try to explain the reasons for things they complain about but they don't listen – they just care about figures on the paperwork."

"How long have you been working in the health

profession Elizabeth?" asked Jim.

"I'm afraid we are going to have to leave it there Jim." Said Gary.

"No, no, let Elizabeth finish please. Its important this – I bet she's tried to get listened to for years and now she's here on the telly and you want to cut her off to play adverts for accident lawyers and panty liners. Let her speak please!" Jim was friendly, but assertive in what he said. It took Hilary and Gary by surprise, and they were unsure of just how to respond. They gave way and sat back.

The caller continued "Thanks Jim. It'll be over twenty odd years now since I qualified."

"Well I think we need people like you running things. People who've been around the wards, seen the changes, been puked on and seen the odd haemorrhage once or twice!"

Elizabeth laughed at the comment as the hosts Hilary and Gary smiled politely but looked extremely awkward, almost as though they had been taken hostage on their own phone in slot.

"They say we can't afford the health service Elizabeth. So does that mean we'll get our tax back if they sell it off. Will we be handed back the billions and trillions of pounds we all pump into the system? They say the population is living longer. Surely that's good, that means more tax for them to spend irresponsibly!"

"Very true Jim."

"Nowhere in the world taxes its people as hard as Britain! Think about how much we have to pay Elizabeth – we pay income tax on our wages, VAT tax on all our clothes and furniture, council tax to live in our neighbourhood, car tax, petrol tax, put the telly on and pay BBC tax, we pay tax on our gas and electric. God, if we decide to cheer ourselves up and pour a beer or a glass of wine, we pay more tax again. Whatever you do, you're taxed for it in this country. Now I wouldn't mind so much if there was actually a good reason for it, but it just gets squandered on madness. With all the money that the government steal from us, how the hell have we got ourselves into debt? We owe billions and billions of pounds to banks. It's a scandal Elizabeth, it really is!"

"We're saying the same thing all the time Jim! If the country can't manage on all the tax it forces everyone to give left, right and centre, there's got to be something wrong with the system."

"Well we know there is plenty wrong with it! They take six hundred billion pounds off us every year in tax and they can't make a do with all that. You know, the tax system was only started to pay for weapons so we could fight in the Napoleonic War. Our ancestors had to pay it in order to keep our country! But now it's just a lazy way for the government to make money, and they take so bloody much they don't know what to do with it all!"

"So true Jim! Everything you're saying is hitting the nail on the head."

"They let it all roll in and let it all roll out again. They don't invest any of it in businesses that'll create jobs – they don't spend it training our young adults with valuable skills. They squander it all Elizabeth!"

"You're right Jim. I see it every day, waste and pointless costs that nobody would pay if it was ran as a proper business. You're spot on – they waste money, so they can get more next year. It makes my fuc…. sorry. It makes my blood boil Jim!"

"Ooh, did you nearly let a naughty word out there Elizabeth?" asked Hilary, giggling into the camera. Jim nodded, looking serious.

"Don't get me wrong – if it's done right, I'm all

for tax. If it was money going in that was used to make the hospitals better, the railways better, the schools and economy thrive. But its not, its just getting wasted every year! I'd love to get my hands on the accounts for this country and see where all our flaming tax actually goes to! I saw a report that the British Army were paying fifty odd quid for a light bulb. But not one, thousands and thousands of normal, household light bulbs, at fifty quid a go. That's where the trouble is – corrupt managers who allow stuff like that to slip through the net, not bothered because its tax payers money and the mentality that there'll be plenty more of it next year and the year after that. It's totally crackers what's going on in this country Elizabeth and it needs sorting out once and for all my love."

"Well good luck Jim, I hope you can save us!"

"Thanks love, and thank you for all your hard work! We all appreciate the thankless graft you do, even if the nerds in the office think you could improve by half a per cent on admissions!"

"Aw thanks Jim."

"You're welcome, lovely to talk to you. And apologies to you guys," Jim turned to the hosts Gary and Hilary. "But it wouldn't have made you look good if you'd have cut her off there."

Gary smiled and brushed the apology aside and in a very British way as he thanked his callers and Jim, for being such an interesting and lively phone in guest, before introducing the commercial break.

Chapter Twenty
Thursday Afternoon

There was absolutely no question that the political mainstream had been presented with a very big headache in the form of Jim Arkwright, particularly because of the public's enormous admiration of him and their insatiable appetite for his views. Whilst Jim was sat in the studio recording "Mock Off" with the rest of the programmes stars, 10 Downing Street had released a statement to the press. It read:

"Following a very urgent meeting between all three Leaders and Chairs of the main political party's in Great Britain, we are all in agreement that the following statement be released with immediate effect:

"Over the past few days an unelected citizen from Clitheroe in Lancashire has been at the centre of a number of politically motivated broadcasts that have caught the whole nation's attention. The three main parties are all in absolute agreement that the topics and matters that Mr Arkwright has raised are of paramount importance.

However, Mr Arkwright is not an elected politician and as thus his views, which appear to be overwhelmingly popular with the electorate are not worth anything of political value in their current format. Despite this, political apathy has been a huge problem in our country for a very long time, starting with the "cash for peerages scandal," and further fuelled by the "MPs expenses scandal," of which all three of our parties were equally responsible.

As senior party politicians on all sides of the House, we recognise as clearly as the rest of the population that our political structure is in particularly bad health.

Mr Arkwright has done an incredible amount for politics within just one week, and all of our collective MPs have been inundated with their constituent's views about this man on an unprecedented scale. We have all listened and we all recognise and respect the great cry from all four corners of the United Kingdom. The inescapable cry is "Jim Arkwright for Prime Minister."

With this unavoidable fact laid before us, all three parties are in agreement that we must work together to utilise Mr Arkwright's enthusiasm, influence and experience to the absolute maximum for the good of our Country.

The outcome of our meeting is the announcement that all three Party Leaders and Chairs have agreed unanimously that Mr Arkwright would make a very strong candidate for Member of Parliament. On that basis, an MP from one of our parties will step down, forcing a by-election in that constituency. This would allow Mr Arkwright to stand as a candidate in the said constituency. If successfully elected, we are all in agreement that Mr Arkwright shall be made the Leader of his chosen party and a General Election will be called.

At this point in time, it is now in the hands of Mr Arkwright to advise which political party he intends to represent. If he decides that he does not wish to represent one of the three main parties – then it is practically impossible for Mr Arkwright to become

Prime Minister in the foreseeable future."

It was signed by the six most senior people in British party politics.

*****

All of the news channels flashed their overly used and over dramatic "**BREAKING NEWS**" banners and read out the incredible statement from number 10.

On this occasion the heightened drama could be justified, but the exhausted graphics didn't really gather enough gusto or drama to fully explicate the true gravity of the announcement.

There was almost a case of "Breaking News" banner fatigue, a "Breaking News" epidemic in the country. BREAKING NEWS was being banded around to kick start a report that the Queen was going to church, or a footballer was arriving at training after a heavy night on the town.

Nobody was prepared for an announcement on this scale. This was undoubtedly the most incredible political announcement of all time and it was obvious that even the newsreaders were in shock – as they breathlessly and animatedly told the nation that the British Government and its two closest competitors had effectively given Jim Arkwright the seal of approval to take over the reins of power.

It was beyond all comprehension for the TV and radio news readers who were audibly and visibly shaken by the enormity of what they were reporting. Veteran broadcasters had not experienced drama in their newsroom like this since the George Michael toilet story broke.

It was even more extraordinary for the TV viewers watching at home and in bars, and for the radio listeners in factories, kitchens, offices and on building sites up and down the UK.

Under pressure from ordinary people, a bloke nobody had even heard of one week ago was practically being begged to sort the country's problems out by the most senior politicians in the land.

Chapter Twenty-One
Studio 2B- Mock Off recording session

"Okay and CUT! That's great guys, thanks. Let's take a fifteen minute break please everyone." Tim was talking into a microphone to the cast, crew and the audience.

"Not you Jim – come with me please. Karen, Karen love, over here a minute please." Jim was red hot from the stage lights and looked disappointed that he couldn't head straight out into the fresh air with everybody else. Still he was absolutely buzzing to be taking part in the recording, and had to keep reminding himself that it wasn't a dream - and that it was actually happening.

"I need a word with you both in my office. Follow me please." Tim seemed quite stern and stressed, he didn't seem like the relaxed, care free media mogul he had appeared on previous encounters as he walked off the set and out onto the corridor at some pace. The Arkwrights followed as requested, struggling to keep up. Karen looked puzzlingly at Jim and at the back of Tim in a way that confirmed that she too had noticed the alarming change of attitude.

"Is everything alright Tim?" asked Jim as he and Karen briskly followed Tim around the maze of identical corridors. The executive kept on walking and replied into the space straight ahead of himself.

"All will be revealed. Karen, if your mobile phone goes off please don't answer it or attempt to read any text messages until I've spoken to you. Just down here now, we're nearly there."

Karen glared at Jim, he could see that there was a real fear in her eyes. Jim fervently grabbed Tim's shoulder and forced him to stop marching ahead.

"Tim, what the fuck is going on? You're starting to scare us." Jim was practically hissing the words as other studio people were milling past carrying boxes and running with scripts. Karen appeared to be close to tears as Jim looked squarely at Tim.

"Has something happened with one of my kids?" asked Karen, the tremor in her voice was unmistakable. The look of panic was etched on her face.

"What? No! no, fucking hell, no. It's nothing like that. We just need some privacy and we're on a tight schedule. We need to be quick. Jesus, sorry." Tim put his hand on Karen's shoulder and shook her gently. Karen let out an audible sigh of relief. Tim's comment about her phone had panicked her. It had panicked both of them.

"Well what's that about her phone? Don't scare people like that mate, its not nice." Jim grabbed his wife's hand and clutched it firmly as they carried on walking and made their way into Tim's office.

"Shit, I'm so sorry - I didn't mean to scare you guys." Tim spoke as he closed the door behind him and gestured his V.I.P's to sit down at the large board room style table. The walls of Tim's office were decorated with awards and certificates. Tim sat down facing the Arkwrights.

"Listen, I didn't think I would scare you there and I'm really sorry I did. But something has happened that is of major significance. Something that nobody saw coming, least of all you Jim. Now, I know what it is," explained Tim, but he was interrupted as Karen's phone started ringing in her handbag.

"Please, Karen don't answer it. Let me have it. It's got nothing to do with your family or anything like that I can promise you – its about the broadcast Jim did last night, well its basically about everything to do with

Jims media activity in the past few days. Just trust me." Karen looked comfortable with Tim's apology and explanation. Tim took the bag. He rifled through until he found the phone and switched it off. He placed it back into the bag and stared straight across the table at Jim.

"How much did I say we would pay you to come on the show today Jim?"

"You said fifteen grand at first, but then doubled it. So thirty grand. That's roughly a years wages that for me Tim." The mood was quite tense. Tim was nodding at his guest and had his hands pressed tightly together beneath his chin. It was almost as though the TV executive was praying. He looked troubled.

"Okay, let's cut the shit. Something has just happened that changes everything. Now I can happily give you all the details here and now, and let you deal with the situation in private – or I can offer you one hundred and twenty five thousand pounds to let us tell you in the studio, in front of everyone and film your reaction to it on the show."

Karen gasped, a nervous, shocked kind of noise. The look of tension and concern on her face was undeniable. Jim on the other hand looked just as laid back and focused as ever.

"What's going on? Sounds bloody weird. Is something going to come out about me? Has someone gone to the papers and said I did them a gate that's gone all rusty or somert?" Jim tried turning it into a joke but Tim wasn't letting the mood relax.

"I can't tell you what it is until you tell me what your choice is. I'm in the TV business Jim and if I don't get footage of your reaction to this when you're in a studio, my name will be mud! In fact, thinking about it, the footage will probably rake in half a million quid from the news programmes that'll pay to run the pictures. So I'll make an offer of two hundred and fifty grand to you."

"Done." Jim smiled. He looked really pleased with himself.

"What do you mean Jim? You don't even know what it's about." Interrupted Karen cautiously.

"Look, I've no skeletons in my closet, no genie's I want keeping in the bottle. I've got nowt to fear Karen love, not a sausage! If this fellah is prepared to pay me the price of my house to tape my reaction to something that's read out, well I'm alright with that love!" He was grinning confidently.

"So we've a deal? Two hundred and, no Three hundred grand for your participation on the show. You'll pay about fifty per cent tax on that so we're talking about one hundred and fifty grand in your pocket." Tim was beginning to relax a bit now, softening up a little but he certainly wasn't in the same care-free frame of mind that he had been when Karen and Jim arrived that morning.

"Yes, definitely Tim, you've got a deal."

"Good. Good man. I'm not a tosser – most people in this business would have just come out with it while the cameras were rolling but I'm not like them Jim and that's why I get the best guests on. Let's go back to the studio and get recording. All of the audience will have been given strict instructions not to give the game away. They'll know all about this now – it'll be all over their phones and internet apps."

"Not being funny Tim, but this sounds really, really big." Karen sounded much more nervous than Jim was feeling.

"Its gargantuan Karen love. That's all I can say,

gargantuan. Come on, we had better get on with it and put you both out of your misery."

Tim went over and opened his office door. Jim and Karen filed out and started walking back along the corridors, at a slightly less frantic pace than they had on the way.

"It's like a Scooby Doo corridor this, isn't it love?" Jim was smiling at his wife, whilst repeatedly turning his head from left to right as he walked. Karen laughed at his lame impression of Shaggy.

"How are you so relaxed man? I'm in bits here."

"Oh I'm just trying to enjoy the experience while it lasts. I'll be back to scraping rust off fences again next week. I plan to enjoy every second of this."

"You're a weird bloke you Jim Arkwright. Anybody else would be shitting their pants at what might happen. They're paying a quarter of a million quid to see your reaction to something and you're not even worried?"

"I've told you, I've a clear conscience. I'm so bloody boring they'll have a big job trying to find something bad out about me!"

Back at the studio Jim sat down with the rest of the panellists and a lady from make up urgently began dabbing fresh foundation onto his face.

Tim took his microphone and addressed everybody on the set.

"Okay guys thanks to you all for that brief intermission. Now Jim Arkwright here and his wife Karen who is just making her way back into the audience there, have no idea what's going on. I know most of you do know what is about to be said to Jim, but please lets keep it a surprise so we get his honest, straight from the cuff reaction – and lots of extra publicity for the show that will boost those all important viewing figures!"

The audience gave a huge round of applause, with wolf whistles and some shouting "woop woop." There was tension and raw, electrifying excitement in the air.

"Okay, camera two can you keep a constant feed on Karen? Get her reaction too. Silence in the studio, standby for recording. And action!"

Jed Aye Knight read out the whole statement from the three political party leaders. Jim listened intently, but completely failed to deliver the anticipated camp facial expressions, sobs of joy, Bambi eyed glances of self indulgence or any of the cheesy Americanised fakeness that had come to be expected from the audience - most of whom had grown up watching all the glossy "fake tits, fake teeth" programmes.

Karen on the other hand filled the TV monitors with a series of expressions that spanned a whole range of different emotions, from worry, to joy, concern to jubilation.

Jim just looked relaxed as normal. He simply nodded as he listened carefully to the details that Jed was reading aloud. When the Mock Off host had finished Jim did a little chuckle and launched into the contracted two hundred and fifty thousand pound response.

"Bloody Norah. So the government are basically agreeing with me, saying the country is shafted? Well that's a bloody relief! But lets be serious, I'm not the answer am I? Even this is being handled badly. For all they know I could be the next Adolf Hitler!"

The audience were still in shock at the outlandish Number 10 announcement, as were the rest of the nation. But the studio audience were even more surprised to find themselves hearing reaction about the situation live from the man at the very centre of the story. This was an historical moment that they were witnessing, and the tension was all around – clear on the faces of everybody, from the audience, to the crew and even the celebrity guests on the show.

"Listen right, it's a nice offer – but none of the existing political parties represent normal day to day people like me. More than two thirds of our MP's are privately educated millionaires who are only doing it to please their parents – probably to keep them sweet for their massive inheritances of mansions, millions more pounds and the caravan."

Jim enjoyed the wave of applause and merriment that greeted his speech. "No, seriously - if I accepted this offer and was suddenly voted in and made to be their boss, it would be like the new kid at school turning up and telling the house captain to take the day off. I'd be bullied and ridiculed by them. Don't be daft, think about it - they'd spend their whole lives trying to discredit me, doing their best to show me up and make me fail. This couldn't be allowed to work, because it would change everything about our democracy. All the rich toffs who want a well paid, easy job with fame, respect and lucrative business opportunities won't give up their birthright that easily mate! I just couldn't be arsed with any of that shite."

The remark got a massive roar of laughter and applause from the 250 members of the Mock Off audience. One by one they got to their feet and gave the modest Lancastrian a standing ovation. The host waited until the audience settled down before quizzing Jim on the matter.

"So come on man Jim, the government are practically tossing ya the fucking keys to number 10! Are you saying no?" Jed Aye looked incredulous at the insanity of the whole bizarre situation. The audience laughed again at Jed Aye's facial expression and his rather unorthodox style of political interviewing.

Jim laughed as well, but Karen was watching on from the audience in a state of astonishment. She had gone from the terror of thinking that something bad had happened up in Clitheroe - and then the next minute her husband was being told that he can take over with the running of the country. It was a lot to take in and she was visibly trembling. Jim however appeared completely relaxed and seemed to be enjoying himself.

"Well, I'm not saying that Jed, but think about it in simple terms - if this happened I'd be basically the manager of 650 staff who are doing the job wrong and they wouldn't want some pleb like me telling them how to do it. It would be a disaster – it's just not the answer!"

"Come on them Jim, you seem to have all of this perfectly clear in your mind – if you becoming the Prime Minister isn't the answer – what is?" The question came from the programmes witty straight man David Baxendale, who looked quite cross.

"Well funnily enough David, I haven't got anything straight in my head at all. I don't have the answer to this - it's the whole system that's wrong. If you give me the chance to be the Prime Minister – but my schools minister has never worked a day of his life in a school, and my defence minister has never even been in the army cadets, I'm not really in a position to Govern – I can't help matters with a government who have no expertise in their own departments can I? You wouldn't ask a bus driver to plaster a ceiling would you? I'd have a chancellor of the exchequer in charge of all the country's money and financial planning who hasn't even studied economics! So it wouldn't work, everything's all to cock! Now listen, I already said all this the other day on the news – if our MP's had a bit of life experience, had a bit of work experience behind them then I'd give it a shot. I'd be in there like a rat up a drainpipe if I had the right people to work with. Give me an MP with 20 years of successful Headmaster experience behind him, and I'd happily put him straight into the Cabinet as the Schools Minister. I'd want an MP who previously worked as the head of income and expenditure at McDonalds UK running the Treasury! The person who used to work as the regional manager of the Citizens Advice Bureau can run the Department of Work and Pensions, and Social Services! We seriously need the people who know what is going on in the world to look after our interests, not some slimy, bullshitting, inexperienced toffs who couldn't care less!"

The audience were stood up applauding, stamping their feet and cheering the outburst from Jim. There was a long wait until it quietened down so that he could conclude his point.

"Trouble is, and you know what I'm going to say next David – these people don't actually exist in Parliament. We just have an endless supply of clueless rich people who have never done a real days work in their lives. They're socially inept, well educated idiots, and it doesn't matter which rosette they're wearing – they're no good for purpose. I'll bet one or two of them don't even know what washing up liquid does – so how can they Govern us – and worst still, how could I possibly manage them, to govern us?"

The audience were confused. This was a massive anti-climax. Nobody really knew what they were supposed to do now. There was an awkward moment of quiet as the penny began to drop. Jim Arkwright wasn't about to thank the government for the opportunity that had been presented. It seemed that this was nothing more than a typically British moment of collective disappointment. Another "close, but no cigar" experience.

"Wait! We can't just accept that Jim. We all want you to be our Prime Minister man! You'll be a man of the people! The voice of reason in a world of tossers! You could get rid of all the really shit things in society - like traffic wardens!" Jed Aye was being told frantically in his earpiece to keep the conversation alive, despite the sense that it had seemingly run its course. The question revitalised the audience who laughed at the typical remark from the Geordie.

"Would I heck! If I was Prime Minister mate, all traffic wardens would be given extra pay. They keep our towns and cities moving. Without those guys, people would selfishly park their cars up all day and nobody else would ever get parked!" Jim was smiling, enjoying the banter.

"Ooh, controversial point Jim. Nobody likes traffic wardens, not even their parents - and I doubt that even you can save them!" Jed reached under the desk and picked up the large sign that he used every week for the "shit head of the week" section of the show.

"You know Jim, a fair few traffic wardens have won this fantastic prize down the years!" The audience began applauding the famous sign that was used on a weekly basis to humiliate people who had excelled at, well - basically being a shit head.

"Well, people who are angry with traffic wardens are probably a bit thick to be honest Jed. If you park up for an hour and come back late and you've got a parking ticket, it's your own fault, you should have bought two hours parking. You wouldn't be angry with your front door if you got home and realised you'd left your keys on your desk at work would you? I know a traffic warden who got spat at, right in the face just because the woman he ticketed was angry at being late back to her car. Its disgusting, and the person who did that should have been locked up, made an example of – but instead – as per usual, nothing was done about it."

"I'm just thinking, this is supposed to be a light hearted, whimsical comedy show," interjected David Baxendale, in a smugly patronising voice. At that moment Tim Dixon wandered onto the set and began speaking into the cameras through the portable microphone that he normally used to give instructions to the set.

"Yes, good point David. Sorry to interrupt the show Jed, but this is a very significant episode of the Mock Off programme, a historical episode that could possibly be talked of in several hundred years time. My name is Tim Dixon and I'm the Director of this programme. For eleven years I have stayed behind the cameras, working in the background making this programme the best of its kind – but in light of what is happening on this weeks show I feel that it is appropriate to come on stage and join the panel. Is that okay with everyone?"

Tim got a massive roar of affection and appreciation from the audience, even the panellists on the set stood up and gave the chief a round of applause.

"What a great honour" said Jed once everybody had calmed down and got back into their seats. Tim Dixon was one of TVs best known names but least recognised faces. He preferred life outside the limelight, but despite this it was a well known fact that Tim Dixon had worked on many of the most popular shows of the past quarter century, and the audience were genuinely delighted to see him changing roles on this bizarre edition of Mock Off.

"Can someone get the boss a chair?" shouted Jed in the direction of the crew. "We can't have him standing up!" A couple of runners shuffled onto the stage with an additional chair and the audience were laughing and gossiping and clearly enjoying this peculiar glimpse behind the scenes.

"Okay, right then. What's the plan now then boss?" Jed looked sheepishly confused at Tim, attracting another awkward laugh from the audience.

"Well, good question Jed. My worry is that we are sat here with one of the most exciting people to grace modern politics, he has just been asked to step up to the plate and take over the Government and as if that isn't enough drama - he is saying no!"

The audience booed loudly in panto style, it was a good natured response to Tim's comments. He waited for the crowd to simmer down before continuing.

"I'm afraid that we are all going to have to try a bit harder to convince Jim Arkwright to give this opportunity a bit more consideration! Our country is desperate for Jim Arkwright to lead us out of the crap we're in!"

Tim recounted the story of when he had met Jim a couple of days earlier, and talked about how he had practically had to beg Jim to break away from his work to come on the show. He explained to the audience what a genuinely down to earth and humble man he believed Jim Arkwright to be. Tim turned to Jim and said, "I have never felt so interested, or excited about a politician. Please do it Jim. Please save our country!"

The audience were back on their feet, a thunderous applause was ripping through the studio. Jim was smiling modestly as the audience began spontaneously chanting "Do it! Do it! Do it!"

"But there's nothing I can do!" said Jim,

pleading with his hands held out as the audience settled down.

"Well, there must be something," said David Baxendale, quite frostily. "We take on board your concerns about MPs being out of touch but that kind of culture is going to take decades to change. It would take half a century until the ex Headmasters and ex-Citizens Advice managers became local Councillors, then MPs and then began to work towards Cabinet positions."

"Yes. I didn't say it wouldn't. Look David, I see you are frustrated by the situation – but don't turn your frustration onto me. I wouldn't even be here talking about it if it wasn't for those two weirdo's secretly filming me in the pub with my mates!" Jim was firm in his response. He was annoyed that David felt it was appropriate to speak to him in such a dismissive manner.

"Listen guys, cool it," interrupted Tim. "We're getting ahead of ourselves. We're forgetting the magnitude of the statement that has come out of Number 10 within the last half an hour. Now Jim, if you don't think that the suggestion from Number 10 will work in its current format, then tell us how we could make it work. There's obviously enough appetite to get you in there, so just tell us what you need, and we'll send your response back to number 10."

"Okay. Listen, if all 650 MPs to agree to my conditions, I'll do it."

"Go on," said Jed, relieved that the dead lock finally seemed to have broken. "What are the conditions? Has anybody got a pen? Yes, you, thanks. Anybody got an empty fag packet?" he asked the audience, which got a vague chuckle.

The mood had changed, a tense feeling of anticipation came across everybody once again as Jim reeled off his demands in a very matter of fact way, it was almost as though he was describing a list of ingredients that were needed to make a spaghetti bolognese. The entire studio listened attentively to every word that Jim said.

"First of all, the MP's will have to sign a contract to say that they will support my appointment 100%. I'm not saying they have to agree with everything I say – but it's imperative that they say that they want me there in the first place, and that they will work with me, not against me."

"Okay, that's clear." Said Tim, as he jotted some notes. The programme was quickly turning into a more serious style of political discussion show, and it was beginning to feel more like an episode of Question Team than Mock Off.

"Next, I'd need my two mates, Dave and Phil working with me, they'd have to be my deputies, my right hand man and my left hand man basically. Everything I've said that has caused all this fuss is based on theories, discussions and ideas that me and Dave and Phil have come up with, after work in the pub over a few beers. So, they need to be factored in as my equals. Then, and only then - all of the MPs, and all of the country would need to support me to do whatever it took to implement what the papers have said is my ten point plan. That will mean major arguments and disagreements with the European Union and probably even the G20."

"Well, you might want to expand on that particular point Jim!" The comment from Jed inspired a wave of nervous chuckles from the audience.

"Of course Jed. Sadly, what's happened over the past fifty years is, we've been nice and listened to the advice of do-gooders and it's brought our society to its knees – we have no consequences left, we can't punish anybody for wrong doing and it's causing dangerous problems, the country is rotting like a scabby knee. Finally, once and for all we have to face facts, and realise that being a do-gooder has trashed our country. If people are serious about wanting me to step in as the Prime Minister, we need to be clear on what I'd want to happen!"

"Tell us then!" said David Baxendale. Jim nodded at the famous wit who was today becoming his tormentor.

"I'd want to rip up the Human Rights bill. We stopped smacking our kids and now they don't do what they are told. We got rid of punishments in schools and now they kids hit the teachers. Prisoners sue the bloody prison if their cell is too cold at night. It was a lovely idea, giving people all these rights, but it's been taken out of context and it needs reining in right now. The Human Rights Bill was introduced in Europe by our very own Prime Minister after World War Two to protect innocent people from murder and persecution – not to help people to take the piss out of the law sixty years down the line. It was brought in to ensure that there could never be another Adolf Hitler. So we would need to revise that law straight away, then I'd be pushing to re-instate capital punishment for murder. I'd want us to redesign prisons, make them really dark, horrible, cold, lonely and scary place to go. I'd want to see police given powers to assault the public when they are acting up, encourage them to use tazer guns and batons to get a handle on these feral teenagers and out of control drunks that blight our streets. We need a return to the days when police brutality was enough to make idiots think twice, not a do-gooders wet dream."

This remark attracted a spontaneous round of

applause.

"I'd want all youths convicted of any repeat anti-social or petty offence to be put in the army for a minimum of two years to learn some discipline and team building – to help them get some structure and planning into their lives. Let me see now, I'd want Headmasters given the powers to physically punish kids, a return of corporal punishment in schools. Basically a return to all these punishments that made up the very fabric of a decent, respectful law abiding society. Parents should be confident enough to smack their kids without fear of do-gooders taking the kids into care. Parents can't discipline, schools can't, the police can't, the courts can't and prison is lovely – our criminals can't wait to get back in once they're released. We need to sort this out, it's at the very heart of all the nations social problems. So I'd want all those things to become law – and in order to do that, we'd need to rewrite Winston Churchill's human rights bill and start again, learning from our mistakes."

"It's not going to be very easy to do that Jim." Advised Tim, who was sat, listening intently to Jims demands and scribbling notes.

"Tim, none of this is going to be easy. It's going to be bloody hard work and it'll cause a lot of fuss – but we are all, finally, beginning to realise and accept that it simply has to be done, no ifs or buts. It's inevitable that we're going to become a bankrupt, lawless society if we don't get our sleeves rolled up now, and fix the roof before the storm. If you were driving your car into a wall your natural instinct would be to swerve out of the way. But where our politics are concerned the British people are sleeping through it as certain disaster lies ahead. To start with we must govern our own shores with our own laws, if that means we have to turn our

back on Europe then that's the price we will have to pay. We need to make our own laws that work for us, not work against us. Now then,
if the same party political leaders that signed that document go and speak to their MP's, then come back and agree to all that, and also agree to
slam shut the door to Britain and call an instant halt to our bonkers immigration policy, then I'll stand in the by-election."

The whole audience stood once again and applauded Jim, there could be no doubt in his mind that his views were popular with this studio audience. He could only assume that his extreme requests would hit the buffers once the 650 sitting MPs voted.

"Well, this has been a particularly insane edition of Mock Off" said Ged, wrapping the recording session up. "Thanks to all of our panellists, our fantastic audience and of course our beautiful, beautiful boss, the one and only Mr Tim Dixon!" More applause and enthusiastic cheering transcended from the hot and sweaty studio audience members who were by now quite relieved that this eventful and mammoth recording session was now finally coming to a close.

"And of course, we must thank our star guest this week, coming all the way from up north to be on the show. Ladies and Gentlemen, please give it up one last time for Big, Jim, Arkwright!"

For the final time that day, the muggy, tired and weary audience showed their respect and support with passionate cheers, wolf whistles and feet stamping applause for the star guest.

Once the recording had finished, and the studio began to empty of its crew, stars and audience, Jim quietly asked Tim Dixon if he would please find a quiet room where he could make an important phone call. Tim was eager to oblige and immediately found a small editing suite nearby that was free. Tim showed Jim through and offered him a seat in the dimly lit booth by a bank of TV monitors, knobs, switches and pulleys.

"So, how are you feeling?" asked Tim. "That's a pretty big gig you're being offered."

"I know. It's quite embarrassing really." Said Jim, in his typically reticent fashion. "It kind of shows just how clueless they are doesn't it? I mean, what sort of signal does this send out to other countries?"

"How do you mean?" asked Tim. This perspective on the situation hadn't occurred to him.

"Well, as if the country isn't in enough of a mess, now we're seen throughout the world as the nation that asks some random stranger to run things because he's got a few good ideas. It'll set us back even further in trying to restore confidence in trade deals. It's typical of the British government, rushing in and making a tit's up of everything." Jim shook his head in despair.

"Bloody hell Jim. You see things from some strange angles. On the other hand it could be argued that they are showing great strength in holding their hands up and saying they think you'd do a better job! Depends how you look at it really. I'm personally really impressed that they've all managed to meet up and discuss it, and agree on the matter. Anyway, listen - you were great out there, you did brilliantly. Now I'll give you five minutes to make your call."

"Thanks Tim, I really appreciate this."

"Sure, no problem. I understand." Tim was sympathetic as to what a huge weight this announcement must be psychologically for Jim. He guessed that it must be a difficult thing to accept. "I guess you'll want to talk to your parents about all this? Ask your kids what they think of it all? Oh, no – don't tell me – it's your mates at the pub you're ringing?"

Tim smiled and swung his arm gently so it patted Jim on the back affectionately.

"No, not really. I just want to ring the lads, see how they're getting on with them railings."

Chapter Twenty-Two
Thursday Afternoon #2

"This is total bullshit Clive, something just doesn't add up here!" Emily O'Hara, also known as "MP Punk" was the outspoken independent MP for Hackney, and thanks to her luminous pink hair, outlandish clothes and famously rude, forthright feminist attitudes, she had become a well known household name. "MP Punk" as she often referred to herself in the third person was famed for her boisterous and often obnoxious manner. She was speaking on the phone to her press officer about the Number 10 announcement as her taxi negotiated the capital's busiest period of the day.

"We don't really know the first thing about this fucking weirdo. Get me a fucking conversation with him Clive, and don't take no for an answer you incompetent twat." She pressed the "end call" button on her employee as her taxi lurched and laboured from traffic light to pedestrian crossing and back onto traffic lights again. The traffic was moving about fifteen yards between stops around Trafalgar Square in the hot and balmy rush hour traffic. Emily looked up another contact and pressed the call icon. The taxi slowed for yet another set of traffic lights as a man almost got knocked off his bicycle by another taxi right at the side of them.

"Watch where ya fackin' goin' you useless berk!" shouted the driver at the cyclist as he kept his hand pressed firmly on the horn. The cyclist shouted something back but the monotone blare of the horn bleeped it out as angry obscenities were hurled from the other taxi too. Emily rolled her eyes at the ceiling as the phone she was calling was answered.

"Nigel, its Emily, have you seen the fucking

news? I know, setting him up to be Prime Minister. It's never happened before. No, never. This completely fucks my strategy up. I'm just trying to get a conversation going with the fucking northern pillock. I've got to get a one to one with him, show him up – yeah, rip his fucking arguments up and get him back home to his cotton mill faster than he can spell "thick northern wanker!" Trust me Nigel, I'll make mincemeat of this prick. Expect my google search rankings to fucking explode. Pow! See you tonight." The MP ended the call.

"Are you talking about Big Jim?" asked the taxi driver.

"Yes, why?" replied Emily snappily.

"Well, he's a diamond geezer. Just what we fackin' need in Parliament." The taxi driver was gushing, he appeared to be another of Jim's overnight followers.

"Bullshit. You don't know what the fuck you're talking about you stupid bastard. Now just shut the fuck up. You fat bastard! Why would I want your opinion you fucking idiot? Fuck off!"

The taxi driver just laughed at the outrageous outburst. Emily O'Hara had found fame and notoriety by behaving in this niche manner and it was almost a thrill for her victims when she gave them a personal verbal assault.

The driver was already looking forward to telling his wife about it later on when Emily began speaking into her phone again.

"Clive, I gave you one simple task. How can he not have a fucking press office? What did he say on The Morning? Ha, so, he wants us to reinstate the Death Penalty. He wants us to legalise drugs? Right I'll doorstep him. Where is he? Tell my crew to get there fucking pronto. Fuck off Clive."

The taxi driver glanced up at Emily O'Hara in his rear view mirror. She could be a really attractive young woman if she wasn't so aggressive and untidy he thought. She wore a bright yellow silk dress that clashed with her shocking pink spikey hairstyle. Her dress had a big split which was revealing a great deal of white, skinny leg.

"What the fuck are you looking at? Change of destination, drive me to Elstree studios. And keep your eyes on the road you ugly bastard."

*****

Staff working throughout the British media in its many forms were experiencing a very mixed reaction to the unbelievable news that had come out of Downing Street's Press Office. It was an excitable and confusing mixture of disbelief, shock and nervous, sarcastic laughter.

Radio presenters on every station in the land were quickly trying to get their heads around the story so that they could repackage it for their own audience – be that teenage listeners on the chart stations or pensioners on the BBC local stations. Whatever the audience, presenters and producers were desperate to break this unparalleled story to their loyal listeners as soon as it was physically possible.

But the trouble was, it seemed like such a ridiculous story, the DJ's, newsreaders and radio station managers had a hard time believing that it was actually true. It seemed more like some outrageous wind-up stunt for a charity film or something.

It was a peculiar jumble of emotions that were running very high in the thousands of newsrooms up and down the UK, and further afield too.

Presenters hit the airwaves with a strangely vague air of caution, saying things which only added more uncertainty and confusion to the story. "Well, this is quite hard to believe, but I'll tell you anyway," was a typical introduction that lacked authority and gave the emerging "bullshit" theory more credibility than it gave to the actual truth.

The most experienced journalists knew that it had to be true. They knew that no joke or gimmick would ever be released via the Number 10 Press Office, whether it was part of a charity stunt or not. This is the Press Office that announces Wars, deaths of Royals and reports major Government decisions. It could never compromise its authority, even for a one off charity stunt.

This crazy, incomparable announcement was genuine.

*****

The Facebook page that had been set up in the hours after Jim's appearance on Lancashire FM with Councillor Fred Norton was now being followed by over 6,000,000 people. The page was called "Jim Arkwright – NBP Party - No Bullshit Politics."

In the hours following the Number 10 Downing Street announcement the page had doubled its number of subscribers. Every few seconds several new messages of support appeared on the site.

"You've got my vote Jim! X"

"Finally, a Prime Minister who will actually give a fuck! Good luck Jim!"

It wasn't all positive however. If viewers of the site looked closely enough there were the occasional voices of dissent, airing malicious views and grievances in amongst the well wishing messages.

One pointed to a rival page "Jim Arkwright is a fuckin dick." The page had over 1,000 subscribers and was littered with messages from individuals who had taken personal umbrage at some of Jim's views.

"Like to see that dick down here saying all that about sending us in the fuckin army. He'll need a fuckin army when I've sparked the bald twat out."

It seemed it was open season on the anti-Jim page. Most of the unpleasant, illiterate messages appeared to be in reaction to Jim's comments regarding anti social youths, prisons and immigration. Many of the messages threatened physical violence against Jim.

One read "Hell have a fuckin team of ambulance men asking him what his fuckin name is when I've laid him out."

Another stated "Jim Arkwright is a racist. Why stop immigration?"   Most seemed like spontaneous messages of derision, written in some haste as is often the case on social networking sites such as Facebook and Twitter.

"Big Jim can suck my fat one" was one message that had attracted a dozen "likes" on the page.

It demonstrated that not everybody was in adoration of the new voice of Great Britain. The numbers of opposition voices was fractional in comparison with the overwhelming outpouring of support in all other aspects of "Big Jim's" media and social network coverage, but none the less - this internet activity showed that there were those in society that were not best pleased with all the talk that was coming out of Jim Arkwright's mouth, particularly those who had the most to fear from his massively popular views.

*****

From Dundee to Doncaster, Cornwall to Crewe, there was only one topic up for discussion throughout the United Kingdom – the announcement that had come from Number 10. From Job-centre signing on queues, to hospital waiting rooms, factory canteens and police station reception desks. No matter where you were in the nation, it seemed that there really was no other conversation happening.

It beggared belief that a man nobody had ever heard of before had suddenly appeared from thin air - and within less than a week he had united the country on so many issues. Jim Arkwright had quite unintentionally redesigned the political agenda beyond recognition, simply because his views and attitudes had been craved for in Britain for such a long time, and because he didn't seem particularly bothered whether people agreed with him or not.

Jim Arkwright offered something more than his just his opinion, he offered a quality that had been lacking from modern politicians – he came across as a genuine man who cared deeply about the country.

All of the newspaper, radio and TV political commentators were agreed that the treaty reached between the three major party's about engineering an opportunity for Jim to stand in a by-election and then, if he was successful - an internal party election for him to become Party Leader was the only sensible option available to them within political laws.

All commentators were also very surprised that the arrogant, bloody minded and self assured government had practically admitted defeat to an unelected citizen from rural Lancashire.

Yet despite the historical announcement, the unprecedented decision - the general public who were discussing all of this in coffee shops, and pubs, in vans on motorways and in shop queues throughout the land felt that this announcement somewhat stalled Big Jim. Although the ink wasn't fully dried the signatures of the most powerful players in politics - there was a collective feeling of disappointment that here stood a man who promised to finally tackle the countries most difficult and challenging problems with sensible solutions, but it would be many months until anything could really happen.

There was very little patience for the old fashioned, ancient political protocol that had to be followed. Five months felt like a very long time to the people who were feeling so passionate and revved up about Jims "no bullshit" approach. In essence, it just seemed like even more British red tape "bullshit."

It was beyond most of the public's attention that the deal being offered to Jim was the only time a fast track scheme to become Prime Minister had ever been made available to anybody — let alone a commoner.

But despite the "fast track" label that news and radio reporters were chattering excitedly about, it would still take about 5 months to hold the three legally required elections. The first one to elect Jim as an MP, and then another to elect Jim as the Party Leader, and then for a General Election to take place that would in theory make him the PM.

Almost everybody in Britain liked what they saw and heard from Jim Arkwright and they just wanted him to become the new Prime Minister right away.

"Get big Jim in there right now and stop faffing about! If I never see another normal politician again, it will be too soon!" Said one frustrated caller on Talk-Sport Radio's tea time phone in show.

*****

In between live updates from reporters in locations across the capital, and based across Jim's hometown of Clitheroe – the BBC, CNN, CNBC, Euronews and Sky News channels were re-running the Mock Off footage of the Number 10 announcement and Jims rather laid back reaction to it.

In amongst that, footage of Jim's radical opinions on "The Morning" phone in show was being re-broadcast as well. The clips seemed to be on a constant loop across all of the networks, stopped only for a "re-cap" from reporters about Jim's activities of the day and the Governments spectacular declaration.

The news editors barely had time to catch their breath as video footage from all across the UK was being sent in relentlessly, reports of supportive vox pops, celebratory street parties, opinions from celebrities and senior public figures such as the Chief Commissioner of the Metropolitan police.

This was as big and complex a story as any of the staff working in British news had ever seen, mainly due to the pace of developments rather than the magnitude of the story itself. Most news stories drip and drip and are easily contained by reporters. This one was just flooding the news desks of Great Britain, and it felt that the torrent wasn't even in full flow yet.

*****

The story was so bizarre, and potentially so historical, it was now making the headlines all across the globe. In America, the news was broken by CNBC who reported it on their "and finally" segment of weird and whacky news to end the evenings programme with a smile.

CNBC Evening News presenters sensationally reported "Britain's Prime Minister has asked a general member of the public to take office and run the country, following a bizarre showing of public support for new guy Big Jim Arkwright, star of the smash hit Youtube video entitled Clitheroe Prime Minister. The British public have been unsatisfied with the lack of political choice in the country for a number of years, claiming that all three of the major political parties are identical in real terms, namely that all three parties are run by rich, privileged white males. The new guy is a working class small business owner who has rallied the whole country in a series of broadcasts. His fans are in their millions and claim that Big Jim Arkwright speaks for all of the real people, not just the really rich people or the really poor people. Big Jim has announced that he can boost jobs, boost the economy, get Britain manufacturing again and he also claims that he can solve the country's crime problems. Well, we wish him well here from all the team here at CNBC Evening News, and if Big Jim manages it, we may just be asking him to come over and help us figure out our problems stateside! Stay tuned for more on this incredible story as we get it. That's all for tonight folks, Take care of yourselves, and each other."

Chapter Twenty-Three
Elstree Studios London

Just outside the stage door at the rear of the television studios, Emily O'Hara MP was waiting to pounce, complete with her small film crew that regularly "happened" to be filming just as she found herself in some potentially newsworthy scenario or other.

There were several "paps" photographers and all of the other TV news crews waiting for Jim to appear from the studios, all of them hoping to get the very latest pictures of Jim to accompany the colossal international news story that he was right at the very heart of.

There was still quite a number of audience members hanging around in the hope of getting their photo taken with Jim, though most had given up and left a good while earlier. Filming had stopped more than an hour earlier and rumours had spread amongst the crowd that he had been taken away through another exit. The more savvy ones stayed put, reasoning that if Jim had gone, the news crews would have gone too. The loud, totally random appearance of the eternally controversial MP added a fresh burst of interest to the audience members, and the patiently waiting press staff alike.

Eventually the stage doors opened and Jim appeared with Karen, escorted by their driver. The MP stepped right in front of Jim and Karen, taking them both quite by surprise as their eyes struggled to adjust from the dark interior of the studio complex to the bright, glaring summer light that they were stepping out into.

"Excuse me Big Jim, can I just ask you one question? Who the hell do you think you are?"

"Eh?" asked Jim as he held a hand up to block out the bright sunshine as his eyes attuned from the dark to strong light. He recognised her distinctive voice and was desperately trying to place the woman – he knew that he knew her off TV and that it would come to him in a few moments – but because of the aggressive way that the conversation had begun and the whole temporary blindness situation, camera flashes strobing and clicking in front of him along with all the pushing and shuffling within the crowd, this was an extremely awkward start to any conversation.

"Who are you, sorry?" He asked, struggling to see who he was speaking to. This question seemed to incense the egotistical MP.

"My name is not important Mr Arkwright. What is important is that I am an elected MP who has had to work my way to Parliament – not just bullshit myself onto TV and play the superstar politician!" She was shouting the words at him.

Karen had to control herself from lunging towards the vile young woman who was holding aloft a smoking cigarette as she spoke in a high pitched, pompous manner. As the tirade went on a little longer Jim had had enough time to find his bearings and gather his thoughts. He realised that it was Emily O'Hara and he felt a little disappointed with himself for not getting it quicker.

"You're crackers love. I've always said it." He spoke calmly and with full eye contact. He laughed at her and shook his head as he tried to walk past. The dismissive response only antagonised the MP further and she stepped straight in front of Jim and his tiny entourage. She was deliberately, aggressively blocking the way. Karen was close to losing her temper with the petulant woman, but managed to keep control of herself.

She resisted an overwhelming desire to push the MP to the floor in a most undignified manner.

"I'm crackers? You've got a flaming cheek – going on TV spouting all this crap that you know how to fix the country's problems. Well let me hear it with my own ears! You claim that you're such a political genius, why don't you tell me how you'd rebuild our broken communities that are crumbling apart, plagued with crime, depression and disease?" She was walking backwards, her head was rocking from side to side and she was pushing out her bum in a ridiculous half-hunch, like a heckling chimpanzee waiting to play. It really was an absurd spectacle, but none the less - quite typical of the MP who regularly, shamelessly involved herself in any matters that were making the headlines.

"I don't have to say anything to you young lady. Like I say, you're as mad as a bottle of crisps." Jim had stopped trying to walk now and stood facing his opponent, he took his arm from around Karen's shoulder, pulled his sun glasses case out of his pocket and put the glasses on to help his eyes adjust to the intense light.

"Do you know who she is Jim?" asked Karen, who had no idea who the weirdly dressed, antagonistic woman was.

"Yes, they've got a picture of her at the hospital - it saves them using the stomach pump." Karen laughed out loudly, along with media staff that were filming, recording or photographing the confrontation. Jim pretended the glasses case was a mobile phone.

"Hello?" he said to the case in a daft voice, holding it by his ear.

"Oh yes, thank you, I'll put you on." Jim held out the glasses case and offered it to Emily.

"It's your psychiatrist."

The gesture attracted a further wave of sniggers and embarrassed laughter from the media pack and the small crowd of remaining audience members. Jim laughed along with them.

"You think that's funny? You enjoy poking fun at people with mental health issues?" asked Emily, in a high pitched, overly dramatic shrill. Her cigarette was still being held up at an angle, mainly for the benefit of her film crew.

"Are you saying you've got mental health problems?" asked Jim, calmly, the smirk still clear on his face.

"No!" Emily was urgent in her reply. As she continued her voice cracked a little. "But you're insinuating that, well you're saying…" Emily had confused herself. Jim laughed at her, not out of genuine amusement but disbelief that this serving Member of Parliament had put herself in such a vulnerable situation, and was making such a hash of it.

"Are you saying that having mental health problems is something to be ashamed of?"

"No, I'm not saying any such thing!" Emily recognised the treacherous waters she suddenly found herself in and her mind was racing, desperate to stay in control, but not to put a foot wrong either. Jim would banter with suppliers, colleagues and customers like this all day, every day, at work. It was just a normal bit of a wind up for him – but one wrong word from Emily and it was political suicide.

"It's just, the way that you quickly said no, with that tone of panic and denial in your voice, it made it seem as though you were scared of people linking you with a mental health problem. Most people suffer with mental health disorder at some point in their lives, its nothing to feel ashamed about Emily. If anything, I'd have more respect for you if you admitted it."

"What? Admit what? I haven't got any mental health problems. This is completely and utterly ridiculous!" Emily had been bamboozled by Jim, and she was beginning to realise it. Gone was the brassy, intimidating and downright insufferable manner of the nations self styled "Punk MP" and instead stood a stripped down, vulnerable looking young woman who looked as though she had lost track of what her agenda was.

"Ladies and Gentlemen, this is the kind of person we have representing our communities in the House of Commons. I mean just look at the type of characters you vote for." Jim pointed his finger directly at the MP, who looked embarrassed, dishevelled and confused.

"I wouldn't normally be so rude, but I have never met this person before, and she has come along here to start a slanging match with me. But look at her, she can't even remember what she wants."

Jim's conscience was completely clear, after all it was Emily that had instigated this public confrontation. It was her that saw Jim's new found fame as an opportunity for her own publicity. In Jim's mind, she had made herself fair game on this occasion, and he still wanted to toy with her. "Are you alright?" he asked. Emily dug deep and found a little bit more of her rebellious attitude in reserves.

"Don't be so condescending!" She hissed, but it was clear that Emily O'Hara MP wished that a big hole would appear and swallow her up, especially as this whole, awkward confrontation was being filmed by the main news channels as well as her own little propaganda crew.

"I believe you think bringing back the death

penalty will solve crime as well!" She announced sarcastically, a spark of her abrasive attitude appeared to be charging her up, a flicker of her typical scorn was returning. She waited to hear Jim's response, taking a long, final drag on her cigarette as she tried to regain some authority.

"I don't think it will solve crime, but it will definitely reduce murder rates and I think it will save a lot of money - we've got prisons full of people who have committed disgusting, evil crimes and we know they can never be released. But we turn a blind eye to the fact that we are keeping them locked away, out of sight and out of mind at a minimum cost of fifty grand each a year, every single year." Jim had a look of sheer frustration on his face, he genuinely couldn't understand this government policy and it was clear to see that even though the policy baffled him, it personally upset him too.

"So you think you can save this country money by murdering people?"

"Yes. If you want to talk in stupid, lazy sound bites, yes, I do. I honestly do. I'd send child killers, terrorists, serial killers and serial sex offenders to death in a heart beat love, each execution could be on telly as a reminder to the whole country what will happen to you if you do that. The snuffing out of their life can be dedicated to the memory of the poor innocent person that suffered at their hands, who had their life stolen away. The murderer should never even be named, just put them down like you would a dog that bit someone. Strip them of their life, and even their identity in death."

"Oh, very brave of you Mr Arkwright. An eye for an eye eh? If everyone took an eye for an eye we'd all be blind. Don't you think it's a barbaric notion to kill another human being because you don't like what they have done?"

"You really are a dickhead Emily, I can't believe you've just said that with the blood of tens of thousands of innocents in Iraq and Afghanistan on your hands. I haven't heard you screaming and raving for the rights of those people, the women, kids, babies and men, all genuinely innocent people. You and your kind voted to go to war in Iraq! You're defending child killers on one hand, showing them mercy – but you're cool with blowing little Iraqi kids up, and Afghan mums? You're a hypocrite. Full of shite, hypocrite." Jim was so caught up in his rant, he accidentally made the sentence rhyme by changing the pronunciation of the word hypocrite, so it rhymed with flight. He pointed at the MP as he spoke and a few of crowd laughed, and some gasped at the bizarre spectacle.

"Listen Emily, when a hard working Grandmother who has worked all her life and paid her way, made a good contribution to society all her life finds out she has cancer and hears that she could live a year or maybe two longer with special drugs – but sadly, the country can't afford the ten grand it'll cost, its heartbreaking. It happened to my Mum, I had to watch her die because there wasn't enough money for the drugs. But we all know that we pay five times that amount each year to keep a single prisoner in jail until they die? We allow that kind of total lunacy to carry on! We're all zombies! We're brain dead to allow this kind of madness to happen!" There was a tear in his eye and Jims face made no mistake of his anger and annoyance at what he saw as the injustice of it all. Emily on the other hand was smirking, almost chuckling at Jim.

"That's a very emotive analogy, skilfully presented – but you know perfectly well that health care finances are completely separate from ministry of justice finances; so you are basically confusing the issue Mr Arkwright!"

"Brilliant! Brilliant! You can't beat this." Jim began applauding his tormentor. "You're showing us all what a moronic thought process you MP's follow. What a shambles. Your argument here is based on funds being in the wrong government account? Have you actually got shit for brains?"

"My argument is that I don't think murdering people as a punishment is a very sophisticated thing to do in a country as civilised as ours." Emily was still smirking, almost smug with confidence in herself. She was certainly getting back into her trademark aggressive, guerrilla style of political discussion. But Jim Arkwright still had plenty in his tank too. The news crews were soaking up every blink, every breath of this incredible confrontation. The tension was raw and the atmosphere was filled with nervous energy.

"Civilised? You call this country civilised? What's civilised about drunken yobs stabbing, shooting and punching each other to death every single weekend on Britain's streets?"

"That's besides the point Mr Arkwright, no death penalty will stop somebody punching another person after ten pints of strong lager and well you know it."

"It would. Of course it would you thick get! It would make people think twice, it would get into peoples skin, into their bones, it would be part of a process of altering their carefree attitude to pointless violence, it would stop them carrying knives and guns on the streets. If you brought out real consequences then it would make a real difference. Make it an automatic ten year prison sentence for carrying a knife and see if it makes a difference, see if the random stabbing statistics go down. I'd bet my life on it, its just basic common sense! At the moment the only thing to stop people murdering each other is seven or eight years in a nice warm prison cell with TV, kind and supportive staff and three good meals a day. It's hardly a deterrent to send a murderer to a place where they'll be better treated than our old folks are treated in the nations nursing homes madam." Jim smiled back, smugly.

"I'm disgusted by your appalling views. You have no idea what you are talking about. You can't just lock people away in prison for years simply to prove a point! It won't take long for the British public to realise that you're just another idealist, a day dreaming bigot who is good at talking tough but who has no real substance to your arguments. You're a joke!"

"Thanks for the feedback. But while you've been an MP, you've stood by and watched kids get sent down for stealing trainers! You've stood by and allowed sentences up to four years for people getting involved in the riots. You change your morals to suit your argument. I hate everything you stand for!"

"The riots were different!"

"No it wasn't. It's just that it was on your doorstep and it all got a bit scary for all you toffs to see what Britain can really look like. So you all over reacted about kids smashing up shops and sent a clear message that it won't be tolerated – but you don't agree on my point about knives?"

"No, it's a completely different matter altogether."

Emily's smug look was slipping again, she knew that Jim's point did call into question the riot punishments for the hundreds of youths who got swept along with the mayhem.

Jim was chuckling to himself, mocking the MP's inconsistent views.

"You're full of it Emily. But, you just called me a joke. And since you're wrong about everything else, including that shite hair style, your opinion isn't worth a fart in a gale my dear. I'll take what you said as a compliment. You can continue to argue for people's human rights all you want love, but we've tried all that, and too much damage has been done by it."

"Really? Treating people with human rights has caused damage?" The MP did a sarcastic high pitched laugh, and turned to the cameras with a camp, almost theatrical look of mock irritation. Jim just spoke calmly and methodically, refusing to give way to her childish provocation.

"Yes, it's a joke. We can all hold our heads up high and be proud that we tried it, we can be glad that we entered into all this do-gooding nonsense with an open mind. But it hasn't worked. We can honestly say to all the do-gooders, the softies and meddlers – we did what you said – we gave it our best shot! We got rid of the death penalty and murders increased by five hundred per cent. We stopped smacking our kids and now they refuse to do as they are told. We got rid of punishments in schools and now the kids hit the teachers. We got rid of the slums and built new housing estates and now the police don't dare to go there. We did all that the do-gooders asked, and it's failed, catastrophically. Do-gooders like you Miss O'Hara need to grow up!"

"Is that so? You're beginning to sound more like a dictator with every sentence that comes out of your mouth Mr Arkwright" The MP was shouting defiantly, though her confidence definitely seemed to be fading again and that vulnerability was returning.

"I'm a dictator? Is that what you are called if you have the courage to admit that things are wrong? Am I a dictator if I say that our police are losing the war on crime, our ambulance staff can't cope with all the alcohol related jobs, our experienced teachers are leaving the profession in their thousands and there are not enough young trainees to fill in the gaps? I'm a dictator if I say we need to sort hospitals out, because at the moment they can't work properly because idiot, unskilled, untrained politicians like you have interfered and meddled and made their jobs impossible with your futile changes and targets?"

"You're just ranting on about anything and everything! I could do that as well if I wanted!"

"Well why don't you? Fucking hell woman! Give me strength! You're the one in government love, you're the one who has the opportunity to make a stand for normal, hard working good people – but instead you follow whoever is in the news, trying to hitchhike off the back of some publicity. I'm not even elected love and people are talking about me in a positive light. How do they speak about you Emily?"

"They speak very highly of me actually Mr Arkwright!" The lack of confidence was now totally clear in the tone of her voice. The way that she delivered this statement with a wooden, unconvincing monotone confirmed to Jim that she had insecurities about this issue. Jim laughed to himself and started shaking his head in a really patronising way.

"They don't, love. Stop tricking yourself, people think you're a gimmick. You're the "none of the above" vote, your constituents voted for you as a way of insulting the proper candidates. You're so wrapped up in your hazy little upper class world that you can't even see it. Listen princess, you're nowt but an attention seeking, spoilt little brat."

Emily's chin began to quiver and her jaw looked quite slack as Jim's volley of personally devastating words bashed into her like they were rocks avalanching down a quarry path. Jim could see he had her on the ropes but he wasn't done. This was the moment he had craved for years, an opportunity to rattle a politician with some well deserved home truths. Unbeknown to Emily O Hara, she chose the wrong target, and had totally underestimated the opponent that she personally selected and went after.

"You're only in Parliament because your parents could afford to buy you a career in politics. If you came from a less privileged background, like the vast majority of British folk, the ninety nine per cent - you'd be working in a shop, but you're so ignorant, blinkered and self centred you probably can't get your head around that concept. You're just another bullshitter, in politics for the publicity, privileges and power, not for anybody else's benefit. You're what we call a knob head where I come from. That's all you are madam."

Emily O Hara didn't look capable of arguing back, she looked totally wiped out by the onslaught of words, but her strongest characteristic was her dogged, frustratingly stubborn defiance. She managed to find her voice again, and tried to recover some dignity.

"Getting very personal aren't we, Mr Arkwright?" She said, holding her burnt out cigarette dimp aloft in one hand whilst supporting her elbow with the other. It was almost like she was doing an impression of a crazy sketch show caricature. It was a peculiar moment for Karen as she watched and listened and wondered if all of this was for real.

"Of course I am getting personal. It's a very

personal matter Emily, can't you understand? It's public school throwbacks like you standing for Parliament as part of an ego trip that has turned this country into the joke that it is. My fifteen year old daughter goes to a state school and has better manners than you do, you're a total disgrace. I hope your parents feel deeply ashamed of what they have produced in you. I hope they are watching this now, blushing and crying with embarrassment, mortified to be associated with your idiotic hair style and your gawky, second hand, marijuana inspired ideas."

Jim had finally cracked the veneer. Emily let out an audible sob that was picked up by the cameras and microphones.

"Now listen, I think you should put that cigarette stump down. It's your public duty to set a positive example to our younger people, not act like a sad little dick."

Emily's eyes were bloodshot and watery with tears, as she realised that Jim had won the contest. He had systematically pulled her apart, and totally humiliated her. Her last hopes of finding a recovery, of penetrating Jim's arguments were lost. Politically speaking, he had finished her off. She had nothing left to say, his comments about her parents had gutted her and as she turned to walk away it was clear that all of her outspoken bravado was nothing more than an act. Jim's words embarrassed and wounded her deeply, but he had no sympathy and decided to make one final comment, raising his voice at the back of the retreating MP.

"And next time, ask before you try and jump into my news flash! Good day."

The media crews on the scene had mixed feelings. Many were laughing and sniggering, shocked and amazed to see one of Whitehall's most obnoxious and self assured characters looking so crestfallen. But there was also a number of them who felt desperately sorry for her. Jim had broken her spirit in the most public of ways, and it was painful to see another human being looking so violated.

Whichever side of the fence the crews, TV viewers and public at large sat on - it appeared to many of the news staff and camera crews that Jim simply couldn't help but supply brilliantly entertaining footage wherever he went. This exchange was likely to be shown on TV not just over the coming hours and days, but for decades, on documentaries and compilation shows, and it was all so genuinely spontaneous and unintentional.

Jim Arkwright really did seem to be the biggest star in London right now, and despite the colossal news from Downing Street that afternoon, and consequently Jims "demands" as made out on the Mock Off set - exchanges such as this one were quickly ensuring that he truly was the only story in Great Britain.

Chapter Twenty Four
Tea Time – Hyde Park Hotel

The moment they entered the hotel suite, Jim and Karen collapsed onto the bed. It had been a long, hot, emotionally and physically draining day – and the couple weren't finished yet.

Tim Dixon had booked a table for the Mock Off star guest and his wife to eat at the exclusive Julies Restaurant in Holland Park, a well known celebrity diner - so the day was still relatively young and there was no time to stop.

"I'm so knackered love." Said Jim, remembering how comfortable the bed was as his body sank into the luxurious mattress and bedding.

"I know. Same. How can it be so tiring just sitting around all day?"

"God knows. Tell you what though, we need to find out where this beds from and get one. How comfy is this bed?"

"Are you for real? Jim. Really? They've just said they're making special elections so you can be the Prime Minister and you're talking about how comfy the bloody bed is? You're not right."

"What's that got to do with the bed? I'm just saying, we've got all this money coming – we might as well get a brand new bed. Treat ourselves. We've never had a brand new one. That bed we've got was given to us by your Aunty Val when we bought the house, and it had seen better days then!"

"I know. But come on Jim. Isn't there more important stuff to talk about than a new bed?" Karen was staring at the intricate, decorative coving around the edge of the ceiling as she spoke.

"Yes, course there is. It's so comfy though. I can

feel myself falling asleep already!" Jim's eyes were closed.

"Well get your arse up – we've got to get ready!" Karen sprung up into a sitting position, grabbed a pillow, spun round and whacked her husband in the stomach with it.

"owww!" said Jim, though the weird noise was more from shock and alarm than discomfort.

"Come on, you big bald bastard!" she shouted, grabbing another pillow and threatening him, now with a pillow in each of her hands.

"Nasty little get!" said Jim, scrambling off the bed and trying to grab one of the pillows off his wife. Karen took her chance and whacked him around the side of the head with a sucker shot.

"Easy! Easy!" She laughingly chanted as Jim came at her again. Karen jumped up onto the bed and smashed a pillow around Jims face, just as he made a grab for the other. Karen's speed and tactics had always been a tough match for him in pillow fights, but he still fought as best he could. It was very rarely to his advantage though, Karen was faster and had much greater agility.

"It's not fair. You've got both of the pillows."

"It's not fair" said Karen in a gruff, deep voice, mimicking her husband as she danced around on the bed, while Jim continued to try and grab at the pillows like a big clumsy bear.

"You've got both the pillows!" She bellowed in the deep voice as she landed another pillow blow around his face.

"It's not fair" she repeated in amongst her breathless laughter. Jim tried a final time to grab one of the pillows from his wife and succumbed to another direct hit around the head. He sat down on the bed and admitted defeat.

"Right, bollocks. You win. I'm getting a shower and getting changed. I stink of B.O."

"Say mercy!" Karen was stood behind him, ready to attack again.

"Mercy. You sadistic get."

"Good boy. Now step away from the bed. I'm not falling for any of your dirty tricks Jimmy boy!"

Jim stood and walked away from the bed, his hands in the air as he retreated in the direction of the bathroom facilities. He was in a mood.

"It's not fair though, you always have to cheat," he shouted as he disappeared into the shower room, only to reappear a few seconds later, without his shirt on.

"I'm going to wait until you're chilling out and start smashing the pillows into you one day, see how you like it when you're not ready!" He retreated again into the shower room. Karen sensed he was going to appear again, and crept up to the doorway in anticipation. She crouched down by the side of the wall next to the door, still clutching her pillows. Just a few seconds later Jim leaned out of the door, his mouth was open as though he was about to speak. Karen walloped him right in the face and ran away laughing hysterically.

"See! That's what I mean! You're a chuffin' cheat Karen Arkwright. You really piss me off!"

"Aw, big Jim, I'm sorry!"

Karen also needed a shower as she was feeling a bit sticky and grubby herself after the hot and murky day in the television studio. She began to get undressed, planning to go and join Jim for a second shower with him that day.

Just as she stood in her knickers and bra, her phone began ringing. She grabbed the hotel issue dressing gown and wrapped it around her as she walked across to the bed and rooted in her bag, having every intention of ignoring the call, but wanting to check who it was in case it was important.

It was Albert. Karen's phone very rarely rang with a call from her Father-in-Law, so when it did it always made her feel a little uneasy. It was always viewed as an important call, rather than a general "washing up liquid has gone up twenty five pence" conversation, which Karen had regularly with her mother.

"Hello Albert. Everything alright?"

"Well, apart from the bloody media city that's camped up outside your house, yes, everythings fine! I've just had to go yours to fetch Jonathan's football boots and I had to fight my way through them all, reporters, famous faces off the news, tv crews they're all there. There's about fifty of them with cameras and all vans parked up the street. I'm seriously not exaggerating."

"No way! They must have found out where we live. Are you alright?"

"Course I am. I'm grand. I'm just letting you know though. What time are you back tomorrow?"

"About seven. You still alright to pick us up from Preston? I'll ring you when I know what time exactly."

"Yes, of course don't worry about that. It's a bit strange what's happening though isn't it? How's Jim? Is he coping alright with all the attention?"

"He's in the shower – I'll shout him in a sec. He's just the same as normal, he thinks it's all a load of bull to be honest Albert."

"Yes, well, I thought he would. We can have a good chat tomorrow on the way back from the station,

258

I'm looking forward to it. Don't bother him now, you two have a good break from the kids and I'll see you tomorrow Karen love."

"Aw thanks Albert. I'll tell him you rang. Are the kids alright then? I'm missing them like mad!"

"They're fine. They're just watching telly all the time, watching Jim! You've been on a few times as well, especially before - when that mental MP was mithering Jim. They were laughing their heads off! Lucy thought you were going to swing for her!"

"Ha ha, I very nearly did, stupid little cow! Aw bless them, I bet they love it!"

"Yes, definitely, they're having a great time. So don't worry about them – you have a good night and we'll see you tomorrow love."

"Aw cheers Albert, seeya tomorrow. Send my love to the kids. Love ya."

"Love you too Karen. See you tomorrow love."

As the couple got dressed, Karen had a glass of red wine, and Jim enjoyed a couple of frosty bottled lagers from the mini-bar. Once Karen was happy that she looked as good as she could do, under the "out of an overnight bag" circumstances, they went down and waited in the lavish hotel reception for their Chauffeur driven limousine to pick them up.

Not long after they sat down in the foyer area of the busy hotel, Karen began to notice that a lot of the guests and drinkers in the bar opposite were taking really long and noticeable glances at the couple. It was plainly obvious that people were openly discussing them. One woman even pointed at the pair, as her friend looked over in the Arkwright's direction. Karen began to feel very self conscious, and paranoid as people were constantly looking over and whispering.

"How do I look Jim?" she asked, brushing her skirt with her hand.

"Fit." Jim answered without looking.

"Aw, thanks. Jim, look at all the people over there in the bar. And those at the check in bit. They all keep looking over at us. It's freaking me out." Karen began adjusting her hair with her hand, then went back to fidgeting with her skirt. Even the staff were taking sly looks at them as they wandered past on their duties.

"Yes, I see what you mean actually, they are gawping a bit aren't they? It's because I'm so ace!" said Jim.

"It's because they're wondering how a bald headed beer monster got such a fit bird more like." Said Karen, forcing Jim to laugh out loud and attract even more attention.

"A bald headed beer monster? You're giving me some jip today you are love."

"Just keeping you down to earth. I've heard about these men who get a bit too big for their boots once they get a bit famous. Look what happened to Dave Lee Travis." Karen expected Jim to laugh at her remark but he didn't.

"Yeah, well. I'm perfectly down to earth love – it's everyone else that's making a big fuss about nothing."

Jim's mood had changed, he'd stopped teasing and suddenly became a little more serious and tetchy. Karen looked straight at her husband, and kept eye contact.

"It's a pretty big deal Jim. It's world news. Come on, you're the big know it all about all these things – why are you being so laid back about it? I don't get it."

"Because it's a load of bollocks love, it's bullshit

– like everything that comes out of politicians mouths. I'll bet you all my money there'll be government officials looking through my life's history right now to find something iffy about me. They'll be going through my school, the council records, the kid's school records, your records looking for a story. Then, if they don't find one, they'll leak something out that may not even be true. But rest assured love, I'm not going to be the next Prime Minister. They will do something to put me off, or to put the voters off voting for me."

Karen looked sad, almost tearful at what Jim was saying. Part of her wanted to believe it, and allow a reassuring wave of relief to wash all over her, promising that her normal life was about to return soon. But the other half of her was excited by the adventure, turned on by the uncertainty and most definitely thrilled by the celebrity aspect that just today's activities had provided. Jim got a sense that Karen was struggling to get her head around it.

"I just don't think, like I said today in the Mock Off studio – I just can't see how it could work. I can't see the MP's allowing it to happen. Why would they let a scruffy little commoner like me play with their toys? But anyway, it's their call now Karen. It all depends on what they say."

"But the way people are feeling Jim, if the MP's say no – there'll be who-knows-what trouble happening. They'll burn Parliament down man. Everyone has said that they want you to do it. Even the fucking Prime Minister!"

Karen remembered where she was and looked around to see if anybody had heard her swear. It looked as though a few had as the chattering and glancing at the pair continued amongst the hotel patrons.

"Well, come on right Karen – forget all that shit

about other people wanting me to do it. What do you want me to do?"

Karen thought about it for a moment. She thought about how joyous she had felt during the day, playing the part of the chaperoned wife of a big star, the endless compliments, celebrity meetings and VIP treatment. That aspect was very exciting, but Karen was also extremely concerned about how angry and defensive she had felt at the studios when Emily O'Hara had come over and started abusing Jim. Her instinct was to scream and shout and punch to defend her husband. But there had been another incident that day that had worried Karen and made her feel defensive. She hadn't wanted to bring it up, but this seemed like the most logical and natural moment to confront the issue.

"Well, I know how good you are at all this politics stuff. I think it's boring as paint drying myself. But I never knew you were clever enough at politics to actually become one! So it's all going to take a bit of getting used to. But you know I will support whatever you decide to do one hundred per cent. And I know that you'd do the same for me."

"But?"

"But, well I'm a bit scared – and I know its stupid, I do, but I'm scared that something might happen to you. What if somebody wanted to murder you or something?" Jim could tell that this was a serious concern by the way Karen was looking at him. He laughed at her. In part it was to reassure Karen, but it also genuinely tickled him. It was another bonkers reminder of just how extraordinary life had become for the Arkwright's in just a few days.

"Come on love, that's bollocks! You mean James Bond will come and give me a lethal injection or summat?" Jim laughed again and dismissed his wife's concern – waving her away with an over exaggerated waft of his arm.

"Where's this bloody taxi?" He asked in a bid to move the topic on.

"It's not a taxi Jim, it's a bloody chauffeured limo!" Karen smiled. Even as she was saying it, it sounded far fetched. She grabbed Jim's hand.

"Listen love, I know you think I'm being a knob. But when we were coming back from the TV studio before, I was looking at Facebook on my phone…"

"God, I hate that Facebook. It's a load of shite that." Jim rudely interrupted his wife to make known the opinion that she was already very familiar with.

"Let me finish or I'll give you a nipple cripple right here in front of all these posh people." Karen did the "look" so Jim would know she was being serious.

"Okay. Sorry. You were on Facebook, the world's biggest cause of problems after money and religion?"

"Yes, I was just looking at all the things people were saying – there's over six million people on your page, supporting you."

"Six million? That's pretty good that isn't it? How many has Stephen Fry got?"

"That's on Twitter you dickhead, and stop being stupid. I'm trying to say something really important that I'm bothered about." Karen was still holding Jim's hand to try and keep his attention but it wasn't working too well.

"Sorry."

"Right, well there's this page, well, it'll have about seven million on it now if not more – they're all the ones who are really behind you, they're all writing remarks on there like "we love you Jim" and "One of us plebs for Prime Minister" and all these supportive comments."

"But?"

"Stop doing that Jim!"

"Right, well hurry up and get on with what you're saying. You make me want to book a one way ticket to Dignitas."

"Well there's another page, its only got a few hundred fans, a thousand tops but basically all the people on there are saying they want to batter you, and that you're a dickhead."

"Well, they're not far wrong. So are these my polling stats? Six million against a thousand? That's probably good going!" Jim laughed again.

"But are you not bothered that people want to hit you? They say they'll kick your head in!" Jim laughed again but straightened his face when he saw how seriously Karen was taking all of this.

"Why do they want to beat me up then? Does it say?"

"They're the people you're making the most noise about. They're all the criminals, all the scum - they don't want you clamping down on them do they? They don't want you to make prison hard, or to send the morons into the Army. They say really awful things, like they'll shove your head so far up your arse you'll be able to smell your own breath." The comment seriously amused Jim, he laughed so much it brought a tear to his eyes.

"It's not funny!" pleaded Karen. The comments had shaken her up. This was her husband they had written the nasty, violent threats about. This was a man who couldn't win a pillow fight. The threats were very real and serious to Karen.

"Listen love, it's a load of bullshit. It's just like

that daft MP today, talking a load of shit. Take no notice – these people won't do nothing to me, I bet they don't have the bus fare to come and get me anyway!"

"Jim, stop taking the piss - think about all the gangsters and big criminal gangs – they won't want you closing their businesses down by legalising drugs. Think about it will you. I'm being serious love."

"Right, now you listen to me for a minute. You know why you're saying all this? Because you've gone looking at a Facebook that's set up to slag me off. If you hadn't have done that, we wouldn't be talking about it. And you wouldn't be worrying."

"Well, what good is it saying that?"

"I'm saying – don't go looking for this stuff. It's just a tiny amount of them, that's why there's only a thousand people involved with the bloody thing. Forget them, remember that the country is full of bloody good folk. If we could get all of the shite people sorted out, we could seriously reduce all the bloody taxes so people had a bit of money left for themselves after all their hard work. I bet most of the criminals would vote for an end of crime anyway – an end to their sad and shitty little deviant ways of life. Seriously Karen, with no crime, no troublemakers, no hassle, no dickheads – imagine how much better the country would be overnight. I think the majority of people in Britain would have my back if anyone did try to start on me, so you shouldn't worry love."

"You know I've got a point Jim. I can tell."

"Yes, alright – it's a point, but I'm not worried about it. The only people that should have anything to worry about are the ones in the wrong business! If they don't like my opinion that being banged up should be horrible or that trouble making tossers should be sent in the army or whatever, they could always change their lifestyle choice."

"They'll still cause trouble for you. What if they can't get at you and decide to go for me or one of the kids?"

"Seriously Karen – you're giving these people too much credit. They're just losers and freaks writing some bullshit on Facebook. And that's it. The best thing to do is just stop going on Facebook."

"I am worried about it though Jim. You asked. I'm only answering."

"Okay. Fair enough. Fair point love. I don't think it's a big deal, but I respect that it bothers you. I'll give it some thought."

"I don't want you to think I'm putting a downer on anything Jim, honestly. I just don't like how scared that kind of thing makes me. Sorry."

A courtier turned around from his position by the door and spoke.

"Mr and Mrs Arkwright, your car has arrived."

"Cheers mate," said Jim. He turned back round to face his wife and grabbed her shoulders. "I'm glad you've said it, right. I love you Karen Arkwright. With all this crazy shit going on right now, that's the only thing I actually am sure about. You and the kids are my only priority."

"I know that. I know you love me Jim, and I love you as well. Let's just forget all this politics shit now and have a right nice night out. Julies Restaurant has loads of famous celebrities in there! Try and get me a photo with one of them for my profile picture!"

"Yeah! Come on. Let's bloody do it."

"Do I look alright?"

"Course you do, I already told you a dozen times. I'd say if you looked hanging. I wouldn't go for a night out with a dog."

"Aw thanks love. Give us a kiss."

Jim and Karen had a modest little kiss on the lips as they walked across the immaculate reflective black granite floor towards the entrance.

A stunning dark graphite Bentley car had pulled up outside the hotel and the chauffeur had already got out and had taken position by the rear, ready to open the back door for his VIP passengers. One of the hotel courtiers came across to usher Jim and Karen out towards the elegant entrance as the hotels onlookers excitedly gossiped and watched on.

The couple walked very self consciously towards the posh car as the scruffy rabble of paparazzi descended all around the outside of the hotels entrance and beside the car. It was quite apparent to all of the affluent people that were watching from the hotel reception and through restaurant windows, that the couple were quite bemused, if not embarrassed by the whole spectacle.

"Are you sure I look alright Jim?" asked Karen, adjusting her hair with her fingers as they approached the doors.

"You look totally amazing Karen. Shame I look like a spud."

"Aw, you do, don't you?"

Once they walked out through the revolving doors the press gang were jostling very aggressively as the camera flashes and bulbs burst into life and the reporters and paps were pushing forwards, shouting for attention, desperately trying to get the couple to look their way for a photo.

"Jim, Jim, Karen, Over here!"

"You look amazing Karen!"

"Big Jim!"

"Karen love, give us a smile."

"Jim! Wave to the camera Jim, wave to the

public!"

The press were pushing and shoving, it was surprising how rough and physical it all was. Jim had to put his arm around Karen to protect her as the pair carefully descended the steps, slowly negotiating the short stairway beside a waterfall feature. It was hard work with photographers shoving cameras right up, close in their faces.

"Hee yar, calm down guys. Calm down!" Jim stood still and shouted at the scrum of scruffily dressed people holding expensive looking gadgets. They began to quieten and simmer down, though the camera flashes continued.

"I don't see the need for pushing and shoving for Gods sake!"

"Sorry Jim!"

"Yeah, sorry mate, sorry Karen" shouted a few.

"Just chill out guys. That's what you need to do, just relax a bit. Its hard work trying to pull a nice face for your pictures when you're all acting like that. Right now, get ready and when you count to three, me and the wife will say cheese."

A wave of laughter met Jim's rather naïve request.

"The British public are right behind you Jim!" It was a pale looking reporter with a cockney accent that was shouting from the front of the crowd.

"We've got poll ratings suggesting there's a ninety percent approval rating. How would you like to thank your supporters?" The camera flashes continued illuminating the couple as though they were stood in the face of a tropical lightning storm.

"Chill out guys, I'm getting dots in my eyes. Are you love?" Jim looked at Karen who nodded back.

"I'm a welder you know – and some of them

bulbs you've got are brighter than any bloody welding tackle, I'll tell you now."

"So what would you like to say Jim?" asked the same pallid reporter.

"Well – first of all I'd like to say thanks! Nice one to everyone who is being supportive, and also – thanks for proving my point that politics doesn't have to belong to a certain party with a certain coloured rosette. Common sense is the thing that really counts for anything. People are hearing common sense for once and they can't believe their ears!"

"Jim! How long do you think it will take the MP's to vote?" it was a different reporter who was shouting the question from within the middle of the pack.

"Oh, I don't know. I'm not fussed about that. What I want to ask the people to do is prove something to me. All those who believe in what I'm saying, who agree this country needs a good shake up – I want you to help me demonstrate a point. On Saturday – I want all the people who support me to organise a street party in their neighbourhood at one pm."

The media gang looked confused.

"Eh?"

"What the fack is he on abart?"

"What's that Jim?"

"Well, a street party. Nowt too big or over the top. Listen, the biggest problem this country has today is that we're an island of strangers. I want the so called ninety per cent of people who say they support me on this poll to prove it! Just come out and properly demonstrate that support, by organising a community street party for all of your neighbourhood. Leave off the beer – I mean have a few by all means but I'm not talking about a big booze up. On Saturday night, if

Britain has had a happy day of street parties and has spent time chilling out and getting to know their neighbours, having a bit of fun and making new friendships – then I'll know that people actually do support me. I'll know there actually is something to all of this, I'll know that it's not just a case of folk pressing "yes or no" on the TV remote or on the BBC website."

"So you want every street in Britain to hold a street party on Saturday?" shouted one journalist, a certain amount of ridicule in his voice.

"Yes. Look, you don't need matching napkins and new plate sets. You don't need anything but good intentions. Just drag your tables out into the street and make a plate of jam butties, take some juice out and biscuits. Have a couple of beers and just have a really good, civilised day of getting to know each other. This is a chance to come together, to forgive and forget all the daft fall outs about parking spaces and blocking each others drives or disputes about trees that have grown too bushy."

"That sounds like a lot to ask the whole country to organise in thirty six hours Jim!" shouted another one of the reporters, this time from the back of the rabble.

"It's not a lot to ask! Can't you see? It's so simple. It's so easy to organise. That's just the kind of stupid, negative comment that's holding the country back. You just need to make the effort, that's all. You just need to show willing, all it takes is for folk to mean well and have a laugh. Just keep an open mind guys, see what happens."

Jim grabbed Karen's hand and started walking down the remaining couple of steps and introduced himself to the driver who was patiently waiting by the Bentley's rear passenger door wearing full chauffeur uniform.

"Alright mate? Nice one for this! I'm Jim, this is my wife Karen."

"Yes Sir, thank you Sir." Said the chauffeur, who looked a bit embarrassed by all of the flashing cameras and television cameras pointed at him.

"Don't call me Sir mate. Jim'll do."

"Yes Sir, Jim Sir."

The media pack seemed a bit confused by Jim's request. Jim and Karen got in the car and their driver closed the door behind him.

"Where do you get all this shit from, Jim?" asked Karen, laughing at the confused looks on the media staffs faces.

"Its not shit love. It's really important stuff."

The car drove away slowly and gracefully, leaving the media crews to figure out their next move.

The announcement had gone out live on the main TV news channels. "BREAKING NEWS" banners were already advertising the street party idea before Jim and Karen had even arrived at Julies Restaurant.

Chapter Twenty Five
Friday Morning - Hyde Park Hotel

Jim and Karen Arkwright had been woken from their sleep by a phone call from the hotel staff at seven thirty, much to their punishing despair. Both were feeling extremely delicate following a very heavy night of drinking, schmoosing and celebrating with a new found gang of celebrity "friends" that came from the glittery, showbizzy worlds of sport, television, film, music, stage and comedy.

From the instant that the couple had walked into Julies Restaurant, they had been acquainted by some of the country's best known A list celebs. The stars in attendance showed no shyness as they made a bee-line towards the Arkwrights - it was almost as though the queue of high profile faces were determined to let Jim and Karen know how much they were in full support of the Clitheroe Prime Ministers ideology.

The weirdest moment was when the couple had been asked for a photograph by American actor and singer David Hasselhoff.

The Arkwrights hadn't arrived back at the hotel until after 1.30 in the morning and were met by a very patient gang of press people. The frantic, aggressive mood amongst them had calmed down massively since the couple had left the hotel six hours earlier.

Jim and Karen stumbled out of their limo and sat on the wall surrounding the neon lit waterfall and had spent some time having a chat and a good laugh with the cameramen, journalists, sound people and presenters for ten minutes before finally saying goodnight and heading up into the hotel suite. Once they'd arrived back in the room, they practically collapsed onto the luxury bed, giggling and joking about the evening's crazy, surreal eventualities as they fell asleep.

The hotel receptionist who had phoned the Arkwright's room at such an early hour had been more than apologetic and insisted that it was totally against hotel policy to wake patrons up in this way. At that point, Karen assumed it was a prank call and hung up, only for the telephone to ring again. The receptionist finished what she was saying, explaining that the reason that hotel policy had been broken was due to government intervention.

Karen was fuming, and shook Jim awake from his inebriated slumber. After some confused chatter on the phone, Jim began to realise that some people from Parliament had come to speak to him on urgent business. He asked the receptionist to give him ten minutes to wake up and make a brew before sending them up.

Once he put the phone down Karen groaned, complaining that she felt "as rough as a badgers arse."

"Shut up Karen, some bloody government people are coming in a minute. Get up, get dressed. God I feel like shit." He looked like he did as well.

"No way. I'm staying here!" Karen started laughing at her husband, stood for the second day in his underpants and socks, looking totally confused.

"Ow." The sound of her own laughter hurt her head.

"They're coming up in a few minutes Karen. I stink!" Jim looked lost and baffled as he started wandering around the place, sniffing his armpit. He looked unsure of what he was supposed to do.

"Go and wash your face, and brush your teeth." Suggested Karen, amused by Jims trance like state, but wary not to laugh as the last one had hurt so much. Jim wandered off towards the luxurious en suite under his wife's instructions.

Karen thought twice about staying put, reasoning that it would be really awkward for Jim's guests to conduct a meeting in a hotel room with a stinking drunk woman snoring throughout it. After a couple of minutes of staring at the ceiling and out of the window at the grand Edwardian buildings across the road, Karen reluctantly got out of bed and smiled as she realised that she was still wearing her clothes from the previous night.

"Dosser," she said to herself as she wandered through to the wet room where Jim was taking a cool shower. His underpants and socks were strewn all over the bathroom floor, which made Karen laugh again, then catch her head with both hands as the pain seared through her brain once more.

"Got any painkillers Jim?" Karen was shaking as she stood leaning against the side of the shower, holding her head and looking ashen and unhealthy.

"No. I wouldn't mind some though! My head feels like it's been kicked about. I wonder what these people want?"

"It'll be MFI, come to assassinate you!"

"Thank god for that! Anyway, you mean MI5 you gimp!" Jim got out of the walk-in shower and flicked his hands at his wife, covering her with water and suds from the shower gel.

"Knob." She said as she grabbed a towel and wiped and dabbed at her face in slow motion.

"Loser." replied Jim as he dried himself off. "Get us some undies and socks love."

"No. Don't be such a noddy. Get your own!"

"Karen, come on, there'll be here in a minute. I don't know where they are do I?"

"They're in the bag."

"Well go and grab us some then women, know your place!'"

Karen laughed and again grabbed her head.

"Argh. Don't make me laugh, it really hurts." She half-whispered it as she made a childish sobbing noise and slowly limped back into the bedroom area and unzipped the large bag that contained all the clothes. Karen pulled out a pair of jeans and a t shirt for Jim, along with his underwear and a can of deodorant.

"Cheers love," said Jim as he came back in after brushing his teeth.

"Get a brew on as well."

"Don't take the piss!"

Karen went and had a shower herself. Jim made the coffee and phoned down to the reception.

"Hello, yes its room 209. Can you sort out some ibuprofen and some paracetamol for us? Pretty urgently really. Cheers."

By the time Karen reappeared in the big white fluffy dressing gown, Jim had shaved, got dressed and was looking much more presentable. Karen also looked a little better for the shower and was certainly pleased to see the two cups of coffee on the sideboard.

"Nice one Jimmy boy."

"No worries. There'll be some painkillers in a minute as well."

As Jim said it there was a knock at the door and he walked over to open it.

"Now that's skill," he said as he walked towards the door. It wasn't the hotels room service though, it was the government people. Two smart looking men, dressed in very expensive looking suits.

"Oh shit, I thought it was room service!" said Jim, "but it's the Men in Black." Jim waited for a laugh or even a smile in response but it wasn't forthcoming from the visitors who wore an almost featureless look of disinterest.

"Ah, Mr Arkwright, so sorry to intrude. You had a late night I presume?"

"Yes, you can say that again! It was a brilliant night actually. I did karaoke with Madonna."

"Yes, yes, we've heard all about it on the news this morning." The man attempted a smile, but it was through a straight, almost stern look on his face and it didn't really materialise.

"Oh, right." Jim hadn't considered that his night out with Karen would be making the news, and the mention of it depressed him slightly.

"May we?" The gentleman gestured to come in. His associate was stood to his right, slightly behind.

"Oh, yes, sorry. Like I say, I thought you were the room service. I rung down for some painkillers for the wife, she's got a right hangover. Come in."

Jim opened the door fully and allowed the two men access to the hotel suite. Karen heard that it was the uninvited visitors and had grabbed her clothes and scuttled back into the bathroom to get dressed.

"Thank you Mr Arkwright. Now, my name is Pierre, and this Nathan. We work in the Speakers office at the Houses of Parliament. Now, I must be clear about the reason we're here. May I?" Pierre gestured again, this time to the chair.

"Sure, yeah, take a seat, no problem." Said Jim.

"Thank you Mr Arkwright." Pierre sat down whilst his partner Nathan put his briefcase down and took out a laptop computer. He opened it, turned on the power and waited for it to load.

"Well, you must be wondering what is going on Mr Arkwright? Well, without further ado I will explain.

In order to put a legal vote to our MP's, we must be able to offer some evidence that they are clear on what they are voting for. What this basically means is, I have to gather some further information from you which will be shared with all the MPs later today in the form of an interview."

"An interview? Like a job interview?" asked Jim, without any enthusiasm as he took a swig of coffee from his cup.

"If you like," said Pierre. He smiled at Jim before he continued.

"Don't worry about it. Nathan here is setting up the laptop to record the interview – I'll just ask you some quick questions, then, we'll leave. Is that okay then?"

To say Pierre was getting on Jims nerves would be a radical understatement. Jim felt like talking back in the same condescending, smarmy way but he just couldn't be bothered.

"Do we have to do this now? I'm still a bit pissed from last night."

Jim made no secret of his lack of interest to participate in this interview right now.

"It would be better to do it now. The Speaker and his Deputies are under a great deal of pressure, not only from within the House but also from outside of the House to get this vote underway. I believe that you are travelling back home to the north again today as well. So I really must insist that you do it now if that's okay?" Pierre did another irritating smile.

Jim refrained himself from speaking his mind, which took a good deal of willpower, and he was secretly pleased with his resolve.

"How long will it take?" asked Jim.

"Five minutes. Ten minutes maximus."

"Maximus. What's that?" asked Jim.

Pierre paused and looked down at his papers. He looked slightly embarrassed. "Maximum." He said and looked across awkwardly at Nathan.

"Oh right, got you! I thought you'd said maximus! I was thinking what sort of an anus would say maximus instead of maximum! Completely misheard you, my mistake!"

Pierre was going red in the face and he shifted uncomfortably in his seat. His colleague Nathan was clearly ill at ease with the whole situation and looked like he was about to start giggling. Jim began to feel a bit better about everything once he'd seen how easy Pierre was to wind up.

"Right," said Pierre, rubbing his hands together. "Come and sit down here please Mr Arkwright. Are we all set Nathan?" he asked whilst patting the seat opposite him.

"Ready to go, it's already recording." Nathan replied with a hint of a grin on his face and Jim got the impression that he may have done Nathan a good turn by taking the mick out of Pierre.

"Okay Mr Arkwright, we'll start then. So as I say, all of what you tell me will be played back to the MPs in full, without edits or changes, and to ensure total transparency and clarity – an unedited copy of this interview will be made public on the Houses of Parliament website as well. Is everything okay?"

"Yes, its fine. But I just want to make it known that I'm still a bit pissed from last night, or should I say five hours ago when I got home. I wasn't expecting this, being dragged out of bed, so I just want the MPs to know I got woke up ten minutes ago and my head feels all whoosey, a bit like it's got a puncture underwater."

Jim looked into the laptop camera and rolled his

eyes and wobbled his head. Pierre remained focused on the job he had to carry out but Nathan let slip a tiny laugh before composing himself.

"In fact," continued Jim, "the guy from downstairs will be bringing me and the wife some painkillers in a minute, so there'll probably be an interruption in this!"

"Okay well we'll take our chance." Pierre did another humourless little laugh to himself before continuing.

"We've heard what you have said in the media, and it's all very interesting. The first question that is concerning our Parliamentary Members Mr Arkwright, do you have any idea of the true enormity of Britain's financial problems?"

"Well, I'm no different to anybody else really - I know exactly what I'm allowed to know. I see the same news on as everyone else on telly. I listen to the Today show on Radio Four. I read papers. But I've never actually sat and studied the nation's accounts."

"How bad do you think things are in this country Jim, if like, not bad is one and really bad is ten?"

"If you give me another question like that I'll break your bleeding finger pal."

"Sorry. But we do have to report back. They want to know how well you understand what's actually happening?" Pierre looked slightly scared and his voice had gone up an octave or two.

"That's fair enough, but you don't need to talk to me like I've got shit for brains lad. I'll tell you how I see it all, and you can judge for yourself if I grasp how bad things are. I know that just over a hundred years ago, our government was the richest in the world and started working on the first ideas that would lead onto the welfare state we have now. The first thing they did was introduce the state pension that everybody was entitled to when they reached 70 years old. Except most folk died in their forties and fifties back then, so it was a pretty safe bet. It was a gesture more than anything else, aimed at the richest in society – it would be like if today's government said you can have a free car once you reach 105 years old. But now of course, thanks to all the improvements that the welfare state has brought us in the past hundred years, all the stuff like education, health care and financial support - we all live much longer. So a massive chunk of our tax money goes into paying peoples pensions for anything up to thirty years and its costing more and more money every year as people continue to stubbornly live! And then of course, we introduced the National Health Service after the Second World War, and that accounts for a major chunk out of the countries money as well. Then if we add into it the rest of the cost of welfare, chuck in a war or two, the odd new hospital or motorway - and then take into special consideration that we had to spend all the spare money buying banks out of the shite – it all adds up to a depressing figure. If we then add on the interest we owe out on the debts we've been racking up since the 1980's, that pretty much accounts for all of the nation's purse for the next fifty years."

"Do you have a plan of how to deal with the nations one trillion pounds of debt?"

"Turn the interest off immediately. Its going up so fast we'll never catch it, so what's the point chasing it? You wouldn't go chasing after a formula one car on a bike would you? We need to say to the creditors that we owe all these billions to that they have to halt the interest, call it a certain figure today and that's it, we'll pay it all back, Scouts honour. But right now the

interest is going up a million pounds every few minutes –
and it's inevitable that it's all going to end really badly.
So I'd say, fair enough, hands up, we've screwed up, but
we could never pay it back at the rate its rising. Stop the
interest and we'll make a commitment to pay back what
we owe. Keep the interest going and we'll stop paying
altogether."

"Thank you. You have also publicly claimed
that you can get people off benefits and into jobs?
Would you care to expand on that pledge Mr
Arkwright?"

"Well, firstly, I never said that – I said we have
people getting paid jobseekers for not working, and that
we could and we should get them working – for their
own benefit. I said if we used a little imagination – we'd
have one hundred per cent of unemployed people in
employment. I never said anything about getting people
off benefits and into work – I'm talking about the people
with no work. I'm not talking about the frail, the ill or
handicapped who can't work – don't try and confuse the
facts mate."

"Okay, so you are talking exclusively about the
job seekers?"

"Yes, the three million unemployed."

"That's clear Mr Arkwright. So how could you
do it?"

"I've already said countless times – we have to
stop importing stuff from overseas, and we have to start
forcing shops and businesses to sell British stuff. If we
do that, we can have a national network of factories
making things. If somebody is unemployed, they will
just go and work in the factory nearest them until they
can find a job off their own back. Call it a work-house if
you want – call it what you like, I'm not bothered about
sound bites or details like that. The big supermarkets

should be forced to buy these products, so it would all work beautifully."

"Just a moment Mr Arkwright – I must interrupt you there. You are suggesting that the supermarkets will have to buy certain products from the government?"

"Well, I'm talking more about setting up sustainable businesses that make certain products. There could be toilet roll from a toilet roll factory, light bulbs from a light bulb factory, paper plates from a factory that makes them. Basically, whatever is being imported right now should be made here, creating sustainable work for our people."

"And supermarkets would be forced to sell them?"

"Damn right! These supermarkets have made enough profit by trampling all over British farmers and manufacturers – forcing prices down so low that farmers are actually losing money to supply them. Well, it isn't working, that system doesn't help Britain – it's just beneficial to the shareholders at the top of the chain. They've got away with all this for thirty, forty years but now the games up! Like most of the things I'm suggesting, we need to reverse the trend. If they don't like it, tough titty! They can sod off and we'll run the supermarkets. We'll run them ethically and responsibly, with Britain's own interests and people at the very top of the priority list."

"Thank you. I think that's clear."

"We could take them over. Call them "Brit-Mart" or something. Shop smart at Brit Mart!" Jim laughed at his new tagline. Pierre just stared at him in silence before continuing with his questions.

"On an entirely different matter now - You caused some concern amongst a number of our MP's when you said that immigration has to stop. Can you expand on that point please?"

"Yes, I can. The country is full. The hospitals are full, the motorways and trains, schools and doctors, police stations and prisons, even the sewer pipes are full! It's all full. So stop the immigration altogether until we can stabilise ourselves, and we have learnt how to cope with the people we already have, not keep adding more to it. And if that's taken as racist then whoever thinks that needs to grow up. Britain is the most culturally diverse country on earth. We've done more than our bit, we have folk from every country on the planet living here - but we are over run with people now, including British people - it's as simple as that. So close the door, and keep it shut until we're coping. That's all I meant by that Pierre."

"Another topic that the Speaker wants you to explain – you claim you can boost manufacturing in Britain. Would you care to tell us how?"

"Easy, in a million ways, I've just told you one with the unemployed, but there are endless ways the government can adjust things to boost our output. Everywhere you look there's a way, here's a quick one for you – make it a law that you can only drive in Britain with British made tyres on your car. Imagine how many tyre factories that simple legislation would create, how many jobs it would create. You could roll it out over three years, and as each old tyre is worn down, it's replaced by a British made one. Here's another idea off the top of my head - all those bloody mobility cars that the government give to disabled folk – make it a rule that it has to be British made. At the moment they're Japanese and German and bloody French cars we are buying on the mobility scheme! Which knob head allowed that to happen? There's over half a million brand new cars being paid for every three years by the British government for mobility users – and half of the cars are from overseas! So come on for gods sake, get a grip. We just need to sort out an attitude to invest our own money back into Britain. Stop getting trains built abroad, make them here, stop letting councils buy vans and bin trucks from overseas, just make it the law that all public money has to be spent on a British made product. So the trains, police cars, ambulances, fire engines, buses and flipping bin trucks are all made and manufactured here. I'm not saying it can't be a Japanese company, or a German car company – but they'll have to relocate their factories here - it has to be built here in Britain, creating British jobs if the public are paying for it. It's a no-brainer really Pierre, we just need the champagne drinking decision makers to stop being so stupid with taxpayers money."

"And you'd also like to reform the prison system?"

"More than anything Pierre. Prison should be the worst thing that can ever happen to somebody. Prison should be so shit and horrible that anybody who has ever been there would never, ever want to go back, never in a month of Sundays. It should be made to be hard work, humiliating and bloody horrible. The biggest mistake we ever made with crime was trying to help and support prisoners. Bullshit, it doesn't work – they need punishing and teaching a lesson. Our current prison system has just become a foster centre for inadequate adults. Well its time to turn things around, we should be degrading them, discouraging them from going back to jail, not making it better than it is on the outside! Get them digging out new reservoirs on the moors, or send the bin wagons in there to dump and get the offenders separating out all the glass, paper and plastic waste before they go to landfill for gods sake. Make prison as shit as possible and let's just wait and see if the re-offending statistics go down, let alone the crime statistics."

"Thank you for your answers, one final topic for now, schools. You have claimed on a television interview that you'd separate pupils, to get the best out of them. Can you expand that point also please Mr Arkwright?"

"Yes, course, no problem Pierre. All I was saying was, if the kids who want to muck about all day are taken out of the picture, school will be better for teachers who want to spend their time teaching rather than trying to make kids behave themselves. It'll also be a better environment for the majority of our kids, the ones who try hard and want to learn. The kids who can't do it, who don't want to learn, who just want to piss about all day can go and sit in a cell by themselves. Or better still, you could send them off with all their like minded friends to clear litter off the embankment on the motorway and the railway. And if they refuse to go and do that they could be taken off to special boarding schools where the staff are trained to manage their behaviour. Lets see if there are still as many disruptive kids in class if they get put on a motorway embankment with a bin bag or locked in a prison school for twenty hours a day. All I'm saying is, we've done the soft touch approach and it's almost wrecked our country, our schools are churning out self centred little freaks with no respect for authority or even their fellow people. So let's take a radically different approach to misbehaviour in every sense, from kids to pensioners and let's see if Britain can improve, and thrive in the future. I've got a hunch that I'm talking sense."

"Can you expand on any other areas where you

imagine applying this "radically different" policy idea?"

"Alright then. Think about all the adults that get completely pissed every weekend, you know, to the point that they can't stand up, and an ambulance gets called to take them to hospital to pump their stomachs. Or the ones that punch shop windows and start losing all their blood as a result. If these people could just act more responsibly, we'd save a lot of money, and more importantly, we'd keep hold of a lot of our precious staff in the health service. But the good staff are leaving our hospitals and our ambulance service in droves because they just can't be arsed dealing with all these drunken idiots every night of the week. So instead of just fixing these people up and sending them home, let's introduce some serious penalties that will encourage responsible drinking. If someone injures themselves because they're pissed, they should be liable for the cost of that care, so we should bill them a thousand quid for a visit to accident and emergency, it can go straight on the tax code in their wage until it's paid off, or straight out of their benefits on a monthly basis. If they need extra care, bill them accordingly, a thousand quid for each hospital visit. Let's really start making people think long and hard before they do stupid stuff. Its no surprise that people just don't give a shit anymore – there are no consequences to make anybody think otherwise. If somebody smacks somebody else when they are pissed, it should be a straight one year detention – and that's a year, three hundred and sixty five days hard labour, no appeals, no mistakes – an unimaginably harsh punishment. It's a great idea! Bloody hell Pierre, that's just some ideas for starters. I'm talking about bringing in a direct response to all this ridiculous behaviour that's been allowed to build up to the random chaos we see now. Its time to rein it in! Enough's enough!"

Jim reached across and drank the last of his coffee.

"Some critics might think you'll need to build new prisons to cope with all of the extra people if you adopted such a hard line approach."

"Build them then. We've got three million on the dole, let's build some new prisons and get a load of the builders in jobs! Sounds better than leaving them lying in bed all day, wishing they were dead."

"Okay, well I think we are clear on what the radically different theory is all about. Now, please just tell us how you would plan to implement all of the changes?"

"Ah, yes, good point! Because this will be a big shock all this, so we really need to warn people that serious changes will be happening. Big, horrible changes are coming if you don't pull your socks up guys! So I say, do it in TV adverts on all the programmes, especially on the Jeremy Kyle show, and Loose Women. Right, heres an idea for one - you could have a guy walking up to a policeman, he's stumbling, he's clearly pissed, right, and he's shooting his mouth off, just being a typical pissed up knob. And he goes up to the copper and knocks his helmet off! Then, the voice over guy says "New rules are coming into effect that will see this kind of behaviour punished with 365 days hard labour. Instant justice. You have been warned!" And it shows a video of a prisoner digging a canal out, or cleaning a railway track with a brillo pad, or breaking rocks or something. You could do the telly adverts on everything, like the hospital costs if you break your hand because you punched a wall when you're out on the piss, or you fell off a bus stop roof doing a back flip to impress your mates. Put them on about everything, including in the kids programmes – show the kids an advert with a kid messing about in class, and then show a load of kids picking litter up along the side of the railway, or working in a factory putting stickers on packets of bacon. We would just need to make sure the press and telly and the radio stations are making sure everyone knows what's coming – then there can be no confusion can there?"

"Okay, thank you Mr Arkwright. That will give enough insight into your thoughts and views for our elected MP's to make a judgement about you." Pierre turned to his colleague Nathan and said "and cut. That's a wrap."

"I was just getting into that!" muttered Jim under his breath, he looked slightly disappointed that it was all over as he was just getting going.

If Pierre heard him, he didn't let on. Within seconds of finishing the interview, the Parliamentary officials packed up their things and left the hotel suite politely and with minimum fuss. As soon as the door closed Karen appeared from the bathroom.

"Where are these bloody painkillers? My heads splitting!"

Chapter Twenty Six
Friday Lunchtime - Clitheroe

The glorious weather just wasn't letting up. The school holidays had landed perfectly for children and parents alike, as well as for businesses as diverse as water gun stockists to ice cream vans. This had been a memorably stunning week of hot days with blue skies, but just enough gentle breeze to keep the trees swaying and to keep people comfortable.

North West England's weather would traditionally call a halt after more than four consecutive days of fine conditions -and would trade with a couple of days thundering rain storms. But not during this past week, the climate had remained consistently beautiful and the forecasters were promising many more days of the same.

Due to a combination of the lovely weather and the Jim Arkwright news story that had now become practically inescapable - Clitheroe was seeing a massive increase in visitor numbers. Parents decided against day trips to the Lake District or Blackpool and opted to have a look at the bonny little place that had been on the telly for the past few days.

The sudden interest in Big Jim's home town was unparalleled. By noon there was an unprecedented traffic jam getting into Clitheroe from both Whalley and Chatburn, the nearby villages that sit a couple of miles either side of the Ribble Valley's hinterland.

The A59 was heavily congested around Clitheroe in both directions. There was traffic from both the Yorkshire side and the Lancashire side serving cars full of curious families from Preston to the West and Bradford to the East, and plenty of traffic was coming in from even further afield.

The hourly railway service from Manchester that came through Bolton and Blackburn had remained busy from 8am, bringing a steady stream of inquisitive day trippers, many of whom had never heard of Clitheroe or the Ribble Valley until this week. As each hourly train was travelling to the town with maximum capacity, by lunch time it was becoming obvious to the ticket collectors and station staff that getting this amount of passengers back home collectively on the tea time trains was going to be an impossible task.

The drivers had started warning passengers that return trains may be overcrowded, and advised that alternative means of return travel may be required. Network rail managers were desperately trying to organise extra carriages to travel on the route that normally coped fine with just two coaches per service. Judging by ticket sales on the line for the day, a fourteen coach train would be required to take them all back again.

Business was booming for all of the cafes, snack bars and food serving pubs throughout the area. The town centre itself was bustling, alive with families from all across the north of England, taking advantage of the fine weather and this uniquely victorious and positive carnival style atmosphere that was resonating throughout the place.

Chicken Deli sandwich bar opposite the library clock had a queue running twenty five metres up Church Brow, and one young member of staff was given the unnerving task of standing by the shop doorway shouting "no cold drinks left – no pies left - all sold out!"

Down on the Marketplace, traders had pleaded with local teenagers - begging them to help out with various jobs, such as washing dishes, peeling spuds and slicing salad in the café vans and food stalls. Others were given impromptu casual employment running errands, fetching and carrying for traders and holding up hastily made placards or handing out leaflets advertising particular stalls and offers. Even the longest serving traders on Clitheroe market had never seen, nor had heard of business like it, not even in the markets heyday of the 1960's and 70's.

The Castle park children's play area was over run with happy children and sun bathing mothers sat all along the grass verges enjoying home made picnics and ice creams supplied by Purdy's ices, the traditional white and yellow ice cream van made so famous by Wednesday nights TV news footage.

At the very peak of the Castle Keep itself, soaring high above the town on its rocky limestone foundations, scores of families were enjoying the outstanding sights from the circular platform that surrounds the monument. The spectators were enjoying 360 degree panoramic views of Pendle Hill, the Trough of Bowland and the entire Ribble Valley landscape from the 900 year old defence look-out that was baking in bright, hot sunshine under a powder blue sky.

Laughter and excited noise filled the air all around Clitheroe. Market traders bellowed out their best offers at the top of their lungs as children were shouting and waving to their parents from the top of the Castle. The news crews were still in town and were all over the area, making much of the frivolity and high spirits – especially Sky News who were anchoring all of their output from various locations around the town centre.

Car parking was a huge problem and by early afternoon the towns surrounding streets and residential avenues were completely double parked with cars, adding extra pressure to the already crumbling road system which was failing to cope with such an enormous and unexpected influx of traffic.

Some drivers began to get vexed and irate, beeping their horns in frustration at the gridlock all around the town centre – but the mood was so buoyant that any horn blares were met with triumphant cheers. The tiny amount of hot and bothered, angry motorists couldn't spoil the festival atmosphere that had engulfed the town with an incredibly positive, friendly and happy vibe.

At Stansfield's sandwich shop on Castle Street, a crowd of hungry sightseers were queueing outside the business, which was adding even further confusion to the gridlocked roads as the queue reached out of the shop and onto the pavement alongside the pelican crossing. Cars slowed down to stop at the empty crossing as the sightseers waited in line for their food. Mischievous members of the queue then cheered when the car driver realised what was happening and pulled off again. It was annoying for the drivers, but tremendous fun for those who were passing the time until it was their turn to get inside and get served in the shop, that was very quickly running out of stock due to such astonishing demand.

The day's main headlines concerning the Jim Arkwright story were focused around the MP's vote on whether they were to stand behind a decision to elect Jim as their party leader, which was causing endless speculation amongst political advisors and commentators. This was a unique situation for the Members of Parliament to find themselves in, and for the media to report on.

Details began to emerge about the voting system which was being carried out. The vote was going to be done by recorded telephone conversation, personally undertaken by the Speaker of the House and his Deputy

Speakers. There were 650 MP's that needed to be spoken to and asked a simple yes or no question, by using only one sentence; "Do you, the Honourable Member of Parliament agree to wholeheartedly support Jim Arkwright as your Party Leader if he should be elected as a Member of this Parliament?"

The Houses of Parliament press office released no information other than the method in which the vote was taking place. It left the news people wildly trying to second guess when the survey of all 650 MPs would be finished – there was even a graphic produced that showed approximately how long each call would take to make, how many hours were being put into the task by the Speaker and Deputies, and allowing for missed calls at a ratio of ten per cent, the graphic suggested an announcement could be made late on Friday evening, or possibly Saturday if the Speaker and the Deputies were prepared to do the overtime into the weekend. It was a very reasonable prospect that the calls would continue into the weekend as this situation had been described as a matter of national urgency.

Sky News had been very keen to explore the facts surrounding Jim Arkwright's proposal to the MP's, which were made the previous afternoon in the Mock Off studio. They were continuously asking political commentators how he could get all of the three main parties MP's to agree to support him, when this would effectively mean that if all of them agreed to support him, there would be no political structure left in Parliament – just six hundred united MP's and fifty independent or smaller party representatives.

Sky News were trying to discover if such a level of support was even legal in Parliaments guidelines. Their researchers couldn't find any evidence to suggest that this vote was against any rules laid down in

Parliaments constitution. But never the less, it was such a peculiar situation, senior editors were desperate to try and work out how a united Parliament might look, and more importantly - how it would govern. It would certainly mean the end of the traditional left wing versus right wing political divide that had remained in place since Parliament began.

Chapter Twenty Seven
Friday Night – Preston Train Station

Albert arrived on the famous Victorian era railway concourse at Preston station with a few minutes to spare after driving around the local area until he had found a parking space down a side street, about a quarter of a mile from the station. This peculiarity of Albert's, his complete refusal to pay for parking costs was affectionately joked about throughout the family. He was often compared to being as tight as a drum, or a ducks arse, but he took no offence at any of the abuse he received about it. Albert remained resolute that paying a pound to put a car on a nine foot by six foot plot of concrete for an hour was tantamount to theft and would say "at least Dick Turpin wore a mask."

Many times through the years this conversation had come up, and many times people had tried to reason with Albert, but his response had been a total argument winner – he would take out his wallet and hand a ten pound note to his opponent and tell them to give it to the charity of their choice, clearing up the "too tight to pay" element of the discussion very early on in the debate.

Albert would then make clear his opinion by explaining that he paid his road tax, he paid his council tax and income tax, and on top of that he was forced to pay ridiculous sums of tax on petrol. There was no way, he'd say - that he would then pay to park the bloody thing after all that.

So in typical fashion, Jim and Karen would have a bit of a walk to the car once they had got off the train they'd been sat on for the previous two and a half hours from Euston station. Albert had reasoned to himself that they'd appreciate the chance to stretch their legs anyway.

Albert was quite shocked to find himself in a great mood. It had been a long time since he had felt so content. His son attracting all this positive attention had really made him proud, his house phone had never rung so much with calls from friends and relatives. It seemed everybody who knew Albert wanted to congratulate him on bringing up "such a star." It had all come as a wonderful antidote to the loneliness and depression he had been suffering from. Albert had tried desperately to hide it from Jim and Karen, but it had been totally obvious that he was struggling to accept life as a single man.

The Tenerife holiday was supposed to give Albert a change of scenery and take his mind off his grief. The break had helped to a certain degree, but this past few days had really been the tonic for him. It had been a fun time with his Grandkids, and Albert was really pleased about what an amazing forty eight hours had just passed. The kids had been so excited about everything, and it had been totally surreal for them watching their Dad on the television practically none stop.

Albert made his way down onto the huge platform and wandered up and down the concourse, whistling as he went, waiting for the London to Glasgow train to arrive. He chuckled to himself as he realised he was whistling a tuneless, made up nonsense as he walked along the platform. He hadn't felt happy for a very long time and he had never expected that he would again. But as he waited for the train to bring his famous son and beautiful daughter-in-law home, Albert suddenly felt as good as he could ever remember feeling.

Apart from the praise and congratulations calls, Albert had been mithered by the press pretty much none stop too. He'd had a few interesting offers which he was excited to talk to Jim and Karen about once they were making their way back to Clitheroe. There were some very large sums of money being talked about, vast sums that made Albert nervous just thinking about. He was looking forward to discussing it all and seeing the reaction from his lad.

A modern looking train began approaching the platform from the Manchester end of the station, and the station announcer confirmed that the next train to arrive at Platform 4 was the 19:47 to Glasgow.

Suddenly a group of photographers and film crews appeared out of the restaurant bar and jostled for position on the ramp at the top of the station concourse. Albert laughed to himself as he saw with his own eyes how keen the media were to catch a glimpse of his son, who was now known pretty much exclusively by the media's "Big Jim" tag.

Once the train had pulled in and the doors were opened, there was a great deal of confusion amongst the media crews as over 100 passengers got out onto the platform and started walking quickly towards them. Most looked quite bewildered by such a bizarre sight at Preston train station of all places.

Jim and Karen didn't appear to be amongst the mass of commuters who swarmed up the ramp and onto the bridge, eager to get to their waiting lifts and taxi's at the Fishergate car park entrance.

Karen had earlier arranged for her and Jim to meet Albert in the Upper Crust Café Bar on the platform, anticipating that the press would be crawling all over the station – if their experiences in London were anything to go by.

"Hiya Albert!" shrieked Karen as she ran over and gave her father-in-law a huge cuddle and a kiss on the cheek. It was obvious she was pleased to see him.

"Hi Dad, how's it going mate?" asked Jim as he too gave his father a strong, well meant hug right beside a table with some puzzled passengers looking on, a couple of whom instantly recognised Jim from the papers and TV.

"Oh, I'm great, absolutely great, thanks!" Albert looked really, really happy and both Jim and Karen noticed it straight away. It was a look that had been missing for a very long time and for his son and his daughter-in-law it was a beautiful sight to see Albert with a huge, genuinely beaming smile and eyes lit up full of life.

"Where are the kids?" asked Jim, visibly moved and quite tearful with joy at seeing his Dad looking so contented.

"Oh, I decided to keep them at home, I wanted to talk to you both. Joan from next door's sitting in with them." Albert grabbed Karen's bag and started to turn for the doors out onto the platform.

"Oh, by the way, there's a lot of press people waiting out there for you – I saw them getting ready as the train approached."

"Told you Albert! We've been followed all over the place by them. I thought I'd better warn you!" Karen smiled.

"Where are you parked Dad?" asked Jim. Karen saw the expression on Albert's face and began to snigger.

"Er, not so far son. Just up the road."

The three of them laughed as they made their way out of the railway café, onto the platform and headed up the platform towards the large sloping ramp area that takes passengers from the platform level to the bridge that connects the other platforms and the City centre.

The press crews noticed Big Jim headed their way and started chattering excitedly, starting their clicking and flashing and recordings, shouting the now familiar comments as the family approached. It was becoming quite familiar for Jim and Karen but Albert was totally disorientated by the bright popping lights.

"Christ, they're bright them. I can't see where I'm going," he complained as he reached out for Karen's arm as the cameras took their pictures just feet away from the family. The press were walking slowly backwards up the ramp way, incessantly flashing their cameras and shouting inaudible chants.

"Had a good time in London Big Jim?"

"Have you heard how the MP's have voted yet?"

"Welcome back to Lancashire Big Jim!"

All of the press people seemed to be shouting pleasant and positive things but it all just blended into a big mix of noise. Albert looked like he was seriously struggling and shielded his eyes.

"They're bloody strong flashes them. My eyes can't take it." Albert put his arm in front of his eyes, his other arm was linked to Karen's as he tripped and stumbled into one of the photographers who fell backwards onto his backside, almost taking another cameraman with him. Albert didn't go down, he just about managed to stay on his feet - but it was very close.

Jim saw what happened, concerned but relieved to see that Albert had managed to keep his footing. Jim reacted immediately.

"Right. RIGHT! Everyone stop taking pictures. STOP! Now!" He bellowed the order at the very top of his voice, it was loud and terrifying. Jim had a finger pointing at the press, and his body language was threatening. Nobody in the station was in any doubt of the request as the sudden, alarming noise made a family of pigeons flap suddenly and noisily fly out of the ancient cast iron roof eaves as Jim's shouting reverberated around the historic station. The cameramen did as they were told.

"Are you alright fellah?" Jim asked of his Dad. A single, defiant camera flash went off as he reached out to his Dad.

"I'm alright – just couldn't see nowt lad. Not to worry, I just didn't know where I was stepping." Jim patted his Dads shoulder and reached out to help the humiliated, disorientated looking photographer up onto his feet.

"Are you alright mate?" he asked. A look of unmistakable embarrassment was masking any pain that the man was feeling. He just nodded at Jim and said thanks quietly. Jim turned back to the rest of the press crew.

"Its hurting his eyes, that's my Dad. Just forget it now, you got your pictures. Call it a day now." Jim spoke loudly but without shouting. It was enough to let the thirty or so press hear his instruction calmly but clearly.

The media people looked as though Jim had placed a spell on them. They quietly retreated back, turned and started going away, muttering quietly and seemingly embarrassed amongst themselves. Jim couldn't quite believe his eyes. Within thirty seconds they had all disappeared.

"You alright Dad?"

"Yes, yes, absolutely fine now. Still got a few dots on my eyes but I'm alright. Hey, I'll tell you though, I was starting to panic a bit then." Albert was relieved it was all over, and a bit embarrassed at how vulnerable he'd been made to appear.

"How did you get them all to stop Jim? I've never seen anything like that before." Karen was clearly impressed at Jims no messing approach with the press.

"Aye, that were bloody weird that." Said Jim. "I didn't expect it to be that easy!"

As the three of them came out of the entrance onto Fishergate, a couple of press stragglers took a picture before awkwardly turning and walking off.

"Come on then Dad, let's start the hike to the car!"

"It's not that far, honestly." Albert chuckled to himself and Karen laughed too.

As they walked back at a steady pace, Karen and Jim spent the ten minutes describing the sights and places they'd seen in London. They talked about the stars they'd met and described the crazy situations they'd found themselves in.

Once the three of them had located Albert's trusty old Mondeo and had begun heading back along the A59 to Clitheroe, Albert felt that it was time that the conversation turned to the life altering announcement that had been made the previous day. As they got nearer to Clitheroe, this was the only opportunity he could see before getting home and spending time with the kids. He decided to change the topic from the celebrity fun and frolics, TV studio and hotel stories, and go straight in about the MP's.

"So, anyway, it looks like you're going to be the next Prime Minister before the years out!" Albert said it so casually, it almost sounded alien.

Jim was less than enthusiastic in his response.

"Come on Dad, not you as well? Let's just face

it, the whole stupid idea stops here. The MPs are not going to agree to some northern gob-shite like me coming in and changing three hundred years of history, so let's just agree that its been a good laugh, we've made about three hundred grand out of it, and now we just smile and nod and let it all fade out."

Jim wanted his Dad to see how unlikely it was that the MPs would return a vote in favour of the untried, untested man who claimed to have all the answers. But he was aware that he had to be ultra careful how delicately he put it as he didn't want to crush the obvious excitement and pleasure that his father was getting from it all.

Albert had a completely different point of view.

"Jim, you're missing the biggest detail out. It's a gamble for all of the MP's whichever way it goes. If they vote against you, they risk upsetting the public, and they'll not get voted in next time. But if they do vote for you to take over, they stand a chance of you choosing their party! So they probably will vote in agreement in order to save their own backsides, because with you in charge of their party – they'd be in Parliament a hell of a lot longer."

Jim considered Albert's theory for a minute or so.

"That's a bloody good point Dad. Jeez, I didn't think of that!"

"Well, self preservation is their best quality. They just voted themselves a thirty per cent pay rise, remember."

"Yes, because they can't take the piss as much with their expenses Dad!" Jim laughed mockingly at the embarrassing sordidness of it all.

"Well, like I say, you'll be able to sort all this

out – you'll be the next one in Number Ten lad. And you'll not have long to wait – the news said at tea time that the vote is taking place as a matter of national urgency, MP's are being phoned up one by one by the head honchos of Parliament and asked if its yes or no. They've been ringing MP's up all day apparently!"

"Does that mean he is going to be voted in then Albert?" asked Karen, not quite understanding any of this long and complicated process - mainly due to the fact that she had deliberately avoided any interest in politics throughout her whole life. Karen had always considered politics as boring, pointless and dull. With everything that was going on, she suddenly found herself trying to absorb a hell of a lot of complicated information.

"Well, put it this way love, I'll bet you a pound that Jim is voted for. That's all I'm saying!" Albert's eyes were filled with sparkle as he looked at Karen through the rear view mirror.

"Christ on a bike! He must be confident!" laughed Jim. "If he's prepared to lose a quid it must be serious!"

Albert turned off the A59 and onto Whalley Road. He took his eyes off the road momentarily and looked across at his son beside him in the passenger seat.

"Listen Jim, you can muck about all you want but I'm telling you, there's going to be a lot more of this to go yet, and you need to be ready."

Albert averted his vision back to the road.

"You've been saying since last weekend it'll all blow over, it'll all die down. Well it isn't doing, it's just getting bigger and bigger, just like Karen warned you it would. You need to start treating this seriously and get yourself prepared. If they come back in the morning and say yes, the MP's have agreed – they are going to ask you which party will you be standing as MP for? You need to be ready Jim."

"Aw come on now Dad, give me a break fellah. I've already said, its not going to happen so please just let me have a rest from it all! I've had a week of all this lot none stop. Can you just tell us about what the kids have been up to?"

"Yes, go on Albert! Have they been good? Did they miss us?" Karen was excitedly leaning forward and popping her head between Jim and Alberts.

"Course they've been good. They've not had a chance to miss you though, they've been too busy watching you both on the telly most of the time!"

"Seriously? Has it been that big?" asked Karen, with a real tone of surprise in her voice.

"It's the biggest news to do with politics in our lifetimes. Wait until you see how much press is parked up outside your house. You might be best coming back to mine tonight you know."

"Aw, I wanted my own bed!" pleaded Karen.

"Hey though, it's not all bad news. The newspapers are all queued up to buy your story Jim. There's a card from the Star who say they'll give you a hundred and twenty five grand for an exclusive interview."

"Shit! Where does all this money come from?"

Karen looked excited, Jim was enthusiastic to hear more, he could tell his Dad was leading up to something.

"The Sun said they'll pay you one hundred and fifty thousand."

"Shit!" said Karen once again. Jim laughed at her and looked around to the back seat. The dreamy expression on her face told Jim she was already spending it in her head.

"And the best offer you've got up to yet was two hundred grand from the Times. They all want an answer pretty quick too, they want the interview in the paper on Sunday."

"But its Friday now!" said Jim, trying to figure out how there was physically enough time.

"How do you know all this Albert?" asked Karen.

"Oh some beggar gave them all my phone number, I had them on from bloody ten o' clock last night! I pulled the wire out of the wall in the end. But I've written the messages down, I said I'd give them to you."

"And what about you Dad, have they tried interviewing you?"

"Yes. I wanted to speak to you about it. I wasn't sure what you wanted me to do."

"Albert, sorry to interrupt, but can you pull up at Tesco's for me?"

Karen remembered she wanted some bits as they approached the junction.

"No problem love," replied Albert.

"Oh, if you're going towards Tesco, I want to go and look at the railings – let's see how the professionals have done!" Said Jim,

"Right. Well you can have a quick look at that while I'm in Tesco but don't be all night!"

"Don't *you* be all night more like. You take half an hour in there just to get a bottle of wine. You're a gossip, that's why. What are you going in for anyway?"

"I'll grab a couple of pizzas to bung in the oven for supper."

Albert took a slight detour from his route and indicated to turn right towards the supermarket.

"Do you want some garlic bread with that?"

asked Karen tapping Jim on the shoulder.

"Garlic bread?" asked Jim in a confused voice.

"Garlic bread?" repeated Albert chuckling at the familiar joke.

"Garlic? On bread? No thanks love, not in my lifetime!" Jim was laughing as he said it, knowing that it really tickled his Dad. Albert was giggling away.

"Do you want some or not?" asked Karen.

"Yeah, go on then! Get the baguette ones though, I don't like the pizza ones."

"Right. Sorry Albert – I do appreciate this."

A minute later Albert pulled up in the car park, at the pelican crossing by the entrance to the store. Karen got out of the car.

"Cheers me dears" she said as she slammed the door shut.

Albert and Jim both looked at each other and quietly said "don't slam the door" as they always did when Karen got out, then laughed. Albert crossed over the pelican and turned the trusty old motor back towards the car park entrance.

"Right, that'll be her for an hour, talking to half the town in there. We should have said we'll meet her back at home."

"Oh leave her alone. It's exciting for the lass."

"Anyway, go on Dad, what were you saying? You'd had an interview?"

"Oh, yes. I got sidetracked. Yes, well I haven't had one, I was offered one. Twenty thousand quid!"

"Twenty grand? There's some mad money flying about Dad! I went on The Morning yesterday and got a grand a minute! Twenty grand for twenty minutes! I'll tell you, we'll be getting that conservatory now, no mistake!"

"Aye, that's a lot of money. So what do you

think?"

"About doing the interview? I can't believe you haven't done it. Why haven't you?"

"Oh, I just thought I'd check with you, make sure you were happy with it."

"Course I am Dad, Jesus man, just get in there, grab as much brass off them as you can get hold of."

Albert looked quite surprised that Jim was so laid back about the press. He pulled the car over at Peel Street car park and got out with Jim, who was keen to see how the second part of the railings job had gone. Jim had planned to come and have a proper inspection first thing the following morning, but for how he was just relieved to see that the job appeared to be completed.

"Nice one. Job done! That's great that. I doubt I'll get any more work off them though Dad." Jim certainly looked pleased with what he saw.

"What's Karen doing?" asked Albert as he noticed his daughter-in-law walking along the road towards them. She was empty handed.

"That didn't take long!" shouted Albert in Karen's direction.

"Where's the pizza?" bellowed Jim.

"And the garlic bread?" chuckled Albert.

"There's none left." Said Karen as she approached the pair who were standing by the new railings, close to where Tim Dixon had come and disrupted everything a few days earlier.

"There's nothing left in the whole shop except shaving stuff, cat food and soap powder! Everything food and drink wise has been sold. The staff don't know what to do, they're all just stood about talking."

"Eh? What do you mean there's nowt left?" asked Jim, he couldn't believe what Karen was saying.

He stood there beside the school railings shaking his head, he had a confused smirk on his face, as though he was waiting for the punchline.

"There's no bread, no frozen stuff, no drinks, no booze. The place is practically empty!"

Chapter Twenty Eight
Saturday Morning

All of the national morning papers had been carrying Jim Arkwright's exploits on their front pages since Wednesday. A couple of them had started on Tuesday, following Jim's triumphant radio appearance.

Although the papers were today focused on the "Great British Street Party" and some even printed fold-out union flag posters in their centre pages, to be used as table cloths – it seemed that the media people had finally started to get their head around the situation now. They were beginning to calm down and write or report more of a measured and less hysterical response to Jim Arkwright's sudden and blistering popularity amongst the British people.

Several papers were running in depth analysis on the topics that Jim had covered so far. They listed arguments for and against on complicated political debates such as remaining a part of the European Union, bringing back capital punishment and the legalization of drugs. Other topics such as immigration, crime and punishment, unemployment, education, welfare and the economy were all tackled with excellent reports analysing the pro's and con's of Jim Arkwright's ideas.

There was no opposition in any of the papers, but reports were balanced and listed a fair account of both arguments for each topic, leaving the reader at liberty to make their own mind up.

Journalists and editors from all sides of the media seemed besotted by this new, common as muck "politician of the people." Even if his views weren't necessarily shared by the all of the reporters, or all of the public for that matter - it was still a hell of a news story, and the press were determined to help it reach its full potential, whatever that may be.

On the internet however, voices of doubt and concern were becoming louder and more obvious. Facebook was continuing to see a small percentage of anti-Jim comments, though very few held much merit for grammar, let alone depth of thought.

"Face it Jim your a fuckin knob" was about as structured as most posts got. Through links posted on Twitter, blogs and online articles of a more ordered nature were receiving good audience figures as a growing number of people became intrigued by the small, but noisy anti-Jim people.

One Blogger, going by the anonymous moniker of "Reason Able" had managed to attract a steady audience of readers to his or her blog by blitzing Twitter with links to the "Reason Able" blog page using hashtags that ranged from complimentary to downright nasty, launching personal attacks against Jim's policy ideas, his broad Lancashire accent and his physical appearance. Reason Able's most recurring theme against Big Jim's ideas and policies was based around the fact that he lived in the Ribble Valley, which was one of the UK's least deprived areas, with practically full employment, excellent education statistics, low crime figures and with way above average health in its population.

"How can this bigot preach to us about anything when he lives in a part of Britain that comes out of a fucking fairytale?" asked the critic in caps lock. "Why are people listening to this fucking pub bore? He's just a piss head, one clue is the pint of beer he's constantly holding." The rants went on and on, all of which followed that kind of angry, venomous tone.

But even for the most cynical of people, Jim

Arkwrights sudden rise to fame, and the excitable reporting of his views brought a refreshing change to the usual dreary, unproductive, argumentative and senseless political news. Jim Arkwright's almost universal popularity was beginning to cause the press and broadcasters legal headaches though. Seasoned journalists were actively, continuously trying to find legitimate voices against Jim Arkwright and his ideas – but it was proving a tall order. The difficulty journalists and broadcasters knew they would soon face was in trying to report this story in a balanced way, which is the legal requirement where political reporting is concerned. It wasn't a major breach of the rules at present, while Jim was unelected and remained independent of any particular party. But if and when he was elected as an MP, reporting on Jim Arkwright's A-list popularity was going to be an extremely difficult task.

Jim himself was in a bad mood. The press had been incredibly inconsiderate, making ridiculous amounts of noise all night long outside the house. The letter box had been slamming shut as new letters and offers were posted through. The six huge media trucks that were taking up the whole length of Jim's street were running their power generators which had been humming and rattling all night long. The house phone had been ringing none stop until it was unplugged – then Karen and Jim's mobiles had to be switched off and then even Jonathan and Lucy's mobile phones had needed to be switched off.

The media people had somehow managed to get their hands on the children's phone numbers. This fact disturbed Karen and Jim greatly, but the whole situation with the press was becoming a major pain and was finally wearing Jim down.

He put it down to being tired after the lack of sleep he'd had through the week and tried to go for his Saturday morning jog. To his frustration and total confusion he found that media cars were following and filming him as he jogged off down Edisford road towards the river. He felt as though his life was just turning into some strange documentary. Jim tried to carry on but realised how ridiculous he must look. He gave it up and walked down a path to the river to lose the cars that were tagging beside him.

When he'd got back after a brief jog home through the nearby village of Waddington, Jim found that he was struggling to get through the swarms of media camped all along his road and crowding around the bottom of the drive.

"Where are you holding your street party Big Jim?" shouted one reporter as Jim tried to push through the hundred strong crowd of press and curious onlookers.

"Not here, am I?" replied Jim snappily, looking totally despondent and tired. Since his protest at the school railings four days earlier this would be the first time that Jim Arkwright would have appeared looking anything other than a laid back, happy go lucky family man. In this footage, he looked agitated and far from relaxed.

Karen had planned to go out with the kids in the family car and it took almost five minutes of photographers shouting questions and flashing their bulbs through the windows before the assembled pack finally moved and allowed enough room for Karen to reverse out of her own driveway.

Jim had watched the shambles unfold and it made his blood boil. In his view, he and his wife had been more than accommodating. For the life of him he couldn't understand the need for such an aggressive and over zealous approach from the press. It just seemed over the top and unnecessary. Despite his fury, Jim had somehow managed to stay inside and watch from the window. He knew that if he'd have gone outside, he would have lost his temper.

It seemed that the mood of the press was changing with each passing day. The already intense media coverage had progressively built up to fever pitch and it was now becoming a major intrusion into the Arkwright family's life. Jim had supplied such extraordinary coverage throughout the week – he was now unwittingly becoming a victim of his own success.

Since Tuesday, he had managed to supply unforgettable television almost every time that a TV camera had been pointed on him, the demand to film him had grown quite organically to this present, unmanageable level.

Lucy had been the first to celebrate the mass media coverage of her parents – but the tide now seemed to be turning and she was becoming sick of it. Her friends too were starting to get bored of the constant coverage of their friends parents and the "awesomeness" was beginning to turn stale.

Jonathan wasn't too bothered by all of the media on his doorstep – he was a very laid back young man who took things in his stride. For Jonathan, this was a really interesting and exciting experience and he especially loved the fact that his lime green bike that was leant up against the front porch had become the most famous BMX in the land, due to the television coverage it was receiving.

Victoria, the youngest of the family didn't really care either way. She was more concerned that the "design-a-home" bedroom she had put together on the computer hadn't saved properly and that she would have to start it all over again.

Clitheroe's wider community were revelling in all of the sudden media interest, and the positives of becoming the most famous little town in Great Britain were far outweighing the negatives. Local businesses had seen a boom in business, local people had rejoiced with a renewed sense of pride and passion for their town – and with the sweeping, beautiful shots of the landscape and its incredible panoramic views of the idyllic Ribble Valley, the area was gaining millions upon millions of pounds worth of completely free tourism publicity.

With the house to himself, Jim had intended to chill out for a few hours, and maybe nod off on the settee listening to Pick of the Pops on the radio, as he did most Saturdays. Other than that, Jim had made no concrete plans for the rest of the day and was hoping to just spend the time relaxing and taking it easy.

It occurred to Jim as he made himself a cup of tea, that it was exactly a week ago that Lucy had shouted at him to come and look at the video on the internet. The thought gave him a jolt. It seemed so long ago now, so much had happened. It really had been the world's longest week. Jim stared out of the window, daydreaming about the past seven days, and for the first time, he began thinking seriously about the money that this crazy week had generated the family.

The excitement he began to feel about the money perked his mood up a little and he decided to have a little bit of fun to cheer himself up.

The previous night Albert had given Jim a piece of paper with the names of various journalists and the cash sums they had offered to pay for an exclusive interview. Jim plugged his telephone back into the socket and the phone began ringing immediately. It made Jim jump.

He answered it. "Hello?"

"Jim. Is that you? My name is Tom Horsefield from the Tribune. We're, well I'm just phoning to ask if you…"

"Nah, sorry mate." Jim put the phone down. He left it a second and then lifted it back up to put to his ear, ready to dial the number he had on the piece of paper in front of him. The line was still open.

"Hello, hello?" said the caller –Tom, from a paper that Jim had never even heard of.

"Here mate, put the phone down. I'm trying to make a phone call."

"I'm, I'm just phoning to ask you a few questions about the…"

"I'm not answering the question mate. Get off the line will you." Jim's voice was getting louder as his irritation grew.

"I'll get off the line in a minute Jim, but I just need to ask you a few questions first."

"Listen mate," snapped Jim, "You better put the fucking phone down and clear my line because I'm trying to ring out."

"I'll hang up when you've answered my questions, come on Jim, give me a break I've been ringing this number since seven o clock this morning."

"Mate, you are seriously pissing me off. Just put the fucking phone down, now!" Jim realised he was shouting down the receiver. His adrenaline was pumping, and he could feel that his blood pressure was rising to a dangerous level.

"Can you not just answer my questions and I'll clear the line."

Jim felt that he was going to either smash the

phone to bits or burst into tears out of sheer frustration. He placed the phone down on its cradle and sat down on the sofa, staring out of the window fruitlessly at the Castle Keep on the horizon. A single tear rolled down his cheek, which he wiped away quickly.

"What a fucking dick." He muttered. There was a knock at the door and a voice shouted through the letterbox.

"Jim, this is Graham Appleton, Daily Mirror. Let me in now, I've got a cheque here for a quarter of a million quid for you." Graham Appleton had a recognisable voice, a very well known journalist and columnist, mainly thanks to his popular current affairs television series on the BBC. Jim hadn't seen or heard of Graham in any of the press packs that he'd encountered all week so assumed he must have only just got involved with the story.

"Make it half a million, and I'll let you in," shouted Jim. There was a brief pause. Then the letterbox lifted again.

"I can go to that figure. If you can just let me in now, and we can discuss everything."

"Put the cheque through for half a million and I'll let you in mate."

A minute passed before the letterbox lifted up again. A cheque landed on the welcome mat, made out to J Arkwright, for the sum of £500,000. Jim couldn't believe it was for real. He went and opened the door, and let Graham in. He was a fat, slightly greasy man, but he had a warm, trustworthy face. Jim felt a bit like he already knew him from watching so much of his stuff on the telly.

"How do you do Jim?" asked the seasoned journalist as Jim shook his hand.

"Hiya mate. I'm alright, getting worn out with

all this media shit to be honest. It wears you down after a bit. Do you want a brew?" Jim was holding the cheque, staring at all the zero's. The moment was too surreal for Jim to take it in.

"Please, yes, I'll have a coffee. You'll have to get used to the media camping outside wherever you are from now on Jim. This is just going to be the norm."

"Really? Bollocks to that, I'll be busting peoples lips. I've had a guy there on the phone – won't let me ring out on my own phone! He's keeping the line open. What an absolute wanker!" Jim was wandering into the kitchen as he spoke, putting the kettle on.

"Well, that's the way things are going to be. You'll soon get used to it!" Graham laughed as Jim returned.

"Coffee you said didn't you?"

"Yes thanks, one sugar plenty milk, thanks."

"Well, anyway, what do I have to do for this cheque then?"

"Oh, right. Well, we want to run a week long serialisation of your story. So I'll just need to hang about with you, have exclusive access to you between now and Friday."

"Bloody Norah. That sounds a bit full on mate. What do you mean by having exclusive access? You're not watching me having a shite."

Graham laughed. "Well, you know – I'll become your right hand man, wherever you go, whatever you do – except shitting, or shagging."

"Right, deal. Is there a contract or anything I need to sign?"

"Yes, I'll sort all that stuff out. Main rule is you don't talk to another paper or broadcaster without my say so, or the deals off."

"Fair enough. Did you say two sugars?"

"One. Cheers."

Chapter Twenty Nine
Saturday Lunchtime

At The Day newspaper offices in East London, the editor Julia Grantham was more than disappointed by the news that was coming back from Clitheroe. One of her reporters outside the Arkwright residence had phoned to say that Graham Appleton from the papers closest rival had gained access into Jim Arkwright's house, and hadn't come back out.

"You're telling me a fucking lie!" She shouted. "We've offered two hundred and fifty thousand grand to that fucker! Right – well, if he's not going to be our story for next week we'll have to go with plan B then."

"Plan B?" asked the reporter, eager to know what the next move was.

"Oh, don't worry about that, you're not involved with plan B. You'll just have to buy the paper in the morning!"

*****

Rolling-news staff were still feverishly reporting on the Big Jim story. If anything, the press interest was now reaching its peak, as crews from overseas had also cottoned on and realised that a major story was unfolding.

All of the media crews were convinced that an announcement about the MP's vote was due imminently. Television reports were to'ing and fro'ing from the media packs assembled outside the Houses of Parliament, complete with Big Ben in the background - to the media teams that were up north.

Clitheroe was over run with news vans and reporters. Teams from all over the world were either reporting from Jim's street, from outside the New Inn or from various places dotted around the town centre –

including a crew outside Banana News, another at Castle Chippy. Another team were situated at the Castle Keep with Pendle Hill as their dramatic backdrop. There was a Japanese crew who were sending their reports back to the Far East from the Bus Stop outside The White Lion pub in Marketplace, with the town's library clock as their backdrop.

It was beginning to get annoying for the television viewers all around the country who just wanted to know the result. All the television and radio reporters ever seemed to be saying was "we're expecting an announcement very shortly."

They had been saying that practically none stop since the previous night. The obvious lack of new information was becoming very frustrating, considering the sheer enormity of the decision and how much was hanging in the balance.

There was an infectious, growing excitement amongst the British people that justice was about to be seen – that there was finally, incredibly going to be a Prime Minister who actually "got" real life; who genuinely understood day to day living in modern day Britain. It seemed beyond belief that an ordinary man, who went to an ordinary school, who came from ordinary working class parents was this close to seizing power. Never before had an average citizen been able to influence politics in such a glorious way.

Big Jim Arkwright was just a normal man who could see what was wrong with society. He said it as it was, as though he was describing a faulty vacuum cleaner and advising how to get it working better. The thing that made the public so enthusiastic was the very real possibility that this man who talked like them, thought like them and behaved like them could actually become their Prime Minister. This was more exciting than any developing news story that the British people had ever witnessed.

It was punishing work waiting, and waiting – not knowing how much longer they would be waiting until the result was announced. It really seemed that the whole nation were desperate to hear the news, and throughout the land, people were feeling a tense, stressful sensation of nerve jangling anticipation.

*****

In between reports from Clitheroe or London, the TV and radio news channels were padding for time with vox pops and videos from all around the UK. There were hundreds of crews on standby from every network imaginable, waiting to hear about street party's starting, which they had been tasked with reporting from.

On Sky News, a live report showed a group of about twenty young ladies wearing plain white T shirts that said VOTE BIG JIM in huge black letters, copying the simple design of the 1980's "Frankie Says" t shirts. The ladies were making their voice heard for the MP's who were supposedly still voting. The women were laughing, smiling and singing as they were shown marching through Bristol City Centre chanting a supportive song to the tune of "You'll never walk alone." The gang of ladies were making a hell of a noise as they marched past the camera crew singing "Please vote for Jim on the phone" as the correspondent tried to talk back to the studio over the racket.

In Edinburgh, Birmingham, Hull, Cornwall and Belfast, similar scenes were unfolding on live TV – the British public seemingly wanted to give one last big push and let the MP's know how strongly they felt about Big Jim.

Parliaments press office staff had never been so busy, even at the height of the MP's expenses scandal. They were taking calls from the public, from press, senior politicians and even members of the royal family. All enquiries were asking the same question; when will the result be announced? The press office remained tight lipped, and phone operatives read out a general comment; "in the interests of democracy, no announcement will be made at all until the official result has been verified." The reason for releasing such a pointless disclaimer was that they simply did not know themselves.

The media were adding fuel to the fire, keeping the nervous, excited pressure on the department. But it was obvious to everybody who contacted them, regardless of how nail bitingly nerve jangling and frustrating it all was – that no announcement was coming. No hints, clues or exclusives were going to be given away, and no amount of interference or impatience could affect that simple fact.

Because MP's were not permitted to talk to anybody about the vote until after it was all over – it seemed that the public would just have to sit it out and wait patiently, and television and radio news reporters would just have to come up with other topics to discuss to pass the time.

BBC Radio Five Live had been running a programme throughout the morning asking listeners if they were having street parties, and if so, how were the preparations going. It made a great programme as scores of listeners enthusiastically and passionately described how simple it had been to arrange their street party, and how "up for it" the whole community had been. Callers talked of endless examples of good will and kind gestures that were being seen in streets and neighbourhoods throughout the land, spurred on even more by the crisis caused by the supermarkets running out of stock.

Indeed, it wasn't good news for everybody, and the news that the vast majority of Britain's supermarkets had run out of food the previous day was just as bizarre and unbelievable as the rest of the story surrounding the Clitheroe Prime Minister. A spokesman for the British Supermarket Standards Agency had been all over the media reports since the previous afternoon, pleading with people not to panic buy.

"We have instances of people just going totally over the top. One woman in Doncaster bought forty eight, two litre bottles of Coca Cola. We are not trying to spoil people's fun," he said, "but we do need shoppers to buy things responsibly."

Normally in the lead up to busy party periods such as Bank Holidays, Christmas, New Year and major football events, supermarkets are able to plan ahead and build up huge stock piles of their most popular products. But Big Jim's street party idea had come completely out of the blue and the supermarkets had been cleared out, almost within hours, partly due to their twenty four hours a day operation.

The logistics required for the restocking of all of the nation's supermarkets were not clear. Nothing like this had ever happened before – and the national networks of supermarkets were sold out of alcohol, soft drinks, wine, biscuits, crisps, sweets, chocolate, frozen foods, sandwich foods, tinned foods and fresh bakery items. One experienced member of staff at Telford's Tesco had described the previous day of mad buying as "like one hundred Christmas Eves in a single day!"

The senior management teams of all

supermarket chains had no idea where to start in restocking their stores and urgent meetings were being organised between all supermarket chiefs and the government's emergency planning committee to discuss the strategic nightmare that lay ahead. It was not an exaggeration that it would take several months before the nations supermarkets were back up and running at their normal standard.

*****

Shortly after 12 noon, the nation's streets began turning into no-go areas for cars. Wheelie bins were pulled to the ends of streets by children – hand written signs saying "road closed – street party!" were stuck on the temporary barricades. Mums and Dads were walking out into their streets with the kitchen table, random kids were wandering about with neighbours chairs and bowls of jelly, while old couples were struggling out into the street with their dining tables.   Neighbours that had never previously spoken to each other before were now walking in and out of each others houses, carrying bottles of pop, big bowls of crisps, trays full of sandwiches and arms full of cakes. Everybody was on their best behaviour and people looked determined that they were going to have a good time.

The same scene was being repeated throughout Britain. In an unprecedented show of solidarity and public support – the whole nation seemed to be doing as they had been asked and were dragging their tables out into their streets. Jim Arkwright's supporters were showing their backing by embracing their local community, getting to know their neighbours and seemingly being glad of the opportunity to do it.

More than anything, there was a positive

attitude reverberating around the UK, people seemed happy to have been given this brilliant opportunity to make new friends and to have a good time doing it.

Neighbourhoods were still in the process of setting up their own event, but early indications were showing that this was a very popular idea, and everyone was up for their own street party. No matter which town or city you went to, it looked like it would be a hard job to locate a street that was not participating in this completely chaotic but admirable spectacle.

Chapter Thirty
Saturday 1pm – Jims House

Inside the Arkwright house, Graham was interviewing Jim about his childhood in the area. Everything that Jim was saying was being recorded on a dictaphone that the journalist had placed on the living room table, but Graham was still writing down notes in short hand. Throughout this first part of Grahams interview there was constant knocking at the door, dozens of journalists were visiting one by one, shouting various questions through the letterbox.

"Have you got a minute, Jim?"

"Have you heard anything from Parliament yet Jim?

"Which street party are you attending Jim?"

If the idea was to wear Jim down, and make him come out to satisfy the media crews, it might have worked if Graham wasn't on hand to explain the tactic.

The doorbell sounded twice in quick succession. Jim assumed it was just another visit from the press and ignored it as he had been doing since arriving home the previous night. But then Dave and Phil appeared at the front room window, staring in with their hands beside their faces, pretending they couldn't see anyone.

"Nope, there's no one in there Phil," shouted Dave, staring through the glass directly at Jim. Graham looked puzzled but Jim laughed and stood up to let his mates in. As soon as he opened the door his pals burst in.

"Booths have run out of beer and wine!" shouted Dave. "And we are holding you personally bloody responsible!"

"Tesco's and Sainsburys have closed the shops down – they've put signs in the windows saying they should be back open on Monday."

Phil was talking quickly and excitedly, like an old gossip at the Bingo.

"There was even a queue to get in Spar this morning." Added Dave. "That bloke with the dirty fingernails was only letting folk in two at a time."

"Look at all this chaos you've caused Jim!" said Graham, chuckling. Jim just laughed.

"Cor, bloody hell – its Graham Appleton! What are you doing here?" asked Dave.

"Shiver me timbers, so it is. Alright mate?" asked Phil.

"I'm good, thanks. I'm just writing an article about Jim. In fact we were just about to break off there."

"Oh, right well sorry to intrude Graham, sorry Jim, but as we can't go for a pint anywhere with our mate, and we can't even phone up, me and Phil decided to go and buy a few beers and come and have a few here with you." Dave was explaining to both Jim and Graham.

"Except, there's no beer left anywhere!" said Phil.

"But then, I cast my mind back to your garage being full of beer after the New Year party!" said Dave, grinning at the very cheek of his suggestion.

"Oh aye, its still got plenty left in there men. Let's go and have a gander. Come on."

The four men excitedly ventured out onto the drive, Jim tippy toeing on the gravel drive in just his socks. The press crews were taking photos of Jim and his pals and the famous journalist looking through several piles of alcohol that were piled up in the garage. There were crates of lager, cases of alco-pops and boxes of wine all across the work surface at the back. Eventually Jim found what he was looking for, there were two trays of bottled Timothy Taylor's ale hidden behind a crate of Fosters. Phil grabbed one pack and Graham grabbed the other.

"Right, let's get pissed." Said Dave, rubbing his hands together as the jubilant men emerged from the garage laughing and joking, and headed back towards the house.

"Put telly on Jim, put the news on – let's see all these street parties you've told folk to have!"

"You mad bastard Jim!"

Jim was suddenly feeling back to normal again. After a completely weird week, he'd begun feeling quite down and overwhelmed earlier. But with his two mates and his real ales, he could feel his spirits lifting – suddenly Jim felt ready to face anything again.

"Cheers!"

"Cheers!"

The men all sat down and started watching the rolling coverage of the street parties that were now in full flow.

"Where's Karen and the kids?" asked Dave.

"Oh she's gone to Sarah's, it's a bit of a headache here for them so they're at the party on Sarah's street. Do us a favour Dave, ring me Dad up on your mobile and tell him to come over and watch this with us if he's not doing nowt else."

As the four men watched the telly and enjoyed the beer, the mood in the Arkwright house was becoming ecstatic. The room would erupt with laughter at footage of Mums getting pushed in paddling pools by kids, Grannies dancing, toddlers wandering around with "Big Jim rules O.K." t shirts.

There was also plenty of scope for the pals and their celebrity drinking partner to make sarcastic comments when news presenters would interrupt people's parties to ask completely pointless questions like "sorry to interrupt your fun, but we're just wondering if you're having a great time?"

It was made abundantly clear from the footage on all the news channels – this idea had been a major success. If this had been what Jim had imagined when he had asked the public to hold this party – he must have been delighted with the results. Across the country, old arguments were being settled, new truces were being made. Neighbours who had always "got on" were making commitments to do more – planning days out, and evenings in together.

Everywhere in Britain – from the Isle of Man to Skegness, from Dundee to Portsmouth the streets were full of people promising each other that they would do this more often. All around the British Isles the air was filled with laughter, joy and positivity.

Sky News were showing how differently the parties ranged from area to area. Some streets had the full bunting up from house to house, there were streets that had DJ equipment and dancing competitions for all the family, others had paddling pools and water fights. There were streets being shown that had huge posh marquee's erected and celebrities mingling with the local community.

Other parties were much more humble, one showed a small row of pebble dashed council bungalows in Teeside with just a few deck chairs taken outside. There was a few old ladies chatting away over a pot of tea and a plate of chocolate digestives – but even that demonstrated that the people had responded to this idea enthusiastically. The nation's streets were buzzing with the general public having a great time in their own way, in their own neighbourhoods. Young people were speaking to older generations, white people were talking to Asians, professional people were chatting with their unemployed neighbours.

If this was what life under Big Jim Arkwright was going to be like, it was quite apparent that the people of Great Britain were glad that they had been given this taster, and they now felt even more involved in the process and passionate about Big Jim than ever.

BBC One had suspended normal programming to report on the street parties. A reporter was interviewing a young woman at a street party in Manchester, and when asked if she had a message for Big Jim, she lifted up her top and shouted "marry me Jim!" The screen was filled for several seconds with the giggling woman's naked breasts as her mates all laughed hysterically – quite unique footage for the UK's most popular channel in the middle of a Saturday afternoon.

The gesture got a huge laugh in Jim's front room. The reporter looked completely embarrassed as he stared at the woman's chest and began apologising to viewers. The screen turned to a test card image for a second before the studio newsreader came back on.

"Our apologies there, obviously the high spirits are getting a little *too* high in Manchester. Let's talk now to our South Yorkshire correspondent Helen Crossley who's attending a street party in Sheffield."

Albert arrived as the men were laughing and joking about the women on the telly.

"What have I missed he asked?" as he let himself in.

"Hi Dad – some woman just flashed her tits on the telly – asking me to marry her!" Everyone laughed again. Albert smiled as he sat down between Graham and Dave on the settee.

"Want a beer Dad?"

"Aye, please. The shops have run out, I might have known you'd have some in you bloody alkie." Albert's comment got a laugh from everyone – and Graham introduced himself to Jim's father. Jim got up and poured Albert a pint as Phil grabbed the TV remote and changed the channel to Sky News and saw a street party taking place in Clitheroe – unmistakably because of the Castle Keep that had become such an instantly recognisable and iconic structure over the past week.

The screen was filled with over two hundred happy, laughing people of all different age groups participating in a shambolic conga, weaving past dining tables and patio chairs up and down the length of Highfield Road.

"This is just unbelievable Jim!" announced Dave, awestruck at the images.

"Aye, you can say that again," added Albert.

"I know, its amazing, I can't believe it!" said Jim, the pride was obvious on his face, he looked absolutely delighted and overwhelmed with the footage that was coming in from all around the UK on BBC, Sky, CNN, CNBC, Fox and EuroNews as the channel was being changed every few minutes.

"You know what, I bet they've already got the vote back – but they won't reveal it while all this lot is going on. Imagine if it's a no from the MPs? These streets will be burnt down!"

It was a good point that Phil made. Jim was staring at the screen intently, he recognised so many faces in the conga line up – and he realised that he was grinning like an idiot.

"I doubt that they have got it back yet," said Graham. "To phone up six hundred and fifty people is a tall order. If there are only four people doing it, that's more than a hundred and fifty folk they have each got to phone. I don't think it's going to be finished today." Graham took a sip of his beer.

"No – Jim said that all of the MP's had to agree. So surely the moment than an MP has said no – it's the end of the vote isn't it?"

"A good point. I didn't think of that Dave!" said Jim.

"Well, they'd still have to phone all of them. They couldn't just ring three and then if the third one said no, call it off – they'd want to see how the MPs voted. Besides," said Graham, "It wouldn't matter if independents or members of the minority parties said no – Jim is only allowed to stand for one of the three main parties – Labour, Tory or Liberal."

"Shit, yes – that's a good point that Graham – I thought it was pretty obvious that Emily O' Hara would say no – just to spite Jim after he tore her a brand new arsehole the other day." Dave's statement received a huge laugh, so much so it brought tears of joy to Jim's eyes.

"Well, listen guys," said Jim after he'd stopped laughing at the vulgarity of Dave's last comment. "If, and it's a big if mind, – if the MP's did say it was a goer – that I could stand for one of the parties and become leader – I'd be turning it down."

Albert, Phil, Dave and Graham stopped concentrating at the street parties on the TV and turned to look at Jim. This was a big shock. Jim was saying that he'd be turning down the biggest opportunity of his life, one that he had personally dictated the terms of just two days earlier.

"No – don't say nowt," said Jim, raising one hand in the air. "Hear me out." The others looked on with a range of curious, concerned and puzzled expressions. Jim grabbed the remote off Dave and turned the volume down.

"If the vote comes back as a yes – you'll just have to wait and see what I do. But what I need from you three," he pointed to Albert, to Dave and then Phil. "I need your backing to the absolute max. No shitting about – I'm talking about full support."

Jim was talking in riddles, mainly because he didn't want to reveal the full details of what he was thinking in front of Graham Appleton. Albert, Phil and Dave couldn't really understand what Jim was on about.

"You know you always have our support anyway, Jim." Said Albert.

"No, I didn't have your support just then when I said I wasn't doing it, I could tell from your faces."

"Look Jim, just cut the bullshit! What are you saying?" Dave looked like he had no time for enigma.

"I can't really go into it now – no offence Graham, but it's not really something I want to discuss in front of you."

"Why?" asked Graham.

"Because…" Jim realised that he had to think for a minute about the answer to that question. "Well, I'm not sure really. Its just I don't know you do I? I know all these knobs – and their advice is important to me."

"Oh fucking shut up Jim and say what you want to say!" Dave was raising his voice.

"Right then, okay. Listen – if I did get voted in, which I still maintain that I won't do – but if – then I'm not standing for any of the three main parties."

"But they're the terms Jim. That's what all the voting is about."

"I know – but I've not slept last night, been up all night thinking about this. The problem with

Britain's politics are the bloody political parties. I'm starting a new party. I know I can do it, look at the support people are showing me. It won't be left wing, it won't be right wing. If those MP's say I can be their leader – I'm going to tell them I will, but they'll have to join a new political party – a party that isn't just trying to change and adapt to win votes, I'm on about a brand new party that doesn't just exist to have an opposite point of view from other parties – this will be a genuinely new party that does the right thing, that fights for good, battles for common sense, rewards its people, punishes wrong doing. I'm going to tell the MP's that if they want me as their leader – they have to resign from their buckled, broken political party and join mine!"

"That is a brilliant idea Jim!" said Phil. "It solves all the problems!"

Jim spent the next five minutes explaining the logistics of his idea. He told his small but captive audience that all the MP's would have to do is resign from their current political party, join as a member of the new party, and they would remain a Member of Parliament until the next election. At that election they would have to stand as a candidate for the new party. In Jim's opinion, this would be the biggest and best opportunity to start a brand new political party that would be able to do away with all of the nonsense and tradition that had helped to corrupt British politics and make the MP's so ineffective against Britain's main problems.

"This is genius Jim. Really, this would work!" It was Graham Appleton who was speaking. "What are you calling the party, Jim?"

"Oh, that's easy – that's the first thing I came up with. I'm going to call it the Crisis Party. Right, glad that's all sorted. Shall I sort us out something to eat?"

After a few more bottles of Timothy Taylor's, a home made dinner of egg and chips, and a couple more hours of watching the phenomenal footage from all around the street parties – the small but very merry group of men in Big Jim's sitting room were having a great afternoon.

Graham Appleton felt as though he had known these people for years and was genuinely enjoying the good natured, down to earth company he was keeping. The thought was interrupted as Grahams phone dinged with a new text message. Throughout the day Graham had been receiving texts from colleagues informing him of any developments that were taking place with the story. The latest one was significant. The well known television presenter read it aloud to Jim, Albert, Dave and Phil.

"Hey, guys listen up - Just got this from my editor – it says "Speaker just seen outside Parliament talking to press officer, results expected shortly, setting up press conference on Downing Street now" so it looks like we're pretty close to finding out!"

The news was greeted with an almighty cheer by Phil, Albert and Dave – though it made Jim suddenly need to use the toilet. The announcement churned his insides around, his tummy felt like it was a washing machine load that had suddenly gone onto spin cycle.

"Shit!" he said as he quickly stood and left the room.

"God, I feel really nervous now!" said Albert.

"Same," said Phil. "I think Jim is as well!"

A few minutes passed, the mood had changed from relaxed and jokey to tense and slightly irritable. The toilet flushed and Jim came back downstairs. He looked pail and quite worried.

"Jesus. Anymore news?" he asked Graham.

"No, not yet. It could be an hour or so yet Jim, these things always drag out. But it's great that we can finally see the finishing line though, eh?"

The question made Jims stomach flip around again. He was starting to feel sick.

"Listen Jim, if you want me to help you with your announcement, I can write something for you and e-mail it to the right people. I've got my laptop with me."

"Yes, that's a good idea! Lets do one for if they say yes, and one for no."

"Bloody hell Jim, are you soft in the head? Its pretty obvious they're going to say yes." Dave looked like he was getting himself worked up.

"I agree." Said Phil. The comments from Jim's friends weren't doing anything to settle his nerves.

"Well I want to do two. So zip it." Jim gestured to his friends to be quiet.

"Right, type this up please Graham."

"Okay," said the Journalist as he got his laptop ready. "Just wait a sec, and don't go too fast though."

"Right – this is the e-mail to send out if they say no. Right, start it off by saying "Dear Britain, over the past few days, and especially today – you've shown that the people of this country are brilliant. You are kind, hard working, polite and friendly people. The street parties that have been taking place are a credit to each and everyone of you – and the pride of the nation. For me personally…"

"You sound like a right wanker." Dave was always known for his straight to the point honesty. His remark got a big laugh from Phil and Albert, and even Graham struggled to keep a straight face.

"Oh, right nice one." Jim looked embarrassed. "So how would you put it Dave?"

"I'd just say – "Thanks for your support guys, I might have known the dickhead MP's would vote against me. But anyway, thanks again."

The comment was blunt and to the point. Jim thought about it for a second as Phil nodded his approval at Dave's plain talking suggestion.

"It'll cause riots that. Think about it. Everyone's had a few beers now, folk have been drinking all afternoon. We can't be saying stuff that will wind people up."

"Good point Jim, excellent point lad." Said Albert.

"Yes, that is a very good point. If Jim says something that gets the public angry there'll be serious consequences – and he'll be blamed for anything bad that happens. It'll be a classic case of hero to zero. You need to be extra careful here." Graham was being very sincere, and he was completely spoiling the general perception that the others had of journalists being bloody-minded, reckless and irresponsible.

"Build 'em up and knock 'em down!" said Phil.

"Precisely." Graham nodded.

"Okay, well if its no, we say I'll release a statement on Monday. Let the mood die down a bit."

"I still say its yes, though." Said Dave. "I'll put my flipping house on it."

"So shall we just prepare your statement for if it's a yes?" asked Graham.

"Yes, definitely!" said Dave.

Albert looked at his son and nodded encouragingly.

"I think it's a bad omen, but we might as well," said Jim as he sat forward in his armchair and began dictating the contents of his statement, in the event of the MP's vote coming back as a unanimous yes.

"Right – if they say yes, which I am sure they won't,"

"Yes Jim, you said you boring twat!" interrupted Dave.

"Shut up you stupid get! Sorry Graham, ignore that dick – he's going to be waking up in a bleeding oxygen tent if he carries on!"

"Right, well, if you can just tell me what to write…" Graham was trying to neutralise the edgy, nervous mood.

"Okay. Thanks for voting for me MP's. You obviously feel that I have made some good points – so why not go a bit further and join me in a brand new political party that is set up strictly to serve Britain in its time of crisis, a party that will involve British people in its work of rebuilding this damaged nation every step of the way. This party will be called the Crisis Party. I will stand as a Crisis Party candidate if a majority of you are prepared to defect from your current party and see out your current Parliamentary term as a Crisis Party MP. If you do that, I would stand as your Leader, and my manifesto would be quite simple. I would instantly call for simple yes or no referendums on the following topics; Capital Punishment for murder, Life imprisonment for sex offences, Return of corporal punishment in schools,
Police given back powers to police effectively, Prisons reformed to become places of punishment and rehabilitation, All street drugs legalised, Prison for absent parents who don't pay for the upkeep of children. Finally, a yes or no on all public money spent exclusively on British manufactured goods.

"Bloody hell Jim," said Phil. "That would

change everything!"

Chapter Thirty One
Saturday Afternoon

The general mood in Britain was weird, people were feverishly excited but also apprehensive, scared almost. It was like waiting for the final whistle in the World Cup final when your team were playing really badly, but scrappily hanging onto a lucky one goal lead. But much more was at stake here than just a game of football.

A hyper new level of nervous tension was replacing the carefree, happy go lucky atmosphere that had engulfed the nation all afternoon. The people had all been enjoying the street parties and the revitalising optimism of a bright new beginning within their local communities.

But since it was announced that the result was finally about to be revealed - the streets of Great Britain suddenly cleared. It was the same scene everywhere, in posh avenues and on run down terraced streets - people had deserted the patio chairs, the sausage and pineapple sticks and literally millions of gallons of fizzy pop on a mish-mash of random table tops as they went inside to await the result. In most properties up and down the land, you could hear a pin drop. Houses, flats and maisonettes were crammed full of people huddling around to hear the news first. Even children seemed caught up in the drama and sat quietly awaiting the results.

Every major television channel had suspended normal programming to broadcast this "news flash" and the media's cameras were trained on the front door of Number 10 Downing Street. It was unclear who was supposed to be coming out to announce the results, but the newscasters seemed pretty sure that it would be the

Prime Minister due to the choice of location. Outside the world famous black door a lectern and microphone had been set up. Each time the door of Number 10 opened, the excitement levels rose a little further, but it was just government officials coming and going, inadvertently toying with the nerves of a whole nation of frustrated, excited and hopeful viewers.

Finally, at half past four, the Speaker of the House came out of Number 10 and walked briskly, almost marching across the street, towards the waiting audience of television cameras - behind which sat an entire nation of panicky viewers in tortured expectation. The Speaker looked tense as he cleared his throat and began to read the statement out.

The nation was silenced.

"This has been a historic week for Britain, and for British politics. For many years, those of us who work in politics have dreamed of a day when the entire population would take an interest in the work that we do. Most of us in politics came into the profession because we wanted to make a difference. Most of us wanted to be able to stand up for what we believe in, and most of us have Great Britain's best interests at the very core of everything that we do. Politics affects every single aspect of our daily lives, from getting our bins emptied, to running the country. I speak on behalf of all local Councillors, party activists and volunteers, MPs and government workers when I say that we are indebted to the British population for showing us all that you really do care what happens here at 10 Downing Street, and over at the Palace of Westminster."

The speaker shuffled his paper and looked awkwardly at the cameras, it was almost as though he could hear the millions of viewers telling him to "get on with it."

"For some time, and as a result of some disgraceful behaviour by some Members of Parliament in recent years, the public have felt more and more alienated, disenfranchised, disinterested and frankly let down by Britain's political system. However, despite all of this - in just one week, one man, Jim Arkwright has somehow managed to unite the entire country. He has managed to provoke a genuinely passionate response from the general public, and everybody in this country seems in agreement that this is exactly the kind of person that we should have in Government."

The speaker paused and took a sip of water from a glass that was hidden away on a shelf within the lectern. It gave just enough time for the viewers to calm down from their shouts and chants of "yes!" "go on Big Jim!" and "you got that right!"

"Now, apart from taking a break to get a few hours sleep last night, myself and my Deputies have spent almost all of the past twenty four hours contacting every serving MP from the Conservative Party, the Labour Party and the Liberal Democratic party to ask them all the question: "Do you, the Honourable Member of Parliament agree to wholeheartedly support Jim Arkwright as your Party Leader if he should be elected as a Member of this Parliament?" and I can now announce that we have a result."

The tension was now electrifying, it was becoming unbearable. To many it felt like this was the very moment that the phrase "put them out of their misery" was intended for. Viewers were staring at television screens with open mouths, they could feel their pulse beating hard and fast as their breathing grew quicker and deeper. This was it, this was finally the moment of truth. This could be the announcement that nobody ever expected to hear, that one of Britain's ordinary people was about to take over the reins of power.

As the Speaker paused a moment longer, deliberately building the tension even further, the only thing that people could hear was the sound of their own heartbeats in their necks.

"All MP's of the Labour Party, the Conservative Party and the Liberal Democratic Party have agreed that if elected as an MP in a forthcoming by-election - on a date to be confirmed, in a constituency to be confirmed - Jim Arkwright WOULD receive their full support as the leader of the party that he chose to represent."

*****

The reaction was completely predictable. All of the street parties reconvened almost immediately, within moments the conga was back in full flow. The jubilation was everywhere – inside houses and on the streets outside, the families, friends, neighbours and newly acquainted citizens were hugging and dancing, kids were spraying each other in fizzy pop, small children were being thrown in the air and caught by joyous parents as the streets were once again alive with indiscriminate demonstrations of unrelenting euphoria.

This moment, this day was destined to become a life long memory for everybody that was involved. This was finally the day that Britain got rid of the rich, out of touch aristocracy that governed the shores. Britain was now practically in the control of a scrubber, a pleb, a peasant, a dosser as the rich and privileged would describe Jim's standing as a working class man from a working class background.

The television presenters, analysts and commentators were excitedly chattering away amongst themselves, oblivious of the fact that there was practically no audience watching. The people that had come inside in their tens of millions to hear the news had now, armed with the information that they had longed to hear – were back outside to celebrate with their new found community of friends and neighbours. Now, with this inexhaustible feeling of triumph and elation, the street parties were really getting going. The people of Britain felt that there was something really special worth celebrating, and it was completely unique and genuine, and it didn't involve sport or the Monarchy.

*****

At Jim's house, the media were desperate to get the potential new Prime Minister outside and hear his reaction to the news. The press had left their positions at the bottom of Jim's drive and were now surrounding the house. There were ten of them stood at the front room window, looking inside, taking pictures and shooting live footage of Graham, Albert, Phil and Dave and a coffee table full of empty Timothy Taylor beer bottles.

The four of them were laughing and joking, smiling and waving to the media people – but Jim was nowhere to be seen.

"Where's Jim?"

"What's his reaction to the news?"

"Can you get him out?"

"Graham you fat wanker!"

Jim was upstairs, sitting on his bed. It had all proved too much for him and he felt himself becoming panicky and emotional at the announcement, so he had decided to sneak upstairs and settle himself down. He'd been knelt over the toilet for the first few minutes, the news had played havoc with the contents of his stomach.

Jim was shaking uncontrollably, he just couldn't believe that the MP's had agreed to his ludicrous request. He was in a state of panic and deep shock, and he just wanted his wife Karen to come and speak to him. Jim anxiously wanted to know how Karen and his children were greeting this life changing news.

*****

Karen Arkwright was dancing and singing and drinking bucks fizz on Sarah's large cul-de-sac estate on the edge of town. Jonathan. Lucy and Victoria were all milling about with gangs of happy friends, having the time of their lives through the snaking avenue that had over a hundred families bobbing about, hoola-hooping, joking and playing all manner of street games like hop-scotch, tig, rounders, skipping and kerby.

To the Arkwrights, this wasn't about their Dad; it was just an absolutely brilliant street party that was being powered on laughter, fun and celebration. The party really was back in full swing now and despite Karen's nagging insecurities about everything, the people of Colthurst drive weren't about to let her go on a downer and worry about tittle tattle today.

Clitheroe people were absolutely filled with civic pride and a true sense of victory. The people of the town, and all of those in the surrounding villages were determined to celebrate this monumental day more passionately than any other district could.

Big Jim belonged to the Ribble Valley and its occupants were chuffed to bits for him. The week long

"Big Jim" story had really put the town, the area and its no nonsense, hard working, "salt of the earth" people on the map.

*****

The celebratory mood was all consuming, people of all age groups were being swept along by the high spirits and positive energy that was pulsating through every road, every town, district and city in Britain.

Barnsley, Nantwich, Kirkcaldy, Brighton, Pontypridd and Walsall's street parties were all receiving the most airtime as the BBC flagship channel continued to travel up and down and all around the UK with their reports on this most remarkable day of unity. The happiest faces were also being shown endlessly on TV's all around the world as nations across the globe became fixated by this extraordinary carnival that was taking place in the United Kingdom.

Some iconic pictures were being captured, and it was clear that these were images that would stand the test of time and would be used to illustrate this day in ten, twenty, even fifty years down the line. The image that appeared to be getting the most attention so far was taken by an amateur photographer who had posted it onto the Sky News Facebook page – an image so striking that Sky immediately adopted it as its background graphic.

The photograph showed a happy policeman holding aloft a little toddler at a street party, the little kid was wearing the officer's helmet and grumpily pointing in the police mans face, as the officer was laughing out loud. This photograph was a beautiful portrait of this incredible day. It was the iconic image that would forever be immortalised with Britain's pleasant revolution, this jolly revolt.

The nation's history was being changed over a few million egg and cress sandwiches and endless glasses of Dandelion and Burdock at the nice, friendly street party uprising. Politics had become so confused, tangled and bitterly despised by the hard pressed British people that this day had long seemed inevitable. And it was the inevitably which was bringing closure. The slate was being wiped clean and it was the street parties that promised an optimistic, positive new dawn.
Through the hundreds and thousands of streets and crescents, lanes and roads – the British people were happy, they were smiling and it all felt so right and proper.

*****

Emergency services had all been placed on amber standby in full strength. Since Jim Arkwright's announcement on Thursday, all leave for police, ambulance and fire service staff had been cancelled and the services had been warned to expect high demand across all sectors of the emergency services.

Accident and Emergency departments had extra staff on rota, and the army were on standby to provide relief cover if needed. Where high spirits, raised expectations and alcohol are mixed together, it usually always ends up with high demand on the police and medical services.

This simple fact was understandably enough reason for the government to panic, and ensure extra resources were available. Britain had become a place where blame for not doing enough in a crisis was far worse than expensively doing too much and wasting millions upon millions of pounds on "over-do."

But things were suddenly and glaringly different. The wind of change was blowing a gale across the land, and the majority of ambulance crews were left watching telly at their stations, A&E staff were stood by vending machines talking about the event, rather than dealing with the drunken consequences of it. By 7pm, the nation's emergency departments were practically empty – it was almost as though routine A&E complaints such as a burst appendix or a sprained wrist were being put on hold until after the party.

There were still the inevitable routine incidents such as kids falling out of trees and giddy Dads slipping discs in unfortunate skateboard incidents, or tipsy Mums walking into patio doors believing them to be open. But in the main, hospitals, police stations and ambulance depots were so quiet, the extra staff that had been drafted in were trying to get permission to leave, and join in with the party themselves.

*****

The mood at Jim's house wasn't so triumphant. Albert, Graham, Phil and Dave had endured enough of all the banging on the door, the tapping at the windows, the constant flash bulbs of the cameras going off through the window. They had discussed going out somewhere to get away from it all but it was quickly dismissed as a fruitless idea. They had tried to close the blinds but couldn't work them and only one half had dropped down. There was lots of laughter from outside as Phil and Dave tried to sort it out, only to draw one side up and the other side down. Some of the press started humming the tune from Laurel and Hardy and were enjoying a good laugh at the bungling pair's expense. Dave retaliated with a flash of his middle finger, which attracted another wave of laughter and derisive noises.

After a short while, it was all getting too much and the four of them had taken their beers upstairs and joined Jim, trying in vain to just chill out and watch the spellbinding television reaction to the Speakers announcement. But it was no good – the letterbox kept slamming, the shouting continued and the pounding at the doors and windows just wouldn't settle down. The swelling numbers of press, telly and radio reporters were determined to get the man of the moment out of the house and onto their reports.

Jim wasn't in the mood at all. He had been completely overwhelmed. He felt spent, he was emotional, tired and quite drunk from all the beers that had been supped at a steady pace all afternoon. The constant banging, shouting and harassment from the press had really begun to anger and disturb him. Following Albert's advice he had lay down on the bed with Lucy's headphones on, and under the influence of the beer, he nodded off listening to music on her walkman.

With Jim snoring away, Albert felt more and more on edge because of the hostile atmosphere. He just wanted to go home and relax by himself at his own house, but he was worried about the stress of facing all the media crews again. It had been a rough experience for him the previous evening at Preston train station and the media presence there had been tiny in comparison to the circus that was taking place outside Jim's. Albert wasn't confident enough to face anything like that so decided that staying put was likely to be the best option for now.

Graham was sat on the landing floor, with his legs on the staircase as he was busily working on his laptop. He was writing out his report for the following day's paper along with the first part of his exclusive interview. Dave and Phil just sat at the bottom of the bed, either side of Jim's feet and watched the telly, once again making sarcastic comments to one another whenever the opportunity arose, but the mood was much flatter now. Albert was sat in the big armchair that Karen had nursed all of his Grandchildren on, though these days was used more as a resting area for dirty clothes and Jims oily overalls.

The noise of the banging and shouting that was coming from downstairs was seriously getting too much, it was threatening and intimidating. The whole group were feeling the strain from the none stop media intrusion and harassment. As a result the atmosphere was very tense, and it was also quite worrying for the four men who were sat, wondering what to do next. It felt like it was only a matter of time until the front door was knocked off its hinges altogether and the press would just run amuck throughout the place.

"I've never known anything like this. This truly is a first for me." Despite many years of being part of press groups that would "doorstep" a celebrity or crook in the news, Graham appeared to be shocked by the relentless ferocity of the media's yearning to get Jim outside.

"Does somebody want to wake Jim up? If we release his statement, that might get them off our backs for a bit. Maybe we could escape?" Dave and Phil laughed at the way Graham put it.

"No, seriously – I could organise a chopper to come and pick us up. Get us out of the area."

"And who said today couldn't get any more weird, eh?" asked Dave with a humourless smirk all across his face.

"You better ask Jim," said Albert. "He'll want Karen and the kids with him."

"Well, I'm not waking him up," said Phil.

"Me neither." muttered Dave. "Just let him be for now."

"No, tell you what, executive decision – book your chopper Graham, and we'll wake him up when it arrives. How's that?"

"Okay, leave it to me. It's fields behind this house, isn't it?"

"Yes mate," said Phil, "watch you don't land on a cow though."

"And is there a gate into the field or will we have to climb the fence?"

"There's no gate," said Albert. "It's just a six foot fence all around the back. And I tell you now, I'm not climbing over that for nobody." None of the group looked particularly agile but Albert was in his seventies, and wasn't about to throw himself over a garden fence. He felt keen to remind everybody of the fact.

"Right, this is getting fucking stupid!" said Dave, standing up and walking across to the window. His appearance at the upstairs window restarted the noise from the press below. He opened the window and stuck his head out.

Phil watched in amazement as this simple act caused a BREAKING NEWS banner to appear on the television screen and Dave's face was broadcast on the television in the bedroom. Phil and Albert could sit and look at the back of Dave at the window, and the front of him on the telly.

Dave was just looking out at all the media personnel. The entire street was full of them, their vehicles and equipment. Their number was doubled if not trebled by nosey neighbours and inquisitive kids that had broken away from their street party to take a peep at what was happening round at Jim's house.

The magnitude of what had been announced earlier was really beginning to sink in and more well wishers and nosey parkers were making their way towards the house. Dave's appearance had prompted an even louder barrage of shouting and questioning from the journalists and photographers below. Dave just kept his finger over his lip for a couple of minutes until they all shut up.

Eventually, and it seemed quite grudgingly, there was finally quiet.

"Listen guys" said Dave, "If you reckon Jim's going to back down and come out while you're all being this naughty – you've got it wrong."

The crowd started jeering, shouting and heckling at Dave.

"Get Jim? We want the organ grinder, not the monkey!" shouted one photographer.

"Tell Jim to come out mate." shouted another.

"Tell Jim he's letting the side down, shafting us lot who got him to where he is!" shouted another angry media voice. The newspaper people were the most riled, they were desperate to get the triumphant pictures of Big Jim for the mornings Sunday papers, which would be hitting the presses within a few hours.

Dave put his finger on his lip again, like an infant school teacher settling a rowdy class of excitable four year olds. Eventually it went quiet again.

"Right – sort your heads out and behave and we'll get Jim to come and speak to you. Carry on like this and you'll get nothing!"

"You'll have to come out eventually!" shouted one defiant voice.

"Yes, we know that – but you don't know where

the tunnel leads to, do you?" Dave tapped twice on his nose and pointed at the heckler before he turned away and closed the window, leaving the audience trying to figure out what on earth Dave was talking about.

"What the bloody hell are you chatting about?" asked Phil as Dave walked back over to the bed and sat back down.

"Don't know! Graham made me think of the tunnel in Escape to Victory earlier."

Finally, after such a tense few hours, the small group of stressed out men laughed. The banging on the house, the shouting and tapping on windows had stopped. It felt strange for a minute, returning to relative quiet after the constant racket and knocking all day. It almost felt like the men had gone deaf, the silence seemed loud, it was unnatural and foreboding.

"Nice work Dave." Said Graham as he grabbed his mobile. He realised that he hadn't gone deaf thanks to the dong sound that alerted him to a new text on his phone.

Once he'd read it, he looked around the room at the others.

"Oh shit. I don't fucking believe this," he said, as the colour drained from his face. Jim was still snoring, but the others were looking straight at Graham, and they could all tell instantly that something was wrong. The famous journalist and television personality handed the phone around. The text message was from Julia Grantham, the editor of The Day. It said;

"Well well well, you got the scoop of the century. Well done. But we'll still beat you on sales tomorrow – we've got the wife's tits."

Chapter Thirty Two
9.30pm – Arkwright House

Although things had now finally simmered down with the press outside, the tension within the house was now suffocating and intolerable. Albert had been tasked with waking Jim up and breaking the news about the text message. Phil, Dave and Graham had respectfully gone through and sat in Jonathan's room to allow some privacy.

Once Albert had woken his son up with a strong coffee, and spent a minute or so making small talk about Dave managing to quieten down the media outside – he took a deep breath and got stuck in.

"Jim, listen - you're not going to like this one little bit lad, but listen to me." Albert was beginning to get worked up, and he looked upset.

"What's up Dad? What's happened?" Jim knew it was serious and pushed himself up in the bed so that he was sitting, looking straight across at his Dad who was sat on the bed.

"You know you've done this deal with Graham, to be exclusive to The Mirror?"

"Yes."

"Well, the main boss at The Day has sent Graham a message saying that they will still win on sales numbers because they are printing nude pictures of Karen in tomorrows paper."

"Eh? You what?" Jim's complexion was draining. He could hear what Albert was saying, he could understand what his father was explaining but it made no sense.

"Look." Said Albert. He showed Grahams phone to Jim, and the photo of the newspapers front page that the editor had peevishly sent – which showed a full length nude shot of Karen smiling with just the words "BIG KAREN" covering his wife's modesty. Beneath it said "See EVERYTHING inside."

Jim didn't say anything for a minute. He was trying to figure everything out. He quickly worked out that the picture was recent as Karen had the short hair and that had only been cut last weekend for the "snogerversary" meal. At first he thought it must be a fake picture, his wife's face airbrushed onto someone else but he knew it definitely looked like Karen. And then it all clicked, the picture had been taken on Thursday morning – at the Hyde Park Hotel. Suddenly, everything came rushing back – Karen had been trying to get Jims attention as he looked at the newspapers on the bed. He was on the cover of them all, and Karen had playfully dropped her dressing gown on the floor and stood there naked to grab his attention.

"There must have been a photographer with a zoom lens in the building opposite." Said Jim, to himself mainly as he stared at The Days front cover. A minute passed before Jim spoke again.

"They can't print that Dad. Karen will fucking kill herself. What about the kids? How will they cope with a picture of their Mum in the paper with nowt on?"

Graham had been listening from outside the room and he came in.

"It's a rotten trick that Jim. It's the most rotten trick I've seen." Graham was shaking his head as he spoke, he looked completely ashamed of his profession.

"Well, it's not happening Graham. I'm not having that – so you fucking tell this newspaper to forget it."

Once again, Jim's naivety of the media business was plain. Graham wanted to explain the situation, without upsetting Jim anymore than was necessary.

"Jim, I'm afraid there's very little you can do, or anyone can do to alter this. They'll be publishing those pictures tomorrow – and even if they don't – even if you bargained with Julia Grantham – cut me loose and signed a deal with them – they'll still print them at some point, or if not they'll sell them to another paper. Trust me Jim, you're stuck with this."

Jim was remarkably calm, it was almost as if he was discussing which train to catch. As far as he was concerned, those pictures were not being published, and that's all there was to say on the matter.

"Graham, get me on the phone to this Julia who sent you the picture please."

Dave and Phil came back into the master bedroom as Graham handed his phone to Jim.

"It's ringing," he said. Jim put the phone to his ear.

"Ah! Graham! Phoning to congratulate me are you darling?" said the voice, a weird, almost witch-like cackle followed the comment.

"This is Jim, Jim Arkwright love." Jim could tell that Julia was stunned by that announcement and she changed her tone immediately.

"Oh, hello. What a pleasant surprise, nice to speak to you, Big Jim."

"Yes, thanks – well what I'm ringing about really is these pictures of my wife. You can't print them, seriously – it's out of the question." Jim was being friendly, he wasn't aggressive or nasty. He was just being his usual, laid back self – which completely wrong footed Julia Grantham, the woman who once boasted that she was "the most hated bitch in all of Britain." She took a moment to respond to Jim's refusal to letting her print the pictures.

"Jim, sorry – I don't think you understand. I've

paid a lot of money for those pictures. They belong to me. With the best will in the world Jim, you can't stop me from printing them."

Jim could feel himself getting annoyed but he managed to keep his cool.

"No, sorry – we're talking at crossed purposes love. You don't understand what I mean – I'm saying you can't print the pictures – it will cause too much damage to my family. My wife would never get over that. She doesn't even wear a bikini at the beach, she'll be destroyed by that – all her friends and work colleagues, her family and everyone in town having naked pictures of her. Seriously Julia, it will destroy my wife. And my kids – what are my kids supposed to say when all their mates have seen pictures of their Mum in the nuddy?"

There was another long pause before the editor spoke again. It sounded to Jim like he had explained the situation and done just enough to make her change her mind.

"I totally understand your concerns Jim," said Julia. "But there's nothing I can do. The paper is already in the print shop – four million copies of it will be getting delivered to distribution centres around the country in the next two hours. I'm sorry." If the editor of the biggest selling tabloid in the country genuinely was sorry – she certainly didn't sound like she was.

"So there's nothing you can do?" Jim was crushed. He thought that he had made a strong enough plea to her. He honestly thought that he would have appealed to her better nature and she'd just say that she was cancelling the story.

"There's nothing at all I can do. I wish I could."

"This will ruin our lives. Seriously, you've got to understand – this is way out of line."

"I understand – really, I do. But if you had told me this would be such a big deal earlier, I could have done something."

"You're bullshitting me. I only just found out about it. Listen, you could cancel that story right now and we both know it. You managed to change the front page at five in the morning when Princess Diana died! You changed the whole bloody paper!" Jim was starting to raise his voice. Julia on the other hand remained calm and patronising in her tone.

"Well, that was totally different. And besides I didn't work here then – so I don't know how they managed that. I'm really sorry."

"You will be love." Said Jim.

"Oh, will I?" asked Julia in a cold, nasty tone, giving Jim his first taste of her acerbic nature.

"Yes, you fucking will. Print those pictures and you'll be sorry love."

"No, I won't Jim. Don't be a silly billy." The editor disconnected the phone.

"What a fucking horrible bitch!" said Jim. "SHIT!" he shouted. "What am I going to do now?"

"Well, the first thing is to sit Karen and the kids down, explain everything." said Phil.

"No. No way." interrupted Jim. "Not doing that. Not a cat in hells chance."

"You have to Jim," said Albert, softly.

"Nah. Bollocks. I need to get Karen and the kids out of the way. I'll take them abroad – go and grab our passports Dad – they're in the business draw in the dining room."

"Righty ho," said Albert as he made his way out of the room, feeling slightly less weighed down by the affair now that he could see Jim was tackling it proactively.

Phil was the next to speak. "I can't believe with everything that's going on, with you practically becoming the Prime Minister – that she's not doing what she's asked – you were perfectly bloody reasonable. She must have a right cob on her." Phil shook his head. Jim wasn't listening, his mind was racing, he was staring out of the window at the darkening night sky, lost in his own little whirlwind of conflicting thoughts and ideas.

"She's used to telling Prime Ministers what to do mate, it's not the other way round." Graham knew the editor well, and knew how corrupt they could become when they were influencing four million people on how to vote in elections. Such a responsible job brought with it plenty of power.

"She couldn't care less about Jim or Karen, or the kids – all she gives a shit about is selling more newspapers than anybody else. It really is as simple as that I'm afraid to say. She can't grasp the human side of the stories she prints. She's been described as the anti-Christ on many an occasion."

"Don't worry. I've got it all in hand." Jim said it slowly, and he didn't sound like he had anything in hand at all.

Big Jim looked beaten, his whole demeanour had somehow shrunk slightly. He was in need of a shave, a good nights rest and a break from this constant, relentless pressure that had started on Tuesday and hadn't let up at all since.

It had all just got bigger, deeper, thicker, higher, wider. It was all consuming and Jim had now come to realise that he was on the edge.

"Graham, do me a favour – type down what I say."

"No problem – give me thirty seconds, the

laptops in your lads room." Graham went out as Albert made it back to the top of the stairs, trying to catch his breath.

"They're all here. Yours, Karen's, Lucy's, Victoria's and here's Jonathans. I've checked all the expiry dates and they're all valid." Albert had put an elastic band around them and handed the passports to Jim. Graham came back into the room clutching his laptop.

"Thanks Dad. I appreciate your help. Right – Graham, I need you to write something down for me for tomorrow's newspaper – and then as soon as that's done, I want a lift to the airport. I don't care where I go, but me, the wife and the kids are going off on a jolly before The Day gets in any paper shops."

"Fair enough Jim." Said Phil.

"No, that's a good idea Jim, it's definitely the best thing to do. Lie low for a bit, eh? Ask Graham to get you on his chopper!" said Dave.

"Eh?"

"Jim – I was saying to these before – we have a chopper available to the paper, twenty four seven, it's at Barton Airport, just near Eccles. If I ring them they'll probably have it here within an hour – we could fly you to the airport. It carries six passengers so that will be enough won't it?"

"Yes! Nice one! Book it please Graham, definately." Graham rang his superiors and made the necessary arrangements.

"Do you want to come Dad? There's room for one more there!" asked Jim, a twinkle starting to return into his eyes, the beginnings of a smile appearing on his lips.

"Where are you bloody going? I've only just come back from Tenerifey!"

"I don't know – but while you're thinking about it, bung some stuff in a suitcase for everyone please – undies, knickers, socks, toothbrushes – grab a few shorts and t shirts for them all – I'll buy them new stuff wherever we end up. They'll love this, the kids." Jim was now starting to enjoy the idea of just turning his back on all of this weirdness that was taking over his usually perfectly normal life. Albert smiled and went off to set about the chores he'd been asked to carry out. Graham finished his call.

"Chopper will be here in half an hour – so what's that, half past ten."

"Nice one Graham, brilliant job. Phil, Dave – you need to go down to Sarah's on Colthurst Drive and tell them to go across and wait at the Grammar School – we'll pick them up from there. Don't tell them we're coming in a bloody helicopter though! Make it a surprise. We'll be there at about half ten."

"No worries – right, well have a good holiday Jim. Hope everything works out alright with Karen and that." Phil shook Jim's hand.

"What a day!" he added.

"Cheers Jim, see you soon then mate, thanks for a really weird day!"   Dave was smiling, but he looked deflated, a little lost and confused.

"Cheers lads, off you go. If the media people start giving you any jip – just tell them we're working on a statement now, and we'll be out soon."

Dave and Phil went downstairs, and shut the front door behind them as they walked directly out into the hundred deep scrum of people waiting outside and along the street. Jim watched them trying to make their way through the crowd for a minute through the blinds in the girl's room. In just over one minute, the two men had managed to advance forward no more than three metres. It made Jim wonder how he stood any chance of getting out. Then a getaway plan came to him, just out of the blue.

"Dad, have you got that suitcase sorted yet?" Jim was still watching his friends trying to get through the dense gathering of people outside.

"Nearly."

"Right, Dad, – Graham, come on chaps – we can make a move now – out the back. Phil and Dave have got everyone's attention!"

Graham started quickly packing his things together and Jim wandered round the upstairs rooms grabbing bits and pieces like shower gel and toothbrushes, sun-cream and books for the kids. He found Albert in Jonathan's room and threw the items into the suitcase that Albert was packing neatly. He zipped it up and headed off down the stairs.

"Dad, Graham, come on – let's go."

Albert and Graham did as they were instructed and quickly followed Jim down, then round through the lounge and into the kitchen. Jim went out of the back door and told his Dad and the famous television star to get out behind him quickly. As Jim closed the back door he checked that he had the passports and his wallet.

Within seconds, in the fading light, Jim had walked to the back of the garage and lifted the fencing panel right up into the air, quietly gliding the wood up on its concrete supports.

"Come on, quick." He whispered urgently. His heart was in his mouth – he couldn't believe that it had been so easy to dodge the mass media. Albert and Graham bent down and stepped through, into the open farm land. Jim eased the fencing panel back down into position and laughed.

"The amount of times I've been through there

when Jonathans booted the ball over the fence! Never knew I'd get to use it for such an exciting mission!" Jim laughed again. Albert couldn't believe what he was witnessing. With everything that was going on, with the MP's and now with the newspaper trouble, he couldn't understand how Jim was laughing.

"Right, listen fellahs, sorry to be bossy but lets just move away from here, head over to the bushes up there and then we'll walk up to the top of the field out of the way - then if them lot realise we've done a bunk, we'll be well out of the road."

Jim turned and led the way as the light was almost faded now and the field was close to darkness. Eventually, after five minutes of careful plodding along, the three men reached the area that Jim had in mind.

"I'm too bloody old for all this malarkey Jim. I can't be doing stuff like this no more!"

Jim laughed at his Dad. "What do you mean no more? You've never done anything like that in your entire life man! Here, lets sit down here – Dad, sit on the suitcase here, take a breather."

A couple of quiet minutes passed as the three of them caught their breaths back. They sat, staring at the back of Jim's house at the bottom of the field.

"I wonder if they've twigged it yet?" said Jim.

"Probably not. They'll go bloody ballistic when they realise though Jim!" Graham laughed, amused and rather proud of himself for being caught up in such an exciting few minutes.

"Right, Graham, turn your laptop on please – here we go. This is my letter to Britain. Tell me when you're ready mate."

"Alright, while it's booting up I'll phone the office and tell them we're in the field at the back of your house – I'll tell them to look out for the light off my laptop screen."

"Nice one!" said Jim, he was getting really excited about the helicopter coming. After Graham had finished giving instructions for the pilot, he sat down in the grass with the laptop on his legs.

"I'm ready. Just don't go too fast, I'm shit at typing."

"Right, okay, here we go. Oh you know that statement we did before – you've not released that have you?"

"No, I didn't do anything because you were asleep." Said Graham.

"Right – no problems mate. You can still use that, but you'll need to explain in your reports that I said all that before I saw The Day – I want you to really show what a piece of shit that editor is."

"Understood – you still want to use the Crisis Party statement – so what's this that we're doing now Jim?"

"This is my goodbye letter to Britain. Are you ready?"

"Go."

"Right. Dear Britain, thank you for the support that you have shown towards me, and to each other. The street parties that have taken place today have been absolutely unbelievable, and you all owe yourself a big pat on the back. It just proves my theory that we are a top country, full of top people. We're a nation of kind, friendly, funny folk and we like to get along with each other and have a nice time. I really believe that practically every person in this country is a good, solid, decent person who would help us out if we were in a fix. We should always remember that – and learn to look past the bullshit that we are brainwashed to judge people on; the clothes they wear, the car they drive, the shops they go into, the size of their telly. We've spent forty years doing that and look where it's got us. We're all in debt, we all ignore our neighbours and we are all so caught up in our own little worlds, we're oblivious to the fact that our country is quite literally falling apart. Let's all start judging people on their merits, not their material goods – just like you all did today! Maybe then we can start to rebuild our most valuable asset – our community spirit. I've had a mad week, and I've learnt some things and seen some stuff I'll never forget. But what has happened tonight has left me in no doubt that there are evil, nasty people around with too much power and influence afforded to them. I have asked the editor of The Day newspaper to refrain publishing some sad, pervy, peeping tom images that will cause my family irrepairable damage – and she has flatly refused. At 9.40pm tonight I explained that I wanted her to refrain from publishing and she said she can't. In response, I am flatly refusing to stand as an MP. Sorry if I've let anybody down – but if that's the kind of treatment that is to be expected, I'm alright thanks, I'm staying well out of it! I'm going off now for a holiday with my family – and I'll have no further involvement in politics on my return. Good luck, and once again, thanks to you all."

Jim smiled. Albert looked despondent and Graham actually looked as though he was close to tears.

"Really?" said Graham, the concern on his face illuminated by the vivid white reflection from the laptop screen. In that precise moment, Jim realised that he had made the right decision. It felt right. By stark contrast, nothing else that happened throughout the week had felt right. He finally felt at ease, almost happy, despite the emotional problems that were inevitably going to follow regarding the nude photo. No, it felt just right and Albert could sense that his son was feeling a huge weight had lifted up off his shoulders. It almost felt as though Julia Grantham was doing Jim a favour in some respects.

"I'm so proud of you, lad."

"Thanks Dad. I'm really proud of you as well fellah." The two men hugged and shed a tear together as the sky began to fill with the rumble of a distant helicopter engine making its way towards the town.

"I love you, Jim." Said Albert as he clenched his son tightly.

"Come with us then. Please Dad, come on. We'll go to yours, get your passport and your anusol cream, then we'll pick the others up. Come on!"

"Yes. Why not? Why bloody not?" The two men laughed.

Graham felt awkward by everything that was happening between the father and son and the emotions that were on show. He also felt a huge emptiness wash over him, realising that he was totally and utterly gutted that this was the end of the journey. At that very moment he got his first sense of just how big a blow this announcement was going to be for Jim's besotted British public.

THE END